WINCHESTER VALLEY

"You do anything but breathe, Mister Morgan, and you'll be all over that bed." The man who spoke was wearing a business suit. So were the two men with the shotguns. The bathroom door opened and Morgan tensed. He was ready to roll to his right when Emmy screamed. It might just give him the time he needed. The Colt was ten feet away.

"My God," Emmy said, "you sure as hell took long enough." She was fully dressed. The man without the shotgun smiled weakly.

GUNSMOKE GORGE

Morgan stayed put. He caught a glimpse of a shadow just to his right. He turned and heard the doors open. Two shots rang out. Both from outside. *Culpepper*. Morgan thought so. He took advantage of the distraction and took a chance. He movd three feet to his right, removed his hat and tossed it onto the end of the bar, just above where he'd been, and then he stood up.

Morgan's hat flew from the bar, just as he shot Louie Blanchard, one of Jess Blanchard's brothers, right between the eyes.

The *Buckskin* series published by Leisure Books:

WINCHESTER VALLEY
GUNSMOKE GORGE

BUCKSKIN

KIT DALTON

LEISURE BOOKS NEW YORK CITY

A LEISURE BOOK®

March 1991

Published by

Dorchester Publishing Co., Inc.
276 Fifth Avenue
New York, NY 10001

WINCHESTER VALLEY

Dedicated to
Robert Vaughan, fellow writer who gave me a boost
when it was badly needed.

1

Lee Morgan liked the cool, slick feel of the silk sheets against his bare skin. He pulled the top sheet up high enough to cover his privates and smiled as he wondered why he'd bothered. After all, he'd been with Emmy for two nights. She knew every inch of his body. His modesty suddenly seemed a little ridiculous.

Morgan was still somewhat in awe of his recent streak of good luck. He rarely got anything he didn't work or fight for . . . most of the time at risk of his life. In this instance, a sick horse had been responsible. The animal had taken ill while stabled in Manhattan, Kansas. After it died, Morgan took the last of his cash to buy a stage ticket to Denver. It was on that stage that he met Emmy.

Emilia Christine Venable! Slim of waist, full of bosom, dark haired, dark eyed and very, very rich. She was the daughter of a Colorado Senator and gold baron. How ironic! Morgan had been bound for Denver to look up an old saddle companion and put the touch on him. Suddenly, there was Emmy. She introduced him to a lifestyle he'd rarely known.

They were quartered in the fabulous Windsor Hotel at 16th and Larimer. They had a four-room private suite, the best food and liquor money could buy, and all the privacy Morgan could handle. He hadn't even bothered to contact Jim Buttrey. He'd do that when Emmy tired of him. And he was sure she would.

"Do you like it?" Morgan blinked, his attention abruptly brought back to his present circumstance. He looked up. Emmy was wearing a black, lacy Merry Widow corset. It pushed her breasts up and together. Their creamy flesh overflowed its top. Morgan eyed them, then let his gaze trace the long, shapely legs from ankle to thigh. He licked his lips in anticipation of again visiting what was between them.

"I like it," he said. "But I like what's in it even better." Emmy smiled, coyly. She let her hands slide along her thighs and waist and then paused teasingly beneath her breasts.

"I'm glad, but champagne first. Right?" Morgan didn't care. He shrugged his reply. "The boy will be here with it in a minute. Let him in. I just want to add a finishing touch." She winked and wiggled her bottom as she disappeared into the water closet. Morgan shook his head in wonderment. She did have a way of renewing his thirst . . . no matter how short a time between trips to the well. A knock at the door.

"Yeah . . . c'mon in." Morgan scooted up a little so that he might rest his back against the headboard. The door opened, Morgan looked over. He was staring into the business end of two shotguns.

"You do anything but breathe, Mister Morgan, and you'll be all over that bed." The man who spoke was wearing a business suit. So were the two men with the shotguns. The bathroom door opened and Morgan tensed. He was ready to roll to his right when Emmy screamed. It might just give him the time he needed. The Colt was ten feet away.

"My God," Emmy said, "you sure as hell *took* long enough." She was fully dressed. The man without the shotgun smiled, weakly.

"Sorry," he offered. Morgan's mouth was half open. He'd been taken! Set up! It didn't happen often but when it did, it was *all* the way. "We had to be sure . . . absolutely sure about our man. Your father insisted on that."

"But he didn't give a damn that his daughter might have to go to bed with the man . . . right one or not."

"You don't look any the worse for wear," Emmy sneered. She walked to the nearby desk, picked up an envelope and took it to the man, pushing by him as she held it out. She got to the door and then turned back.

"Only one night was part of the set-up, Morgan . . . if that's any consolation." Morgan didn't respond. He was pondering how long he might have left to live.

"Get dressed, Morgan, we've got an appointment. Get out of the bed on *this* side. Charlie," the man continued, addressing the man on his right, "get his clothes and bring them over here." Charlie did as he was told. So did Morgan.

9

2

The mansion was pretentious, with ornate iron deer and marble statuary gracing the front lawn. Morgan caught a glimpse of a private coach being readied for a trip. As the surrey pulled up in front of the portico, Morgan saw the wrought iron fancy work between the center pillars. It was woven into a name and verified what he already suspected:

Venable

Morgan was ushered into the library and ordered to sit. One man accompanied him while the others took up guard duties nearby. A few moments later, a tall, graying gentleman entered. He was wearing a monogrammed silk shirt, broadcloth suit and a cravat held in place with a diamond stickpin.

"Give him back his gun, Mister Denton." Denton assumed a look of surprise but didn't move. "I said, give the man his gun."

"Senator . . . this man is . . ."

"I know who he is . . . and what. Now sir, give him

his gun." Denton gritted his teeth but he complied. The tall man then moved to a nearby liquor cabinet, poured two shots of whisky and walked over to Morgan. "I'm Senator Charles Wingate Venable, Mister Morgan. I must apologize for the circumstances under which we are meeting."

Morgan accepted the whiskey and downed it in a single gulp. "Under any other circumstances, I doubt that we would meet at all."

"Perhaps not, but I'm certain you must have many questions."

"Only one for right now," Morgan said. "What kind of a man would use his daughter the way you did?"

Venable assumed a rather quizzical expression. Denton took two steps in Morgan's direction, but Venable held up his hand.

"Hate is a strong motivator, sir. All I ask is that you do not judge either of us until you've heard the facts."

"Shotguns pointed at my belly make me very hard of hearing," Morgan said.

"Then you will listen?"

"Why not? The whisky's good and the last few days at the Windsor must have some price on them. Listening seems cheap enough."

"Mister Denton," Venable said, "you and your men go on to the dining room. They will serve you breakfast." Denton started to speak but the Senator held up his hand. "I'll be just fine, don't worry." Morgan could tell by Denton's expression how the man felt but, one way or another, Denton was on Venable's payroll. He did what he was told.

11

"Another whisky, Mister Morgan?"

"Why don't you just bring the bottle over. Interruptions are distracting." Morgan strapped on his rig, checked the Colt for load and then pondered an escape through the French doors. Venable caught the look.

"I dare say you'd get off the grounds, Mister Morgan . . . but you'd never get out of Denver."

"And after I listen?"

"I'll speak frankly, sir. As of this moment, you're facing charges of kidnapping and rape. Your life depends on those charges never leaving this room. That, sir, is up to you."

Morgan downed a whiskey and started to pour another. He looked at Senator Venable, smiled and put the glass on the table. Then he tipped the bottle up and took several good-sized swallows.

"Do you always drink this heavily, Mister Morgan?"

"No, no. Just on those days when I'm facing kidnap and rape charges." The men eyed each other for a moment . . . a considering of strengths and weaknesses. Morgan half smiled. "I could add murder to the list," he said, "it wouldn't go any harder on me."

"I don't like this," Venable said. His face contorted and his tone had changed. He meant it. "I just can't run the risk of being turned down."

"For *what*?"

Venable walked to his desk, pulled a *Wanted* poster from a drawer and handed it to Morgan. "I want you to hunt down and arrest this man . . . or kill him." Morgan looked at the name. It was Henry Jared.

"Doc Henry?" Morgan laughed. "Hang me, Senator. It'll be a damn site quicker."

"I know you're not afraid of him, Morgan. I know you faced him down, and I don't know anyone else who has. If you do . . . get him here and you're free to go."

"I can give you the names of a dozen men who faced Doc . . . but you wouldn't want them here. They're all in pine boxes."

"You're not."

"And you don't have your facts as straight as you think."

"It's all right here, Morgan." Venable held up an envelope. Morgan recognized it as the one Emmy had given to Denton earlier.

"And that says I faced down Doc Henry?"

"You don't remember? Laramie? Two, maybe three years ago?"

"I don't remember because it never happened, Venable. The man I faced was Doc Henry's brother, Johnny. I've still got a chunk of lead in a rib bone to remind me."

"No matter, Morgan. The fact is . . . you're not afraid of him . . . either of them. Are you?"

"Makes no difference," Morgan replied. "I don't intend to go looking for trouble. Plenty of it comes my way without looking."

"How much, Morgan? What will it take to buy your gun?"

"Save it, Senator. If you'd have thought you

could buy my gun, you wouldn't have gone to all this trouble."

"I'd prefer to pay you. Officially, of course but . . . well, I have to have some assurances."

"Here's one for you Senator. I assure you I won't go looking for Doc Henry Jared."

The door opened and both men turned. Emmy Venable walked in.

"Emilia," her father said, "I told you . . ."

"I know what you told me, father, but after what I did, I've earned the right to be here."

"For what it's worth, lady," Morgan said, cynically, "you did a helluva job on me."

"I told you, Morgan, only the first night was part of the plan."

"*Emilia!* Surely you didn't . . ."

"Don't sound so shocked, father. You can't be that naive. How did you expect me to hold his attention for three days?"

"Your money of course. The hotel. Your *name.*"

Emmy's eyes suddenly filled with tears and she assumed an almost hateful expression. She spat the words at her father. "All that didn't help Carla did it? Or Carl? Or Momma . . . none of it helped them, *Senator* Venable."

Morgan realized a more complex issue was at stake than some politician wanting to gain a vote or two by ending the career of a notorious gunman. There was emotion here . . . family emotion.

"Just what interest does a millionaire politician have in a man like Doc Henry?" Morgan could see tears now in the Senator's eyes.

"He . . . he killed my family, Morgan. Or at least

he was responsible for their deaths. My other daughter, Carla. My son. God! Poor Carl. He had to watch . . . Carla with . . . with those men. He tried to stop them . . . to stand up against them.''

"And your wife?"

Venable blew his nose, downed a swallow of whisky and regained some of his composure. "She put a gun to her head."

"How in the hell did Doc Henry's men ever get that Goddam close to the family of a man like you?"

"They were on the way to the wedding of the daughter of the Mexican Ambassador, Senor Juan Diego Valesquez. His home is near Juarez."

"Publicity?"

"A great deal of it, Morgan. It was to have been a major breakthrough in our relationship with Mexico. A new beginning. Emilia and I were in Washington."

"And you let the rest of your family make that trip without escort?"

"Of course not! As a matter of fact, there was a troop of Cavalry and the usual personal body guards. More than twenty men all together. The party was attacked by a band of renegade Apaches. The Indians traded the survivors, which included my family, for guns."

"From Doc Henry?"

"Yes. He's been running guns to them for a long time. They've been stirring up much of the trouble between our country and Mexico. The fight has been over who is responsible for bringing them to justice. The Apaches ignore the international boundary."

"Yeah. Since they owned all of it once, I can see

where they would. I still can't figure why Doc didn't demand payment from you, though."

"He did! Unfortunately, a hot-headed army Lieutenant tried to take action on his own before I even knew about the events or the ransom."

Now Emmy joined in. She was no longer crying, she was *mad*, damned mad.

"Doc Henry turned Carla over to his men. When they were through with her, they gave her back to the Apaches."

"And just how and when did you find out about all of this?"

"Only a month ago, Morgan. Until then, we didn't know the fates of any of them."

"And me, Mr. Venable? Just how in the hell do I fit in?"

"There was a man who once worked for the Pinkertons. When I was elected, he went to work for me. He undertook the job of getting the truth, paying the ransom, whatever he had to do."

"And where is he?"

"Dead, I suppose. I'm not certain." Venable took another envelope from his desk. This one was thicker, its contents dog-eared. He handed it to Morgan. "Read it, Morgan. It's his complete report."

Morgan read. The author had been thorough. Sickeningly so where it related to Venable's family. There had been many other victims too, over a long period of time. Women and young girls from emigrant trains headed west, mining camps, even small towns sacked. The gang, growing in numbers and in the vileness of their atrocities, had become an empire of evil. Somewhere they hid themselves away between attacks. A fortress, probably impregnable. Morgan had read enough. He started to hand the papers back. Venable shook his head.

"The last page, Morgan . . . read it . . . read the signature." Morgan read again.

I was never able to pinpoint the exact location of Jared's stronghold, but there is someone who knows and there is one man who might get in alone. He is Lee Morgan. Have him contact Irish Molly. This is probably my last report, sir. I've been discovered.

J.B.

Morgan looked up, frowning. "J.B.?"

"James Buttrey, Mister Morgan, the man you were coming to see."

"I'll be damned!" Morgan looked at Emmy. "Jim Buttrey, a Pinkerton agent. This has been a week of surprises."

"Do you know this woman, Morgan? This Irish Molly?"

"Yeah, I know her. She runs a whore house in Creede."

"And just how would she know where Doc Henry's gang is holed up?" Emmy asked.

"She's known Doc for years. He likes his women and he likes to take care of the men who ride with him."

"Will you take the job, Morgan?" It was Emmy asking. No threat now. In fact, more a plea.

"How can I do what Jim Buttrey, the U.S.

17

Cavalry and a Senator with a million dollars couldn't do?''

"One man Morgan . . . alone. That's what Buttrey said."

"*He* was alone."

"But he was . . . involved."

"Working for you, you mean?"

"I mean . . . Jim was in love with my other daughter."

"Lost his edge," Morgan said, almost in a whisper.

"What? What was that about an edge? Jim mentioned that once."

"You ought to know about that, Senator. Politics is full of it. It's what you've got . . . wealth and power. For Buttrey . . . for me, the tools are different but the edge is the same. Lose it and you'll die."

"Have you got it, Morgan? I mean in this case . . . with Doc Henry?"

"Mebbe. If Irish Molly will help, just mebbe."

"Morgan," Senator Venable said, softly, "I'm sorry . . . terribly sorry for the way I got you here. Ashamed too. And the threats . . . forget them. I want you to do this job officially . . . as a Pinkerton agent. That way, Jared and any of his gang members who might survive can be legally tried and hanged." Venable paused. Morgan knew he wasn't a man accustomed to apologizing or backing down. Venable stood up and pulled himself to his full height. "Unofficially, I'll pay you any amount you ask. Just name it."

"I've got a dodger or two hanging over me Senator. No murders, just mistakes . . . small ones. I

don't like them dogging me. Wipe the slate clean . . .
if I make it. Clear them for me. Pay my expenses.
You can call what it's worth to you after that."

"Then you'll . . ." Emmy looked up now too, her
eyes wide. Morgan looked from one to the other.

"For Jim Buttrey," he said.

3

Creede, Colorado had the dubious distinction of being called "Hell at Heaven's Gate." It was a lawless, rip-roaring mining town some ten thousand feet above sea level. Just to the north were the La Garita Mountains and the south, the San Juans. Northwest lay the Spring Creek Pass, primary access into the wilds of the Uncompahgre Valley. Few men had reason to ride in there. No one came to Creede itself without a damned good reason. Most of those who did were seeking their fortunes. The gold and silver mines were some of the best producers in the territory. Then too, there were those who followed the men who were following the rainbow.

Creede had once boasted a sheriff and two deputies. They now reposed on Calvary Hill. Legend had it that Creede had once enjoyed three summer months without a single shooting. The reason was a visitor from back east. He agreed to wear the tin star of the law in exchange for room and board. At summer's end, Dr. John Holliday quit Creede and returned to warmer climes.

Lee Morgan came to Creede by stage. Butterfield

ran two into the town; they tried to time the once-a-month runs to accommodate passengers going in either direction. Most of the time there were two or three day lay-overs. The runs were rugged enough given the country. Men like Doc Henry made them more so.

Senator Venable had advanced Morgan $1,500 for expenses. He was ready to outfit himself in Creede and maintain a low profile until he could develop a plan, hopefully with Irish Molly's help.

Morgan was surprised at the growth since his last visit. He'd come to Creede then following a trail he hoped would lead him to his father. Creede had often offered respite to Buckskin Frank Leslie when he was alive.

Morgan had no trouble finding Irish Molly's place. It too had grown, nearly tripled in size. He stood in the street and read the sign, which appeared to be fairly new.

Irish Molly's
Keno Poker 21 Whisky Beer
Women
If you're honest . . . you're
Welcome!
If not . . . you're
dead!

Morgan grinned. He could hear Molly speaking the words with that deep, Irish brogue. Her place had a fancy facade, covered half a block and sported three entrances. The center one, into the dining room, was high with fancy cut glass windows. On either side were bat wing doors leading into the casino and the saloon. Upstairs was Molly's private quarters and the rooms of pleasure. Molly's place, like Creede itself, never closed.

Morgan, noting the two armed men at each entrance, opted to enter the casino. Inside, he found himself confronted by another armed man.

"Check your weapons with the young lady." Morgan glanced around. No one else was carrying a gun. He nodded.

"Now, sir, your pleasure?"

"I'm here to see the owner. Just tell her Lee is here and that it's very important."

"I don't believe Miss O'Flynn is up for the day yet, sir. I will see to it she gets your message, however. Meantime, take your stage ticket stub into the dining room and enjoy Irish Molly's free breakfast." Morgan's eyebrows raised. He was impressed. He remembered Molly talking about something like that a long time ago.

"Thanks," he said. "I'll do that."

The breakfast lived up to Molly's promise. A sizeable cut of steak, some potatoes, flap jacks, and all the coffee a man could hold. The steak was actually antelope or venison, and sometimes even bear meat. Honest to God beef steak was at a premium and Molly saved that for her dining room dinner business. Morgan was just finishing his third cup of coffee when he heard the rustle of a satin dress. He saw the hem of the Emerald green garb and the slim ankles below it. He looked up.

"As the Good Lawrd is me witness, if it ain't Lee Morgan himself." The brogue was still there, the face pixie-like, the hair a flame red. Molly's eyes matched her gown. She pushed aside the tin plate, leaned down and gave Morgan a long, hard kiss. He nearly choked on the coffee he had not yet swallowed.

"You can still take my breath away, Molly."

She sat opposite him, eyeing his every feature and smiling. "You've not changed a bloody bit. I should be angry with you. You promised a letter a month you did. Blarney! I've not heard from you since you rode out. Let's see now, that's been . . ."

"Let's just say it's been too long, Molly, shall we?"

"That it has, Morgan." She tilted her head and cocked one eye at him. "An' what brings you back, I'll be askin'?"

"This will tell you as much as I could." Morgan handed her Jim Buttrey's letter. She read it and then looked up. "Did you see him, Molly . . . lately, I mean?"

"We buried him Thursday week."

"Who did it?"

"Who knows?"

"You do, Molly. Was it Doc Henry or one of his gunnies?"

"Does it matter? He's gone, he is, an' nobody can get them all, can they now?"

"I'm going to try, Molly," Morgan said, "but I need your help."

"You'll not be gettin' it, Mahrgan. I'll not send you to your death."

"If you don't tell me what you know, Molly girl, that may be exactly what you'll do. See, I'm going to find him, with or without you."

"You're a damned, bloody fool you are. Nobody can take Doc Henry. Most can't even find him."

"But you can." She was already shaking her head.

"Not even me," Molly said. "Not unless Doc wants me to. He hasn't. Not for a long time now."

"Jim said you knew."

"I know that Doc holes up in the Uncompahgre Valley. That's the same as tellin' you there's gold in the Rockies. There's a site more mountains than there is gold. A man could ride for a year up there an' niver seen another human bein'."

"Then," Morgan said, standing up, "I'd best get started." Molly reached out and gripped Morgan's arm. "Wait! Stay the night!"

"With you?"

"You owe me, Mahrgan. After all, you niver wrote."

" 'Til tonight then, Molly."

Morgan picked up his rig but left the Winchester checked. He went first to the Creede livery stable, where a hulk of a man greeted him.

"I'm looking to buy a horse. You sellin'?"

"Fer packin' er ridin'?"

"One of each," Morgan said. He'd learned that the death of his riding mare in Kansas had also been part of Venable's set-up. It was one reason for the sizeable advance of expense money.

"I got pack animals, mister. Best ridin' mounts you'll have to get from the Halsteads."

"And where are they?" The man pointed south. "How far?"

"Two . . . three miles, mebbe." The big man took Morgan to the rear of the stable and pointed to a corral. "Six or seven good pack animals out there. Take yore pick."

Morgan found a good, strong pack pony. He then

went to the mercantile and bought his supplies, leaving them until he could return later. He also bought a saddle. Then he rode the pack pony to the Halstead ranch.

"The livery man told me you sold horses."

"The best in the mountains, mister. I'm Luke Halstead. This is muh daddy's spread. You lookin' for a runner or a climber?"

"You got one that'll do both?"

"Sure do." He eyed Morgan carefully. "Most men can't afford 'em."

"I'll pay cash, right now!"

The man shrugged. "Got a big roan gelding out back. Runs like the wind, climbs like a mountain goat. Fella what owned him got himself kilt a week or so back. We bought the horse so there'd be buryin' money."

"You happen to know the name of the man who owned him?"

"Nope. That make a difference to you?"

"Not really. Let's have a look."

The horse was obviously a good one. He'd been treated well and seemed to take to Morgan quickly.

"You can saddle 'im up if you want. See how he gets on with you."

"No need. I'll take him." Morgan paid Halstead and while Halstead was getting the paper, Morgan checked the horse over. He found what he was looking for . . . a brand. It was simple and personal. The letters were J.B.

Morgan was looking over several other animals when Halstead returned.

"You change your mind, mister?"

"No."

"You lookin' for somethin' special?"

"You get all your horses the way you got the roan?"

"I don't figure that to be your business, mister. They're all bought, paid for, an' I got papers."

"And you don't care where they come from?"

"Nope. Don't care where they're goin' neither . . . or the men who rides 'em."

"You bought any horses from a man called Jared? Doc Henry Jared?"

"You're pushin', mister . . . way too hard." Morgan heard a twig snap just behind him. He crouched, spun and leveled the Colt at the man who stepped on it. The motion was fluid . . . all done at once.

"You're mighty edgy, mister."

"When somebody gets behind me, I tend to get that way."

"You'll find no trouble here, mister . . . unless you make it. I'm Henry Halstead. This is my place. I buy horses from any man who'll sell 'em to me at a fair price. That's my business. Where the horses come from in the first place, *ain't!*"

Morgan rode away but he wasn't easy with it. He'd found three animals with cavalry brands, two others with private brands the same as Jim Buttrey's, and one Indian pony.

The curtain swayed to the night breeze. The air was crisp at this altitude, even in the dead of summer. Morgan slipped out of his long-johns and sat on the edge of the bed. In the dim light, Molly came from the next room, naked.

Her breasts were not large but they were firm and jutted upwards at the nipples. The little buds were hard and a soft pink in color. Her pubic hair was not the flaming red Morgan remembered. It was softer in color and seemed less than he recalled . . . but no less inviting.

"Kiss me, Mahrgan . . . the way you used to." She stood in front of him, her legs slightly apart. She clamped her hands together, behind her head. Morgan reached up and tweaked the nipples, rubbed them and filled his hands with the rubbery softness of Molly's tits.

"Stay still," he said. "Stay still . . . no matter what."

Morgan's tongue circled Molly's navel. She sucked in her breath but she didn't move. He pulled at her waist and she leaned forward just a little. He licked each nipple until they were as hard as rocks. He could feel Molly's body tensing against the urge to move. His hands tightened around her ass and he let his tongue work nearer to her pussy.

"Oooh Gawd . . . it's been so long . . . ooh."

"Shh!" Morgan found the slit. It was slick, wet . . . almost pulsating. He teased her, avoiding her clitoris. She moved ever so slightly and he tightened his hands against her as a warning.

He flicked at her love bud, even closing his lips around it briefly. Then he'd stop and repeat the procedure again. Molly's body was covered with goose pimples. Her eyes were closed and she was biting her lip to keep from screaming with the pleasure of it all.

Morgan pushed her back, gently. Now he dropped to his knees and buried his face in her softness . . . his tongue found her clitoris. The fingers of his hands were on her nipples. The sensations were

27

shooting through her body in waves, each moment increasing in momentum. He licked faster and faster . . . she moaned . . . she stiffened . . . she thrust her hips forward . . . hard! Morgan stopped!

"On the bed," he said. His voice was firm, commanding. Molly obeyed. She knew what to do. She got up on her knees, spread them wide apart and then reached behind her and gripped the headboard with both hands. Morgan got on his back, his face beneath her pussy. "Lower yourself," he ordered. She did. Morgan's tongue went to work again. This time, he'd attack her clitoris, then thrust his tongue up, inside her. Again, repeating the process over and over.

"I can't Mahrgan . . . I can't take it . . . oooh God. God . . ."

"Quiet!"

"Oh *please* . . . please, Mahrgan. . . ." He stopped completely. Molly's breathing was the only sound. It was heavy and rapid.

"Are you ready to be quiet, Molly . . . or do you want it the hard way?"

"Oh no . . . please. It's just that it's been so long . . . I . . ."

"Which is it going to be Molly?"

"I'll be quiet . . . I swear it."

"And still?"

"Yes . . . I'll not move again, Mahrgan."

Once again, Molly lowered herself to Morgan's tongue. He couldn't help but smile to himself. He knew he was torturing her but it was the most pleasant torture he could imagine. He continued to tease her for another ten minutes. Even in the cool night air, Molly's body glistened with sweat. Finally, Morgan stopped.

"You were a pretty good girl this time. Lay down." Molly moved quickly and Morgan positioned himself so that his cock touched her lips. She licked the tip, the shaft, the swollen head and finally took it, deep, into her mouth and throat. Gurgling sounds punctuated her effort. It had been a long time for Morgan as well. He suddenly pulled back, slipped atop her and thrust himself deep inside her.

"Don't tease me anymore," she cried. He didn't. Their bodies became a single, human piston until Molly exploded inside. Morgan was only a split-second behind her. Their moans and words were lost in the fiery passion of climax. Molly seemed insatiable but finally, she too fell limp beneath him.

"You're still the best I've ever had," she finally said. Morgan knew she meant it. He always felt guilty about not saying the same thing. It wasn't that he couldn't have said it . . . Morgan just wasn't certain it was true. Instead, he kissed her.

4

Morgan had only the most vague recollection of
Molly's departure the following morning. He was
very much aware, however, that he had slept well
past his usual time. He was fully dressed, save for
his shirt, when Molly returned. She was followed by
a man with a huge tray of food.

"We got some talkin' to do," she said. "May as
well do it over a good breakfast." After the hired
hand left, Molly walked over and kissed Morgan,
long but soft. "Top o' the marnin' to you."

"And to you, Molly my girl," Morgan replied. He
made a half hearted attempt at an Irish brogue. It
didn't work. Molly laughed.

Throughout breakfast, Molly spoke of many
things. Among them old times she remembered with
Morgan and Jim Buttrey. By the last of the coffee,
her mood had turned solemn. Morgan didn't push
her but he didn't have to wait long.

"Charlie Bojack rode in this marnin'. He's a
gunny. Works for Doc Henry. He brought this."
Molly reached inside the top of her blouse and

extracted a folded paper. She handed it to Morgan.
He opened and read it.

> Molly,
>
> I know you won't come personal, but I'd
> like to ask you anyways. My men need some
> ladies. Nine will do. $200 a girl for two nights.
> Meet Charlie at the pass in five days. He'll
> bring you in.
>
> My love . . .
> Doc

"You've got something in that scheming red head
of yours. What is it?"

"I don't have nine girls here that I can spare. I run
a small house down at South Fork. You came
through it comin' in." Morgan nodded. "I can close
it down for a week or so. I got five girls there. You
can go get 'em, Mahrgan. Ride out tonight. There's
an old stage coach down there. You can bring them
and yourself back in it. Then," she said, smiling,
"you'll be workin' for *me*. Just make certain Charlie
Bojack don't see you today."

"Whoa, Molly. I can't risk other people going
after Doc. He finds me out . . . or someone else
does . . ."

"It's a chance we'll have to take, Mahrgan.
There's no other way to get into Doc's camp."

"*We?*"

"This is a trip I'll be makin' too."

"Not on your life, Molly."

"Then we'll be strikin' no bargain."

"I don't need your bargain, Molly. I can follow
Bojack and your girls from a nice safe distance. I'll

get in."

"Not with busted legs you won't, and if you won't be dealin' me in, I'll see to it that's what you end up with." Morgan knew Molly meant what she said. She had enough men to get the job done.

"What changed your mind, Molly? You didn't want any part of Doc Henry yesterday."

"With this note from Doc, we got a chance to get in. I've got some good men that'll come in mighty handy when the shootin' starts and then there's Jaimie boy. Cold dead he is. Sod coverin' 'im up 'cause o' Doc Henry Jared. I don't need any more reasons."

"Fair enough."

"Not quite, Mahrgan. I got a feelin', deep down, that Jaimie's shootin is not your only reason. Am I right?"

"You are. Money is the other one."

"That's all?"

"Isn't that enough?"

Morgan whiled away the day in Molly's casino. One of the girls kept Charlie Bojack occupied for most of it. Toward sundown, Morgan made his way to the livery. He had just finished saddling the roan when he heard the creak of the door. He stepped back into the shadows.

"Your daddy ain't gonna like this, Luke. Not one little bit he ain't."

"Don't you worry none about my daddy. Just you git up in the loft and make sure we get this Morgan fella alive. He's got some questions to answer."

Morgan moved quietly until he could peer between two boards. He could see Luke Halstead's outline by the light from the door behind him. The other man was half way up a ladder to the loft. Morgan didn't want any shooting . . . if he could help it. He found an old horseshoe and tossed it into the air, behind him. It fell into a stall several feet away with a rattle and spooked a horse.

Luke Halstead, shotgun in hand, made a dash for the other end of the livery barn. When he got even with Morgan, Morgan thrust his boot out and Luke went ass over appetite.

Morgan planted the butt of his Colt on the back of Luke's head and there was only a soft grunt. The other man had jumped from the ladder when the horseshoe hit and was frozen to the spot.

"You come tend to your friend here," Morgan said. "I'm riding out of Creede and I'd like to do it with no dead men left behind me. I hope you'll cooperate."

"Yes, sir, yes, sir. You'll git no argument out o' me." The man moved slowly up to where Morgan stood over Luke. Morgan backed the roan out of the stall, mounted and then told the man to lie face down and stay put. The man complied. Minutes later, Morgan was galloping south.

Luke Halstead was scared. He'd always promised Doc Henry that he'd handle any problems at his end. So far, Luke's father had believed the stories he'd been told about the origin of the stock Luke bought. He loved his son and he trusted him. Jim Buttrey had come snooping around the Halstead stock too. Luke had handled that . . . with a shotgun. Lee Morgan, if he was more than he appeared, would be another matter.

"I want that sonuvabitch dead," Luke said. He

was still groggy.

"He tol' me he was ridin' out o' Creede. Maybe we'd best let it be, Luke. We don't want Doc Henry on our asses do we?" Luke looked up. His little friend was right. Luke nodded.

"Yeah, okay for right now. But if that bastard comes back, I'm taking 'im out."

South Fork was a whore house which also happened to provide a livery barn, mercantile, stage stop and five saloons. The only women in the settlement were those of ill repute. Most of the men were either on the run or in between illegal activities.

Morgan contacted the girl named Gretchen who ran Molly's house in the community. She told him she'd have the girls ready to leave by the following morning. He lined up the stage coach and then found his way to the most raucous of South Fork's saloons. He was soon immersed in a six-man stud poker game.

By midnight, though down about two hundred dollars, Morgan was still in the game. Now he was one of only four men playing. He had barely noticed the entry of two new faces in the saloon, but he had a feeling he was being watched. After a win, Morgan stood up and announced he was going to get himself a cold beer. As he turned to walk to the bar, one of the two new faces appeared in front of him.

"I been tryin' to figure you, mister, and now I don't have to anymore. You're Lee Morgan." Morgan eyed the man carefully but he was also aware of the movement of the second man. Off to his right, the man had circled and now flanked him.

"You find something wrong with who I am?"

"You gunned down my brother," the man said. "It was in Cheyenne, a year back."

Morgan remembered. "Davy Wickett wasn't it?"

"Yeah. I'm Tom and that there's my brother Joad."

The Wickett boys were sometime bounty hunters and all-time bastards. They had never brought a man in alive and most of the dead ones had been shot in the back.

"You should have told your little brother who he'd be facing. Maybe he'd still be alive," Morgan said. The man's face twisted into a scowl and he stepped back. Morgan could detect a similar move by the man to his far right. Chairs scraped across the old wooden floor as men jumped up and scurried for neutral corners. The saloon girls were huddled in a little knot at the end of the bar.

"I heard you back shot 'im, Morgan."

"You heard wrong."

"I don't think so," the man replied, pausing only long enough to curl his lips into a sneering smile, "but either way, I'm sayin' you did."

"You're a liar, Wickett." Morgan's voice was soft but his demeanor displayed his readiness to back the allegation. He punctuated his words with a slight shift in his own position. He was now facing in a diagonal direction between the two men. He could see both but faced neither head-on.

"You ain't good enough to take us both," Tom Wickett said.

"Then I'll make damned sure you're the volunteer for the one I do get." As Morgan spoke, his eyes shifted, for just a split second, to Tom Wickett's six gun. It was an old Navy Colt, hung low on the man's leg and tied down. Morgan could take this man in a heartbeat. He couldn't see Joad Wickett's rig so he'd have to take him out first.

Just as Morgan had anticipated, it was Joad who made the first move, and it was fast. Morgan drew, dropped into a semi-crouch and felt the sting of splintering wood strike his right cheek. His own bullet had already struck Joad Wickett, killing him instantly. The Bisley's barrel was levelled at Tom Wickett's heart when a shotgun went off. It nearly tore Tom's arm from the socket and Morgan's own reflexes precluded stopping his own action. Tom didn't feel much pain from the shotgun blast. He was dead a split second later.

Morgan's brain relayed still another signal to his deadly right arm. Maybe the shotgun was meant for him. The Colt found its target even before Morgan's eyes could focus on it. There, half way up the staircase, stood Emmy Venable!

5

Emmy Venable refused to take "No" for an answer when she told Lee she planned to accompany him. The following morning, he purchased some chloroform from the town doctor, drugged Emmy and put her on the eastbound stage. By ten o'clock, he and his girls were well on their way back to Creede. Gretchen had opted to ride the shotgun seat.

"Molly told me she had five girls working for her. Where'd the extra come from?"

"I don't know," Gretchen replied. Morgan detected a deep, Southern drawn. "She just come bouncin' in one evenin', pretty as you please. Told me she'd work for room an' board. Ah don't think she's slept with a customer since she's been heah."

"She looks pretty young." Morgan turned and looked at Gretchen for her reaction. She was nodding.

"Ah think she said she was twenty but ah don't believe her. Why I doubt the girl's a day ovah seventeen."

"Yeah," Morgan said, "that'd by my guess." He

didn't know why but the presence of the extra girl, young as she was, bothered him. Morgan didn't like things out of the ordinary or last minute changes or new faces. At least, not while he was on a job that would probably bring him face to face with the likes of Doc Henry Jared.

The trip back to Creede was uneventful. Morgan had found himself some dude clothes, as he called them. Gretchen kept his things with her own, including his Colt. It wouldn't do for him to be seen wearing a gun while he was posing as pimp for Molly. He did carry a Derringer, but it afforded him no comfort.

Molly arranged for rooms for the girls, and Morgan stayed in her quarters. He'd simply stay out of sight for another day and then the little party would head northwest to meet Charlie Bojack. Molly was ready to bed down with Morgan again that night but, in a rare instance, Morgan wasn't.

"You're a mite fidgety," Molly said.

"You know anything about this extra girl?"

Molly looked surprised. She smiled. "Lee Morgan is worried about a snip of a girl? You've gone daft on me."

Morgan was on the bed, his back against the headboard, fingering the Derringer. He looked up at Molly, then back to the gun and said, "It isn't just the girl. Someone else showed up and I've got a hunch she'll show up again."

"She?"

Morgan nodded. "The daughter of the man I'm working for."

"And just who might that be?"

"I'd sooner not say," Morgan replied. "The less you know, the better."

"She after the same thing you are?" She paused and then placed more emphasis on her words. "Or is she after you?"

"Probably both." Now Morgan looked up. "But I told you before, I'm in this for the money." There was a knock at the door. Molly opened it, noting Morgan's reflexive tension. Morgan saw a tall, thin man dressed in a black suit, like an undertaker. Molly invited him in. It was then that Morgan spotted the man's gun.

"This is Trigg," she said. "He's my right hand." The tall man nodded when Morgan spoke to him. "He's a mute."

Morgan watched as the man scrawled a note to Molly. She read it, wrote a short reply and sent him on his way. Morgan saw that her face was somewhat paled.

"A problem?"

"Maybe a big one, Mahrgan. Doc Henry's brother is back in the territory. He was spotted in Durango four days ago."

"What was the note you wrote?"

"I told Trigg to put two o' my men to watchin' for him. He'd likely recognize you right off."

"More than just likely, Molly. He'd gun me in a heartbeat."

"My man figures Johnny Jared is the contact man for whatever scheme Doc Henry is into now. You know what it is?"

"Gun running to some Apache renegades."

"My men can take him out." Morgan shook his head. "Why not?"

"He's the only trail I've got right now. I can't be sure of finding out what I need to know in Doc Henry's camp . . . not even with the help of your girls. Johnny Jared is my back-up plan. I don't like it, but I'll have to use him."

"You sure you don't want me to have Johnny eliminated?"

"I'm sure."

'An' how about spendin' the night with you, Mahrgan? You still sure about *that*?"

Morgan eyed the swell of her breasts and the flair of her hips. He felt the tightness forming in his groin but it passed quickly. "Sorry," he said.

The sun was still struggling to climb above San Luis peak when the stagecoach reached the summit of Spring Creek pass. The horses' sides heaved under the weight of the load they pulled in the oxygen-thin air. The girls climbed down from the coach and gaped at the valley below them. It ran east and west for a hundred miles or more. Just a few miles to the northwest, it took a sharp rise up again, all the way to the summit of Slumgullion pass.

"You been to the Uncompahgre before?" Molly asked.

"Nope. Never had a reason."

"She's beautiful, Mahrgan . . . but she's deadly. In winter, the drifts get twenty feet deep and a blizzard can whip up in no time an' bury man an' beast alike."

"Yeah," Morgan said, taking in the entire panorama below him, "and it hides a few side-winders as well . . . the two-legged variety."

"There's a man comin', Miss Molly." One of the girls was pointing down trail.

"Charlie Bojack," Molly said. She walked toward him, catching him about fifty yards from the coach. Charlie didn't look at her. His eyes were squinting into the morning sun, trying to identify Molly's male companion. " 'Lo, Charlie."

"Who's the dude?"

"Name's Wilfrid Butler. He runs some girls for me over in Walsenburg. Law got nasty and run 'im out. I brought 'im up to Creede to help out."

"Doc Henry ain't expectin' no dude."

"Doc Henry ain't expectin' me, Charlie. You want to tell 'im we're not comin' in because I had a dude with me?"

Charlie eyed her. Molly was smiling. Doc Henry would have Charlie's hide if he turned Molly down, dude or no dude. "Let's ride. We got some hard country to cover."

"Will we make it by dark?"

"We'll make it." Charlie looked toward Morgan again and then turned his horse and waited.

Charlie hadn't lied. The terrain was rugged. The trail led from the main road, itself only little more than a trail, down into the very depths of the Uncompahgre. It was early afternoon before they finally reached bottom. Another two hours passed as they followed a river along its course where it flowed down from the melted snows of Sheep mountain. Finally, Lake Fork river began a rushing trip into the final depths of the huge valley. Atop the last ridge before Doc Henry's hideaway, Charlie Bojack stopped the party.

"All guns git dumped right here. You got a gun, dude?"

"No, sir," Morgan said.

"I catch you lyin' to me an' I'll have your ass." He turned to Molly. "Any o' them girls got guns?"

She grinned. "They didn't come here to *shoot* anythin', Charlie." He nodded but Molly and Morgan could tell he wasn't completely convinced.

The coach finally came to a halt in front of a huge log house. It was, even by city standards, a fine residence. The door opened and out stepped Doc Henry Jared.

"I'll be a sumbitch," he shouted. "Molly!" He grabbed her around the waist and whirled her around several times, then he kissed her, hard. He finally put her back on the ground, pushed her away gently and made a wide, sweeping gesture with his arms. "Welcome to Winchester Valley," he said.

Morgan had taken note of every twist, turn and rock along the way. Even he was impressed. Doc Henry might only have nine men, but it would take a cavalry regiment to get to him. Besides, Morgan harbored no misconceptions about Doc Henry's men. They'd all be the best and he knew there would be more than any nine. These were his closest gang members, the leaders. Doc would have men riding in about every day before his next operation.

While Charlie directed Morgan and the girls to their quarters, Doc Henry met with Molly in the main house.

"I smell somethin' gone rotten," he said. "You never come before."

"I never had a reason before."

"You had me. Ain't that reason enough?"

"You can't buy me, Doc. I told you that before. I do business with them what can do business back."

"An' now you need ol' Doc Henry. Is that it?" She nodded. "What for?"

"Makin' money."

"I'm not in the whore business," Doc said.

"An' I want out of it. Runnin' guns to the Indians pays better from the look of it."

Doc Henry frowned and eyed Molly carefully. She had to tread ever so carefully, and she knew it. She struggled to keep smiling.

"What do you think you know?" he asked.

"The army is about to bring in twenty wagon loads o' guns . . . brand new guns. I know when and I know where. Seems to me that ought to be worth somethin' to you, Doc."

"Like what?"

"A third."

Doc laughed. "I got men up here what'd blow my head off if I give some whore a third o' their take."

"Winchester model '73's," Molly continued. She was acting as if Doc had said nothing. She walked to the window but she didn't turn to face him as she spoke. "They'd be worth fifty dollars each just to the Apache." Now she turned, quickly. "But to the Mexicans? You guess, Doc. A hundred apiece? A hundred and twenty-five maybe?"

"An' all in gold too," Doc said, sarcastically. He was surprised at Molly's response.

"Hell no, Doc. Silver! It's comin' out o' the ground at 225 ounces to the ton. The Mexicans will work for nothin' to mine it just to buy guns so's they can take over their government."

"An' you're tellin' me you know somebody who

43

can make that kind of deal." Doc got up. "That right, Molly?"

"I didn't come all the way up here to sleep with you, Doc . . . not for two hundred dollars . . . not for three times that much."

"Who and where?"

This time it was Molly who laughed. "I tell you that, Doc, an' what would you be needin' me for? Now, you interested?"

"What if I'm not, Molly my girl? What if I just tell you to go on back over the mountain?"

"Then that's exactly what I'll do. I meet a lot o' men in my profession. Hungry men, most of 'em. I'll find one that's hungry enough."

"But will you find 'im in time?"

"A third o' the take, Doc. That's not for dealin' about, so don't try."

Doc Henry poured them a drink. He downed his in a single gulp.

"You brought a dude with you. How's come?"

"He's not what I told Charlie he was. He's my contact with the Mexicans."

"What Mexicans, Molly?" Doc Henry turned surly. He hadn't stayed alive as long as this by being careless.

"Only one. You had a chance at him once but your men messed it up for you, didn't they?" Doc was caught off guard. "A girl, a woman and a young man."

"You whored with somebody, Molly. One o' my men. They opened up to you."

"Blarney! If you can't trust your own kind, Doc, I'm not wantin' to do business with you. But don't think you're the only one can make a fortune and a contact in these mountains. You're not!'"

"Yeah," Doc said, softly. "I'll deal with you Molly
. . . a third." He turned and pointed a finger at her.
"But I've got my own deal to make first."

Molly shrugged and said, "Fine. It'll take a bit to
set mine up anyway. Now I'll be askin' you to let my
man come and go as he needs to."

"Charlie Bojack rides with him . . . everywhere."

"No. If Butler rides in with a gunny on his back
there'll be trouble. He goes alone. I trust 'im and
you'll have to trust me." Doc grabbed Molly's arm,
up high. He nearly lifted her from her feet as he
pulled her close. The stubble of his beard scraped
across her cheeks and his breath was hot and reeked
of bad whisky. "You're hurtin' my arm," she said.

"It'll be a whole lot worse than that, Molly, if
you're lyin' to me. You think I won't put you under
same as anybody?"

"No, Doc . . . I don't think that."

"Then we'll deal, Molly, and you an' me, we'll
make it official tonight." The idea revolted her but
Molly knew she had pushed as far as she could.

6

Jim Buttrey had told Molly everything he knew. Morgan knew it now, and he didn't like it one damned bit. Unfortunately, there was nothing he could do about it. Molly had planned her vengeance even before Morgan entered the picture. Buttrey's death was only a small part of her motive. Doc Henry had also been responsible for the death of Molly's little sister. The outlaw didn't know that but Molly did, and Morgan knew she'd get Doc even at the cost of her own life.

"You've put a lot of people's lives in danger," Morgan told her, "just to kill Doc Henry."

"I'd as soon see 'im hang, Mahrgan, but I swear to you on me sister's grave, Doc Henry will die. I'll play along with you for now but if you don't get him, I will."

"The Mexicans? Is that legitimate?"

"To be sure, but I don't want him to get that far. I think he'll tell me what I need to know about his deal with the Apaches. Once he's done that, we can make a plan to stop him." Molly walked across the room, stood quietly for a moment and then turned back to face Morgan. "I've told you everything," she said. "Now who are you workin' for and why? I know it's not all for the money."

"U.S. Senator Venable. Doc killed his youngest daughter, his son, and his wife. Emmy Venable is the girl I told you about . . . his other daughter. I'm working for him, officially. I'm a Pinkerton agent, same as Jim was."

"This Emmy woman can do us in," Molly said. "Can you control her?" Morgan mentally smiled to himself. Control Emmy Venable? It was laughable after the way she'd set him up. Morgan knew better than to let Molly in on that part.

"I can handle her," he replied.

"Sure you can, Mahrgan," Molly said, grinning, "but can you control her?" Molly didn't wait for an answer. She had a meeting with her girls. They would be instructed to elicit as much information out of Doc Henry's men as they could. Most were experts at it. While Molly was doing that, Morgan decided to play his hand. He'd simply go out into the open, ask to see Doc Henry personally. If there was anyone in camp who recognized him, he might as well get it over with fast.

Charlie Bojack ushered Morgan into Doc's house and then left. Doc was studying a map. Finally, he fired up a Cheroot and looked up. He eyed Morgan carefully.

"I seen you before, dude. That bothers me 'cause I don't recollect exactly where it was."

"Probably in Creede. Walsenburg maybe."

"Yeah . . . maybe. Maybe not. Anyways, when I finally recollect you'd better hope it was someplace right. Now dude, what Mexican do you work for?''

"Senor Valesquez. I am his aide."

"Can you speak for him—official, I mean?''

"I can."

"How's come? You're sure no Mex."

"I served with the American delegation for five years. He trusts me because I put him onto a source for weapons, women and other things he needed to support his revolution." Morgan was more than a little surprised at Doc Henry's grasp and knowledge of such matters. He suddenly realized he'd have to be on guard.

"So you know who his best field general is . . . don't you?''

"General Quesada? Of course." Morgan relaxed a little and made himself comfortable in a nearby stuffed chair. "You will not deal with him, however; you will deal with me and me only."

"And maybe when I'm through dealin' with you . . . I'll kill you, dude." Doc Henry smiled and his hand flashed to his hip.

"From all I've heard about you," Morgan replied, calmly, "I hardly think you'd risk a hundred thousand dollars just for the fun of putting a bullet in me." Doc's eyebrows raised and Morgan took advantage of the reaction. "Yes, Mister Henry . . . one hundred thousand. That's the sum I've been authorized to offer as payment for the rifles."

"In cash?''

"In silver, just as Miss O'Flynn told you."

"When and where?" Doc asked. Morgan chuckled. "You laughin' at me?''

"At your question. As you were told earlier, if you have that information, you have no need for my services or those of Miss O'Flynn, do you?"

"Okay, dude, what's next?"

"I will make contact with Senor Valesquez and tell him we have made a bargain. By the time you finish the job you have to do, the arrangements will be made." Morgan stood up and walked to the door. "Incidentally," he said, "just when will you be finished?"

"Ten days," came the reply. Morgan's nonchalance had paid off. "I'll want half the silver then and the balance on delivery."

Morgan turned around and said, "You'll have two thirds of the silver then and the rest on delivery. Miss O'Flynn wants her share up front as well." Morgan gave Doc Henry a little smile, a wave and walked out.

Charlie Bojack came back into the room, having entered the house from the rear. Doc looked up at him.

"You know that dude?"

"They's somethin' familiar about him," Charlie answered.

"Yeah . . . yeah there damned sure is, and I don't like it. Put a man on 'im, Charlie, a man what'll stick like flies to horse dung."

"Jake Trist just rode in. How 'bout him?"

"Good choice. If the dude is what he claims, Jake'll have no trouble findin' out. If he ain't," Doc continued, grinning, "Jake'll have no trouble killin' 'im."

Jake Trist was a quarter-breed Mescalero and one of the best trackers in the Southwest. He was also lightning fast with his guns. He wore two and was equally skilled with either hand. He'd ridden with

Quantrell, served as a deputy marshal for Wyatt Earp, and scouted for the army. Mostly, Jake Trist was a killer.

While Charlie Bojack was meeting with Jake, Molly sat down with her girl Gretchen, from South Fork. They thought they were alone. In fact, within earshot was the new girl who'd shown up in South Fork. Even now, no one knew anything about her but her first name. It was Elizabeth, but most just called her Beth.

Molly confided everything in Gretchen. She too had been a victim of Doc Henry and was seeking revenge. Gretchen was both surprised and relieved at the news about who Lee Morgan really was and why he was there. Beth was shocked. A few minutes after Molly and Gretchen separated, Beth slipped out of the room and made her way to the bunk houses used by Doc Henry's men. She singled one of them out, a young one. They left together, laughing.

Alone, hidden by a cluster of boulders, the young man finally spoke.

"What's this all about, Beth? I told you last night, I'm not leavin' and I'm not quittin' Doc Henry. This here is the only way I'll git enough money for us to live on and help Momma too."

"It's a trap, Billy . . . ever'thing is a trap. Miss Molly is in on it and that new man that come with her, that man named Butler. Well he's really a Pinkerton man an' his name is Lee Morgan. They plan to do somethin' to trap all o' you."

"Little sister, are you sure? Absolute sure?"

"I heard 'em, Billy. I heard Miss Molly and Gretchen talkin'. I'm sure, and if we don't light out o' here right now, Billy Frye, we'll both be daid."

Elizabeth Frye was only nineteen. She had been looking for her brother for more than a year, off and on. Billy had ridden away from their run-down little farm after his father died. He'd been sure he could earn enough to take care of the family of eight. He drifted for a few weeks, finally ending up in Creede. There, because of his way with horses, Billy fell in with the Halstead family. It was through Luke that he finally joined Doc Henry's gang. The money was easy, regular, and there was no law within a hundred miles.

When Beth's mother fell ill, she asked a neighbor for help and then went off in search of Billy. The trail finally led her to Molly O'Flynn's whore house. Now she was scared and shocked at the life in which she found Billy. Too, he'd taken to wearing a six gun and had even bragged to her about his skill with it. He was, in Beth's eyes, a gun fighter.

Billy escorted Beth back to the girl's quarters and reassured her that he would be safe. In fact, Billy wasn't exactly sure what he was going to do. He suffered no ill feelings about stealing army guns and selling them to the Apaches. But he had learned recently about the atrocities perpetrated by Doc Henry's men upon innocent victims. He'd already planned to do only one more job for Doc, collect what was due him, and ride out. Now he was facing the most difficult and dangerous decision of his young life.

While Billy struggled with his feelings, the safety of his sister and the knowledge she had shared with him, Lee Morgan rode out of the camp. He had been on the trail less than an hour before he knew he was being followed.

The discovery was no surprise to Morgan. Doc Henry was certainly not above a lie or a double-cross in any deal with anybody. Morgan's problem was simply one of keeping Jake Trist from finding out the truth. It seemed to him that the best way to do that would be to actually meet with the Mexican Ambassador. Morgan knew that he could gain such an appointment by merely using the Venable name. The Ambassador's men would deal with Jake Trist, and the situation would lend credibility to Molly's story. Ambassador Valesquez maintained an office in Farmington, New Mexico Territory. Morgan would telegraph his request and set up the meeting at the Chimney Rock Indian agency. It was about equal distance from Farmington and Creede.

Morgan spotted his pursuer more than once, but he made certain he wasn't seen. He had hoped to identify the man but the distance was too great. Finally, Morgan decided simply to ride on back to Creede and execute his plan. It was, he was satisfied, a good one. What he didn't and couldn't count on was Emmy Venable!

7

Morgan's timing couldn't have been better if he'd planned it. He rode hard and fast out of Winchester Valley and back to South Fork. The less time he spent in Creede now, the better. It was from South Fork that Morgan sent his telegraph to Senor Valesquez. That done, he found himself a room.

His arrival back in South Fork was timed almost exactly with that of Emmy Venable. She had managed to entice the Butterfield stage driver to return her to South Fork the very same day Morgan had chloroformed her. In the days that followed, she learned enough facts to formulate a plan of her own. It included sense enough to stay clear of Creede, which was where she believed Morgan to be. It was no small shock to her when she saw him enter the very rooming house where she was staying.

Emmy watched and waited. Morgan finally left his room and made his way to a room down the hall. It was equipped with a cattle tank that served as a bath tub. Morgan had a towel wrapped around him and his Colt in his hand. Emmy slipped into his room. Fifteen minutes passed. The door opened. Morgan closed it behind him, walked to the bed and slipped the Colt into its holster.

"Drop the towel," Emmy said. Morgan was half way between the bed and the chair which held his britches. He looked. She was leveling the sawed-off at him. "Don't get the idea I won't use it. I'm not that sure of anything right now, especially you." She motioned with the shotgun. Morgan looked down just a little sheepishly, then let the towel drop.

"You're a threat to this whole operation, Emmy," Morgan said. "That's why I bush-whacked you. Any one of Doc Henry's men could recognize you."

"I'm not stupid, Morgan, but I'm also not as full of blind trust as my father is." Emmy's eyes had really never left Morgan's groin. The idea that he was again being victimized by this woman somewhat angered Morgan, but the anger was tempered with his memory of the Windsor Hotel. Too, bedding her one more time would offer him his best chance to gain the upper hand. Emmy Venable had other ideas. "Lie down," she said. Morgan didn't hestitate. Even the minimal anticipation of her against him began to manifest itself and by the time he was on the bed, his cock was semi-rigid.

Emmy kept the shotgun pointed at him even as she fumbled through her handbag. Morgan's eyes widened when she produced a pair of handcuffs. She threw them at him and said, "Cuff your wrists to the center post." Morgan's mouth started to move but Emmy pulled the hammers back on both shotgun barrels. Morgan complied. Emmy leaned the shotgun against the wall, removed all her clothing and used the drawstrings from her corset to secure

Morgan's ankles to the footboard.

She positioned herself over his chest and then leaned forward. Her breasts brushed his face, their hardened tips caressed his lips. She chuckled. She was enjoying the power as much as, maybe more than, the act itself. She reversed her body, eased her bottom directly over Morgan's face and then lowered it. "Lick it." The words weren't a feminine plea but a demand. "Do it until I say stop."

Lee Morgan wasn't accustomed to taking orders. Even this one stirred irritation deep within him. Partly, his mind conjured up flashing memories of the power he exerted over Molly O'Flynn. The tables were turned and the role was a new one. Those things aside, Morgan's expertise was in no way hindered.

Emmy increased her own pleasure with timed movements of her hips and settled lower so that she might savor every movement of Morgan's tongue. In just a minute or so, her hands found the softness of her own breasts and she kneaded the flesh and toyed with the nipples. Her eyes were glazed with passion and she licked her lips with every prod of Morgan's tongue.

She scooted back just a bit farther and then leaned forward onto her forearms. Her own mouth went to work now. She sucked and licked and caressed Morgan's blood-gorged shaft, his balls, inner thighs and lower abdomen. This too was new for Morgan, at least from Emmy Venable. She had made no such overtures while they were in Denver. She was an expert as well.

Emmy's whole body suddenly stiffened. She was on her hands and knees and her breathing sounded almost labored. Morgan couldn't see her face but her eyes were rolled back, her teeth clenched and sweat trickled down her cheeks onto her neck. She shuddered. A moment later, she eased herself off the bed, stood up, spread her legs and placed her hands on her hips.

"You are very good, Morgan . . . really. Thank you." Morgan reacted inside. He felt a gut wrenching tension. His balls ached and his cock twitched reflexively. Emmy's head went back slightly and she laughed.

"You've made your point," Morgan said. It was all he said. Anything else would probably sound like begging. That he didn't intend to do. Emmy sat on the edge of the bed. She thrust two fingers down between her legs and rubbed until they were shiny with her own juices of satisfaction. She rubbed them along Morgan's cock and then repeated the procedure, this time wetting his nipples. She leaned down and licked first one, then the other. She felt the muscles tighten, the breath sucked in. She raised up and laughed again. She studied Morgan's face, closely. His teeth were clenched but it was not from passion. He was determined to resist.

"You'd like to finish, wouldn't you?" Morgan didn't answer. Emmy stroked his cock again. It's head looked so swollen it appeared on the verge of bursting open. She stopped. "Well, wouldn't you?" Morgan nodded almost imperceptibly. Emmy laughed. "Not good enough, Morgan. Say it! Say," she lowered her tone slightly, "Emmy, I'd like to cum.' "

"Go to hell." She laughed and lowered her head to his chest. Her tongue flicked over his swollen nipples and her hand was pulling, slow, even strokes on his cock. Morgan felt all his own juices rushing to their release. He tensed and strained against his bonds. Emmy stopped. Morgan's breath stopped too. He tried to concentrate on completing his desire but her timing had been perfect.

"Say it, Morgan. Say the words," she paused, caressed his cock again and added, "and say 'Please, Emmy.' "

Lee Morgan had been around a lot of women, a lot of experienced women. Molly enjoyed her submissiveness and Morgan had bedded down with more than one who enjoyed a certain sexual dominance. Emmy was not like any of them. It was not the sexual satisfaction she enjoyed but the power she wielded. Suddenly, Morgan was feeling something else. A feeling with which he was a hundredfold more familiar. It was a feeling of danger. This woman, this seemingly innocent victim of her father's wealth and her family's fate, was dangerous. Sex was the bait but death was the trap. Morgan knew, suddenly and certainly, that Emmy Venable would use the shotgun.

"I'd like to . . . to cum, Emmy . . . *please!*" She laughed. She stood up, hovering over him for a moment, like the Black Widow just before it devours its male mate. She went to her bag and returned to the bed with the handcuff key. She undid the manacles and then hurriedly crossed the room, picked up the shotgun, turned back and levelled it at Morgan's head.

"Then please do so," she said. "I'd like to watch." Morgan hadn't masturbated since he was nine years old. He'd never done it in front of a woman. The

. order had a predictable effect. His cock softened somewhat. The reaction only made matters worse. "Looks like you'll have to play with it a little, doesn't it, Morgan?" She cocked the shotgun again. Morgan played. He stroked, trying hard to concentrate only on Emmy's naked and still inviting body. His eyes half closed and in a moment it was over. Sweat rolled from his muscular body and his face burned from a combination of involuntary embarrassment and increasing anger. It had all been done to a background of Emmy Venable's sinister laugh.

Morgan reached for the draw strings around his ankles. Emmy stopped him. "Just before you do that, you'd better understand one thing." Morgan looked at her. "I've got two men with me, good men. They know you but you've never seen them. If you have any ideas about getting rid of me again, I'd suggest you forget them."

"It's your neck," Morgan said. He freed himself and got dressed. Even watching Emmy dress, Morgan realized he'd probably never be aroused by her again. It wasn't what she had forced him to do but her own state of mind which bothered . . . even frightened him. Most of the men he faced were predictable. Their skills could be judged by their actions, the gun they wore and the way they wore it. Emmy Venable could not be so judged and Morgan wouldn't drop his guard again.

As Morgan figured it, he had nothing to lose by telling Emmy the entire plan. She wasn't about to go away and in this case, Morgan reckoned that what she didn't know could kill him. She listened, nodding occasionally. When he finished, Emmy spoke. Her voice was once again that of an innocent girl with vengeance in her heart.

"You know you were followed." Morgan nodded. "Do you know the man?"

"No. Haven't got that good a look at him yet."

"My men did. He's called Trist."

"Jake Trist! Shit! He's one of the best trackers in the country."

"And one of the fastest guns too, I've heard."

"Yeah, that too."

"Well he doesn't know about me . . . or my men. We can handle him."

"You do that and we'll all be in trouble. Stay put Emmy, and stay out of it . . . just for now. Let me meet the Mexican Ambassador and let his men handle Jake Trist."

"You mean trust you?"

"Yeah, Emmy, that's exactly what I mean."

Emmy was about to protest when a knock took her attention to the door and Morgan's to his Colt.

"Got an answer fer ya Mister Butler, from down in Farmin'ton." Morgan opened the door just far enough to accept the telegraph message and hand the messenger a dollar. "Thanky, Mister Butler, thanky." Morgan unfolded the paper and read its contents aloud.

"The Ambassador regrets to inform you that he will be unable to meet with you at this time due to the press of affairs in our country. He will contact Senator Venable when his schedule permits such an appointment." Morgan looked at Emmy and frowned.

"What now?"

"I ride to Chimney Rock same as before. We know

the facts, but Jake Trist doesn't.''

"He'll find out when he gets there."

"Not if you stay here and send a message down ahead of me. I'll make certain he gets that one. I'll just fake one to confirm the gun purchase and the amount, with regrets that the Ambassador couldn't meet me in person.''

"How do you know somebody else isn't following you?''

"Because I know Jake Trist, at least by reputation. He doesn't need any help.''

"I don't like this, Morgan, not any of it.''

"You don't have to like it, Emmy, just do it.'' She hesitated a moment and then nodded. The reaction still surprised Morgan. How suddenly demure and obedient Emmy seemed. It was, he concluded, all the more reason to be cautious.

If Ambassador Valesquez's message was a minor setback in Morgan's plans, a major one was even then riding into the Chimney Rock stage station. The lone rider, sinister in appearance, dismounted and paused after pushing the bat wing doors open. His eyes adjusted quickly to the dim light. He satisfied himself that there was no danger. He walked over to the long bar.

"A whisky.''

"Just got some ice in, mister, if'n you'd be wantin' a cold beer.''

"I said whisky.'' The bartender shrugged, noting the long, deep scar on the man's right cheek. That was the only feature which distinguished Johnny Jared from his brother Doc Henry. "When's the next stage for Creede?''

"Tomorrow noon, if'n it don't git way-layed.''

"I need a room."

"Upstairs, mister. Two dollars with a bath."

"I just want it for sleeping."

"Dollar, then. Clean linen but no towels."

Over the years it had been Doc Henry Jared whose name and occasional likeness appeared on lawmen's *dodgers*. There were many stories, however, about just which of the Jared boys was the fastest. Ironically, one of the stories focused on Johnny Jared being shot in the leg by a man who, so said the witnesses, was the fastest they'd ever seen. As the story was told and re-told, the identification of the man with the fast gun came into it. Now it was generally accepted that it had been Buckskin Frank Leslie. Few people knew that Frank had fathered a son. Among those who didn't know was Johnny Jared. What he did know was what the man who'd bested him looked like. He really didn't care about the man's name.

Jared retired early that evening. It was unusually quiet in Chimney Rock and Jared felt at ease with himself. He'd returned to the territory at the request of his brother and he'd done the job that had been asked of him. He rode into Durango, staked himself to adequate supplies and then rode into New Mexico territory. He rode down to Chaco creek and there met and made a deal with a Jicarilla Apache renegade named Naschitti. In just ten more days, Johnny and Doc Henry would deliver twenty cases of army rifles and ammunition to Nashitti. In return, Naschitti's warriors were to raid an army pay wagon as it journeyed from Farmington to Durango. They would net about $50,000 for their efforts and were obliged to give only a thousand apiece to Doc Henry's men. They'd split the rest and be done with the Apaches at the same time.

It was nearer to two o'clock than noon the next day before Johnny Jared finally boarded the Butterfield stage for Creede. It was a full load. Two saloon girls, a drummer, an army sergeant, a young lawyer and Jared. There was no money aboard so there was no shotgun rider. The driver was a craggy-faced old freight skinner and knew every rock, bump and bend in the trail. By suppertime, they'd reached Pagosa Springs. The run, well into the evening, would finally end at Wolf Creek Station. It was on the western slope of Wolf Creek Pass, nearly 11,000 feet of pure hell. It was a climb not even the best skinners would try at night. On the eastern side of the mountain was another stage stop where, by mid-afternoon, the stage would stop and change stock.

Bearing down on that station, as Johnny Jared dozed off and on in the stage coach headed toward him, was Lee Morgan. A couple of miles behind him rode Jake Trist. Unknown to either of them, Trist had his own shadow. At Molly O'Flynn's order, her man Trigg was not far behind. The tiny stage stop might also become a permanent rest stop for any one of them.

8

It was summertime but the air smelled of fall. It was
cool, crisp and clean. It poured down from the San
Juans and carried with it the scent of pine and the
sound of rustling Aspen. Morgan stepped outside
the small stage depot, took in a deep breath and let
his eyes scan the terrain around him. He was still
attired in his dude clothes but the Bisley was now in
place. He felt secure again.

The station agent stepped out behind him and
eyed the sky. It was cloudless. " 'Nother mighty
purty day in the makin.' "

"Yeah," Morgan agreed.

"You ridin' on west, mister, or waitin' fer the
Butterfield?"

"I'll be moving on. I'd like to get to Pagosa
Springs by dark."

"You'll be pushin' that roan o' your'n, mister. You
ever clumb the pass?" Lee shook his head. "Well,
'tain't like most of 'em. Got a mean streak. Turn on
ya real sudden. Rock slides, snow and ice bustin'
loose," the agent paused and looked toward the

63

summit, "varmints too. Makes even the best o' horses skitterish. They's the bones o' horse and man alike . . . some say a foot deep . . . at the bottom o' one o' the drops."

"You know another way into the Springs from here?"

"Nope."

"Then I guess I'll have to chance it." Lee smiled at the agent, in part about the tall tales. "I'd best get to it." Lee slapped the man on the shoulder and headed for the stable.

Morgan was about two-thirds of the way toward the summit when he was forced to dismount. The agent had been right about the rock slides. Half the narrow trail was blocked and the outside edge of it looked none too safe. He began to clear some of the smaller rocks away but he doubted there'd be room for the stage to pass. He decided to wave it down when he finally met it and warned the driver.

The stage itself was already at the summit but not without its own problems. A hub had snapped and it had lost a wheel. The male passengers were helping the driver to get set for repairs, and Johnny Jared was chopping down a small pine to assist them in raising the rear of the coach when the time came.

"Fella ridin' our way," the drummer said, pointing. Everyone stopped their work and looked up. Jared was still working on the tree, about fifty yards away. "Howdy, mister. S'pose you could spare us a hand?"

"Yeah," Morgan replied, dismounting. "You got more troubles about half way down. Rock slide. I cleared some of it but you'll have to lever a couple of big boulders out of the way." Morgan looked over the passengers carefully, studied the heavy coach's position and then turned back for a last glance at the trail he'd just come over. Somewhere behind him, he knew Jake Trist was still coming.

"Hey, you at the coach . . . give me a hand with this log." Morgan was surprised. The voice came from the opposite side of the stage . . . a man's voice. Another passenger. He was tense with a sudden alertness.

"Had a fella choppin' down a pine to use fer some leverage," the driver said. Morgan nodded and started around the coach.

Johnny Jared was bent over at the waist, wrestling the log loose from between two rocks. The stage driver, the army sergeant and Morgan, who was out front, were headed toward him.

"Hang on, mister, and we'll give ya a hand," the driver hollered. Jared straightened and turned. His eyes met Morgan's. Both men squinted. Morgan's features seemed to leap from his face and reform themselves in Jared's mind. A voice. A threat. A flashing Colt. Jared's mind recalled the grunt he'd heard and the searing pain in his right knee.

"Jeezus! Lee Morgan!"

Morgan's own thoughts had been hurtling through his head with the speed of bullets . . . but he had that all-important edge. This time, it was his recent visit with Doc Henry. Even as Jared's mind was recreating their last meeting, Morgan's right hand was in motion. A split second had passed. Jared's fingers tightened around the butt of the gun strapped to his left leg. Morgan's peripheral vision registered the movement of a man's body off to his left. The stage driver was diving for the ground. The army sergeant stood, petrified by the scene unfolding a few feet from him.

The Bisley's barrel belched out blue smoke and the crack of shot bounced against the rocky surroundings, echoing down the slopes of Wolf Creek Pass. Morgan had shot to kill. The sergeant's eyes had blinked and he'd missed the draw. The bullet struck home . . . Johnny Jared's heart . . . dead center. His own gun barked and the bullet ripped through Morgan's pant leg about boot high, tearing away the boot's pull strap. Jared blinked. He coughed. Blood filled the cavity that was his open mouth. His left hand jerked, reflexively, and he fell, face down.

Morgan whirled. "Stand fast," he ordered. No one moved. His brain sent him another warning. The shot! Jake Trist must have heard it. He'd want to know about it.

"I saw it all, mister, ever' move," the army sergeant said, "the man pulled on ya. It was self defense fer sure."

Jake Trist pulled back hard on the reins. A shot! Two! They were from different guns. He jerked his rifle free from its boot, tucked it under his arm and spurred his mount. He crouched low and dug the spurs deeper still into the big animal's flanks. He could see the figures of two men near the coach. A third was on his hands and knees, trying to get up. Trist's eyes scanned ahead of him. Another man was face down, not moving. He saw a horse nearby and recognized the animal. He'd seen it, recently . . . Durango! It was Johnny Jared's horse.

"Look out!" It was the sergeant. They were his

last words. The Henry repeater barked once and a small, red spot appeared on the sergeant's forehead. Morgan dropped to one knee, swung his right arm in a leading movement and squeezed the trigger. The shot lifted Jake's hat from his head. Morgan rolled. The Henry barked again and Morgan heard the shell splintering the wood of the coach door.

Lee Morgan came to his feet, still crouching. His eyes flashed back and forth over the short distance the horse had traveled, but the animal was riderless. Jake Trist had leaped from its back, dug in his heels to control his forward momentum, spun around, and dropped behind a tree stump.

Morgan's right arm moved forward about two inches. The Colt was waist high. He squeezed the trigger. The shot was deafening . . . too much noise for a Colt. One final, ear-shattering *craaack* echoed through the rocks. Lee's eyes caught the shiny movement of the Henry's barrel. Its bullet struck, digging up the dirt twenty feet in front of Lee's position. The Colt's bullet struck Jake Trist right between the eyes, but only because his body had been lifted up by the force of a missile from a .50 calibre Sharps. That bullet had caught Jake in the side, just below his rib cage.

Now there was silence, a macabre stillness. A twig snapped and Morgan's body turned, tense, the Colt ready again. He saw Molly's man, Trigg, riding slowly toward the coach, a Sharps cradled on his free arm.

"I don't like my trail being dogged, not even by friends," Morgan said. There was no answer. "Shit!" Morgan remembered—Trigg was a mute. The tall man dismounted, slipped the Sharps back into its scabbard and walked over to Morgan. He extended his hand. Morgan stared at him. Trigg was half smiling. Morgan shook his head, and then shook Trigg's hand.

Morgan had plenty of problems and he knew it. He might get away with an explanation about Jake Trist's death, but he dared not mention Doc Henry's brother, and there would be plenty of questions about the sergeant. And no matter what he said, he knew no one on that stage coach would keep their mouths shut. On top of that, the Chimney Rock station had just been equipped with a telegraph.

By the time they'd reached South Fork again, a cavalry patrol was waiting.

"Everyone inside." The two women left the coach first and Morgan could see who was barking the order. A leathery-faced old sergeant-major. He assisted the women, half smiling, and then wrinkled his brow as the men emerged. Trigg and Morgan climbed up and aided two troopers in lowering the trio of bodies to the ground. That done, they joined the others inside. The driver had already given his account of the activities and so had the women.

A young lieutenant with a shock of blonde, touseled hair and pink cheeks confronted Morgan and Trigg.

"Lieutenant Tyson Yates, U.S. Fifth Cavalry, sir. I have been charged with determining the cause or causes and the party or parties responsible for the death of Sergeant Henry Willis."

"Only one cause, only one party, lieutenant," Morgan said. "Man named Jake Trist fired a rifle at me, missed and hit the sergeant instead."

"And the reason for the attack?"

"I figure Trist and his companions were planning a holdup. The busted wheel messed up their schedule and this fella," Morgan continued, pointing at Trigg, "just happened along."

"Is that right?" The lieutenant addressed himself to Trigg. Trigg nodded. "Your name, sir?"

"He can't tell you lieutenant. He's a mute."

The lieutenant frowned, rubbed his chin in a nervous gesture and then said, "Then your name, sir?"

"Butler. Wilfrid Butler."

"And your line of business?"

"I'm a gambler . . . mostly."

"By the accounts I heard a few minutes ago . . . Mister Butler, it would seem you're a mighty handy man with a gun."

"It was self defense, lieutenant. We caught them by surprise and came out on top. I don't know anywhere that has a law against that."

"Nor do I, sir, if that's what happened." The lieutenant turned to the others. "You are all under army detention over night. Let's hope we can clear this up by tomorrow, in which case you will be free to go." He turned back to Morgan. "I am requesting that you and your mute companion accompany me."

"Are we being arrested?"

"No, sir, but there are some additional questions."

The army had taken over a run-down hotel at the far end of town. It was there the lieutenant took Morgan and Trigg. Inside, they were asked to wait in what had once been a small dining room. After a few minutes, they were joined by the lieutenant and a captain who introduced himself as Phillip

Torrance.

"I haven't a great deal of time," he began, "and even less patience. I want the truth and I want it now. If I do not get it, gentlemen, then I will execute my rights and declare this community and those in it under martial law."

"Since when does the army take such a direct interest in territorial law?"

"A sergeant was killed. Perhaps you've forgotten."

"Not at all, captain, but there were several witnesses to the incident and they all told your lieutenant the same story." Morgan sat down, leaned back and half smiled. "Or have you forgotten, captain?"

"I'm looking for a gang of gun-runners. Sergeant Willis was enroute from Durango with information about one of them. I have reason to believe that the entire affair at Wolf Creek station was deliberately staged to eliminate him."

"At the cost of two innocent men?"

"This gang, mister, uh . . . Butler, wasn't it?" Morgan nodded. "This gang wouldn't hesitate to eliminate everyone on that stage if they felt threatened."

"And we're your best bet right now, right?"

"You are!"

Morgan carefully removed a letter from his pocket and handed it to the captain. It was his confirmation as a Pinkerton operative and bore the signature of Senator Venable. The captain read it twice and then looked up.

"How do I know you didn't lift this from one of the dead men?"

"Because I can tell you who they were as well. One of them was no doubt the very man your sergeant was looking for."

"And who might that be?"

"John Jared, the brother of the gang's leader, Doc Henry Jared."

"And the other man?"

"Jake Trist."

"Mister Morgan," the captain said, handing Lee the letter, "I'm going to verify what you tell me and I'm going to ask you to remain in town until tomorrow. You and your mute friend." Morgan pondered his position for a moment, even considering a quick verification by Emmy—but, somehow, he didn't feel comfortable with the choice. He simply nodded. "There are quarters here, not fancy, but I'm sure you've suffered worse."

"No doubt I have," Morgan said.

Sore-ass tired, Morgan slept fitfully that night. Half a dozen times he woke up, each time with a knot of discomfort deep in his belly. A good plan had gone sour and he couldn't be sure that Doc Henry didn't already know it. Molly and her girls could all be dead by now. He was glad when morning came.

It was near seven thirty before the captain finally asked Morgan and Trigg to meet with him. Morgan thought he looked grim. He soon found out why.

"I've substantiated your story, Mister Morgan, and I was told to give you your head."

"And you don't like that, do you, captain?"

"I not only don't like it, sir, I don't intend to abide by it. I don't take my orders from United States Senators. I stayed out of this situation when the last Pinkerton man showed up."

"Jim Buttrey?"

"I believe that was his name, yes. I won't make the same mistake again. I intend to stop these men before they supply those guns to Naschitti."

"I'm on the inside right now, captain, and so are several of my friends. If you go off on a half baked raid, they'll all get killed."

"And if I let you handle it and you fail, a lot more people will get killed. No, Mister Morgan, not this time. I'll work with you, but not for you."

Morgan was as tied up right now as he had been when Emmy Venable had him hand-cuffed to the bed. He didn't like being tied up at all, and this time there wasn't even any pleasure in it.

"What have you got in mind?" Morgan asked.

"An ambush. You and your friends set it up. I don't care how, but I do care where." The captain walked to a nearby desk and unfolded a map of the territory. Morgan joined in. "I know that Henry Jared is somewhere in the Uncompahgre Valley. I know it would be suicidal to attempt to take him on his own ground. You bring him out, Morgan; I'll do the rest." The captain pointed to a spot on the map. "Here, along the San Juan river, is an old mission called Gato. It's nestled in the closed end of a box canyon. Get him there and I'll do the rest."

"Sounds simple enough," Morgan said, "but just how the hell am I supposed to convince him to ride in there? Doc Henry hasn't stayed alive all these years by being stupid."

"Guns," the captain said, smiling, "lots and lots of guns. Among them, for bait, two Napoleon guns and one Gatling. It's a lot more than he expected."

"And because it's a lot more, Doc Henry will smell a skunk."

"Not if he has government confirmation and a personal request to deal on those guns only from the renegade Naschitti."

Morgan frowned. He looked Captain Torrance square in the eye. "The official confirmation I can understand, Captain, but how do you propose to get Naschitti's cooperation?"

"I have something the Apache wants perhaps even more than the guns." The captain smiled wryly. "I have Naschitti's son!"

9

"*Sumbitch!*" Doc Henry downed another shot of whisky and got up from behind his desk. "You're smarter'n ya look, dude." He winked at Molly. "This here pimp o' yours brought us back a fortune. Them Mexicans wanna deal an' we got more'n we figured on from the army to sell to Naschitti." Doc's Colt was suddenly levelled at Morgan's belly. " 'Less'n you're lyin' to me." He was grinning but Morgan knew he was still questioning such a lucrative proposition. Morgan decided to play his Ace.

"The deal is made, Jared, but it didn't come for you, Doc."

"Whatta you mean?"

"You were told not to have me followed. That was your first mistake. Senor Valesquez's men didn't take to Mister Trist."

"Jake?" Doc's eyes widened.

"He's dead, Jared. And so is your brother, Johnny."

The Colt's barrel caught Morgan a glancing blow, high up on his right cheek. His head snapped and a razor thin line of blood appeared.

"You're a lyin' sumbitch, Butler."

"You think I'd tell you that kind of news if it wasn't true?" Morgan wiped his cheek and feigned a dizziness he didn't feel. "Why risk my life for nothing?" Molly got to her feet and stood between the two men. Doc Henry was glowering but the look was slowly turning to shock.

"How?" Jared asked, weakly.

"I only know what I heard. Two men, Pinkerton agents, I heard, they ambushed your brother on the trail between Durango and Chimney Rock."

"Charlie! Get your ass in here . . . now!" Doc Henry screamed the order, downed three huge gulps of straight rye and hurled the empty bottle toward the door. It shattered just over Charlie Bojack's head. "You git on down to Creede. You find out about Jake and Johnny. You find out if this dude is tellin' me gospel. Soon as you do, you git on back."

Charlie Bojack eyed Morgan carefully. Morgan could tell he was still trying to recall where he'd seen him before. Eventually, he'd remember. Morgan didn't. Maybe it was a poster, maybe a poker game, maybe even a shoot-out. It made little difference. Morgan remained calm. When he spoke, it was softly.

"You'll lose too much time with that, Jared. The deals are made. If they don't come down on schedule, they won't come down at all."

"You tellin' me my business, dude?"

"I'm telling you mine. You do whatever you want with the Apache, but if you're not at the meeting place with Senor Valesquez on schedule there won't be any hundred thousand in silver."

"Maybe you should be givin' up on the Indian," Molly said, smiling. "Just take the deal I've made for you Doc."

"Pass up Naschitti? You are tryin' to set me up. I double cross him an' there'd be hell to pay, Molly girl." He turned back to Charlie Bojack. "Tell the men we'll ride out day after tomorrow. Follow the usual procedure. I don't want anybody stumblin' into Winchester Valley."

"I know you don't like changes," Morgan said, half smiling now and displaying some nervousness, "but after all, your brother did give his life for the deal. It's just a stroke of luck that I stumbled into it when I did."

"Yeah," Doc Henry said, "it was a lucky break. Now we'll find out if it was good luck or bad luck for you . . . dude!"

As Molly and Morgan left, young Billy Frye brushed by them on the way in. He stared at Morgan, hard. Inside, he cleared his throat, hefted his gun to display his newfound bravado and started to speak.

"Well, if'n it ain't little Billy Frye." Doc Henry uncorked another bottle, took a long drink from it and then handed it to Billy. "Wet your whistle, boy. You look like you need it." Billy nodded and complied. He nearly choked on the rotgut. Doc Henry laughed. "You git one o' them girls yet?"

"Uh . . . well no, boss, not yet."

"Well you'd best do it quick, boy. We're pullin' out day after tomorrow. Hell, what's the matter with you? Your dick rot and fall off? Why when I was your age, I'da had 'em all fucked by now . . . oncest anyways." He laughed again and took another drink.

"Boss . . . I . . . I come to . . . talk to you about somethin' important."

"That right? Well Billy boy, just you talk away. Few more days an' you'll be so damned rich you won't even want to talk to me. You can buy yourself as many fancy women as you want. Not whores like these but fancy, N'Orleans women. Besides, these here'll all be pushin' up daisies."

Billy frowned. "What?"

"Daisies, boy. Sod. Dead, Billy boy, cold, stone *dead*. Ever'one of 'em 'cept fer Molly."

"I . . . I don't understand, Mister Jared."

"Simple, boy. They seen too much an' they know too much." Doc Henry walked over, wrapped his arm around Billy's neck and half dragged him across the room. "You'll learn aplenty ridin' with me, boy, but if you don't learn nothin' else you'll learn not to trust nobody but your own kind." He slapped Billy on the back, laughed and then added, "An' only trust them when you can see 'em."

"Yes sir."

"Now what was it you wanted to tell me that was so all fired important?"

"Uh . . . well I was wonderin' if you thought I was ready to ride with you on the next job."

Doc Henry looked into Billy's eyes. The request puzzled him. It didn't seem to match Billy's concern when he first walked in. If Doc Henry Jared was short on anything, it wasn't his judgment of men.

"That's it?"

"Uh . . . yeah, boss."

"Bullshit!"

"Well . . . I was hopin' you'd let me ride as a gun

77

an' not just a lookout or watchin' the horses."

"A gun? So you think you've got that good, eh?"

"I've been practicinjg near ever' day now."

"You as good as Charlie here?"

"Well, I . . . I don't know."

"Then let's find out." Doc Henry jammed his hand into his pants pocket and pulled out a coin. "Draw when it hits the floor." He tossed it up. Billy's eyes were still on Doc. Suddenly they went up. At the same moment, the coin struck the wooden floor and bounced. Billy reached, but he was already staring into the barrel of Charlie Bojack's .45.

"I . . . I wasn't ready."

"That's right, boy, you wasn't an' you'd be dead. An' if'n you was ridin' with me, you'd have somebody else to keep an eye on and they'd be dead too. I'll tell you when you're ready, boy . . . me, not you." Billy nodded and eased toward the door.

Outside he took a deep breath of air and tried to settle his nerves. He'd had two close calls and he was more confused than ever. Doc was going to kill all those women. Maybe even Molly and for sure he'd kill Lee Morgan. Beth might talk too, if she thought Billy was in danger. He didn't know what to do.

Alone with Molly for the first time since his return, Morgan filled her in on the events which had transpired. By the time he was through, Molly was pacing and cursing under her breath. Suddenly, she stopped.

"You know, don't you, that Jared won't take every man he's got to meet Naschitti. Hell, Mahrgan, men been ridin' in here, steady, since you left. There must be thirty or more by now. "

"Yeah I figured that."

"If the army even gets half of 'em they'll be lucky."

"Yeah . . . I figured that too."

"Damn you, Mahrgan! How can you be so bloody calm about it?"

"I took a little extra precaution, Molly. I telegraphed Senator Venable and asked him to see to it that there were some minor changes made in that gun shipment."

"Like what?"

"Like only one in five crates of rifles will actually contain rifles, and the shipment will be in that canyon two days ahead of schedule. The wagons bringing the shipment in will bypass the army and go direct to Gato mission."

"Can you be sure o' that, Mahrgan?" He handed her a dispatch. It was Senator Venable's reply to the request. "So you've done that much. How do you get the word to the Apache?"

"Your man Trigg handled that for me. Seems he has an Indian friend." Molly looked puzzled for a moment and then smiled. Trigg had been bedding down with an Apache maiden.

"I told you Trigg was a good man." Morgan nodded his agreement. "There's still Doc Henry. How do you convince him?"

"I'll handle that when we get to Creede. Remember, Doc Henry thinks I'm a man with all the right connections. I'll convince him of it by a simple visit to the good Captain."

Almost as though she'd been struck a blow, the whole scheme suddenly revealed itself to Molly.

"God A'mighty Mahrgan! You plan on runnin' half o' Doc's men into that canyon so's Naschitti can open them crates and find out he's been duped."

"That's about the size of it, Molly. By my reckoning, he'll be one mad Apache."

"An' we'll be rid o' half our worries."

"And the army should be able to take care of the other half. Captain Torrance commands three cavalry companies, that should be enough."

"And when he finds out he's been duped too . . . an' missed a chance to get Naschitti?"

"That, Molly, is Senator Venable's problem."

"The girl, Mahrgan . . . the Senator's daughter. What of her?" It was the only question Molly had asked for which Morgan had no answer. He still felt uneasy about her and he knew she wouldn't simply be sitting idly by.

"It's the only hand we've got, Molly . . . and she's the draw card."

"So it is, Mahrgan, so it is. I just hope it works." Morgan smiled. "There's an old Irish saying that covers it if it doesn't, Molly. I think it goes something like . . . I hope you're in heaven half an hour before the devil knows you're dead." Molly nodded but she wasn't smiling.

Throughout the next day, Morgan, Molly and her girls watched men ride into Winchester Valley. By nightfall they estimated Doc's gang had swelled to more than 60. Many of the girls spent time with Doc's top hands, mostly trying to keep them half drunk. One, however, stayed out of sight. Beth Frye was scared out of her wits and she hadn't spoken to Billy since the day she told him what she'd overheard. She was crying to herself when Gretchen walked in on her.

"What is it, Beth, what's wrong?" Beth shook her head but continued crying. Gretchen tried a second time. Still Beth resisted. "Did one of these jackasses hurt you?" Beth shook her head. Gretchen sat beside her and put an arm around her shoulder. "You're not the girl you claim to be, are you?" Now Beth looked up. Her eyes were wide and her expression gave Gretchen all the answer she needed.

"I lied to you," Beth blurted out. "I lied so I could get up here and help my . . . my . . ."

"Your what?"

"My brother." Beth confessed all to Gretchen, finally calming down enough to express her more immediate concerns. "I don't know if Billy's told anybody yet."

"I think we're safe in figuring he didn't," Gretchen replied. "We're all still alive." Gretchen stood up, walked a few feet and turned back. "You go fetch Billy right now. Get him back here."

"What do I say to him?"

"I don't give a damn what you say, Beth. Just get him here."

Gretchen watched Beth cross the compound and then hurried off to find Molly and Morgan. Just her tone, when she found them, was enough to get them to return to her quarters. She hastily informed them of Beth's real reason for being there. She had barely finished when Beth and Billy walked in. Billy saw Morgan and reached for his gun.

"You go ahead and kill me," Morgan said, "and then hope you can keep Doc Henry from killing you . . . and your sister." Billy holstered his gun.

"Have you told Doc Henry the truth?" Molly asked.

"I went to do it yesterday."

"But you didn't. Why not?"

"He's gonna kill ever'body, Mister Morgan. Ever'body but Molly. That's what he tol' me." Billy shook his head and looked, helplessly, at Beth. "Jeezus! What have I done?"

"The right thing," Molly offered. She looked at Morgan. "The thought had crossed my mind. I lost five girls up here once before. Doc Henry paid me well but he tol' me the Apache got 'em."

"Yeah, Molly, but the Apache wouldn't have killed them until they'd had their fun."

"I know that now."

"What do we do?" Billy asked.

"Just as you're told," Morgan said. "When, where, and how."

"Beth . . . what about her? One o' Doc's men has already talked about havin' her?"

"I'll handle that end," Molly said. "I'll tell Doc that one o' the Mexicans asked for a young girl . . . a new, nice young girl. I'll pick Beth. He won't argue about it."

"An' what do I do for now . . . anythin'?"

"Yeah, Billy," Morgan said, "keep your ears open and your mouth shut." He eyed the boy's rig. "Can you use that thing?"

"I can, yes sir. I been practicin' near ever' day now."

"I mean, can you kill a man with it?"

"I . . . I think so."

"You'd better decide, Billy, and fast. One of them will kill you while you're thinking."

A few of the newly arrived gang members had planned a little party with the girls that night. Gretchen promised to keep an eye on Beth. They all knew that some of those men would even ignore Doc Henry's orders if they got too drunk. Billy returned to his quarters, scared but feeling better. Molly sat quietly for several minutes, got up and walked to the door, and then turned back.

"I think I'll add just a wee bit o' spice to the pie."

"How's that?"

"A little double-cross talk to Doc. I'll let him think I don't give a damn about anybody but him an' me. A little larger share for both of us if you're out o' the way." Morgan pondered the idea for a moment and then nodded.

"Can't hurt a thing," he said. "It's Doc's kind of thinking."

"One thing does bother me, Mahrgan. Me girls. I don't want 'em gettin' hurt . . . or worse."

"Don't worry. Doc won't risk doing anything until both deals are over."

"He wants me to show 'im where those wagons with the Winchesters are comin' in."

"Do it. I'm supposed to talk to him too, in the morning. I'll remind him that Senor Valesquez will be expecting both of us. You and me."

"I'm prayin' you got this all figured right, Mahrgan." Molly walked out. Morgan watched her.

"So am I," he said to himself. "So am I, Molly girl."

10

The thunder of hoof beats jarred Morgan from his sleep. It was still dark outside, but he could see the silhouettes of the riders as they galloped by. Doc had moved the schedule ahead. Morgan was witnessing the departure of thirty-three of Doc's gang. They would ride to Gato mission and make the deal with Naschitti. The gang included four of his top guns, one of them a half-breed Apache named Brazo.

Morgan dressed hurriedly and made his way to Doc's house. He found Doc in an unusually jovial mood which Morgan attributed partly to Molly's double-cross talk of the day before.

"I made a couple o' changes, dude. I figure there's just enough time to make sure the deal with Naschitti comes off before we have to ride out and meet with the Mexican boys." He looked for a reaction.

"Smart move," Morgan said.

"An' I'm having Charlie Bojack lead the raid on them Winchesters. Me, Molly, an' a couple o' my

boys will ride with you, dude . . . back to Creede.
That way, we'll all be there together when everything gits confirmed." Morgan didn't like that, but
he couldn't afford to tip his hand.

"Another good move, Doc. Now I understand why
you've stayed alive so long." Doc liked the
compliment. He grinned and then pulled Morgan to
a nearby map.

"You pick the spot fer that raid on them Winchesters?"

"Yeah. Anything wrong with it?"

"Not if'n you're levelin' with me, no. If not, it'd
sure be a good spot fer an ambush. You'd best remember I'll be watchin' ya, dude . . . real close like."

The ride to Creede seemed to take forever, and
Molly was visibly nervous. Doc picked up on it and
Morgan knew it. Doc's two gunnies rode behind him
all the way. Nonetheless, Morgan's luck was
holding. He managed the phony dispatch
confirming a time and place for their meeting with
Senor Valesquez. Doc was impressed.

"A hunnert thousand in silver," he said. He
looked up and laughed. "Sure beats holdin' up them
Butterfields, wouldn't ya say, Molly?"

"It does that, Doc, surely it does."

"Now, dude . . . part two. You git on down to that
Army cap'n an' bring me back the word that ever'
thing is still okay with Naschitti. Army's not
supposed to meet up with them guns fer three more
days, that right?"

"Right," Morgan said. "But tomorrow, your boys
will have already ridden into Gato and made the
deal."

"Well, I'd still like to make sure. An' I'd like to see you walk into that army office."

"Let's go."

"Jess here'll do it." Doc looked up at the big, scar-faced man who stood near the door. He was cradling a scatter gun on one arm. "Watch 'im, Jess . . . watch 'im close."

The army's small office in Creede was at the far end of town. Morgan stayed to the back alley until he reached the main street. There was little activity there and he hurried across, cast a brief glance back at his unwanted shadow and entered the office. His luck was still holding, but he'd just walked into a hornet's nest.

Inside, he found himself facing a pink-cheeked private.

"I'm here to see Captain Torrance." The boy looked up, a quizzical expression on his face.

"I beg your pardon, sir."

"Captain Torrance . . . your commanding officer. Tell him Mister Morgan is here to see him."

The boy frowned and stood up. "Sir . . . you must have been out of town."

"Yeah, but what the hell does that have to do with anything?"

"Sir . . . Captain Torrance died four days ago. The Fifth cavalry troops stationed here are now under the command of Brevet Lieutenant-Colonel Yates."

"Jeezus," Morgan mumbled. He took his hat off, rubbed his forehead and glanced back at the window. He could see Doc's man eyeing the office. "Yates then, where is he?"

"In the field, sir. Acting on his own responsibility, Lieutenant-Colonel Yates took two companies south to hunt down and arrest . . . or kill . . . the renegade Apache, Naschitti.''

"Shit! When?''

"Two days ago, sir. He took the action following a raid of hostiles on our stockade. During that raid, we lost a half a dozen men and our prisoner . . . Naschitti's son.''

"The crazy sonuvabitch,'' Morgan mumbled. He put his hat on, quickly forced a most uneasy composure and walked out. He had cleared about half the distance between the office and where Doc's man, Jess, was standing when someone called out to him.

"Right there, Morgan . . . that's far enough.'' Morgan looked at Jess, dived for the cover of a horse trough and yelled at the same moment.

"Pinkerton men!'' The reaction was predictable. Jess cut loose with both barrels of the scatter-gun. There was a howl. By then, Morgan had the Bisley working. There had been three targents. The shotgun took out the middle one, the biggest. It ripped open his whole belly. Morgan recognized Luke Halstead. His own shots dropped the other two.

The sudden appearance of the trio, Morgan's swift action and Jess's reaction were closely followed by stark reality. Jess suddenly realized the name which had been called out. He'd heard the sharp crack of the .45 . . . a weapon the dude wasn't supposed to be carrying. Now he found himself staring into it. He reached but it was too late. Jess took the shot high in the chest.

The melee had brought the pink-cheeked army trooper and a couple of his companions into the street. Morgan's options were slim to none.

"Get one of your men out of here and find Yates. Tell him Creede is threatened." Morgan rushed over to the young trooper and held his Pinkerton letter in the boy's face. "Get word to whoever is in charge of the reserve company to get those men *off* and *on.* Tell them to ride to where the Rio Grande cuts the trail to Wagon Wheel Gap south of here. Don't argue, don't ask questions, just do it. Now, trooper."

"Yes, sir!"

Morgan double-timed it back to Molly's place, once again through the back alley. He couldn't figure who tipped Luke Halstead to his presence in town or, in fact, how Luke had learned who he was. All he did know what that Doc Henry would have heard the shots.

The shots had drawn many of Molly's men out of her place by the front way. The commotion was what Morgan was counting on to distract Doc long enough to give him a plausible account of the affair. It didn't work.

The shotgun blast was the only sound Doc needed to hear. He forced Molly out the back way, scattered the horses save for hers and his own, and left his other man beneath the stairway to wait for whoever returned. He and Molly rode, hard, back toward his waiting men.

Morgan saw the still open office door. He knew it wouldn't be long before some of her men would be checking the alley. He didn't see his horse . . . or anyone's. He turned to see if there was anybody behind him and the voice brought him forward again.

"Where's Jess?" It was Doc's other gunny.

"They got him . . . but he saved my life. Where's Doc?"

Even as Morgan spoke the words he knew they weren't doing him any good. The man's eyes had shifted to the Colt.

"You ain't no fuckin' dude at all . . . never were." The man stepped out of the shadows, smiled and pulled the trigger. The gun flew upwards, the shot buried itself in the thick wood of one of the stairs and the man dropped into a crumpled heap. Now the Colt was in Morgan's hand, but the man who stepped over the body of Doc's gunny was Trigg.

"This is getting to be a habit." Trigg walked up and handed Morgan a note.

My Apache woman reached Naschitti. He waits at the mission. My woman also reached Yates. He rides in the wrong direction.

Morgan looked up and smiled. "Don't take me wrong, Trigg, but you're sure as hell a man of few words and a helluva lot of action." Trigg smiled and scribbled something else.

Do I ride with you?

"No. Your note might just be what I need to convince Doc Henry that nothing has changed. Meantime, you've been to his stronghold. Keep clear of his men, wait 'til they've passed, and then ride back into Winchester Valley and wait." Trigg looked quizzical. "Yeah, I know it doesn't make sense but do it, Trigg . . . for Molly. I got a hunch

Doc Henry has an ace or two of his own. If he happens to get out of this alive, he'll head straight back there. You and your Sharps will be ready." Now Trigg smiled broadly and nodded. The two men shook hands and Morgan went in search of his horse. It was obvious that Trigg's presence had kept the rest of Molly's men off his back, and for that too he was grateful.

As he'd suspected, Doc Henry's anger was at it peak. Morgan ran into the gang less than five miles outside of Creede. It was probably only Molly's presence that kept Morgan from being gunned on the spot.

"Mahrgan . . . what . . ."

"Shut up, Molly!" Doc screamed. He had his own gun on Morgan and Charlie Bojack's was on him as well. Morgan had once again shed his Colt, slipping the gun into one saddle bag and the rig into the other.

"I'll let this do my thinking," Morgan said. He handed Doc the note Trigg had written. Doc had met Trigg only once, the day they first rode into Doc's stronghold. Nonetheless, he knew Trigg was Molly's man. He gave the note to her.

"That from your dummy?" She nodded. "What the hell happened down there, Butler?"

"Captain Torrance died a few days back. Some hot-headed West Pointer took over and decided to make a name for himself by killing Naschitti. The few men still there intended to detain me. Your man Jess cut down two of 'em and gave me my chance. Trigg helped out."

"And Jess?"

"Sorry, Jared. He didn't make it. Neither did your

90

other man, but it doesn't change anything. You saw that note and you saw what I got from Senor Valesquez. We need those guns. Now I'd suggest we break your men up into smaller groups and take a wide berth around Creede. We can't be sure what else may have happened, but there are no troops to worry about if we don't waste any time."

"I don't like it one Goddam bit, Doc," Charlie said. Morgan eyed some of the men. They too were restless and craning their necks in both directions looking for anything suspicious. Doc himself was staring straight into Morgan's face. Molly's stomach had a sinking feeling and her throat was bone dry.

"He give the orders now, Doc?" Morgan finally said.

"You're lyin' to me, dude. I know it. I can feel it. It's like poker when you know you got a hold hand."

The two men's eyes were locked in a silent struggle. Neither man blinked. Morgan knew Doc was right . . . it was a poker game and Doc held all the cards. All Morgan held was the bluff.

"Play it out, Doc. Play your hold hand. I'm calling you."

Doc frowned. "How you doin' that dude?"

"Your hundred thousand against my life."

Doc could feel the eyes upon him. Charlie's . . . the other men's near enough to have heard the exchange and . . . Molly's. The hair on the back of his neck bristled, and his cheeks felt flushed. Still, Morgan hadn't blinked. A wrinkle, just the smallest of wrinkles, appeared at one corner of Doc's mouth. His lips parted ever so slightly and the wrinkle spread across them into a half grin. He too was an old poker player.

"You take this pot, Butler . . . but the game ain't over. There'll be another hand dealt."

"We'd best ride," Morgan said. He turned his horse and as he did so, his eyes met Molly's for a split second. They both knew that the next hand Doc was talking about would be settled with Colts.

Miles away to the south, the half breed Brazo held up his arm and halted the column of men. They were at the entrance to Gato mission canyon. He turned to a gunny called Ferret and said, "You wait. I will ask to speak to Naschitti."

"This smells rotten," Ferret said. "This is a fuckin' box canyon and we ain't even sure them guns are in there."

Brazo smiled and pointed to the ground. There were deep ruts leading into the narrow gorge. "Wagons . . . heavy loaded." He nodded a self-confirmation. "The guns are there . . . but maybe army too. I will see."

Ferrett dismounted the men, all of them eyeing the canyon walls and the ridges above for any sign of trouble. Brazo rode carefully. He followed the tracks, but also looked for signs of shod horses . . . cavalry mounts. He saw none. Suddenly, almost as if by magic, two Apache warriors appeared in front of him. He could hear two more drop to the ground behind him. He smiled and raised one arm in a gesture of greeting. It was not returned, but one of the warriors motioned for him to follow.

Half a mile into the ever narrowing canyon, the party rounded a sharp bend. Brazo saw a line of army wagons—a dozen, perhaps fifteen. Near them stood a group of Indians. One of them he recognized at once as Naschitti.

Brazo dismounted, walked over and again offered a silent gesture of greeting. Naschitti's rifle butt was the reply and Brazo doubled over in pain and dropped to his knees.

"The dog of no color rides for Jared? Where is he?"

"Johnny's dead." Brazo struggled for breath enough to speak. He coughed. "Bush-whacked. Doc is tryin' to find his killers," Brazo lied.

"Naschitti thinks you have learned the white man's ways very well. You lie!" He kicked Brazo and then held the barrel of his rifle to the half breed's forehead. "The blue coats trapped my son. I believe it was because of Jared. Yesterday the blue coats rode into our land to kill us. I believe it was because of Jared. Today . . . you and not Jared come to deal. Why, half breed?"

"I swear to you, Naschitti, I speak only true words. I would not lie to my brother." Naschitti kicked him again.

"You are not my brother. You are no man's brother. You do not fly with the birds or run with the deer." Brazo was scared. He swallowed hard. He licked his parched lips and then raised his arm ever so slowly and pointed to the wagons.

"The rifles . . . as Jared promised. They're the proof. The cannon too and the gun of many bullets."

"Perhaps the rifles are no good. Perhaps they will not fire. Perhaps they will blow up in the faces of my warriors."

"No Naschitti, no! Open them, see for yourself."

"Now it is Naschitti who will say . . . no! Bring Jared's men into the canyon. Then we will open the boxes. They will fire the guns. Then I will believe your words." Brazo nodded, weakly.

Ferret and the others wanted no part of entering the canyon but they were also aware that Naschitti commanded more than a hundred braves. Running might prolong their lives but it most certainly wouldn't save them. Nearly an hour had passed before all of Jared's men were at the clearing near the mission. Above and all around them were Naschitti's warriors.

"You, half breed," Naschitti said, "you open the first box. You fire the first rifle."

Brazo nodded and waved. He moved over to the nearest wagon and, with the help of two of the men, opened the first case. They looked at each other with relief when they saw rifles. Brazo broke open an ammunition box. loaded the weapon, took aim at a cluster of rocks well up the side of one of the canyon walls and let go four rounds. The rocks disintegrated into dust. Brazo held up the rifle.

"Your proof, Naschitti." Now many of the other men rushed to the wagons and began breaking open cases. They simply wanted to complete the negotiations, get their payoff and ride out. It was not to be.

Many of the crates on the second layer had already been opened. What the men found were pieces of lead pipe. Brazo checked box after box. Two . . . four . . . seven. He began backing up. Slowly he turned and looked toward Naschitti. The Apache bent over, picked up something and then mounted his horse. He held up a length of lead pipe.

"Fire it . . . dog of no color."

"Naschitti . . . we didn't know . . . there's been . . ." Naschitti's arm came down and the canyon was suddenly filled with the roar and smoke of gun fire and the less audible *twang* of bow strings and *whoosh* of arrow and lance.

Jared's men huddled together and returned the fire but in less than ten minutes, Gato canyon fell silent again. Brazo, Ferret, three or four others tried to slip out. Their ultimate fates made them regret the effort. They would have died much quicker had they stayed. By noon, the gun deal with Naschitti in Gato canyon was over.

Doc Henry Jared's thoughts were running to many things and the Gato deal was one of them. He no longer trusted the man called Butler. He was not certain of Molly, and he particularly didn't like the idea of splitting his already inferior force. Doc had spent time in the army and he knew the rule. Only the element of time prevented him from riding into Creede and snooping around. Instead, he kept Molly with him and his small band, about seven men. He sent Butler with a little larger group, a dozen, under command of Charlie Bojack. Two other groups were also formed for a total of twenty-eight guns.

One of the first groups which neared the trail along the Rio Grande was the one led by Charlie Bojack. Morgan's eyes scanned ahead carefully. He was hoping the troopers were in place and hoping even more that they wouldn't mistake this group for the whole gang. He coudln't see any signs to indicate they were even there, but Charlie wasn't riding to the river until Doc ordered it.

"We wait here," he said to Morgan. Morgan nodded and continued his surveillance of the terrain, adding to it a possible escape route if things went suddenly sour.

The men in the second group were less cautious than Charlie. They appeared out of the woods, off trail, riding hard and loud. The instant they had mingled with Charlie's men, the old sergeant decided he had them all. Troopers stood up on both sides of them as well as to the front and rear and began firing.

Morgan caught Charlie a good, solid backhand swing to the chest and knocked him from his horse. At the same moment, he dug his spurs into the roan's flanks, jerked the big gelding's head hard to the right, and plunged into the trees. He felt the burning slash of a bullet as it dug a ridge high up on his left arm. Another severed the left stirrup link and Morgan had to shift his weight. A third grazed the horse and he snorted and seemed to dig harder for more speed.

Once out of the main line of fire, Morgan turned north and rode hard and low in the saddle. He worked the Bisley out of his saddlebag . . . and none too soon. Two men crashed through the brush just ahead of him. Doc's men. He cut them both down.

Less than a mile away, Doc Henry heard the shooting. He reined up. Suddenly a rider appeared before him. The rider spoke and Doc Henry's face wrinkled into a mask of hatred. He struck Molly a solid blow to the face and she slipped from her horse unconscious.

"Tie her to the saddle. We ride for the valley."

"The men?"

"To hell with the men!" Doc screamed.

Billy Frye was with the last group. It had stationed itself about midway between Doc's position and the rendezvous point when the shooting started.

"Ambush!" he screamed. He turned his horse and rode back toward Creede. As he did so, he yelled. "Every man for himself." The others took him at his word and scattered. Billy was counting on it. Doc had left two men behind to keep an eye on the girls, including Beth. He had to get to them before Doc did. Given Morgan's position, Billy was certain that he was already dead. Now, it was all up to Billy.

By the time Billy Frye had ridden around Creede, moving far more slowly than he wanted to, for fear of discovery, the gun fire behind him had stopped. Most of the men, he reckoned, had given up. Carefully, he gauged, the distance back to where Doc had left the women and tried to approach it from the back side. He found the spot but not the women. Even as he searched, he heard several lone riders gallop past on the nearby road. Stragglers, headed back to Winchester Valley. He sat down and wept.

11

Billy felt a hand clamped over his mouth and the cold steel of a gun barrel at his temple. He opened his eyes to find it was dark. He'd slipped into a sleep of utter fatigue. He blinked.

"It's me, Billy . . . Lee Morgan." Morgan released his grip. "No need for noise . . . just in case." Billy nodded. The day's events rushed back to his head. He sat up.

"They're gone . . . the girls. I . . ." Morgan was shaking his head. "I know. Doc got here first. By now they'll be back in the valley."

"They'll be *dead*. God! Oh God, Beth."

"Easy boy. Doc won't have killed them . . . not yet."

"Why the hell should we wait?"

"They're the bait, Billy . . . the only reason for me to ride back and face him."

"How can you be so sure?"

"Because I know how Doc thinks. Besides," Morgan added, standing up, "Doc will want me to watch them die . . . one by one. Particularly Molly."

Billy got to his feet.

"I'm riding with you."

"I'd counted on that," Morgan said. He smiled at Billy's look of shock.

"Why can't we get some help from the army?"

"We can . . . when Yates gets back. Right now there aren't enough troopers left. They've got their hands full keeping tabs on Doc's men."

"And when will Yates be back?"

"That's the problem, Billy, we don't know and we can't wait. I stayed out of sight and rode into Creede after dark. I spoke to the sergeant. He'll give Yates the word as soon as they ride in."

"You an' me . . . that's it?"

"And, if he didn't get spotted, Molly's man, Trigg."

"Doc had seven men with 'im. Top guns. I heard more later, five or six, mebbe."

Morgan motioned to Billy to follow him and they walked over to Morgan's horse. He lifted two sets of saddle bags from around its neck and handed them to Billy. They were heavy. Billy opened the flap on one of them.

"Dynamite!"

"Those bags and mine. Maybe we can cut down the odds a little."

They climbed the pass and found a decent spot to camp. It would have been both foolish and dangerous to try going down in the darkness. The two men hadn't spoken a word since they left their meeting place. They dined on cold beans and jerky, not daring to risk a fire. Shortly after midnight, a light but steady drizzle started to fall.

"Mister Morgan . . . you awake?"

"Yeah."

"You really think we got a chance o' savin' the girls?"

"If we work things right . . . mebbe we do, Billy."

"You got a plan?"

"Yeah . . . in a way," Morgan lied.

"I got somethin' itchin' at me," Billy said. He didn't wait for Morgan to respond. "I come near to high-tailin' today . . . even though I knowed my sister was likely in there . . . or already daid."

"What stopped you?"

"Ain't real sure. Even if we save the women an' git Doc, I'm facin' jail. I rode with 'im. Done what he done."

"Kill anybody, boy?"

"Nope. Doc wouldn't let me ride gun for him. Don't think I'm good enough yet."

"You're good enough, Billy . . . you've just got to put aside your judgments. If a man wants to kill you, then you've got to want to live."

"You mean I gotta want to kill *him*?"

"No. I mean just what I said. You've got to value life more than death. It just so happens, in that case, the life you value most is your own. In this case, right now, maybe the life you value most is Beth's. You can't win a gun fight just because you're better. Remember that there's never a horse that couldn't be rode and never a rider that couldn't be throwed."

"Meanin' there's always somebody better'n you?"

"Yeah. Somewhere. But that's okay providing the only thing he cares about is proving it. Then, Billy, you got the edge."

"You ever faced a man better'n you?"

"Faster mebbe . . . but with the wrong reasons for trying me."

"Ya know, Mister Morgan. I think I understand what you're sayin'. Doc, he tol' me oncest that Charlie Bojack was the fastest man he'd ever knowed with a gun. I asked him . . . was Charlie faster'n him? He tol' me that Charlie was . . . but in a showdown Doc said he'd win 'cause Charlie wouldn't want to kill him. Doc said he wouldn't give a damn 'bout killin' Charlie."

"That's about it, Billy, that's an edge. Just remember, it's not only the edge. Doc Henry don't give a damn about life at all."

"Even his own?"

"It's never really been put on the line. He hasn't had to make the decision."

"But what if he did have to?" Billy asked. He was sitting up now and looking at Morgan. "What if it was you an' your edge an' him? What if he decided his life was more important than yours an' what if he was faster'n you?"

"I'd kill him, Billy."

"Damn, Mister Morgan . . . how the hell can you be so sure?"

"Because he'd have to take the time to make his decision. Mine's already made. I'd kill him in the difference."

The rain had stopped. A silky mist crawled along the valley floor. As they rode toward it, Billy commented that he thought it looked like snow. By the time they reached it, it was gone. The sun was half way to noon and Lee Morgan's thoughts were miles and years from Winchester Valley.

He remembered back . . . back to the Spade Bit. Then too, he was riding in to face one of the best . . . a man with the speed, the skill, the edge. He was looking for Buckskin Frank Leslie. He was looking for his father. No, not his father but the man who'd sired him and then left. Then Lee thought there was a difference. He also thought Frank Leslie was living on his reputation. Lee couldn't gun the old man. He'd had the chance. He couldn't.

The next time he saw Frank Leslie he also saw the edge. Harvey Logan had come looking for Lee. A greenhorn kid with a nasty black snake whip and a vast draw. Harvey Logan was faster. Harvey found Lee, but he found Buckskin Frank Leslie first. It was over in the blink of an eye. Frank still had the edge, but he'd slowed just a hair. He died that day. He left his son a borrowed name . . . Lee. He left him the name of his unwed mother . . . Morgan. He warned him about the black snake whip. He left the boy a ranch . . . the Spade Bit. He left him half a reputation, but most of all, Frank Leslie willed to Lee Morgan . . . the edge.

"Smoke, Mister Morgan."

"Wha . . ." Morgan must have almost been dozing in the saddle. His eyes opened, his muscles rippled to respond to the signals his brain sent them. *Danger!* Then reason . . . he shook free of the cobwebs of his memory.

"Up ahead . . . comin' from the valley." Morgan saw it. He held up his hand and Billy Frye reined up. Morgan looked over the lay of the land. He pointed wordlessly to a stand of Aspen near the river.

"You stay here, Billy. Today and tonight. Keep the horses out of sight. No fire. No nerves. If I'm not back by sun-up," Morgan now turned and looked Billy in the eye, "then you do what you have to do."

"You ain't goin' into the valley alone . . . not on foot?"

"I've got to look . . . get some idea what we're up against. You sit. I'll be back."

Billy watched Morgan change his clothes. He wasn't a dude anymore. He carefully slipped cartridges into his rig's belt, checked the Bisley, and half smiled as he caught a glimpse of the initials W.F.L., William Frank Leslie. Morgan slipped the Colt into the holster, pulled it, put it back, pulled it again. Billy thought it was like breathing . . . natural, easy, smooth.

Morgan checked over the Winchester with equal care. He slipped a cartridge belt of rifle ammunition over his shoulder, then untied his bedroll, laid it down, and rolled it open. Inside, Billy saw a Black Snake bull whip. Hand woven. Snake skin, leather grip with silver inlay. Eight thongs, silver tipped, at the business end.

Morgan eyed Billy. His own father's words echoed again in his ears. "*Better shoot a man than use that thing on him.*" Morgan laid it behind him in a single, easy move of his arm. He eyed a tree. Six feet up there was a bare branch with a knot of wood on its end. Billy's eyes shifted to the limb. Morgan flexed his grip, made a slight dipping motion with his wrist and then a long, smooth forward motion. There was an almost inaudible *swish* in the air. A sharp, short-lived *craack* . . . the limb was still there. . . the little knot of wood was gone.

103

He could still use the whip. Some men deserved worse than shot. Some deserved to hang, but not all of them could. The whip might make it possible for *one* man to hang . . . or so thought Lee Morgan about Doc Henry Jared.

Doc Henry sat at his desk. He was swilling whisky. The window shades were pulled. Doc fingered his hand gun as his mind conjured up fuzzy pictures of Lee Morgan standing before him. Johnny Jared had been fast; Doc had taught him. Doc wanted Morgan . . . the old way. Just the two of them. He took another swallow of whisky, sloshed it back and forth between his cheeks, and then swallowed. It wouldn't be that way, he knew that. He'd take Morgan alive . . . partly alive anyway. Then there were the women. Morgan could watch before he died.

The door opened, easy . . . quiet. Doc looked up. It was Charlie Bojack.

"All the whores is locked up an' watched. Took their clothes off'n 'em." He laughed, nervously. "*Keerist!* The boys was cuttin' cards jist fer the privilege o' keepin' an eye on 'em."

"Molly?"

"Nope. Did jist what you ask, Doc. She's up in yore room, hawg tied."

"Anybody else ride in?" Doc asked.

" 'Fraid not. Two o' the boys rode out yesterday . . . found four o' the men 'bout two, mebbe three miles apart. All shot with a buffalo gun."

"The sumbitch with the Sharps. Who the hell is he?"

"Cully Bright thinks he put a slug into 'im . . .

ain't fer sure, though, but Cully got on it. So did Hightower. Want we should go lookin'?''

"Hell no! If the sumbitch is hit or dead, it's over. If he ain't,. he'd get ya one at a time. We'll wait it out.''

"Doc . . . well . . . some o' the boys figure we're waitin' fer nothin' but trouble. Army's bound to come after us soon. Well . . . they ain't too sure Lee Morgan'll come in, not even fer that Irish bitch.''

"I don't give a Goddam what they think, Charlie, nor you neither. You all want to ride out, fuck you. Ride out. Morgan'll be here . . . and when he gets here, I'll be waitin'.'' Doc picked up his pistol and then got to his feet. "How 'bout you, Charlie?''

"I'll be here, Doc. You know that.''

"I don't know nothin' fer sure anymore . . . 'cept I'm gonna have the personal pleasure o' killin' Lee Fuckin' Morgan.''

"Okay, Doc. If that's your word, then that's what'll happen. We got eleven men. They's only two o' them.'' Doc said nothing else and Charlie Bojack slipped quietly out.

Doc took another long pull of the bottle. He wiped his mouth with his shirt sleeve and picked up his pistol. "C'mon,'' he whispered to himself, "c'mon to Doc, you sumbitch.''

Morgan spent most of the afternoon climbing. The sun was already behind Pole Creek mountain when he finally settled onto an overhang that had a small cave behind it. The shadows were long and purple, but below Morgan could see all of Winchester Valley.

He could see the curl of smoke from Doc Henry's

house. The smoke from the other building, the one housing the men, was thicker, darker, and spread out, creating a haze. Two men stood watch at a third building. Morgan smiled slightly. The women. They were still alive.

Morgan counted stock. Fifteen riding horses, four pack mules. A dozen men? He wondered. It seemed a fair amount, but Doc could have twenty in hiding. Then again . . . maybe there were only six. He stowed his gear, got himself situated for any emergency, and half settled in for the long night ahead.

A rock, it was small, almost a pebble, dropped beside him. The Colt came up. He could see a dark patch dart between the boulders above him.

"Damn," he whispered to himself. "Who the hell dogged me?" He wondered if it might be Trigg. He hoped so. Another pebble. Footsteps, some gravel slid. He levelled the Colt. Whoever it was didn't seem to care about being heard.

"Mor-gun . . . Mor-gun?" Morgan got to his feet. He stepped nearer the edge of the drop for a better look up the narrow path that led back to the ridge above him. He saw his visitor.

"Jeezus. Who the hell are you?"

"Tonsika . . . I am the woman of the man who does not speak." Trigg's Apache! She'd dogged him and Billy . . . then him. Why? "I find the Buffalo gun man here?"

"No." Morgan helped her the last few feet. He got her inside the small cave. "You shouldn't be here. You could get us both killed."

"No one follows Tonsika. I come to find . . ."

"Yeah, yeah, Trigg. His name is *Trigg*."

"Tuh-rig?"

"Close enough. Did you follow him or me?"

"I follow you. I come from the blue coats with a message."

"*Yates?*"

"The boy blue coat," she pointed to her shoulders, "with gold thread here."

"Yates. What about him? What's the message?"

"In two suns he is to meet with his blue coat chief . . . he say Gen-rul Coombs."

"Then what, Tonsika? Then what?"

"Many pony soldiers ride here to the Uncompahgre. They will kill the evil white eyes."

"How many days . . . uh . . . how many suns before they do that?"

"The boy blue coat tells Tonsika . . . four . . . maybe five."

"Shit!"

"Tuh-rig?"

"I don't know. Dead maybe. Down there," Morgan pointed, "maybe."

"This night . . . I stay with Mor-gun."

"Yeah, that's how it looks."

Morgan slept hard for a couple of hours. Then it rained. The wind blew in and he and Tonsika both got wet. The rain stopped. He could hear, ever so faintly, men's laughter from Doc's compound far below. Tonsika was cold. She stripped. He turned his bedroll to the dry side.

Tonsika was young . . . *very* young. Morgan tried to put his desire out of his body and her age out of his mind. She was too close . . . it was too cold and, Morgan thought, they'd both likely be dead in a few days. If there was still a doubt, Tonsika

107

removed it. She moved his hand to her tiny breast.

It was firm, almost hard. It had not yet fully developed. Morgan looked into her eyes. They revealed only an adolescent yielding. Tonsika was exploring . . . searching for her womanhood. She was trapped between little girl and passionate lover. Morgan was her choice only because he was there.

He moved his hand and lowered his head until he could rest it on her body. His tongue flicked the tiny nipple, already hardened from the cold air. She moaned softly as he continued his ministrations. His fingers too began an exploratory movement along her inner thighs. She reacted by spreading them. He continued licking and sucking at her nipple and with his free hand, reached beneath and around her to toy with the other one.

His other hand found her pubic hair. It was fine, soft and covered very little. He was more accustomed to the thick, wiry hair of a mature woman. He found it fascinating and stroked it for several minutes before his fingers dropped lower.

"Go inside me . . . Mor-gan." She whispered the words. Morgan replied, "Shh! In time Tonsika . . . in time." He found the tender flesh between her legs and parted it gently. He was surprised at the moistness. He rubbed. Tonsika's back stiffened and arched, pressing her pussy against his fingers.

He found the bud of her passion. The clitoris was the smallest Morgan had ever touched. Merely a pimple . . . but far more sensitive than that of a white woman. The combination of his breast play and his light touch between her legs prompted a premature climax. Morgan cursed himself for not realizing what might happen.

Tonsika let out a little howl. Her legs went farther apart and she bent them at the knees as she pushed against his hand. She gasped. He could feel more liquid, thicker and slimy . . . like cactus juice. Her body went limp. She opened her eyes. She smiled.

"Again . . . Mor-gun." She raised her legs into the air, spread them as far apart as possible and simply waited. Morgan didn't. He resumed his touch, his stroking and the use of his tongue. Slowly, he shifted his own position until he was on his knees between her legs. He lowered his head and his tongue found her navel. He circled it and then traced a path below it until he felt the line of her hair. He moved from side to side now, flicking his tongue over the protrusions that were her hip bones. He lowered his head, licking at the inside of her thighs. Then he thrust home.

His tongue moved sideways first, then up and down. She closed her legs around his head and pushed. He licked her clitoris. The body stiffened again, held its suspended position for a few seconds and then relaxed again. This time there was no moan, nothing but a body reflex. Morgan raised up. Tonsika smiled again.

"Go inside me, Mor-gun . . . *please.*"

Morgan removed his pants and dropped his underdrawers to his ankles. Tonsika spread her legs for the third time and Morgan was ready. He was concerned about hurting her . . . she was so small and Morgan didn't lack from either thickness or length. He needn't have worried. He thought it was like slipping his cock into a half-ripened honeydew melon. Moist, very tight and without a bottom. He began a rhythm, and soon Tonsika had found it and

109

joined him. They were fucking . . . pure, simple fucking. He couldn't remember the last time he'd done that. He'd forgotten the *feel* of it . . . the pure enjoyment of sex between man and woman which used only the tools God had given them for the act.

Morgan and Tonsika remained connected for a long time. Slow, loving, tender strokes. She grew more passionate with each and Morgan's juices built to a crescendo exactly timed with that of the Indian maiden. They burst forth together, writhing bodies no longer two . . . but melding into one. Oblivious to the cold . . . to artificial stimuli . . . a man . . . a woman . . . a climax of physical passion.

Afterwards, they kept each other warm, huddling close but saying nothing. Morgan finally raised up to his elbows, leaned over and very gently kissed Tonsika on the mouth. He pulled away, looked into her eyes and said, "Thank you. You made pleasant memories for me tonight." Tonsika just smiled.

12

Tonsika was gone! Morgan was furious at himself. He'd never even heard her leave. He'd told Billy Frye he'd be back by sun-up. He guessed it was eight thirty, maybe later. He didn't excuse himself for being bone weary from the climb and drained from fucking half the night. Even if they were legitimate reasons, they could cost him . . . or other people . . . their lives. He resolved not to let such a thing happen again.

His stomach was growling. He wanted coffee, but settled for half a can of beans. He readied his gear and then studied Doc's compound again. He could see some action but nothing out of the ordinary and, more important, nothing to indicate the arrival of more men.

The trip back down the mountain seemed much easier, barely more than a morning stroll. He stopped to rest and estimated he was now within three miles of where he'd left Billy. He hoped the boy would have sense enough to do nothing immediately. By now, Morgan was sure that Billy would be plenty worried . . . perhaps even panicky, but with luck, he'd still be at the camp. Morgan had also considered the possibility of Tonsika finding Billy.

He had barely resumed his trip when an ear-shattering blast reverberated through the canyon. He thought it had come from behind him, but such sound echoed so in the mountains, it was difficult to tell.

"Stupid little sonuvabitch," Morgan mumbled. He'd concluded that Billy had put some of the dynamite to use. He'd barely recuperated from the explosion when another tore loose, followed by two more. Morgan made a quick decision. He hid most of what he was carrying beneath a boulder, took only his Winchester, and broke into a trot. He figured he'd either cross trail with Billy or get back to their camp ahead of him.

He'd gone nearly two miles when another sound, more faint but just as easily recognized, caught up to him. It was the deep, guttural discharge of a Sharps . . . .50 calibre!

"Trigg?" Morgan turned. Another shot . . . a rifle. A Henry maybe or Winchester. There was the Sharps again. Morgan made his decision. Billy was a maybe, but Trigg was alive. He turned to run in the direction of the gunshots.

"Mister Morgan . . . Mister Morgan." He wheeled. There was Billy, mounted, and with the roan gelding in tow.

"I'm a little late," Morgan said, "sorry."

"I thought all of the noise was prob'ly you."

"Well it wasn't," Morgan said, as he jumped into the saddle, "so let's find out who the hell did make it."

Moving fast, but carefully, deep in the woods, Morgan and Billy finally reached a point where the trail into the valley narrowed. They saw no one, but they did find the cause for the blasting . . . and the results.

"Goddam!" It was all Morgan could manage. Billy couldn't even muster up that much. The trail was completely blocked with huge boulders. A lone man would have a tough go at getting over them, let alone doing so without being seen on the other side.

"Army boys can't get in now, can they, Mister Morgan?"

"Oh yeah, Billy," Morgan replied, sarcastically, "if they want to take the same losses the Mexicans took at the Alamo. Shit!"

"An' we don't know how many's in there, either."

"Yes we do." Both men wheeled around at the sound of the strange voice. Morgan's Colt was in his hand, but his mouth dropped open. There stood Tonsika and next to her . . . Trigg. "I overheard one o' them this marnin' . . . he figured the eleven of 'em . . . plus Doc Henry himself . . . could hold off the army long enough if it came to that. There's two less than that now."

Morgan walked up to Trigg. "You talk, you sonuvabitch . . . and you talk *Irish*."

Trigg grinned. "There's a reason for that, Mahrgan . . . I am Irish. I'm Molly's big brother, come over with our sister."

"Holy Jeezus!"

Trigg motioned with his head for the two men to follow him. "We'd best get out of sight. They could be watchin' too. I've moved me spot again an' I think it's good enough for the lot of us. I'll fill in all

113

the holes when we get there."

Trigg . . . or whatever his name was . . . had picked out one hell of a spot to hide. He could no longer simply pick off Doc's men from there, but if they happened to ride out and find him, they'd play hell ever getting to him. It was a cave, high up, good shelter, and an excellent view below. There was open ground for nearly half a mile leading to its base. And it was only a mile to the main trail.

"Helluva fortress, Trigg," Morgan said.

"Name's not Trigg. It's Patrick Sean Terrence O'Flynn." He grinned. "Covered me father, grandfather, and me uncle." Morgan was listening, but he was also looking. He was more than a little surprised. There was fresh meat, tinned food, whisky, some medicine, several rifles and hand guns, appropriate ammuntion, coal oil, lamps, and half a dozen cases of dynamite.

"You've proven to be a damned handy man to have around," Morgan finally said. Then he pointed to the various items and added, "But I don't think you're this damned good."

"Hardly, Mahrgan. I've been slippin' in an' out o' here for more'n six months. I knew there'd be a time . . . a day o' reckonin'. I'm thankin' the Good Lawrd I'll still be around to see it."

"The dummy act, Trigg . . . uh, O'Flynn. What about that? Just covering the Irish accent?"

"Call me Paddy . . . most do." Then he nodded. "The dummy act, as you call it, was a God-send. It did cover up the accent, sure . . . but I didn't plan it." He pulled down the neckerchief around his throat and revealed an ugly, deep scar. "Minie ball. Took quite a chunk o' me throat. I couldn't talk for quite a spell. It happened on the same raid that took me other sister. I managed to crawl off and hide."

"You and Molly figured out the rest?" Paddy nodded. "Sorry I haven't introduced you . . . this is Billy Frye."

"I know about Billy Frye and his sister. We'll get her out, boy . . . Molly an' the others too."

Tonsika cooked some breakfast. The cave was deep and her Apache upbringing paid its own dividends. She could build a fire and cook on it with almost no smoke at all. The quartet of friends ate and then Billy fell into a deep sleep. Tonsika climbed a nearby rock ledge and stood watch while Morgan and Paddy O'Flynn split a pint of whisky.

"I can't help wanting to call you Trigg," Morgan said. "Maybe we should keep it that way."

"No matter to me. It's a name I'll not likely ever forget, anyway."

"There's another little matter," Morgan said. "I'm not sure just how you'll take it, but we'd best get it out."

Trigg smiled. "If you're meanin' the Indian girl, she already told me. I've no mark on her, Mahrgan, nor she on me."

"I'm glad you're on my side," Morgan said. "I got a hunch you'd be as mean an enemy as you are a good friend . . . and a good man."

"It's as much trainin' as anythin', Mahrgan. I was an officer in the Queen's Own fer fifteen years."

"Jeezus! That explains a lot of things," he gestured at the surroundings with a sweep of his arm, "this among them."

"It might help, but maybe not. Not if Doc Henry kills an' runs. There is a back way out o' that valley."

"He won't take it, Trigg. He knows I'm coming. He wants me."

"It's the only thing we've got goin' for us, Mahrgan. The only chance we've got to save Molly and the others."

"It's enough."

"Have you got a plan, Mahrgan?"

Morgan grinned now. "Sure, but I'd damn sight rather use yours."

"It's had to be changed some, you know."

"I'd say that's one hell of an understatement. The Goddam army fucked everything up back down on the Rio Grande. I figured to be chasing Doc Henry and maybe one or two of his gunnies . . . but not a dozen and not with him holding the women or holed up in this valley."

"Don't blame the army fer everything, Mahrgan. He had some help."

"From where? Who?"

"I can't answer that one yet . . . but he did. I got that much out of one of his men, a young one I shot up two days back. He told me about everything he knew. Too bad my shootin' was better'n my doctorin'. He didn't make it."

"What's your plan, Trigg?"

"Well, now that you an' the boy are here, I'd say it was best to send a message on back to the army. The Indian girl can do that. Get them movin' a bit faster, maybe."

"I'll buy that, but then what? I figured to slip into the compound and do as much damage as possible. Maybe entice Doc Henry into an open confrontation."

"The dynamite?"

"Yeah. I've got some myself."

"Nothin' wrong with the plan on paper, Mahrgan. But it has to include gettin' one or more o' his men *ever'time*. Right now it's three to one an' I don't think they'll be comin' out again so's I can pick 'em off with the old Buffalo gun."

"Agreed." Billy Frye sat bolt upright. Both men thought he'd been sleeping hard. "Someone's comin'," he said. Both his guns were drawn and even Morgan was impressed with the speed. A moment later, Tonsika entered the cave.

"A white man . . . alone near the rocks on the trail. He carries the white man's sign of talk."

"A white flag?" She nodded. "Then they know they can be seen."

"Yes, Mahrgan," Trigg said, shaking his head in bewilderment, "an' they still expect we'll act as honorable men . . . even when they don't."

"Are you suggesting that we don't?"

"Not at all. We've no choice while they hold the women. Well then, let's have a look."

The closing of the narrow trail into Winchester Valley with the blasting of the rocks was a two-edged sword. It would make it impossible for any sizeable number of men to get into the valley without being seen, but it also limited the number coming out to one or two. By the time Trigg and Morgan reached a spot where they could see the trail, the man had gone. There was a pole in the ground which bore the white flag and a note. Tonsika walked down and retrieved it.

Sun up tomorrow, Morgan. You and me, right

here. Every hour goes by you don't show, I kill
a girl.

"Shit! I've been afraid of this," Morgan said.
"He's got a hold hand again."

"An' more back-up guns than we've got," Trigg
added. "He won't face you without them, Mahrgan
. . . you know that, don't you?"

"Yeah, Trigg, I know it."

"Me'n Trigg here will back you. We can keep
under cover."

"We could that, boy . . . but we can't be sure we'd
get 'em all."

"And if I don't show?" Morgan wadded up the
note and threw it down. "He'll do it, Trigg. He'll do
it just to prove he can."

"Then we'd best plan on goin' in there tonight and
gettin' those girls out."

"Sure, Trigg . . . just like that."

"Young Billy, here. I was thinkin'. They don't
know what's happened to the lad. So he's a day or
two late gettin' back. If he rides in, they'll not argue
with 'im . . . will they?" Morgan's eyes lit up. So did
Billy's. "We can sweeten the pot a bit, too. I'll give
the boy my Buffalo gun. He can tell his own story."

"I can do it, Mister Morgan. I *can*. He's right an' I
can keep 'em all busy long enough fer you to get the
women. I know I can."

"It just might work," Morgan said.

"An' we'll get the girl here on the way back to the
army . . . just in case."

Less than an hour later, Tonsika, using Billy's
horse, slipped through the woods and headed
toward Creede and safety. Morgan climbed to some

high rocks after bidding his farewell to Billy. There, he fired half a dozen shots from his Colt and his Winchester. Below him, Trigg fired the old Sharps once, twice . . . and then again. Billy scrambled up the pile of boulders at the entrance to the canyon. He let himself be seen, fired behind him several times, and then scrambled down the other side. He holstered his guns, put the old Sharps over his shoulder and started walking.

"Hold it, kid." Bill turned. He saw Frank Potts, one of Doc's top hands.

"It's me Frank, Billy Frye." By then, several other men had reached the spot. Charlie Bojack was out front.

"Goddam if it ain't the kid. We thought you was dead." Now Charlie spotted the Sharps. "Where'd you git that?" he asked. His voice had changed tone. Billy knew he was suspicious.

"From the son-fo-a-bitch that tried to way-lay me with it," Bill answered. His voice was firm, cool . . . even proud in tone.

"Is that right? We'll see, kid, we'll see. You tell that one to Doc."

Two men remained behind . . . the front line watch. Billy took note of their positions. He'd already formulated an addition to the plan which even Trigg and Morgan didn't know about. A few minutes later, Charlie ushered Billy into Doc's office.

"Well, sumbitch . . . if it ain't the gun-slingin' kid." Doc spotted the Sharps and frowned.

"Claims he. got the sharp shootin' bastard," Charlie said.

Billy's head jerked sharply toward Charlie Bojack. "I don't claim nothin', Charlie. I did git 'im."

Doc grinned. "An' you brung in his piece to prove it."

"Hell no. I got it 'cause I wanted it. He's got no more use for it."

"An' nobody else was out there? Morgan wasn't out there? You just picked off the sharp shooter, walked up and took his piece and here you are."

Billy stood the Sharps against the wall and backed up. "You callin' me a liar?" Doc was clearly surprised.

"You got a heap o' grit all o' the sudden, boy."

"It come from ridin' with yellow bellies." Charlie Bojack took a step toward Billy. Doc held up his arm.

"What yellow bellies you talkin' about, boy?"

"Them what I was with when the army hit us. Them you hired an' trusted. Most scattered like chickens. Damn near come gettin' kilt because of 'em." Billy rattled off the names of two men he knew had died. "They was the only ones besides me what fought. I barely got away, and when I finally got back this far an' that bastard shot my horse . . . well, I just plain got mad." He turned toward Charlie. "An' I'm mad right now. Don't need nobody callin' me a liar."

"That sharp shooter took out some good men, damn good men. Only one got through was Cully. He did enough shootin' so's Hightower could make it too. Now Cully, he's a better man than you, boy."

"Who says? You, Doc?"

"You got a smart mouth, boy." Doc walked over and backhanded Billy. At the same instant, he felt the barrel of a Colt against his belly.

"I come back, Doc, 'cause you did me right. But I'm no boy anymore. I did what I said I did an' I ain't takin' no slappin' around." Billy backed up and looked Doc square on. "Not even from you."

Doc Henry grinned. "Sumbitch! You *have* growed boy, a whole fuckin' heap in a week. Why I bet you figure you could take on ol' Charlie here now."

Billy holstered his gun. "I got no fight with Charlie, an' I don't need to be provin' I'm better'n him. Only thing I'm willin' to prove is what I tol' you. I got the Sharps man. You want, I'll ride out an' fetch his carcass back here."

Billy Frye had just turned in the performance of his life. It rivalled anything ever done by Edwin Booth or the great Sarah Bernhardt. Within himself, Billy felt it. But even more surprising, he felt, at that moment, as though he could have taken out Charlie Bojack and Doc Henry Jared too, if it had come to that.

"Sumbitch!" Doc laughed. "Hell, boy . . . you showed some real guts just now. Yessir, real guts. You got nothin' to prove to me. I believe ever' word ya said." Billy smiled. Doc stopped smiling. "An' one more thing, *boy* . . . you ever pull on me ag'in, you're fuckin' *dead*. You unnerstan' me?" Doc's sudden attack on Billy's manhood had its affect.

"Yeah, Doc. Sure. I . . . I'm sorry." He glanced at Charlie Bojack. Charlie too was sneering. They still held him in contempt. He felt the fire of anger and hatred in his belly, but Morgan's words were in his ears: "Value life . . . value life." He'd have a chance at them again . . . another time . . . another place.

Billy now played his own ace in the hole. He'd picked up the wadded note from Doc, unseen by either Morgan or Trigg. He pulled it from his vest pocket and handed it to Doc. Doc read. He looked up. He was truly impressed.

"Where'd you git this boy?"

"The man with the Sharps had it tucked in his shirt pocket. I went through his clothes, lookin' fer who he might be. I ain't seen 'im before . . . nowhere."

"You didn't see nobody else out there, no tracks . . . *nothin'*?"

"No, Doc. I rode in clean. They wasn't nobody out there but the man that owned this." He picked up the Sharps and held it out.

"Sumbitch! Morgan *ain't* out there."

"You don't know that for sure, Doc."

"Yeah, I do, Charlie. I do now. This here boy ain't lyin' to me. I got no *feelin'* about it."

The *edge*, Billy was thinking. There goes Doc Henry's *edge*. "Doc, lemme go do some snoopin' out there." Billy walked to the window and peered up at the sky. "There's enough daylight left. I know where I left that old man. Lemme see if'n I can find where he was camped. Who he was, mebbe."

"Yeah, boy . . . good idea. You do that. You take my horse too." When Bill was gone, Charlie Bojack stood quiet for a minute and then he hit one fist against the open palm of his other hand.

"I don't like it, Doc. It stinks like the shit house."

"Ever'thing stinks to you, Charlie."

"I was right before . . . right about that dude. I knowed I'd see 'im somewhere. Lee Morgan! I shoulda remembered."

"Yeah, Charlie, you *shoulda*. That's what I pay ya fer." Doc sat down. He took a drink. "I'm gonna kill 'im, Charlie . . . one way or another. The sumbitch is good, real good. Beat Johnny.''

"You figger he's better'n you, Doc?''

"Fact is, Charlie . . . I ain't too fuckin' sure about it.'' Doc took another pull on the bottle. "But it makes no never mind. I don't figure to face 'im alone. I just want 'im dead. Him, an' that Irish whore an' her girls.''

"Then what, Doc?''

"Then we clear out. Mexico, mebbe. We'll find us some good men. We'll be back.''

Billy Frye made double certain he wasn't followed. He'd had no trouble getting out of the compound and expected even less getting back in. Now he was Doc's man . . . at least for the moment. He tethered his horse well away from the trail leading to the cave and made his way quickly over the path until he was close enough to toss a rock at the cave's entrance. He did so and Trigg peered around the entrance wall.

"It's Billy Frye.'' Trigg waved. Inside, Billy quickly described the events at the compound. He had observed two men guarding the entry to the valley and two watching the building where the women were being held. "Get them four,'' he finally said, "an' it'll be five to three.''

"Not quite that easy,'' Morgan said. "The instant that happens, we've got to get those women the hell out of there.''

"That's true enough, Mahrgan. But young Billy here is right. If Doc has swallowed his story that you're not around and I'm dead, then we've got to do somethin' fast. He'll soon figure out you're not comin' without the whole damned army behind you. He's just liable to kill those women . . . or decide to move out the back way."

"I was thinkin' about that ridin' in," Billy offered. "I got a plan." Both men looked at him, then at each other.

"Let's hear it, Billy."

"You write a note to Trigg. Tell 'im to sit tight and keep 'em pinned down 'til you can steer the army away an' then git here. Uh . . . today's Thursday. Write that if ever'thing goes accordin' to plan that you'll be ridin' in Saturday mornin' early."

"Then you'll take it back to Doc."

Billy nodded. "That's what I'm out here for, to snoop around. I think he'll believe what I bring back."

"Sounds to me like the boy's makin' sense."

"Not this time," Morgan said. "Doc Henry will want to see your body, your camp, *everything*, if Billy goes back with a note like that. It's no good. We're going to have to slip in, try to cut the odds, get the women and get out. We might even have to give up Doc in the bargain."

Rocks, jostled loose by someone, suddenly slipped from the ledge outside the cave and rattled down the hill. All three men levelled their guns at the entrance. In a moment, they were looking into the face of Tonsika. She half smiled, took a step forward, staggered and then fell. High on her back, between her shoulder blades, protruded the broken shaft of an Apache arrow.

Trigg moved quickly to treat her wound, assisted by Morgan. Several times they had to force her to lie still. Trigg finally managed removal of the arrow head itself. It had been deep. Morgan had seen such wounds many times. He looked into Trigg's face. Trigg's head moved from side to side, almost imperceptibly.

"No blue coats . . . Tonsika failed her Tuh-rug."

"Stay quiet, girl."

"Naschitti . . . he comes. All whites are his enemies." She coughed. Time was short. Tonsika reached Trigg's lips with her fingers as he started to speak again. Morgan knelt near her now too. "Naschitti will come with the sun . . . many braves . . . many guns."

"Tonsika . . . where will Naschitti come from?"

"From . . . from where the sun sleeps."

Tonsika fell into unconciousness. It was a sleep from which she would not awaken. The three men all knew it. She had never reached Creede. Naschitti's warriors were converging on Winchester Valley from all directions.

"Looks to me like Naschitti is goin' to do to Doc Henry what we'd like to do."

"If he gets the chance, Billy. His main force will come through the Uncompahgre from the west. He'll no doubt attack here first . . . draw the fire of whoever is in the valley . . . test the strength."

"The girls!"

"Yeah Billy. The girls."

"I . . . I didn't think."

"I knew it wouldn't take you long. Life, Billy . . . their lives or our hatred of Doc Henry."

"Well," Trigg said, drying his eyes as he shifted his gaze from Tonsika's form, "we've got no bloody choice, have we?"

"Not really. We either team up with Doc, and he

lets us . . . or we're all goners."

"Doc won't believe this," Billy said. "Not even from me. It's worse than the note . . . he won't believe it. He won't."

"Easy, Billy . . . don't lose your grip now. We need you. We need each other."

"But how? How do we convince Doc Henry?"

Trigg had been at the cave's entrance. He'd heard something. He called Morgan and Billy to his side and pointed. On the trail they saw three Apache warriors.

"He'll bloody well believe *that.*"

"How far ahead o' the main body you figger 'em for, Morgan?"

"The main force is with Naschitti off west. I'd say three or four miles back there's probably forty, mebbe fifty Apache."

"Let's get it over with," Trigg said.

"Billy, slip back to your horse. If one of 'em gets away from us, cut him at the trail. We'll give you two minutes."

The three Apache warriors were taken out with ease, and the firing drew the attention of Doc's men. Billy scampered back into the compound; it would still be better for Doc to believe Billy was riding with him. Doc's own men brought in Trigg, Morgan, and the Apache bodies.

Billy reported to Doc Henry that he had encountered the two men while searching the area for the camp of the sharpshooter. Billy said his only chance to run had been when the Apaches attacked. Charlie Bojack didn't believe him, but Doc went outside.

"I knowed you come, you bastard. You figger to

scare ol' Doc off with some Apache shootin'?''

"There's no way out, Doc. The main force, Naschitti . . . he'll ride in from the west with the sun tomorrow. First, you'll get hit at the gorge. The boulders will help but the only chance any of us has is being ready.''

"Git down, Morgan. Let's you 'n' me settle it.'' He grinned. "One more gun either way ain't gonna matter . . . now is it?'' Morgan dismounted.

"I suppose not, Doc. It's your hand again. Play it . . . I'll call you.''

One of Doc's men from the entry gorge rode up fast. "Apaches, thirty, mebbe forty of 'em. Jeezus! They've built a fire, they're dancin' around hootin' and hollerin'. They'll be hittin' us fast, Doc.''

Doc Henry looked at the man and frowned. He looked into Trigg's eyes and then at Morgan.

"I've got some dynamite,'' Morgan said. "The army's due here in two or three days. All we have to do is hold 'til then.''

"Sure, Morgan. Then the army gits me instead o' the Apaches. That what you want?''

"If we hold . . . and if the army gets here . . . they'll have their hands full of Naschitti's warriors. Once they've distracted the Apache, you and I can settle our differences. We'll have plenty of time, Doc.''

"You fucked Naschitti . . . not me.''

Morgan laughed. "Then you hunt him out and tell him that, Doc. And make him believe it.''

"I say we settle it now, either way.'' Charlie Bojack stepped back, spread his feet apart and spit in Morgan's direction. Morgan saw Billy's fists clench and unclench and he shifted his own position just slightly.

"Pull on me, Bojack. Try me. Like Doc says . . . one less gun won't matter." Doc stepped between them. He glowered at Charlie.

"You don't say nothin' here, Charlie . . . not yet you don't. You'd best remember that."

Now, even from their own position some distance away, the group could hear the rising crescendo of the Apache war dance. Doc looked once more at Morgan. His face was contorted with hatred . . . perhaps even a little fear. The look slowly dissolved to a sneer.

"You keep low, Morgan . . . I'll be close. No Apache warrior is gonna deprive me o' what's rightful mine. We'll play the hand together . . . for now."

13

No one slept that night. A dozen men, already enemies, were facing what could be their last night on earth. Each knew the horror they faced if they fell into Apache hands. Some had thoughts of spending their last night with a bottle and a woman. Only one carried out his fantasy . . . and for completely different reasons. Billy Frye went to see Doc Henry just after midnight.

"I come to ask for a woman," he said. Doc looked up. He too had thought of Molly, but there was a knot in his stomach and no desire in his groin. "I don't wanna die without havin' one."

"Sumbitch! A Goddam *virgin.*" Doc laughed. "You got balls boy, I'll give you that, yessir . . . you got balls."

"They's a young one out there . . . she's the one I want."

"Shit, boy, take her. Go tell Skeet I said you could take her. Fuck 'er eyeballs out, boy." Doc suddenly turned sullen again. "I was thinkin,' Billy boy . . . I was thinkin' about offerin' them women to

Naschitti. They's nine of 'em. Molly, she screwed me too . . . that's ten.'' Doc looked up. "You think that fuckin' Apache would take them women an' ride off?''

Doc was asking Billy about something. The very idea amazed Billy, but the suggestion turned his stomach. He knew Doc would do it if he could save his own hide. Billy eyed Doc carefully. Right now, he could kill him. Doc was half drunk, slouched down in a big chair. Billy was fast and he could put a bullet between Doc's eyes in an instant. He considered it. Then he thought of the possibility of Naschitti managing to get at Doc. That, he'd like to see.

"He'll be too fuckin' mad," Billy finally said. He pushed his voice to sound tough and confident. Billy hated his voice. It was changing. It sometimes cracked and went high-pitched on him.

"Yeah, kid, we will. *Sumbitch!* That Goddam Lee Morgan brought this on me . . . you know that, boy? *Lee Fuckin' Morgan.* I'm gonna kill the bastard. I'll wait 'til we git rid o' those Redskins at the front door . . . and then I'm gonna kill the fucker.''

"You can beat 'im, Doc . . . you can beat 'im easy.''

"Beat him? Shit, boy, I'll blow his fuckin' head off first time I git a chance. I don't owe him nothin' an' I don't give a shit if he's faster'n me. I'm gonna kill 'im.''

"I'd sure like to see that," Billy said. "Fact of it is, I'd like to kill the other one . . . that there Trigg.''

"Would you now? Sumbitch. By God . . . you can! Charlie wanted him, but by God you can do it, boy, yessir. I'm promotin' you right now. You go on over there and fuck that little whore's eyes out an' tomorrow you can kill that other sumbitch!''

Billy smiled, nodded and hurried away. He felt sick. He fought the nausea. He entered the building where the women were being held. Their fear led them to half cover themselves. Beth was curled up in the corner with her head on Gretchen's lap. Molly got to her feet. Billy placed his finger over his lips and moved toward her.

"I'm with you now," he whispered, "with Morgan. I'm taking Beth out. She'll tell you everything later." Molly frowned. "It's true . . . somehow, it'll all be okay."

Billy led Beth to the privacy of one of the unused buildings. No one paid them any attention. Beth was so happy to see Billy still alive that she chattered on about nothing. Finally, in private, she broke down and wept. Billy let her emotions run their course. That done, he told her everything.

"We've got to hold the Apaches until the army gets here, but I promise you, Beth, no Apache will lay a hand on you. I swear it to you." He didn't bother to tell her how he could make such a promise. In fact, however, he planned to use the dynamite on the building if the Indians broke into the compound. The women would never know what hit them.

"If . . . if the army does come and drive off the Indians, Billy, there's still . . ." She didn't need to finish. Billy nodded. "I'm scared, Billy . . . scared clear inside my bones."

"I was, Beth, but no more. I know now what I got to do, an' Trigg and Mister Morgan, they'll help. It'll be fine." Billy believed what he said but the conviction in his heart was not nearly so strong as the tone of his voice.

They stayed together until nearly four o'clock.

The false sunrise had lightened the eastern sky. Billy walked Beth back to the shed. At least the women would have some hope . . . even about their possible deaths.

Several of Doc's men, working alongside Trigg, had placed dynamite in among the boulders blocking the entrance to the valley. Doc had more dynamite, and Morgan and three other men rode west to the ford in the river. Only here could the Apache cross with ease.

As they rode back toward the camp, the eastern sky was slowly turning pink. Morgan rode a little behind the others and his own thoughts leaped from the Uncompahgre to the quiet valley near Boise. He thought of Idaho, the Spade Bit, and home. He couldn't help wondering what his father would say to him now. Indeed . . . what would Buckskin Frank Leslie do? Morgan knew only one thing for sure, the old man wouldn't have run.

The Butterfield stage, westbound, rumbled into Creede. The driver and the shotgun dropped off the seat and the driver opened the door. A tall, gray-haired man emerged.

"I'm looking for the office of the local army command."

"Down t'other end o' town, mister." The driver cocked his head and stepped back in a moment of wonder and then recognition. "I seed yore pitchur in the *Rocky Mountain News,* mister. Three days ago it w'ar."

"Probably so. I'm Senator Venable."

"Tarnation!" The driver jammed two fingers into his mouth and let go a shrill whistle, which quickly gathered a dozen people around the stage. "I jist brung a Yewnineted States Senator to Creede. This here is Senator Venable." A cheer went up. Venable had recently been pushing lesiglation to approve a railroad spur line into Creede. At that moment, he was one of the most popular men in the territory.

That aside, the Senator was nervous and obviously in a hurry. He made a brief speech, apologized for his brevity, and promised a more formal appearance later. Then he hurried off to the army office.

The recent events in the remote mountain country had made their way to Denver by way of loose-fingered telegraph operators. First there was the missing army gun shipment. Apaches seemed on the warpath. The district commander died of a heart attack, and most recently . . . the reported massacre of more than thirty white men.

"I'm Senator Venable. I'd like to speak to the commanding officer at once. It's a matter of the utmost urgency." The trooper acted quickly and a moment later, Venable was ushered into the office of Brigadier General Brian Utley, late of Fort Carson.

"Senator, sir, I'm honored."

"With due respect, General . . . I'm not paying a social call and I don't have a great deal of time for amenities. Where is the main body of troops you were sent here to command?"

"In the field. Enroute here, sir . . . but still in the field."

"When are they due to arrive?"

"Two days."

"I don't believe we have two days. I have always hesitated to use the power of my office to exert authority directly, but in this instance, general, I intend to make an exception."

"Sir?"

"A Pinkerton agent assigned to my staff was sent here a week ago to determine the progress of my efforts to hunt down and capture a band of gun runners. I received this telegraph cable from him three days ago."

Senator . . . Morgan's fate uncertain. Part of Jared's gang in army custody . . . Jared not among them. 30 of his gang massacred by Naschitti. Jared not among them. Naschitti seeking revenge . . . Army troops in the field. Am riding into valley to continue investigation.

Denton

Senator Venable quickly told General Utley the background and other details of the situation. He asked for a drink, and the General noticed Venable's sudden nervousness and the much more sombre countenance.

"I sent a backup man, one who would keep out of sight . . . to watch Agent Denton and look for Mister Morgan. He too is working for me through the Pinkerton agency. That man is here in Creede. And Agent Denton is dead." Senator Venable swallowed, tears filled his eyes. "He's dead, sir . . . at the hands of my own daughter!"

"My God, Senator . . . are you certain of this?"

"I found a letter from Doc Henry Jared among her things. My daughter, Emilia . . . God, she . . . she has been his lover. He murdered my family . . . my son

134

. . . my other daughter. My God, how could she . . . how could Emmy do it?''

"Senator Venable, sir, I have 75 men here. They are yours, sir, at once.''

The Senator, obviously shaken, struggled to regain his composure. In a few moments he stood up. "We must ride into the Uncompahgre valley . . . into wherever those men are. We have to find Morgan and warn him. My other man, John Myers . . . he's been to the valley. He knows the way."

"I've been getting reports of Apache Indian movement . . . a large number of them."

"Naschitti?"

"I wasn't certain, not until now. We do have many of Jared's men, and the others were killed. There can't be many left. Let me send a trooper from your agent, Senator. Please, you stay here, rest. I'll have my men ready to ride within the hour."

"It will leave Creede undefended, general."

"It's a risk we must take. I only hope that we're not already too late."

The first line of attackers charged the entry trail into Winchester Valley a few minutes after five o'clock. There were no more than a dozen of them, and only two were hit. Trigg was among the five men defending the position. Doc Henry, Billy and Morgan stayed back with five others. Trigg had urged Doc's men, all excellent shots, to hold their fire. He wanted to create the illusion of even a lighter defense than actually existed. The hope was to draw in the Apache, withdraw to a line manned by the others and fire to detonate the dynamite.

The second attack involved nearly thirty warriors,

three quarters of the immediately available force. As planned, Trigg and the others withdrew slowly, firing but not really aiming. Suddenly, most of the Indians were astride the pile of boulders. Trigg and the others scattered and the men behind them cut loose with rifles.

The blast rocked the compound's buildings, shattering window glass and oil lamps. Debris ripped into the cool, morning air, and through the smoke and soot, the bodies of men were hurled like rag dolls to their deaths.

As the dust settled, Trigg and his group moved forward. The surviving Apaches were dazed, confused. Those outside the compound, watching in hypnotic astonishment, all became easy targets. The leader, an eagle-nosed young buck, fell under Doc Henry's sights. He killed him with a shot between the eyes and the others fled.

"Round one," Morgan said to Trigg. Billy tensed as he saw Doc Henry walking toward Morgan. Suddenly Doc laughed.

"We won't need the fuckin' army at this rate. We didn't lose a Goddam man."

"And Naschitti won't be so easy," Morgan replied. "He had a man or two out there somewhere, watching. In a half an hour he'll know what happened. I'd suggest you give those women their clothing and whatever weapons you've got. They may be able to help hold the line. If worse comes to worse . . . we can herd them back inside."

"You don't give no orders here, Morgan . . . remember that."

"Then forget it, Doc. Do as you please." Doc looked menacing. He took a step toward Morgan but Charlie Bojack walked up just at that moment.

"I sent Cully west, Doc, right after we blew the hell out o' them Apaches. Tol' 'im to check the fork at the river. He's comin' in." Charlie was pointing. It was Cully's horse and Cully was riding it, but Morgan frowned. Trigg squinted in the morning sun, focussing on Cully's body bouncing in the saddle.

"He's dead," Morgan shouted. Half a dozen Apaches leaped from the gullies just to the west of the compound. They all had rifles. They were too far away for hand guns. Trigg fired first and one of them dropped. One of Doc's men, a young gunny named Beau, took a shot in the head. Morgan dropped two of the Indians. Cully's horse trotted by and Billy looked up. Cully had five arrows in his back and he'd been scalped!

Three of Doc's men, still near the narrow gorge where the fight had taken place, opened fire. They were flanking the remaining Apaches and dropped two more of them. The last one fled on foot.

"Sumbitches! Run, you bastard, run! Come back and we'll blow you to fuckin' hell!"

"Not at this rate of exchange we won't," Morgan said. "We lost two men."

"Get them women dressed. They's some rifles in the house, an' a shotgun too. You stay with 'em, Charlie, ever' minute. One o' them whores tries somethin' funny, blow her tits off."

Morgan found Doc's order and his tone promising. Doc Henry Jared was scared shitless. Morgan knew if he needed an extra edge with Doc, he had it now.

"Billy, you be the youngest an' prob'ly the best runner. Git on down to the fork. Keep your hair but find out if them Apaches is comin' in yet."

"Okay, Doc." Billy cast a side glance at Morgan. Morgan winked. Billy smiled and trotted off toward the river. The women were dressed and armed with a variety of weapons. Two old Springfield army rifles, three Henry repeaters, a couple of Winchesters. There were two old Remington pistols, a Colt .44 and two shotguns.

"I got a line shack up the side o' that hill yonder. If them Apaches git acrost that river, anybody at that shack would have a good clean shot at some of 'em."

"Agreed," Morgan said. "Why not put Trigg up there, too. Between him and Charlie and the women, they could buy us some time to use that dynamite."

"Yeah . . . yeah," Doc said, reluctantly. "Put the dummy up there too."

A scream! One of Doc's men was running toward them. One of the men from the entryway. He raised his arms, waved, then fell. A lance teetered for a moment and then layed over to one side.

"Jeezus!" Doc pointed. Ten or twelve Apache scrambled through the rocks and began firing. Doc looked helpless.

"Looks about right to me, Trigg," Morgan said. Trigg nodded. Morgan raised his Winchester and followed Trigg's finger along an invisible line-of-sight to a small pile of brush. Beneath it, Trigg had placed half a case of dynamite. Two Indians dropped, Morgan fired. Nothing. "Low, dammit." He aimed, fired again. Pay dirt!

The explosion was ear-shattering. The Apaches were gone. So was another of Doc's men.

"We got nine men left . . . nine," Doc said. He took

off his hat and wiped his forehead with his shirt sleeve. It wasn't that hot. Doc was sweating. He watched as Trigg, Charlie, and the women climbed to their positions. He yelled for the other men to gather 'round. Suddenly, an explosion. Another! *Another!*

"The river," Morgan said.

"Look . . . it's the kid." Billy was running, hard and fast. He was carrying a broken Apache lance. He reached the group and handed Doc the weapon.

"They . . . they blew it. They seemed to know where it was. They . . . they must have been watching us." There was a note wrapped around the lance. Doc removed it and held it out.

> Tomorrow is the day of
> your last sun

"Sumbitch!"

"Naschitti is going to make us sweat it out."

"Not me he ain't, Morgan. There's a back way outa this valley."

"Where is it Doc? Up there?" Morgan was pointing to a hill behind the house, its summit perhaps a mile away. Doc looked. The hill was lined with Apache warriors!

14

Trigg and Morgan bedded down that night near the entry of the valley. Billy volunteered as one of the guards at the building where the women were being kept. Two of the other men went up to the line shack to keep an eye on the western approaches to the compound. Doc Henry ran Charlie Bojack off, early in the evening. He did so on the pretense he wanted to be alone. In fact, he went to an upstairs bedroom about ten o'clock.

"We're gittin' out," he said. Emmy Venable laughed. "I tol' you before, woman . . . don't never laugh at me."

"Getting out? Don't be ridiculous, Doc. I've seen and heard what's going on. How in the hell are we going to get out?"

"You think I'm stupid don't you, woman? You think 'cause you're the fancy pants daughter o' some hifalootin' Senator that you know ever'thing an' I don't know nothin'."

"I didn't say that, Doc."

"You don't have to say nothing'. I know what you

think. I seen your kind before . . . Southern mostly, durin' the war. Well, I'm tellin' you, we're gittin out . . . tonight!''

Emmy suddenly realized that Doc Henry was serious. He did have another way out of Winchester Valley. "We're sure to be spotted."

"We go on foot, due east. We got some climbin' to do, but then we come down on the river. I got me a boat hid away down there. We go down river 'til we're south o' Creede. We can get horses and supplies from Luke Halstead."

"Luke Halstead is dead, Doc . . . cut down by Morgan and your man Jess. Didn't you *know* that?"

Doc looked at her. "Sumbitch," he mumbled. He thought for a moment. "No," he finally said, "I didn't know it. I knowed there was a fracas o' some kind, but I didn't know Halstead was in on it. Well, no never mind. We'll take what we need from Luke's daddy. He argues . . . I'll *kill* 'im."

"It still sounds risky to me but it's better than the Apaches laying their hands on us. Besides, the two of us might stand a chance."

"Three, woman . . . they'll be *three* of us."

"Charlie! You're tellin' Charlie Bojack about this?"

"Charlie, hell. We're takin' that Irish whore. Just in case somebody trails us . . . just in case that sumbitch Morgan lives, I want that Irish whore along."

"Damn it, Doc, she's dead weight. She'll slow us down."

"She goes," Doc said. Emmy knew it was useless to argue the point. "Get changed. Nothin' goes with us but money an' guns. I'll go git the whore."

Across the compound, Morgan leaned carelessly back against a boulder. Trigg was rolling a smoke. "How 'bout it, Mahrgan . . . want one?"

"No thanks, Trigg."

"You look to be a man thinkin' about somethin' more than tomorrow marnin.' "

"As a matter of fact, I was. I was thinking what I'd do if I was in Doc Henry's spot."

"You mean run?" Morgan sat up and looked at Trigg with surprise. Trigg smiled. "I was thinkin' the same thing, Mahrgan . . . 'bout an hour back."

"Okay, Irishman, which way?"

"I'm not knowin' the country all that well, Mahrgan, but the bastard don't have a lot of choices does he now?"

"He's got east."

"An' what's over the hill?"

"The Rio Grande . . . flowing south."

"A boat?"

"Why not?"

"Makes sense. Where would he end up?"

"Creede mebbe . . . or South Fork and the Butterfield."

"An' his men?"

"He'll let the Apaches have them, Trigg . . . and us and the women too."

"I know the kind, Mahrgan, I've seen 'em before. Alright then, do we stop him?"

"One of us has to try, don't we?"

"I'm no gun fighter, Mahrgan. A fair hand with a rifle. More than good with the old Sharps . . . but no gun fighter."

"And who stands against the men he leaves here? Billy Frye isn't that good."

"So I go now . . . wait and . . ."

"Without a second thought, Trigg. If you hesitate, Doc will kill you."

"I'll have no trouble with hesitation, Mahrgan. I'd just like to see the bastard hang."

"So would I, Trigg . . . but that doesn't seem too likely." Morgan leaped to his feet when he heard footsteps. Out of the darkness came Billy Frye.

"I told Doc I ought to check the posts. He agreed. The real reason I'm here, Mister Morgan, is . . ." he looked at Trigg. Trigg understood.

"Molly?"

Billy nodded. "He came and got her a few minutes ago."

"He's taking her along."

"I hadn't thought of that," Trigg said. "I can't let that happen."

"You can't stop it, Trigg . . . not without a full-fledged showdown right now, tonight. We're not ready for that."

"I won't let him take her, Mahrgan."

"Trigg! Use your head. He won't hurt her. He wants her for protection."

"And if you're wrong?"

"I'm not, Trigg. Think about it, man. Don't let your feelings slow you down. You do that, you're a dead man."

"You really think Doc's gonna run?"

"Yeah, Billy, I do. So does Trigg, here. You get on back to the others. Keep an eye on them, close. Be ready to make a move in the morning. We're going to try to get the women and make it to the river as well. Trigg, take Doc out. Wait for us . . . with Molly."

Doc took Molly back to the house. She assumed he intended to take her to bed. Minutes after they got there, she was wishing he would. He bound her ankles together and tied her hands behind her back. Then, he gagged her. Emmy walked in, looked down and winced at the pleading look on Molly's face.

"I still think taking her is a mistake."

"You don't run with me to do the thinkin'," Doc said. "You ready?" She nodded. "Then you wait. I'm gonna make a final round o' the compound. Let ever'body see me . . . let 'em think ever'thing's fine. When I git back, we go."

After Emmy was certain that Doc was outside the house, she returned to the bedroom and knelt beside Molly. "Just do as you're told and you won't get hurt. I promise you that . . . you won't." Molly frowned and tried to speak but the effort was futile. "If you don't do what you're told . . . I'll kill you, personally."

Less than fifteen miles from Winchester Valley, Senator Venable was finishing a cup of coffee and lighting a cigar. He offered one to General Utley.

"Thank you, sir. It's not often I'm privy to a really good cigar."

"The late war, General . . . I assume you served."

"I did. I was Lieutenant Utley then. Eastern theatre. Served with Little Mac, Joe Hooker, Burnside and, finally, old Grant himself. How about yourself?"

"No . . . no, General, I wasn't in the war. I was a Congressman then. I was offered a commission and a command . . . from Lincoln himself." The senator smiled. "He was desperate at times."

"I'd wager you'd have made a fine field officer. We had more than our share of a shortage."

"Yes, that we did. I've often pondered the outcome had the South been able to sustain the brilliance they enjoyed in the field."

"We'd be riding out under the Stars and Bars most likely."

"The enemy we're facing now wouldn't have made the distinction, would they?"

"Hardly. The Apache nation has been at war for two hundred years. They fought the Spaniards, then the Mexicans, now us. They're a harsh and determined lot . . . not without just cause either."

"But losing to Manifest Destiny. I was opposed to it," Venable said. "It elevated land thievery to lofty heights, I thought. There should have been another way."

"Hmm! But in another hundred years, the Indians, all of them, will be gone. Wiped from the scene as though they had never been there. It seems as foolish as it does shameful. They have much too offer."

"Naschitti too?" Venable asked.

"Once. No more. Naschitti lives for only one thing," the General said, smiling sadly, "he lives to die."

"And what will tomorrow bring?"

"A nasty fight, the deaths of good men, both white and red. Maybe tomorrow Naschitti will die, maybe not. Either way, he will lose."

"Your plan, General? What is it?"

"We break camp at four o'clock. It is my intent to scout ahead and determine Naschitti's main thrust. We'll wait him out, let him become fully engaged

. . . then we attack.''

"How do you know we're even in time?"

"I sent a patrol ahead of the main column, Senator. It left Creede several hours ahead of us. They reported back to me just before suppertime. The Apache have covered every trail in and out of Winchester Valley, but there are hold-outs. I'm afraid I can't tell you just who is among them.''

"No matter. Whoever it is, tomorrow's confrontation will bring an end to the troubles in the Uncompahgre.''

It was well past two a.m. when Doc finally led Molly and Emmy out the back of his house. They moved along a stand of trees, keeping to the shadows. The night was cloudless, but there was no moon. The scent of pine was strong in the air and a light breeze rustled the leaves of the Aspen.

As Doc had said, the climb from the compound to the east was difficult. In the dark, jagged rocks slashed at bare hands and solid footing was at a premium. Doc forced Molly to climb first, putting Emmy second in line. He toted only his handgun and a Bowie knife; a rifle would have been cumbersome and an added burden.

Twice, Molly nearly fell. Only Emmy's assistance prevented it. Doc cussed at the women, urging them on with subtle threats. It was nearly four when they finally reached the first level of the treacherous mountain.

"Please,'' Molly said, "let me rest here . . . just for a short time.''

"You got five minutes,'' Doc replied, harshly. "I don't plan to git caught half way up the side o' this hill come daylight.''

"How do you know there won't be Indians at the top?'' Emmy asked. In fact, Doc didn't know. He'd thought about it but decided it was a risk worth taking. He knew damned well where else they were.

"Won't be no Apaches up there,'' he finally said, pointing. "Only way to it is from the river, and it looks even tougher from that side.''

A few minutes later, the trio had resumed the climb. They were within a hundred yards of the top when they heard the first shots. They were faint and distant. The sky was barely light yet, but they knew Naschitti was beginning his last charge. Emmy stopped and turned toward the firing. She looked forlorn . . . lost. She looked down at Doc Henry Jared and he scowled at her.

The last few feet were pure hell. Molly's palms were torn and bleeding, her clothing shredded, her feet covered with blisters. Emmy too had suffered, but her clothing was more suited to the endeavor. When at last they reached the top, it was daylight. Doc's gun was drawn and he eyed the terrain to the east very carefully. He could see the first rays of the morning sun as they struck the ribbon of water that was the Rio Grande, some two miles distant.

"That shootin' won't last too long,'' he said. Then, Doc laughed.

By the time Doc and the two women had covered about a mile, a new round of rifle fire began. It sounded closer and it had a dull crack to it that stopped Doc in his tracks. He cocked his head. More shots.

"What is it?'' Emmy asked. Molly knew. She smiled.

"It's the army," she said. "Those are Spring-
fields." Then they all heard it. The bugle, sounding
the charge.

"Sumbitch!" Doc started running toward the
river. He motioned for the women to follow him.
Molly hesitated, and Emmy pushed her along. The
firing was more intense now, a mixture of weapons.
Even a few war whoops could be heard as the
Apaches realized they were themselves under
attack.

The meadowland spread out before the trio,
undulating in gentle waves down to the river. Doc
tripped and fell. He rolled once and then came back
to his feet. At that moment, the Sharps cracked
once and the air was split with its booming discharge. The .50 calibre shell, easily able to down a
full-grown bull buffalo, dug up the dirt for six feet
just short of Doc's position.

"Trigg," Molly screamed. Emmy struck her and
she went down. Emmy was on top of her instantly.
At the same moment, Doc looked at the rut in the
dirt. A furrow almost as straight as a string. His
eyes followed its direction while his right hand went
into play. He drew and fired in a single motion. The
bullet ricocheted off a tree, pulling some bark with
it. He was far short of his intended target.

"Git that whore up here." Emmy had easily won
the battle with the exhausted Molly. She had her by
the hair and Doc pinned Molly's arm behind her,
placing the barrel of his gun to her temple.

"Come out where I can see you, sumbitch. Come
out now or I'll blow this whore's head off." Doc
looked at the horizon. He was squinting into the
rising sun. He didn't like it, but it was Emmy who

finally spotted Trigg.

"There, off to the right. There he is." Doc looked. The target was still too distant.

"Let her go, Doc. Send her to me and go on your way."

"Sumbitch! That's your dummy, whore . . . the sumbitch talks."

"Let her go, Doc . . . please." It was Emmy who spoke, and Doc was now showing his true colors. He swung the heavy pistol back and to his right, striking Emmy hard on the temple. She went down in a heap.

"Now you, dummy sumbitch. Toss that Sharps away and walk this way. Keep them hands high, real high. You breathe wrong, dummy, an' the whore dies."

Trigg pondered his options. He'd reloaded the Sharps but it would take time to aim and fire it. It wasn't the light weight Winchester or Henry. He was wearing a handgun, but he hadn't lied about his skill. Trigg was no match for Doc Henry Jared.

"I'm coming," Trigg finally said. He hefted the Sharps high where Doc could see it, then he tossed it aside.

"Don't do it," Molly screamed. "Don't, Sean! He'll kill you!"

"Shawn? That sumbitch is your man?"

"My brother, Doc. For God's sake, don't kill 'im, I'm beggin' you."

Now Trigg had come within range. He stopped.

"You're not much of a man, Jared . . . not much at all. Shoot me, then . . . and Molly there. The other one, too. She's already unconscious. No threat to you. You should be able to handle her with ease."

In a single move, Doc raised the barrel of his gun, brought it down on Molly's head and turned her loose. She dropped to her knees and then collapsed. Doc had his pistol holstered before she hit the ground.

"Now you dummy Irish bastard . . . now tell me I'm no Goddam man." Trigg reached. He'd practiced. He'd learned accuracy. Even some speed. He could have impressed his many fellow soldiers back in Ireland. He looked impressive and might have bluffed his way through a saloon brawl or two in the West. But against Doc Henry Jared, he wasn't even a novice. He never cleared leather. Doc's shot went straight through Patrick Sean Terrence O'Flynn's heart. He blinked once and his lips formed a single word. "Molly," he whispered. Then he fell dead.

As Doc glanced up, he thought he saw movement near the river. He dropped to his knees. There it was again. A hat. Another. Blue.

"Shit! A cavalry patrol." They were checking the river bank for Apaches. He could still hear gunfire back to the west but it was even more distant. The Apaches were running and the cavalry was hard on their asses. "The compound. They'll have it searched by the time I git back."

Doc waited until he could no longer see signs of the army patrol. Both women were still out. In fact, Emmy looked dead. "Too bad," Doc muttered. "I liked your style, Emmy. Liked the way you figgered things. Too fuckin' bad. We'd a' done good, you an' me." Doc got to his feet and trotted back toward his compound in Winchester Valley.

Even as the events by the river were unfolding, Morgan had his hands full. General Utley's troopers had disrupted the main Apache attack and most of the Indians had pulled back, uncertain of the number of troops confronting them. But two dozen or more had gained the compound itself. Morgan, the remaining members of Doc's gang, Billy Frye, and four of the women were holding them at bay from the main house. The other women were taking shifts reloading the weapons. At about six thirty, there was a lull in the fighting.

"By my count, there's still fifteen or so out there. They'll be back."

"Where the fuck is Doc an' that bitch he was with?" Charlie Bojack was beginning to wonder if Doc Henry had run out on him. Morgan, of course, assumed that the woman Charlie was referring so unkindly to was Molly.

"My guess is he ran out on you, Bojack."

"I'm gonna kill you, Morgan . . . even if them fuckin' Apaches git in here. I swear, I'm gonna kill you."

"We can't be fightin' amongst ourselves," Billy said. "Take it easy, Charlie. There's time fer that. Hell, they's still five o' us left . . . they's only one o' him."

The Apaches resumed their attack and rendered the exchange academic.

"Now," one of the man yelled, "hit that dynamite case." Seven warriors had gained access to the yard area just west of the house. Their position now afforded them possible entry unless they were stopped. Charlie, Morgan, and Billy all cut loose on the dynamite they'd buried overnight. Three of the warriors died instantly, Morgan and Charlie dropped the others. One of the gang was fatally hit during the fight, along with one of Molly's girls.

The Apaches had sufferred all the losses they cared to endure. Only a few had not been driven off by the army, and the accuracy of the fire directed against them, coupled with the open ground they had to cross, had proved devastating. The remainder now fled.

It was one of Doc's men who first realized it. Lefty Hightower saw them riding east. The running battle between Naschitti's main band and the cavalry could still be heard, but it grew more faint with each passing moment. Lefty moved from his upstairs window and carefully edged down to the main floor.

"Can you see 'em?" Billy asked Morgan. Both men were at the windows. Morgan replied that he could not. Lefty caught Charlie's eye, but Gretchen spotted the exchange.

"Look out, Morgan!" Lefty, his gun already drawn, shot and killed Gretchen instantly. Billy darted across the room toward where the rest of the women were located. Morgan went through the window, followed closely by two shots. Both missed. Billy herded all the women through a bedroom window on the ground floor and told them to hide in the woods nearby.

Lefty Hightower, Charlie Bojack, and a man called Petrie remained in the living room. They were trying to pin down Morgan's location. Morgan had taken refuge behind the well in the front yard. The fourth man, Jace Ryker, had watched what Billy Frye did. Ryker now walked onto the back porch. Only Billy stood between Ryker and the women.

Ryker was a gritty-looking sort. He sported a stubble of whiskers where they would grow, but he'd suffered pox as a boy and there were blotches on his face where no hair would grow, making him look all the more sinister. In fact, Jace Ryker was only a little older than Billy. He was alleged to have once ridden with the James boys on a bank holdup, and a wanted poster on him told of his murder of a sheriff somewhere in Oklahoma Territory. The other story about him focused on his lightning fast draw.

He wore a Colt .45 with an Ebony covered butt . . . an unusual and attractive weapon. It was tied to his right leg about midway between his waist and his knee. When he positioned himself to draw it, he didn't take the usual wide-legged stance. Rather, he put most of his weight on his left leg and extended his right leg forward just a bit. The butt of the Colt then protruded from his thigh in a position affording him the fast draw for which he was reputed.

"I figgered you fer a fuckin' traitor, Frye. Figgered it a long time back." Ryker grinned and licked his lips. "One thing you got is good taste in women. That young one, that there Beth." Ryker raised his eyebrows and nodded his head slightly. "Soft pussy, I'll bet. I figger to have it, Frye . . . jist as soon as I kill you."

"You got it wrong, Ryker. I was herdin' them women out o' here 'til we could take out Morgan. Hell, Ryker, you can have that young one," Billy forced a half laugh. "She ain't bad."

"You're a lyin' bastard, Frye. All you had to do was throw down on them women and we'd 'a' had them an' Morgan. Now pull on me, Frye, 'cause if you don't . . . I'm gonna pull on you." Ryker grinned again. "You're a dead bastard either way."

Billy Frye had come of age. There was no more distance. Shooting an Indian or any man from twenty or fifty or a hundred yards was a whole lot different than eye-to-eye. His throat went dry and he couldn't find the spit to swallow. There was only silence save for the faint popping of rifles far to the west.

Billy's mind was reeling with self portraits of his long hours of practice. Draw and fire . . . draw and fire. A split second later, the image vanished and was replaced by Morgan's words. Now Billy Frye asked himself the question. "Can I kill a man in a gun fight?" His answer was less than fifteen feet away from him.

Charlie Bojack stepped through the back door. "What the fuck is goin' on?"

"Frye here decided to switch sides, Charlie. He run them girls up the hill to hide an' then tried to lie his way out. He's mine, Charlie; you an' the others keep Morgan tied down."

Charlie looked at Billy. Billy's face was all the confirmation he needed. "Yeah, Jace . . . good idea. Take the kid out." Charlie turned and re-entered the house. It bothered Billy. He didn't know if it was a display of confidence in Ryker or a show of contempt for Billy. His mind flashed back to Morgan's near shoot-out with Doc Henry.

"You're makin' the bet, Ryker . . . an' I'm callin' you. Show your hand."

Ryker slapped leather. The pretty little Colt fairly flew from the holster and spit lead twice. Ryker's eyes had widened in surprise even as he began the move. He could already see the twin black dots that were the barrels of Billy's guns. Billy fired one shot from each. Ryker's bullets went wide and high. Billy's struck the upper right chest and the belly. Ryker teetered for a moment, managed one foot forward in a vain effort to deny the truth, grimaced in a moment of pain, and fell dead.

Billy darted around the corner of the house to near the front. "Morgan . . . Ryker's dead. I gunned him. The women are hidden in the trees." Billy heard the front door of the house open.

"Morgan, you sonuvabitch . . . show yourself." Lefty Hightower stepped out and stood at Charlie's right. In a moment they were joined by the man called Petrie. "It's three to two," Charlie said, "but you're supposed to be so fuckin' good that won't make no never mind . . . will it, Morgan?"

Morgan stood up. "Get the women, Billy, and get out of here."

"Not yet, Mister Morgan," Billy said. He walked across the yard and positioned himself on the opposite side of the well from Morgan. They were about twenty five feet from the house. The trio of men on the porch came off it and stood in the yard.

"Hightower's fast," Morgan said, "but he bends his knees just before he shoots. It costs him time. I'll take Bojack. I can't tell you about Petrie."

"I've seen 'im," Billy said. "He's not as good as Ryker."

Billy Frye had come from a two-gun-toting loud-mouth to a subdued and skilled gunman almost in the blink of an eye. Petrie went for Billy. Petrie's eyes were glued to Billy's right hand gun. It was logical; Petrie was on Charlie's left and in the line of fire for Billy's right hand. Billy was faster, and he proved it. He was also smarter! He drew both weapons but crossed them in front of him as he fired.

Petrie died instantly. Lefty Hightower got off a shot which Billy felt as it grazed his neck like the sting of a wasp. Lefty took Billy's shot in the leg, staggered, and caught a second shot that killed him. It too came from one of Billy's guns. Even later, he could not recall which one he'd fired twice.

Morgan, for his own protection and to buy Billy another fraction of a second, concentrated on Charlie Bojack. Charlie's arm seemed almost disconnected from the rest of his body when he drew. It was so fast as to make a man wonder if his brain could work that fast. Morgan's hat flew from his head, somersaulting through the air. There was a hole, dead center just above the wide band.

Morgan's own right hand almost tingled from the tension in every nerve ending. There was no feeling Morgan had ever experienced that was exactly like it. He'd often thought the feeling came from a momentary visit by Death itself . . . but if so, Death always passed Lee Morgan by. Morgan's hand and arm and the gun they manipulated all ended up three or four inches lower than that of any other man there. The bullet he fired ended up in the target just an inch or two higher. It defied explanation but the results were obvious. Charlie Bojack died two quickly to show any response. He fell forward, stiff as a board, still looking straight ahead. The impact flattened his nose.

"How bad you hit?" Morgan asked. Billy wondered how Morgan could know. Even Billy wasn't yet certain. He touched the wound.

"Scraped me, that's all."

"You lost time crossing your guns. Against better men, you'd be dead."

"I'll remember, Morgan."

Morgan smiled. "Yeah, Billy, do that. But you're good, damn good."

"What now?"

"I'll round up enough horses for everybody. You get the women down here." Morgan cocked his head. There was no more distant firing . . . only the gentle whistle of the breeze through the pines.

"It's over, Mister Morgan." Morgan looked at Billy, but he said nothing. He knew it wasn't over. He'd come for Doc Henry and he hadn't got him yet.

Morgan found the roan just where he'd left him. Two other animals were nearby, but no others could be seen. He decided, if worse came to worse, he'd have Billy stay with the women and he'd make contact with the army. He led the mounts back to the house. Billy was sitting on the porch steps, hat in hand and staring at the ground.

"What is it, Billy?" Billy looked up. Morgan could see the glisten of moisture in Billy's eyes.

"The women, Mister Morgan. It's all my fault . . . they're *gone!*"

"Jared," Morgan said to himself. "He doubled back."

"What'd you say?" Billy got to his feet. He walked over and handed Morgan the note he'd found stuck to a tree with a Bowie knife.

You follow . . . they're dead.

"It's not your fault, Billy. You did the right thing."

"I want 'im, Mister Morgan . . . I want 'im bad."

Morgan nodded. "Yeah, Billy, but you're at the back of the line. Ride out of here and find the army. Tell them what's happened and tell them about the women."

"I want to go with you."

"Don't argue, Billy. Just do what I tell you to. Don't make me force it." Billy saw Morgan's eyes and the set of his jaw. He knew he'd lose this one. He nodded passively.

Morgan rode to the edge of the tree line, stopped, and turned back. Billy was riding west. Morgan looked at the compound and thought how serene it looked . . . how pleasant now. Then something gripped at his innards. It was the old feeling of hatred. The feeling that went back to Harvey Logan and the death of his father. Out there somewhere was Morgan's Harvey Logan . . . in the body of Doc Henry Jared.

15

The rain was incessant. It didn't fall . . . it was
driven. Drops the size of a man's thumb, and cold.
Billy Frye hunkered down even lower in his saddle.
No one had spoken for the last five miles. The
soldiers were weary and dejected, the column a
morbid snake of men crawling along a mountain
trail, toting their own dead.

General Utley had begun his campaign with considerable zeal and no small measure of success.
Surprise was his ally and Naschitti was clearly on
the defense. Perhaps that was Utley's mistake. He
simply forgot that the Indian, never mind the tribe,
had always fought on the defense. Naschitti was
brilliant in his withdrawal from Winchester Valley.
He ordered his warriors to split up and flee in
apparent terror of the sudden appearance of the
Blue Coats.

In fact, Naschitti had carefully planned his movements, drawing General Utley's main force still
deeper into the Uncompahgre. He used brilliant hit
and run tactics along the way until, finally, his main

force had gathered again. Their counter attack decimated Utley's command and the General himself sustained a serious wound. But Naschitti also knew when his own time had run out. He knew there were more soldiers . . . and he didn't know where. It was the only thing that saved Utley's command from being wiped out.

Billy caught up with the returning force just as it broke the trail north of Slumgullion pass. General Utley was too feverish even to accept Billy's report. It made no difference anyway. He'd simply ride with them back to Creede. The rain began on the mountain top and grew increasingly worse.

Senator Venable had argued to try and force entry into the valley where Doc Henry had been holed up. Soon, even he realized the effort would be futile. Reluctantly, with a small detachment to accompany him and, he hoped, lead Yates back into the fight, the Senator headed back to Creede.

As Billy rode along in silence, he couldn't keep his imagination from conjuring up the worst possible scenarios. They included Doc Henry's cold-blooded murder of all the women, or his rape of Beth and their abandonment in the high country. Billy knew that Lee Morgan wouldn't give up, but that was little consolation where the safety of the women was concerned.

Morgan was frustrated. The country over which Doc Henry had chosen to go was not suited to riding a horse. Morgan led the roan through some rugged terrain and could only hope the animal wouldn't slip, go crippled on him, or simply bolt from Morgan's almost impossible demands.

Morgan knew only that Doc Henry had been

working, slowly, back to the west. Morgan's knowledge of the Uncompahgre wasn't sufficient to draw any conclusions about an ultimate destination. Four days had passed since the shoot-out in the valley, and Morgan's only thread of encouragement had come from the women. One of them, maybe Beth, had been marking a trail. A small bit of cloth here, a piece of silk or satin there. Someone lived, someone besides Doc Henry.

Morgan, in spite of the loosely marked trail, harbored grave concerns for the lives of the women. There was no lack of water in the high country, but food was another matter. Morgan had seen no smoke; Doc Henry would never allow a fire. He could feel the drain on his own body from a restricted diet of jerky and hard tack. The open meadow country, and there were many miles of it, did nothing to aid Morgan's efforts. Doc Henry kept to the high country, and Morgan dared not risk losing the meager trail someone was leaving.

Shortly after sunup on the morning of his fifth day out, Morgan spotted a man! He too was seen, but the man made no move to run or confront Morgan. He simply rode toward him, slowly. They met at a crystal clear stream that cut a path through the meadowland.

"Jehosophat! You look nigh on to daid." The man slipped off his horse. He was a giant and made more so by a double layer of clothing . . . buckskin and bear hide. "I be called Stoner."

"Morgan . . . Lee Morgan. I'm trailing a man and several women." Stoner spat a wad some twenty feet and wiped his whiskers. His shirt sleeve was dark brown where he'd done the same thing untold times in the past.

'Them wimmin fo'k looked mighty sorrowful.''

"You saw them? When? Where?"

"It w'ar two day back. Four they wuz . . . an' a surly feller herdin' 'em up trail.''

"Damn. Four is all?"

"Yep. I give 'em som b'ar meat . . . fresh kilt that mornin'.''

The grizzly old mountain man then went to fishing through his many pockets. He finally grinned, exposing short, dingy teeth.

"One o' them wimmin, she sez if'n I meet anybody to be sure an' give 'em this.'' Morgan took the crumpled paper. The note was short, written with a burned stick.

> Molly alive—no here.
> Only four. Silverton.
>
> Beth

Morgan suddenly felt a new surge of hope. Molly must have slipped away. Or had she been abandoned? Not likely, he decided. Beth! Morgan wished he could get word to Billy. He looked up. Maybe he could.

"Where you bound for, Stoner?"

"Wh'ar ever that ol' horse'll carry me a'fore the snow flies.''

"Creede," Morgan said. He pulled out a hundred dollar bill. "You ride to Creede for me. Deliver a message to the army and to a young buck named Billy Frye. I'll write the words so you won't have to remember them. Do that, Stoner, and you can winter it out in Creede . . . high livin'. This hundred's yours now . . . I'll have to trust you to that much. Do what I ask and there'll be two hundred more in it. You've got my word."

"Had me a whole poke full o' hunnert dollar bills oncest. Struck gold up in South Park." The old man reared back his head and let out a war whoop followed by stacatto laughter. "Lost every penny of it to a bunko steerer in a Denver saloon."

"Sorry," Morgan said.

"Sorry? No need to be feelin' sorry, sonny." Stoner once again began rummaging through his pockets and talking at the same time. "I waited fer that feller fer two month er more. He final come ridin' along Cherry crik one night. I cut his gizzard out." Morgan frowned. He needed the old man's cooperation, but he had no time for tall tales. Stoner's face lit up. "Here 'tis." He held up a short length of thong leather. "Took his ear too." The leathery ear dangled from the rawhide.

"I need your help, Stoner . . . I mean those women do. The man they were with was Doc Henry Jared. You ever hear of him?"

"Nope," Stoner said without hesitation. "Don't palaver much with city fo'k . . . don't like cities. Don't like Creede." He shifted the chew in his cheek, lined his sight on a columbine and it disappeared beneath a dark brown blob. "Don't like it none, but I'll do it for ya. Been a spell sincest I wintered indoors."

Morgan quickly penned a note to the commanding officer at Creede and a separate one to Billy Frye. He wasn't sure who was in command by now, but he urged them to return to the compound and began a search for Molly and possibly others. He told Billy to meet him in Silverton.

Morgan sat atop the roan and watched until the old mountain man reached the end of the valley. Stoner stopped, turned back and waved and then headed south. He was going to help.

Two of the women were too weak to continue. Doc Henry finally yielded to Beth's pleadings that they stop for the night. He had managed to snare a rabbit, and Beth along with a girl named Alicia set about to cook it. The wind was out of the east, coming down from one of the nearby high peaks. Doc felt safe that no one behind him would see smoke. The other women fell asleep quickly, and Doc leaned back against a rock some distance from the fire.

"Beth, keep working," Alicia said, "but listen." Beth nodded. "We're traveling west . . . almost due west now. We've been traveling this way for five days. We're very close to the roads. Very close."

"What road?"

"It runs north and south between Ouray and Silverton where Doc Henry said he was going. I worked in Ouray once . . . a mining camp there. I traveled the road south. It went down to Silverton over a high mountain pass. We're real close to it, Beth."

"How can you be sure, Alicia? My God, we're in the middle of the mountains."

"Look up, Beth . . . due west." Beth did. What she saw was one peak with a little snow at its summit and a reddish tinge along its slopes.

"I don't see nothin' but that there funny lookin'

red mountain."

"That's it, Beth . . . Red Mountain. That's the pass I went over between Ouray and Silverton. We look to be a little north of it. If we go west, through that flat country, we'll come out on the trail. There's always minin' equipment goin' back an' forth . . . men too, ever'day between Ouray and Silverton."

Beth's heart pounded hard. If Alicia was right, they had only a few more hours to live. Perhaps Doc agreed to stop here only so that he might kill them. It couldn't be more than a few hours walk to that road. He wouldn't need them anymore, and he certainly didn't intend that they should live to tell their story.

"Alicia, in the mornin' I want you to go tell Doc you're makin' a trip into the woods . . . you know, to pee or somethin.' "

"You mean . . . ." Alicia's eyes got big. "Try somethin'?"

"What choice we got? While you're doin' that, I'll git Doc over to one o' the other girls . . . tell him I think she's daid and ask him to look. 'Stead o' peein', you be waitin'. Git a rock or tree branch, anythin'. If we don't git now, he'll kill us . . . ever' one of us."

"Where's that fuckin' rabbit?"

"Comin', Doc, it's comin'."

Even the women who were asleep were grateful for having been awakened. The rabbit tasted like beef steak, but one of the sickest women couldn't keep it down, and within an hour after she'd eaten, she was sicker than ever.

Just after dark, Doc set about to tying them up as he had done each night. The second one was the sick girl. Beth was nearby and heard a slight groan. Then, with the last dying rays of the sun, she caught the gleam of light off the knife blade!

Doc moved to Alicia next. She pulled back as he squeezed one of her tits and then laughed. He slapped her and she began to sob, softly. He stood up, legs spread, and said, "Think I'll have myself a little treat tonight, after that there rabbit dinner."

Beth had never moved so quickly. She cleared the distance to where Doc was standing in four leaps. He heard her steps and turned, but she was already in position. She kicked, hard. The heavy boot struck home. Doc howled and doubled over in pain. She grabbed for his gun. He swatted at her, but he'd dropped to his knees. She aimed the Colt at his head and pulled the trigger. The hammer dropped onto an empty chamber! They were all empty. Doc had taken no chances.

He was still holding his balls with one hand, but he'd managed to get back on his feet. He never heard Alicia behind him with the branch. It caught the back of his head and he went down face first. It was a solid blow, but lacked force. Doc groaned again, shaking his head.

"Run, Beth . . . run now." Alicia already was fleeing, and Beth was confused. One girl was still alive and it was nearly dark. Doc wasn't dead and she had no way to kill him. She swung the Colt but the butt missed its mark, catching Doc on the back of the neck. He went down again and Beth turned and ran.

Morgan had gotten some beans and dried bear meat from Stoner. The old man also poured a

healthy amount of whisky into Morgan's canteen.
This night, Morgan wouldn't camp. Trail or no trail,
he knew his ultimate destination and he figured to
close the gap between him and his prey. He ate the
beans as the big roan walked easy through the
meadow. He washed down the bear meat with
whisky and felt a new strength. By dark, Morgan
was riding steady toward the darkening sky to the
west. His landmark was the silhouette of Red
Mountain pass.

It was well after sunup when Morgan again found
a tiny piece of cloth. Beth was a smart girl. She
always marked the trees to the right and poked a
hole through the cloth if there was no change in
direction. Where there was a direction change, she
would knot the cloth. Morgan's own tracking skills
more than made up the deficits.

At mid-morning, Morgan rode into the camp. He
found rabbit bones, a still warm fire bed, and two
dead girls. He felt a moment of guilt when he
realized he was relieved that neither of them was
Beth Frye. He didn't tarry long—only long enough
to bury the girls in shallow graves.

He crossed Animas creek near noon and he knew
it was less than five miles to the base of Red
Mountain. He'd found no more cloth and no tracks.
He wasn't sure of his direction from Silverton, but
he was aware of the mining road not too far away.
His fear now was that he would be too late to save
Beth and one other girl, whoever she was.

"Morgan? Oh my God . . . Mister Morgan!" He
looked toward a small pond formed from the creek's
recent overflow and there stood Beth Frye.

"Where's Doc?" Morgan's Colt was already out.

He'd shoot on sight. She shook her head.

"He went south . . . we saw him. We were scared to death he'd find us again. We hit him and ran away last night after he killed Mary."

"He on foot?" Beth nodded. "How long ago did he pass?"

"Two hours, mebbe three. I'm not sure. Alicia . . . I think her leg's broke."

Beth was right. Doc Henry would have to wait, and so would Morgan. He put both women on the big roan and they set out for the road. At least tonight they'd bed down inside. They were headed for Ouray.

The Elk Horn Palace was a sham. The facade would have done any street in New York City proud. Once you walked through the bat wings, it ended. Still, it was inside. The sheets were clean. Yellowed with stains, but clean. Besides, there wasn't anything else in Ouray, Colorado.

Alicia had a room for the night in the sawbone's house, where the doc had set her leg. Morgan got himself and Beth adjoining rooms. After he'd treated her to a fine dinner, he saw to it she got bedded down. He slipped out and wandered into the bar.

"You drinkin', mister . . . or just takin' up space?"

"I'm looking for the sheriff."

"You'll have a long wait mister. Ain't no sheriff hereabouts."

"There's the territorial marshal," an attractive young girl said. Morgan looked at her and she smiled . . . a come-on smile. He smiled back, but he wasn't interested.

"Where might I find him?"

"Don't know for sure. If he didn't ride down south, he'll be in his office, I reckon. It's down at the end o' the street." Morgan nodded his appreciation.

Halfway there, he saw the flicker of a lamp in the office window. He picked up his pace and entered without knocking. The marshal was a big round-shouldered man with thick gray hair. He was engaged in paperwork and didn't look up.

"What can I do for you?"

"I'm Lee Morgan, marshal." The big man shoved his chair back quickly and got to his feet. He was eyeing Morgan's gun. "I'm not lookin' for trouble. I came for your help."

"I got a dodger on you, Morgan."

"Probably. Mebbe two." He handed the marshal his letter from Senator Venable. The marshal shoved some papers back and forth looking for his glasses. He finally found them, and took a closer look at the young muscular man he'd heard about before.

"Lee Morgan, eh?" The marshal read the letter and handed it back. "I'm Ephram Banner." Morgan tilted his head. He was trying to remember where he'd heard the name before. "I knew your daddy."

"Then that's why the name sticks."

"In your craw, mebbe . . . that right?"

"No."

"Well, mebbe it should." Banner walked to a dusty old chest in the corner. It was a roll-top and he blew away some of the grime before he opened it. Inside, in three neat stacks, each a foot thick, there were wanted posters. Banner fingered through the first stack until he reached the halfway point. He lifted the top half and slipped a yellowed sheet out. It nearly tore in two. He turned and handed it to Morgan. It offered a $1.,500 reward for Buckskin Frank Leslie, alias Lee Williams, alias Fred Lee.

Morgan handed the poster back. "He's dead, marshal."

"I heard that. Who backshot him?"

"Nobody. Harvey Logan got him."

"Fair draw?" Morgan nodded. "Then Logan's dead too."

"He is."

"And you're claimin' to be a Pinkerton man."

"I'm a Pinkerton man at the request of Senator Venable . . . that's all."

"Your daddy never asked me for help." He grinned. "I chased him over most o' three states. Felt lucky I never caught up to him when it mattered."

"But you did catch up to him."

"Dodge City. Youngster named Toby Jacobs got shot during a bank robbery. The Tyler brothers, Kiley Haddock from down Missouri way, and little John Ringo. Ringo skedaddled clear out o' Kansas. Drifted south. Me'n your daddy an' Morgan Earp an' Doc Holliday went after 'em. We got 'em. Now Kiley, he was smooth, fast. A right fine gun hand. Frank Leslie beat him clean and drilled a hole through his right elbow. Shattered it." The marshal looked down at Morgan's rig. "That the Bisley?"

"Yeah."

"I never drew against him." Banner laughed. It was a soft laugh, deep from his belly. It reminded Morgan of Frank Leslie's laugh.

"Well, I know Senator Venable sure. If that

letter's on the up an' up, then you've got my help. If it's a scam, son . . . I'll kill you. Want some coffee?" Morgan nodded. Banner poured them both a cup and they both sat down. "Alright, son, tell me your story."

Marshal Banner took in every word without expression until Morgan finished. Then Banner leaned forward. "Doc Henry Jared has never come this far west. We don't want him here, and folks aren't going to appreciate the Pinkertons taking on somethin' they can't finish." Morgan got to his feet. "You goin' somewhere?"

"Back to my room, marshal. I'm dead ass tired. As far as folks are concerned, we'd best get Doc Henry quick. No need for them to know anything if we do the job."

"You're not as smooth as your daddy was."

"Nor as patient," Morgan said.

"Mind if I walk with you? Haven't made my rounds anyway."

"You're welcome."

They were half way back to the Elk Horn Palace before the marshal spoke again. "Any idea why Jared would go to Silverton?"

"Only one. Doc's brother rode back south to help him with his Apache deal. Johnny's dead, but I found out later that he didn't ride south alone. He had three men with him and he left them in Silverton to wait for him. He'd told Doc about it in a letter several months ago."

"And these three men?"

"Largo Johnson, Quint Yokley, and Charlie Hawks." Marshal Banner stopped dead in his

171

tracks.

"Shootists don't come worse than them three, Morgan."

"Damn few I ever heard of do."

"I don't know a man this side o' the divide that'll ride against the likes o' them."

"I know three, marshal."

"Name 'em."

"Banner, Morgan, and Frye . . . Billy Frye."

"I'm law an' they don't scare me none an' you say you're workin' for Pinkerton an' that makes you law. I'll take your word on this fella Frye. The odds are still wrong."

"Four to three. I've faced worse."

"You've faced worse numbers mebbe . . . but these odds, Morgan, these are like your daddy's with Harvey Logan."

Morgan looked puzzled. "Odds? How so?"

"They may be even, boy, and that means no winners . . . just seven dead men."

Morgan didn't know what time it was, he only knew that it was still dark, he was still tired, and there was someone in his room.

"Morgan," came the voice . . . low, soft, frightened. "It's Beth." He fumbled and found a match. He lit it. She was wearing one of his shirts and nothing else.

"Couldn't sleep?"

"No. An' . . . an' I'm scared Morgan."

"Don't be. Tomorrow we'll get out of here and you'll get back to Creede." Morgan had been thinking about what he'd told Banner, about the men who'd stand against Doc. "You'll be back with your brother. I told him to meet me in Silverton. If he's not there yet, I'll send you on and send him back to you when he shows up." Beth sat down on the edge of the bed, then she learned over and layed her head on Morgan's bare chest.

"I need to forget for awhile," she said. "Will you help me?" She raised her head and looked into Morgan's face. He knew what she meant. He didn't think he could do it. Not even if he felt like it and, at that moment, he didn't.

"It might complicate things even more."

"How Morgan? Tomorrow we'll split up. Maybe I won't ever see you ag'in." Beth stood up, removed the shirt and Morgan realized she wasn't really a little girl. Her breasts were full, round, and tipped with large, perpetually hard nipples. Beth was fully matured physically and old enough to make her own decisions.

"Love me, Morgan . . . please." She moved to the bed and slipped over his body. She was warm and smelled like a woman should smell. She kissed him and her tongue darted into his mouth. Morgan began to respond. His hands found the fullness of her tits and he kneaded them gently. She raised up and he continued his caresses. She turned around and bent from the waist, lowering herself until she could close her lips around the head of Morgan's already hardened cock.

She sucked greedily at his shaft and Morgan responded with his own tongue. He teased at first and then found his desires too demanding for delay. He licked furiously at her pussy until it was soaked with a combination of his saliva and her juices.

Suddenly Beth got up, rolled to the bed beside him

and spread her legs. Morgan moved on top of her and entered, slowly, carefully. She had experienced a man before, but he felt a tightness around his prick which he had not known for a long time. She contracted her vaginal muscles and increased the sensation as Morgan began to pump. It was slow at first but increased with each stroke.

They kissed and Beth squealed as every nerve ending in her body responded to his efforts. She had been fucked by a boy, a 17 year old boy. She loved him and he was leaving with his family for California. It was their last time together. She had never regetted it but it had left a smouldering within her which Morgan was now fanning into a full flame.

Beth's body heaved and she closed her arms around his neck, digging her fingernails into his back and shoulders. Morgan was near his climax, he moaned.

"God, Beth. God, you're nice . . . young . . . " His sperm burst forth like a broken water pipe. Beth strained and contracted her muscles so that she might join him. She succeeded and they writhed in those precious few seconds when a man and woman truly become one.

16

Butterfield didn't run stages into that part of Colorado. Instead, Beth was put aboard the Montrose-Durango line. It did make a stop in Silverton, but Beth wouldn't even get off. At Durango, she'd wait for the eastbound Butterfield.

She and Morgan had exchanged little talk that morning but she kissed him as they parted. He thought back to the night before and realized that his own needs had been as great as Beth's. He watched the big Concord coach until it was out of sight and then he walked to the marshal's office.

"This is Ole Swenson," Banner said. "He keeps an eye on things when I'm not around." Ole and Morgan shook hands but said nothing. "I'm ready, Morgan." Banner looked up as he put a final item or two in his saddle bags. "I give Ole here an official swearin' in this mornin'. Mayor was witness, an' I turned in a letter of recommendation on Ole."

"Sounds pretty final to me."

"It was, Morgan. How about you? You settled your affairs?"

"I've got none to settle."

"I recollect hearin' somewhere that ol' Buckskin Frank had himself a ranch." Banner looked at Morgan. "Didn't he leave it to you or was that just a story?"

"There was a ranch. The Spade Bit. Idaho. I sold it," Banner detected there was more to it than that but he didn't push the issue.

"Ole, take care o' yourself . . . an' take care o' Ouray for me."

"You'll be back, marshal," Ole said, smiling.

"Mebbe, mebbe not."

It was 23 miles from Ouray to Silverton. A third of it was up one side and down the other on Red Mountain pass. The base of the 11,000 foot peak was very near before either man spoke again.

"You scared, Morgan?" Banner looked at him for an answer.

"I don't know. Most men that I've heard about who were scared ran away. I've never run away." After he'd said that, Morgan wondered if keeping ahead of Harvey Logan and leading Logan back to where he and Frank Leslie shot it out was running. Maybe it was.

"There's a lot o' ways to be scared. Dyin' scares some men."

"You?"

Banner smiled. "I've already lived longer than most in my business. I looked at myself in the mirror this morning and thought about you and decided we're the last o' the lot."

"Meaning?"

"Me . . . an old timer. A man raised up like your daddy was. You, a gun fighter with fewer men to fight and civilization telling you not to. It's not the way anymore . . . not in most places anyways."

"You saying we're out of place?"

"Yeah," Banner agreed, nodding. "Yeah, I guess that's what I'd call us."

"But that civilization you talked about, Marshal . . . it's people. They want to move west, to build and grow and multiply. They can't quite do it yet because of men like Doc Henry. We may be the last, but we've still got a place."

They rode over Red Mountain, pausing only to eat. They eyed the sluice piles and the rotting timbers of long-abandoned mines. The northbound stage and a half a dozen freight wagons passed them. This was civilization and it expected to be left alone to get on with itself. Thousands of men, women, and children trying to scratch out a new life for themselves and their families yet unborn. Between them and men like Doc Henry, there was a handful of dedicated lawmen. At that moment, Lee Morgan was one of them.

Silverton was not Ouray or anything like it. Half a dozen narrow, muddy streets were lined with wooden buildings. The people, shoulder to shoulder as they went about their business, were a mixture of the old and new that Banner and Morgan had spoken about.

Women in Eastern finery, the wives of those who had already made the mountain yield its hidden wealth, mingled with the saloon girls and plain pioneer stock. Men in broadcloth suits and sporting plug hats rubbed elbows with grimy miners and buckskin clad mountain men. Kids rolled hoops through the streets with sticks. The bunco steerers, tin horns and flim-flam men who often made a bigger fortune than those they bilked were as easy to spot as the camp followers.

Banner rode to the middle of town and reined up in front of a small, rickety-looking wooden building. Morgan could see the faded letters on an old sign above the door.

Assay Office

"Sheriff's office," Banner said, as he dismounted.

"You didn't mention a sheriff."

"No need. He won't fight."

Morgan climbed down, secured the reins to the hitching post, and walked around in front of Banner. "We're short one man," he said. "If Billy Frye shows up, I'm sending him back. He's got a family to care for."

"Good idea, Morgan. I figured I'd mention it to you later, if you didn't think of it yourself." Morgan shook his head. Banner was more like Frank Leslie than Morgan had realized.

"If this fella won't fight, why bother with him?"

"Law, Morgan. Rules and regulations, paperwork. It's all part of this . . . civilization. Funny a little. Law says you kill a man, you have to write down somewhere who he was and why you did it."

The sheriff was closer to Banner's age than to Morgan's. He was a small stocky man with deep blue eyes. They were his most noticable feature.

"Howdy, Banner."

"Josh. This is Lee Morgan . . . Pinkerton man. We've come down to make an arrest," Banner paused, glanced at Morgan and then took a deep breath, "there's going to be trouble . . . big trouble."

"Yep. I figgered it right. Three gunmen rode in a mite ago. Still here. I got paper on two of 'em . . . stacks of it."

"There'll be four. Doc Henry Jared is comin' to your town, Josh."

"Already has. The four of 'em set playin' poker last night down to the Hampton House."

"Any trouble?"

"Not a lick or a spit. Whole bunch been behavin' like kids in Sunday school."

"You got a deputy?"

"Not 'ny more. Quit on me after a bunch o' drovers come through town. Skeered clean out o' Silverton."

"Anybody else in town of meanin'?"

"Yep, they is, Banner, now that you bring it up. Colorado Charley Utter."

"He rode with Hickok," Morgan said. "I've heard his name for years."

"That's him," Josh said, beaming now. "First time I met 'im he was with ol' Bill. They come up from Denver er sum such. Bill, he gambled most of a week. Run a tin horn out an' him an' Charlie faced down the Butcher boys. 'Member them, Banner?" The marshal nodded and smiled. "Meaner'n a kicked hound they was, but turnt plumb to jelly when they found out who they was facin'." Josh had been sacking up a few personal items. He was finished now, and finished talking. "Hope I see ya walk through your office door in a few days, Banner . . . but if'n not, been pleasurable knowin' ya." He turned to Morgan. "You too, son."

"Let's get a room," Banner said. "Get the lay of things. Tomorrow or maybe tonight yet, we'll go talk to Colorado Charlie."

"I gather you don't plan to confront Doc right away."

"You said you wanted help from me, Morgan. I'm givin' it."

"If Doc spots me, there'll be no waiting."

"Can you take him?" Morgan nodded. "Then it'll be three to two, won't it?"

They were just entering the Mother Lode hotel when Josh Stalcup rode by headed for Ouray. Banner smiled. It was a smile of sympathy and accompanied by the thought that he, one day soon, might do the same thing in reverse. "He was a hell of a lawman once."

"I couldn't wear a badge and do that," Morgan said.

Banner pushed the door open, hard. There was some contempt in his tone when he said, "You couldn't wear a badge at all, Morgan. You're out o' the wrong bolt o' cloth."

The two men ate an early dinner and returned to their room. Banner stripped off his rig and shirt and stretched out on the bed.

"Wake me up about six o'clock," he said.

"I'd like to get on with this, marshal . . . one way or another." Banner pulled his hat down over his eyes. "Go ahead," he said. "If you have it done by six, lemme sleep another hour."

Morgan was too restless to sleep. He quietly slipped out about thirty minutes later, convinced that Banner knew he went. He walked most of a block in both directions and finally entered one of

Silverton's less conspicuous saloons. He sipped a beer and watched the comings and goings out on the street. It was Friday and the whole town would be different after sundown.

Morgan knew he had to do something. He left the saloon and made his way to the stage station. The telegraph office was there, too, and he sent a telegraph cable to the army office in Creede. It informed them to tell Billy Frye to stay put if he hadn't already left. Morgan knew that it was likely Billy would still be in Creede. Old Stoner, the mountain man, didn't move that fast.

That done, Morgan returned to the room. It was half past five. Banner was snoring, and Morgan again tried to sleep but he couldn't. At five minutes to six, he got up and turned to wake the marshal. Banner was already sitting up.

"Evenin', Morgan." Banner stretched, stood up and pulled his arms back and forth to loosen up. "Touch o' roomatiz, I'd guess. This is the wrong job for an old man."

"Why don't you quit," Morgan asked.

"Not me! Jake Graybow quit. Next I heard, big New York newspaper payed his fare back east. Bill Cody put him in that Wild West show he does and Ned Bunline had him wrote up in ever' dime novel for the next three years."

"That so bad?"

"Found him broke an' drunk in some county home 'bout two years later. Sobered him up and he got hold of a gun and blew his brains out." Banner shook head back and forth. "No, sir, not me. When I go, I want it to be quick and clean." He pointed. "Right down there in the street, mebbe, or up in

Kit Dalton

Ouray. Wherever, whenever, I want to see it comin'
. . . not sneakin' up on me gradual."

Colorado Charlie Utter wasn't hard to find. He
had just sat down to a poker game when Banner
walked up. It was in one of the two big casinos at the
Hampton House, Silverton's biggest and best.

"Lo, Charlie."

"Well, I'll be damned . . . Ephram Banner. Hell, I
thought you was dead."

"Practical am, Charlie."

Charlie Utter was a stringbean of a man with a
beak nose and a deep scar that ran from just
beneath his right ear, along his lower jaw bone, and
ended beneath his chin. Charlie said it was a gift
from a Sioux warrior. When others told the story, it
was given to him by Crazy Horse. Charlie never
bothered to set the record straight either way.

Morgan noted Colorado Charlie's weapons. He
carried a Buntline special in a cut-out holster, waist
high. He also had a Colt Peacemaker tucked in his
waistband.

"Like to talk to you, Charlie, an' have you meet a
friend of mine. Son of a fella you knew once, you n'
Bill."

"Sure thing, Ephram. Lead the way."

The trio found a table in a semi-darkened corner
and Banner told Colorado Charlie what had
happened and why they were in Silverton. He ended
his story with a more formal introduction.

"Morgan here . . . Lee Morgan, well, he's the
offspring of Buckskin Frank Leslie."

"Hell fire!" Charlie smiled, broadly. "I knowed
your daddy real good. So did Bill. Tell you some-

182

thing, son . . . Frank Leslie was the coolest head I ever saw in a gunfight."

"That's a helluva statement," Morgan said, "considering who you rode with."

" 'Twas Bill Hickok what first said it. They throwed down on each other oncest. No shootin' o' course . . . but they throwed down."

"Who won?"

"Now that is a good one, son, a real good one. I was there an' I can't tell you." Morgan smiled. He was getting a history lesson about his father.

"Well, Charlie . . . you know who's here, you know why, and you know the reputations. It's not your fight, but Banner and I could use you."

"Charlie Utter don't work cheap, son . . . there's a price."

"Name it," Morgan said, surprised at the statement.

Colorado Charlie's face stretched into a big grin. "I git Charlie Hawks . . . jist me. Used muh name once up in Dakota territory. Got a bank loan from it. I had to pay it back. I owe him." Morgan laughed.

Charlie went back to his poker game. Banner told him he'd get word to him when the time came, and started back to the hotel with Morgan. As they were crossing the street, someone called Banner's name.

"Banner!" The marshal stopped, putting his hand up to stop Morgan from too hasty a move. The marshal turned, slowly. Morgan turned as well. "Got yourself a kid deppity now, have you?"

"Hello, Largo."

"You lookin' fer *me?*"

"Don't flatter yourself, Largo. My dodger on you says five hundred. You must have slipped a lot lately. Hell, Quint Yokley's worth twice that."

"You won't live to collect it, no matter what it is."

"Mebbe, mebbe not, Largo. But why don't we find out. Sunday mornin'?"

"What's the matter with right now?"

"I'm here with mister Morgan to bring in four men, not one."

"Morgan?"

"Lee Morgan, Largo. Pinkerton man."

Largo grinned. "*Pinkerton.*" He laughed. "Hell, Banner, I've put more Pinkerton men in a buryin' box than you could count. That all the help you got?"

"Show up Sunday, Largo, and find out."

"Show up where?"

"Empty lot next to the mercantile two blocks over. Seven o'clock."

"You know who else is in town?"

Morgan answered that one. "We know. And you tell Doc Henry if he tries runnin' out again, I'll come after him fast. Got nothing to hold me up this time."

"One more thing, Largo . . . just to keep it official. You and Quint Yokley, Charlie Hawks, and Doc Henry Jared are all under arrest. If you decide to change your mind about Sunday . . . I'm at the *Mother Lode* hotel." Marshal Banner turned and walked on. It took Morgan a moment to catch him.

"I admire your style, Banner," Morgan said, "but times have changed. If Doc Henry—or any of those men riding with him—get a chance at back shooting one of us before Sunday, they'll do it." Banner said nothing, but held the door open for Morgan. Finally, Morgan entered. Upstairs, he had more to say. "Don't ignore me, Banner."

"I wasn't ignoring you, Morgan. Just pondering what you said."

"Then you agree?"

"Not completely. Oh, times have changed but *men* haven't . . . least ways, men like these. Anyways, we'll do somethin' about it . . . tonight!"

"What?"

Banner smiled. "Now that's where you're showin' you're no lawman. We got a town here, Morgan, a whole town. They won't fight, but they like honor. Tonight, I'll show you what I mean."

Banner found Morgan in the saloon downstairs at just after eight o'clock. "Take your gun upstairs," Banner said, "and I'll meet you in the lobby."

"What?"

"Do it, Morgan. Trust me." Morgan looked down. Marshal Banner wasn't wearing a gun. A few minutes later, Morgan appeared in the lobby, still frowning at the latest request of the old lawman.

"Where we headed?" Morgan asked.

"The Hampton House. Friday night, my guess'd be that all four of 'em are there."

The main casino at the Hampton House was so crowded it was difficult to move through it. Morgan noted the smile on Banner's face. It grew even larger when he spotted the four men. He nudged Morgan and pointed.

"Let's walk on over."

"What about Charlie Utter?"

"We'll save him fer Sunday. Besides, I already got word to him where and when to meet us."

Morgan didn't like any of what was going on. He was beginning to question why he'd even agreed to it. He respected Banner, and he'd asked for the marshal's help. But this wasn't what he had in mind.

"Evenin', gents," Banner said, casually. Doc Henry spotted Morgan and leaped to his feet, his chair clattering across the floor behind him. "He's not wearin' a gun, Jared. Me neither." Suddenly the noise in the casino was gone. Morgan slowly looked around. Nearly everyone was looking at the group of men.

"What the fuck you want, marshal?"

"Got to thinkin' maybe Largo's memory wouldn't be so good anymore. Decided to deliver my own message."

"Sumbitch! We got your message."

"Well, just in case, Doc . . . I'll give it to you again. The four of you are under arrest. If you want to turn yourselves in, I'm at the Mother Lode hotel. If you don't, I'll see you Sunday mornin' at the lot beside the mercantile. If you try to ride out before that . . . I'll gun you down on sight."

Doc Henry's Colt was in his hand. He was pointing it at Marshal Banner's belly. A voice from out of the crowd got Doc's attention.

"We don't take kindly to shootin' unarmed men in Silverton."

Another voice. "And with the sheriff gone, be hard to control folks what got mad."

Banner smiled at Doc. "Use it, Jared . . . right now. In ten minutes you'll be hangin' from a rafter."

"You sumbitch!" Doc slowly holstered his gun.

"See you Sunday, Doc," Banner said.

Banner and Morgan moved to the bar. Morgan eyed the old lawman and half grinned. "That was about the slickest bunch of work I ever saw, marshal." Even as he spoke, Morgan could hear nearby men taking bets on the outcome of Sunday's showdown. "The only thing I would have done different was buy myself a little edge . . . just in case."

Banner smiled and pointed to the balcony. Morgan looked up and saw Charlie Utter with a shotgun. Charlie waved and walked away.

17

Saturday disappeared like a puff of smoke in a brisk wind. Morgan lay on his bed, wide awake. It was just after one thirty, Sunday morning. Marshal Ephram Banner was breathing the heavy breath of a deep sleep, but Morgan was worried. Not scared . . . worried. He'd come after Doc Henry Jared. No matter what Banner had accomplished, Morgan knew Doc Henry. If there was a way out, he'd find it.

Morgan jumped. The Colt flew into his hand in response to a light knock at the door. Marshal Banner was awake.

"I'd answer it, Morgan. Don't think those other fellas would bother with knockin'." Morgan walked over and opened the door.

"Don't be mad with me," Beth said. Morgan was, but it didn't last long. "I got off the stage an' telegraphed Creede. I waited for an answer. If Billy wasn't comin', I was gonna leave."

"He is coming?"

"I'm already here, Morgan." Billy stepped out of

188

the shadows in the hallway.

"Not for long," Morgan said. "When I first tried to contact you, things were different."

"Yeah," Billy said, "I guess they wuz." Morgan looked surprised at the firmness in Billy's tone. "Beth tol' me what she done with ya. She's her own woman, an' I'd rather it wuz you than some."

"There's more to it than that," Morgan said.

"Doc Henry an' three gunnies."

"Not gunnies, Billy, not these men. Charlie Bojack was a gunny. So was Cully and Hightower. These men are gun fighters. Professional shootists. That's how they live."

"Morgan," Billy said, stepping into the room. "I'm here. I won't be leavin' 'til they're dead or I am. You can keep me from comin' with you, but you can't keep me from bein' there. 'Less'n you plan to call me out right now."

"That what you plan on doin', Morgan?" Morgan turned. A quizzical expression crossed his face. The question came from Banner.

"No," Morgan said. "It isn't. And this isn't any of your business, marshal."

"I walk into a gunfight with a man, ever'thing he does is my business. You take the boy out now, you'll feel it in the morning. You run 'im off and he shows up, you'll feel it. Only place he *can* be is with us. You thought he was good enough before. What's changed?"

"Shit!" Morgan said. "A helluva lot of things have changed."

"Name just one that'll help keep us alive in the mornin', 'cept for this boy bein' here and offerin' his guns." Morgan felt his face getting warm. He was angry, mostly with himself. He knew better than to tie himself to somebody, anybody, before a fight. He turned and looked at Beth. She smiled.

"Billy could be laid out on slab board eight hours from now. Men here will be collecting money over his corpse."

"I know," she said, "but my momma always said Billy had to earn what he wanted. He wants to be with you in the mornin'. Hasn't he earned that Morgan? Hasn't he?"

Colorado Charlie Utter was just finishing a two inch thick cut of beef, four eggs, and coffee when Morgan walked into the dining room. He saw Charlie, shook his head in disbelief and then glanced at the clock. It was 6:20.

"Coffee, Morgan?"

"Yeah." Morgan took several sips of coffee, eyeing Charlie's shotgun. He thought it looked odd. "What make is your scatter-gun, Charlie?"

"My own, mostly. Fat part there, near the stock," he grinned, "holds an extra shell. Got a roll lever in it. Fire both barrels an' it rolls that third shell into the empty chamber. Left chamber if'n they're both empty."

"Ever used it?"

"Yeah . . . several times. Works right nice."

"Surprises a few people too, I'd guess." Charlie grinned and nodded.

"Maybe this mornin'."

"We've got a fourth, Charlie . . . kid named Billy Frye. Rode with Doc Henry for awhile. No more. He's good, real good."

"But not good enough, Morgan, is that it?"

"I don't think so."

"Run 'im next to me. I'll keep an eye on 'em fer ya.
He sees you watchin' i'm, he's li'ble to git all choked
up at the wrong time."

"Thanks, Charlie."

At 6:40, Marshal Ephram Banner and Billy Frye
came down stairs. Banner gave a black boy named
Zeb a dollar to run over to the site of the meeting
and see if the gunmen were waiting. He returned
after five minutes later and reported that all four of
them were there.

"Let's go," Banner said. The four walked abreast,
Charlie at one end with his scatter-gun and then
Billy, Banner and Morgan. Silverton's streets were
empty, vacant even of the usual drunken miners
who never got back to their sleeping quarters. Faces
could be seen peering from windows and hands
pulled back window shades briefly, but no one
wanted to run the risk of being on the streets and
getting caught up in a running gunfight if anything
went awry.

The foursome turned the corner and half way
down the block Marshal Banner said, "They'll
spread on us so I figger we'd be best to go man on
man."

"Who's the best man there?" Billy asked. He
seemed nervous, edgy. Banner knew the boy was
scared.

"Be a toss up, Billy, 'tween Doc Henry an' Quint
Yokley. I'll take Quint." Banner turned and looked
at Morgan. "Doc?" Morgan nodded. "Then Charlie
gets the scatter-gun an' you take Largo."

"Yessir," Billy said.

"I'd like to take at least one of 'em in. I won't ask

ya to shoot that way, but if one goes down an' can't
do no more . . . try to leave 'im breathin'."

At the corner of 3rd Street, the four men stopped.
Half a block east was the vacant lot. They could see
Doc and the others lined up, waiting.

"Haven't known any of ya too long," Banner said,
" 'cept Charlie. Wish I had."

"Let's plan to see to it you get to know us better,"
Morgan said. The wily old marshal smiled and
nodded.

"Let's get it over with."

Silverton was no stranger to such confrontations.
There had been many men who fought one another,
sometimes with guns, sometimes with knives . . .
even bare-handed. Most were obscure gamblers,
gunnies, or just plain mean. There had also been a
few big showdowns; the day Bill Hickok and Charlie
Utter faced down the Butcher brothers was one of
them. Another day, on a Sunday, Doc Holliday shot
and killed a bounty hunter by the name of Joe
Hedley. John Ringo visited Silverton and shot a
young hot-head whose name was never known. But
none of those measured up to what was about to
happen. The only participant in this fray who had no
reputation was Billy Frye. If he survived it, the
mark it would place on him was one he would carry
to his grave.

"I'm givin' you one final chance," Banner said. As
he spoke, Colorado Charlie, Billy Frye, and Morgan
moved away from him, eyeing the four men opposite
them and positioning themselves accordingly.

"You'll git a trial by a jury of your peers an'

sentenced according to their findings. I'm here to arrest you, and the men with me are duly authorized deputies. If you resist arrest, we'll defend ourselves."

"Pretty speech, Banner," Largo said. "Now you'll have to back it up."

Quint Yokley didn't wait. He drew and fired as fast as any man present had ever seen. No one else moved except Marshal Ephram Banner. Morgan was near enough to hear the crack of bone as the bullet struck home. It came just after Banner had fired his own gun. Banner's face contorted with pain and then a ripple ran through his big-boned frame. His right leg wobbled and gave way and he dropped, landing on his right side. His gun flew from his hand. Quint Yokley had clearly beaten the old lawman, but he was more fast than accurate. Quint was already dead. Still falling, but already dead. The slug hit him in the forehead.

What happened immediately after that not even an eye-witness could have stated for sure, let alone a participant. One voice was heard, that of Doc Henry Jared. He spoke his favorite word.

"Sumbitch!" Doc drew amid the roar of a shotgun discharging. He levelled his weapon at Morgan's chest, allowing for Morgan's possible draw and crouch. Doc's shot went wild. Morgan's bullet just nicked the barrel of Doc's gun, not by design but by accident. The fluke saved both their lives. Morgan proved the fastest and escaped unscathed. Doc Henry's left side was bleeding, he had two broken ribs and he was out of the fight.

Colorado Charlie Utter cut loose, low, with both barrels of his scatter-gun. The shot struck Charlie

Hawks in both legs . . . about knee high. Colorado
had fired the weapon with his right hand, from his
hip. Simultaneously, he drew the Peacemaker from
his waistband with his left hand.

Charlie Hawks was one of the best, and his speed
was even greater than Utter's action with the
shotgun. Colorado Charlie took a slug in the right
shoulder. The Peacemaker's bullet shattered
Hawks' right elbow as he was falling. He'd be
walking on crutches for a long time, and he'd never
fire a gun again with his right hand. Colorado
Charlie stayed on his feet. He knew in an instant
that he wouldn't be able to help Billy Frye.

But Billy didn't need help. Largo Johnson had
Billy pretty well sized up. He toted two guns for
show, but he was a right hander. Largo was not the
fastest of the four . . . but he was clearly the most
accurate. He aimed for Billy's right-hand holster,
and he beat the kid by just a hair's breadth. The
thing Largo didn't expect was that Billy used his
left-hand draw. He'd been practicing harder on it to
develop his accuracy. He killed Largo with a single
shot, but went down from the spinning force of
Largo's shot when it struck Billy's other gun.

Morgan kept his gun levelled at the spot where
the four men had been. "Billy dead?" he asked
Utter.

Charlie looked down. He saw movement. "You
dead, boy?"

"Hardly," Billy said. He got to his feet. "Damn.
He ruint muh rig."

Morgan could see Doc Henry trying to get up. He
got to his knees and a violent cough wracked his
body. He spit, cursed and his arms gave way. He

was finished. Charlie Hawks was beginning to feel the pain. He was doubled into the fetal position and holding his knees with his good arm, howling at the top of his lungs.

Morgan holstered his gun and knelt next to Marshal Banner. "How bad?"

"Hip bone . . . whole damn thing's busted from the feel of it." Banner twisted his head, grimacing with each movement. He managed a twisted smile. "But I'll live, Morgan, I'll live."

"Quint Yokley didn't," Morgan said.

"That's how I played it."

A crowd had gathered. Even from the street, it was obvious who had come out on top. The town doctor pushed his way through the little knot of people. He was carrying his black bag and was followed closely by the town undertaker.

"Three for immediate doctoring," Morgan said. Colorado Charlie had already waved the doctor away. The bullet had gone clean through. "Marshal Banner first." The doctor nodded.

"Only two to be fit fer a box?"

"For now," Morgan said, "but there'll be a trial . . . and I'd guess a hangin'."

Wagons were brought up and the wounded and dead, save for Colorado Charlie, were carted off. He walked away with the crowd. Morgan and Billy Frye stood alone, only the breeze making any sound as it whistled through the boards of an old building.

Billy finally walked over to where Morgan was standing. He'd taken his rig off and it was looped over his shoulder. "Well, Mister Morgan, did I qualify?"

"You did, Billy." Morgan looked the kid square in

the eye. Billy hadn't seen that particular look on Morgan's face before. "Now you don't have to qualify anymore." Morgan pointed to Billy's rig and continued, "You got it off . . . leave it off."

Billy looked down and smiled a weak smile. "Ya know," he said, "I was kinda thinkin' that to muhself, Mister Morgan. Maybe 'bout takin' Beth and goin' home." He looked up. "Tryin' to figger a way to make a livin', but . . . but hangin' these up. This mornin' wasn't like I figgered it'd be. Muh feelin', I mean."

"It never is, Billy. You got a good idea there. Stick with it."

"An' you, Mister Morgan? What you gonna do?"

"Watch Doc Henry hang." Morgan paused in his answer. He looked north, smiled faintly, and then looked back at Billy. "Then mebbe I'll go home too. Back up Idaho way."

18

Charlie Hawks, still recuperating from Colorado Charlie's shotgun, was tried in *absentia* for a dozen or more crimes, none of them related to Doc Henry Jared. The evidence against him was overwhelming, but the jury showed some leniency when they learned that Charlie Hawks would never walk again.

He drew eight years, but the judge put him on probation. He ultimately turned to gambling, worked his way east and plied his trade on Mississippi river boats. Almost two years to the day after the shoot-out in Silverton, Charlie Hawks was shot dead. He was caught dealing from the bottom.

Doc Henry's trial was another matter entirely. It was moved from Silverton back to Creede on a change of venue. The whole town loved it. It was another boom, as good as any gold or silver strike ever found. Few incidents in Colorado's long and often inglorious history had drawn such attention or so much security. Creede even built a special cell to house him.

Colorado Charlie could really offer no direct

evidence against Doc. He left the judge with a deposition, and he left Colorado for his old stomping grounds in Deadwood, Dakota Territory. Morgan wondered if they'd ever meet again.

Morgan, Beth, and Billy returned to Creede even before Doc Henry was moved. Marshal Banner would be sufficiently recovered from his own wound to be there for the trial.

Morgan reined up in front of Molly's place, dismounted and just stood in the street. No one he'd talked to, not even Billy, had been able to supply any information about Molly's fate.

Morgan walked through the bat wing doors as he had done so many weeks before, expecting to have to check his guns. He saw a new man working security. The man walked over, smiled and said, "Welcome, Mister Morgan. Go on upstairs. I believe Miss O'Flynn is expecting you." Morgan smiled and went upstairs.

"Welcome back, Mahrgan." She walked to him, they hugged and she kissed him. "You know, I'd have been mighty angry with you if you'd gone an' got yourself killed."

"I wouldn't have been so happy about it myself," Morgan said. She poured them both a celebration drink and they sat down. "Trigg," Morgan said, softly . . . "I mean . . ."

"Sean? No, Mahrgan. He tried. God, he tried."

"He was a helluva man, Molly. I'm sorry."

"He wouldn't have had it any other way." Molly told him what had happened to her. When she finally regained consciousness, a cavalry patrol found her, wandering near the river.

"Emmy?" Molly shrugged.

"She was gone when I woke up. I didn't even think about her 'til later. The army said they never saw her. They made a thorough search too, for her and others. The valley, Doc's trail west . . . ever'where, Mahrgan. She just vanished. Maybe she was . . ."

"The Apaches?" Molly nodded. "Yeah, it's possible." Morgan stood up, kissed Molly again, softly. "I'll be around," he said, "if you need to talk."

Morgan walked to the army command post. There he learned that General Utley had succumbed to his wounds. Gangrene. Young Yates had over-stepped his authority and was back east facing a court martial. Morgan also learned about Senator Venable's role in the army's rescue efforts and the loss of both Pinkerton agents. Venable had returned to Denver, but planned to be in Creede for Doc Henry's trial.

The trial opened three months after the showdown in Silverton. Creede's hotels, boarding houses and saloons were packed full every day and night. Newspapers from as far east as Chicago were on hand to report the proceedings. Ned Buntline himself showed up.

Doc Henry wasn't present for the two opening days. They were devoted to recording the many depositions and opening statements. The defense attorney, who had been court-appointed, found himself the object of considerable scorn and more security than that surrounding Doc Henry himself.

Morgan was just entering the court house on the morning of the third day when he felt a hand tugging at his arm. He turned.

"Mister Morgan. I'm relieved to see you alive." It was Senator Venable. His face was thin and drawn, and dark patches were prevalent below his eyes.

"I'm sorry Senator. Emmy . . . I was told what happened."

"Some satisfaction will come from this trial, Morgan. I've never been a vengeful man . . . but," he sighed. "I want to watch this man fall through the trap door."

"He will, Senator."

"I'll have your money, Morgan, whatever you say . . . after the trial."

"We'll talk about it, Senator, when the time comes."

Morgan, Molly, Billy, and Marshal Banner sat together, just behind the table of the Mineral County Prosecuting Attorney. He was handling the courtroom work, but also present was a representative of the Colorado State Attorney General's office. There was a stir, then a murmuring, then some unruliness when finally Doc Henry Jared was led into the courtroom. He was bound in wrist and leg irons, and he looked thinner. But there was still the contempt, the look of a man certain he would once again escape death. There was no sign of the wound Morgan had inflicted.

The judge, Clayton Jonas Howell, was one of the most reputable of Colorado's Circuit. He was strict, stern of countenance, and would tolerate nothing less than absolute order in his court. He silenced the crowd with a stern warning and showed irritation at a last minute arrival. No one else paid any attention. Doc Henry started laughing at the judge's pleas. He too was reprimanded, and threatened with gagging. Sullen, he finally slumped into a chair.

Just before the noon recess, Judge Howell addressed himself to the defendant. "Get to your feet, Mister Jared, and come stand before the bench." Doc Henry was led from the table. He stood, looking up and grinning. "When we return from lunch, you will be taking the stand. I expect you do to so in proper dress and without shackles. Nonetheless, there will be deputies on either side of you. They have been ordered to shoot you should any trouble occur. Any man, yourself included, is entitled to a trial by jury and should be considered innocent until proven guilty. I hold to that concept with every fibre of my being." Now the judge leaned forward and pointed a finger in Doc's face. "If, however, there should be trouble out of you, or from someone outside this court, I will personally take it as a confession from you indicating your guilt and I will act accordingly. Is that clear, sir?"

"Clear enough, yer honor." The judge then banged the gavel and called for mid-day recess. He stood to leave the courtroom and everyone else stood as well. Doc Henry turned around and a voice broke the silence.

"I loved you. I hated the boredom of my life . . . and I *loved* you. I could have provided everything for us. You would never have had to rob again. But you . . . the women . . . your filthy debasement of my love . . . you bastard!" Heads had jerked to the center aisle. Deputies were frozen in their tracks at the sight of the gaunt, feminine figure in the man's clothing.

"Emmy," Senator Venable said to himself, "my

God!" He leaped up. "Emilia, no, for God's sake, no!"

Morgan leaped from his seat, the first person to move quickly, but even he was too late. Emmy Venable brought the pistol from beneath her vest, levelled it at Doc Henry, and began firing. One . . . two . . . three . . . four . . . Morgan dived toward her, but she leaped back.

"Sum . . . bi . . ." Two of the bullets struck Doc Henry Jared in the head. The fifth shot caught him in the chest and drove his body backwards into the judge's bench. It hung there a moment, his eyes wide open, his mouth still moving. Then it slid slowly down until he was in a sitting position. Another moment and the head dropped to the side. Doc Henry Jared was dead.

Emmy stepped back again, put the .45 to her temple and pulled the trigger. It had all happened in seconds. Women began to scream and several fainted. Senator Venable, pushing to reach his daughter, stiffened suddenly and grabbed at his chest. Morgan got to his feet and slipped out a side door to fetch the doctor.

Senator Venable survived his heart attack. He resigned his powerful post in Washington and lived out his years, quite a number of them, in the seclusion of his Denver mansion. Emmy Venable's funeral was one of the most attended in Denver's history.

Morgan was paid well for his role in ending Doc Henry Jared's reign of terror. In addition to the money from Venable, reward money poured in from a dozen sources. He gave much of it to Billy and

Beth Frye.

Marshal Ephram Banner returned to Ouray and continued as the chief territorial law officer with deputies carrying out the field work. The showdown in Silverton was Banner's last hurrah.

Even as Creede was returning to some measure of normality, word came about the fate of the renegade Naschitti. He had, once more, outwitted his army pursuers and fled to Mexico. A few months later, however, he and his small band were trapped by Federales and fought to the death.

By the time most of the complexities of Doc Henry's death had been settled, winter snows were falling daily on Creede. Morgan decided to stay the winter. He knew he wouldn't be lacking for warmth and comfort . . . Irish style.

Spring came all too soon. On the night before Morgan was to pull out, he had a late-night visitor. It was Molly's going-away gift to him . . . and he was certain it would do him for quite awhile. The next day, Morgan readied his gear and the roan and then rode back to Molly's. She came out to meet him.

"I won't be askin' you to write ta me. I did that before." She smiled, stood up on her tip toes and kissed him. "Will you ever come back, Morgan?"

"I'll come back Molly . . . someday." He mounted, smiled at her blown kiss, flicked the brim of his hat, and rode out. He headed north, up over Spring Creek Pass and on to Slumgullion pass. Many times he looked down from the high country and thought back about what had happened.

He spent a day in Lake City, a way station for the Gunnison-Creede stage line. There, he heard the story of an old mountain man caught last winter in the high country and found frozen to death. He rode out to the little burying plot. There were only seven head boards. The most recent simply read,

STONER

Just north of Lake City station, Morgan found an overhang. He walked out on the giant boulder and looked over the vast expanse of the Uncompahgre. It was beautiful, but it stirred something deep in his soul.

"Home," he said to himself. "Home to Idaho and the Spade Bit . . . just maybe." He'd often thought of it and wondered what his father would have said about Morgan's sale of it. Particularly after he lost the money from it in a crooked lumber deal.

There were no more Wanted posters on Lee Morgan. Venable had been as good as his word. And the Senator had said that if Morgan ever needed help, all he had to do was ask for it. If the new owners wanted to sell . . . if they would. A new life . . . a life with no guns. Just maybe. "Home," he said again.

Morgan got up, mounted the big roan gelding, and said his last goodbye to Winchester Valley.

GUNSMOKE GORGE

1

The main street of Grover, Idaho, was decked out in banners, ribbons, flags and wreaths. They were all *black!* Many of the store fronts were boarded up and Lee Morgan saw no sign of life. He was still looking up and down the street when he finally dismounted in front of the Sawtooth saloon. Clearly, the little cowtown was in mourning . . . but for *who*? Almost everyone of any prominence had long since died or moved on.

The Sawtooth was empty, save for the barkeep. He was a nervous little man, somewhat porcine in appearance. When Morgan entered, he looked up, over top of the pince-nez glasses he was wearing. He started to smile but then he spotted Morgan's gun. His expression changed to fear and his hands shook as he put down the beer mug he was wiping.

"Y . . . yessir?"

"A beer," Morgan said. It wasn't what he wanted but it was quick and easy. He was too curious about conditions to spend much time here now. He watched the barkeep draw the draught with shaking hands.

"Fifteen cents," the man said.

"Keeps gettin' higher, doesn't it?"

"The distributor out of Boise just raised the price again last week."

Morgan nodded, took a long swallow and then said, "Who died?"

"Beg pardon?"

"Who died?" Morgan repeated. At the same time, he gestured toward the street. "Must have been somebody pretty damned important."

"Then . . . you, uh, you're not from around here?"

"Not lately."

"Lots o' folks," the barkeep said. Morgan considered him. He went on. "They're buryin' eight 's'afternoon."

"Eight?"

"The Winslows. Joad an' his missus. Frank Peters who worked for him an' a cowhand name o' Kane." Morgan pondered the name but it didn't register.

"That's only four," he finally said.

"The others I never knowed a 'tall. Folks had a ranch close by, mebbe three, four mile."

"What ranch? The name I mean."

"Don't recollect right off." The little barkeep frowned and then shook his head and waggled a finger in the air. "Somethin' odd." Morgan straightened up. "Differ'nt," the barkeep added. Suddenly he smiled. "That's right . . . cards. Name had to do with cards. It was the Spade Bit Ranch."

Morgan never finished the beer. He rode the big bay hard all the way . . . all four miles. There was a chill wind sweeping down from the north when Morgan finally reined up. He pulled up his coat collar and jammed his hat down tighter. He was on a rise along the Jack's Fork tributary of the Wickahoney River. He looked at the valley below.

"Jeezus!" Morgan felt the hair at the back of his neck bristle. His cheeks flushed with anger. The once lush valley was charred and only a lone brick chimney still stood. It seemed a mute sentry guarding burned memories against the advent of an unseen threat. The Spade Bit Ranch was gone!

Morgan rode down, slowly. He remembered. The big, white frame house. The old barn and smoke house. The bunk houses and the cook shack. Indians? Morgan doubted that. It was 1877 when the last of the Red Men posed any threat in Idaho. The Nez Perce, a small band trying to escape to Canada. General Oliver O. Howard finally cornered them and their leader, a Chief named Joseph.

Maybe they'd jumped the reservation. Morgan thought back to what he'd heard. Joseph had finally surrendered in the winter snows. The army had lied to him again—even in his defeat. He was separated from the rest of his people, sent to a far away reservation in Washington or Oregon. Then Morgan remembered the old Chief's promise. Morgan repeated the words aloud. "From where the sun now stands, I will fight no more . . . forever!" Morgan looked around again. He felt anger. "The hell I won't fight," he said.

He rode on another mile. The undulations of the land built to another rise, a sharp rise. Atop a quiet hill, beneath a huge, century old Willow, there was a small cemetery. Morgan dismounted and walked to its crest. He sought out a single headstone and stood, quietly, hat in hand, looking at the name engraved upon it.

William Frank Leslie

"I know what you'd do daddy," Morgan finally said. "I guess you got the only peace there is."

Morgan found the nervous little barkeep in the

Sawtooth was no longer alone. He was talking to a big, round shouldered man. Both of them looked up when Morgan entered.

"That's *him*," the barkeep whispered. He stepped behind the bar and the big man stepped away from it.

"Hold it mister." As he spoke, the man produced an old model Navy Colt's. He levelled it at Morgan's belly. "I'm Marshal Rawlings."

"Seth?" Morgan stepped to the bar where the light was better. "Seth . . . it's Lee. Lee Morgan."

"Lee Morgan?" The marshal moved closer, but he didn't lower the gun. "I'll be," he finally said. Morgan started to move toward him, his hand extended in friendship. The marshal backed off. "Who you ridin' with?"

"What?" Morgan stopped. "Seth, maybe you didn't hear me."

"I heard you. Question's still the same. Who you ridin' with?"

"Nobody. What the hell is going on here? I just rode back from the Spade Bit or what's left of it. Jeezus, Seth, I'd like some answers."

"So would I," the marshal said, "an' mebbe I can get some of 'em from you. Ease the gun onto the bar —real slow like." The marshal cocked the old Colt's and Morgan knew he wasn't kidding. Morgan complied and the marshal motioned for Morgan to walk to the door. "Over to my office. You remember where?"

"I remember."

"What if he's got riders with 'im," the barkeep said, softly. Morgan heard the question. "I don't. I haven't seen anybody in Grover since I rode in except you two."

"You start walkin'," the marshal said. "Stay well

ahead o' me but you'd best not try anythin'. No runnin' . . . no signallin'. You try it Morgan an' I may die but you'll go first."

"Let's go," Morgan said. "Let's get over to your office and get this cleared up."

Morgan found himself an old high-backed, wooden chair and sat down on it, backwards. Seth Rawlings layed the Bisley on his desk, holstered his own gun and then sat on the desk's edge.

"How long you been back, boy?"

"I got here today."

"From where?"

"Cheyenne. Look, Seth . . ."

"I'll do the askin' boy, you do the answerin' . . . fer now anyways." Morgan shrugged. "Somebody send fer ya?"

"No."

"You hear 'bout anythin' goin' on up this way before you rode back?"

"No." Morgan was getting irritated. Seth could detect it. He shifted his position for easier access to his gun. "I came back to see some old friends, maybe go to ranching."

"You mean cow herdin'?"

"I *mean* ranching. I was planning to look for a spread."

"You picked a poor time," Seth said. "Poor time fer ranchin', poor time for findin' work, poor time to come back." The old lawman got up, walked behind his desk and began thumbing through a stack of wanted posters.

"You won't find anything on me Seth." The marshal ignored him and finished going through the stack.

"I got nothin' here an' nothin' to hold you on." He handed Morgan the Bisley. "Where you headed now that you know about the Spade Bit?"

"I don't know Seth. Not right this minute anyway."

"Lemme help you boy. Sarah Brownin' is runnin' a boardin' house now. As I recollect, you 'n Sarah thought a little more'n most 'bout each other. Not much business lately, she could prob'ly use your money."

Morgan frowned. "Sarah was . . ."

"Married? Yeah, fer a spell. He was a tin horn. Rode over to Boise one day 'bout two, mebbe three years back. Never come home ag'in."

"Well, then, maybe I will stay with her."

"You do that, Lee. Git yourself a good night's sleep an' then why don't you ride on out? Back south mebbe, back to Cheyenne."

"Damn it, Seth," Morgan said, standing now, "you're right. You got nothing on me in that stack of posters and nothing to hold me on . . . so why you pushing me?"

"I'm not pushin' you boy . . . I'm givin' you some sound advice. Take it. It's free."

"And so am I Seth. Free as a goddamn bird. When you were sheriff you pushed hard. Well, I was a hot-tempered, short fused kid then, I'm not anymore."

"An' I'm not sheriff. I'm a United States Terri-torial Marshal and I don't need any hired guns ridin' in."

"Seems to be Seth, from the look of the Spade Bit, you got plenty of 'em. Maybe you ought to get some of them on your side."

Seth Rawlings walked to the door, opened it and then turned back. "Sarah's place is a block south."

Sarah Browning, like 'most everyone else, was at the funerals. One of her guests, a whiskey drummer, told Morgan she wouldn't be back until late. There was to be a big community feed at the church after the services.

Morgan thanked the drummer and left. He considered going to the church but finally decided against it. There were many, he was sure, who probably wouldn't take kindly to the son of a gunman, himself possessed of a dubious reputation, showing up. Besides, Morgan still had plenty of questions and no answers. He rode northeast out of town. He knew one place he might get them.

2

It was a long, rugged trip from Grover up to the Rocky Barr ranch. Morgan rode onto R-B land a full day before the house would come into sight. It was northeast from Grover, up toward the Sawtooth range.

He forded the south fork of the Boise River and was following one of the R-B's fence lines when he found himself confronted with two surly looking young men.

"What the fuck you doin' here mister?"

"My name is . . . ."

"I didn't *ask* your fuckin' name. I ask what you're doin' up here?"

Morgan eyed both men. They were gunnys . . . no doubt about that. Morgan could remember the days when Judge Isaac Barr would have run such men as these off his property . . . or had them hanged!

"You take me to the *Judge*," Morgan said. "I'll talk to him."

"You'll talk to me or you won't live long enough to see the goddam *Judge*."

The man reached behind him. Morgan could see the stock of the rifle. He looked at the other man who was smiling and fingering the butt of his pistol. Morgan shrugged. He swung his right leg over the pommel and dropped to the ground. The move covered his release of the Black Snake whip from its leather retainer.

The man with the rifle brought the weapon to bear. Morgan's right arm went back in a smooth, flowing arc. The whip lashed out.

"Jeezus!" A long, red gash suddenly appeared on the back of the man's hand. The rifle slipped from his grip and clattered to the ground. Morgan dropped to his left knee, hauled back his right arm, rolled to his left and thus avoided being shot. The whip was ready again and caught the second man, who'd fired at Morgan, across the right cheek. He grabbed at his face, losing his pistol in the act.

Now, there was a double sound. The whip's narrow mass slicing the air and the crack of its tip against flesh . . . horse flesh! First one . . . then the other . . . both whinnied and bolted off, full bore.

Judge Isaac Holston Barr was pushing sixty. Few men knew it for he looked closer to forty-five. He had once boasted that he'd have no man working for him that he couldn't whip. By his look, the rule might still apply.

He was a short man, barely five and a half feet. He was barrel chested, bull-necked and with arms that resembled logs. His torso was nearly as long as his legs, which were bowed from years in the saddle. He walked straight, fast and rarely looked up to any man.

Rumor had it that he'd once been a pugilist back east. He admitted only that he had entered the prize ring to earn extra money while he attended law school. The *Judge* sobriquet was not honorary but a fact. He'd served the circuit for a dozen years.

"I'll be damned," Judge Barr said. Lee Morgan stepped from his mount and secured the reins to the hitching rail.

"Judge."

"I was about to send out half a dozen men to string up the bastard who'd use a black snake on a man."

"It still ain't right," the tall man standing next to the Judge said.

"Beats dyin' Harper." Judge Barr turned to the tall man. "That's what would have happened if this young fella had used his gun instead of the whip. You might want to remember that."

Morgan stopped on the first step. He held out his hand. Judge Barr took it, shook it warmly and put his other hand on Morgan's shoulder.

"If I'd have been anywhere but on Rocky Barr land, those two gunnys would be laying out there right now. It's good to see you, Judge," Morgan said.

"I'm glad you didn't kill them. I need every man I've got." He turned, stepped onto the porch and motioned with his head for Morgan to follow. "C'mon in." The man called Harper stepped between the judge and Morgan just as Lee started to move. Their eyes met. Harper fingered the butt of his pistol. Morgan smiled, sidestepped quickly and walked on by him.

"What'll you be drinkin'?"

"Bourbon's fine," Morgan replied.

"Sit, son," Judge Barr said. He handed Morgan a glass. "Tell me about yourself." Morgan did. "What brought you back to the Idaho?"

"An idea," Morgan replied, blandly. "A bad idea."

"The Spade Bit?"

"Yeah. What the hell's going on Judge?"

"East of the Mississippi they call it progress."

"What do *you* call it?"

"Thievery!"

"Who's doin' it . . . and why?"

"The last part's easy," the judge said. "Land. They've got more beef on the hoof than they can graze. Ten . . . fifteen years back they started leasing land. The locals jumped at it . . . didn't think to the future. Lease money meant a steady income during tough winters and three meals a day for the sod-busters whose crops didn't make it."

"And now?"

"The leases are up and the ranchers are getting their notes called in."

"Notes?"

"The lease agreements all had riders . . . options on them. They allowed the small operations to borrow extra money against the lease contracts. Many of them took advantage of it and got in way over their heads. Borrowed more than the lease money would ever pay back."

"They're foreclosing."

"Uh huh. And anybody who stands against them gets run out, burned out or killed."

"I take it from what you say that it's not gettin' settled in the courts."

"Nothing to settle. The leases were legal, the money borrowed on them is due and payable. Thing is, most of the smaller farmers and ranchers signed direct . . . no legal advice. There was a renewal option in every lease but the fine print was another matter."

"How so?"

"*If* the owner wanted to excercise his renewal option, he had ninety days to do it and signed over half his spread if he did."

"Jeezus!"

"Like I said . . . thievery. Me, the folks down on your old place, Josh Killerman over on the Snake River ranch and a few other outfits didn't sign. Most of us didn't need the help but we also knew what they had planned. We tried to warn the smaller ranchers. Even formed an association. They just saw us as harbingers of doom."

"And now?"

"Most of them are already out. Thing is, it's starting to hurt the bigger outfits like me. I'm hemmed in now on three sides. If two or three of the smaller outfits south of here buckle I'll have no way to move stock."

"They'll own the land and won't let you cross it." The Judge smiled, cynically. "They'll let me cross it . . . sure . . . for a *fee!*"

"And there's not a damned thing you can do about it?"

"Just one. We've already been through the courts. We lost but it did buy us some time. We organized a few of the smaller outfits and pulled them into the Rancher's Association. Me, Killerman, Ben Strada . . . some of the wealthier outfits put up money to tide the little fellows over the rough spots."

"Holdouts."

"Yes . . . and the outfit back east . . . and we don't know for sure just who it is . . . can't wait. They've got *really* big money in this. Railroad money and buyers who are waiting."

"You hoped to bust their backs that way," Morgan said. "Figuring they'd back off?"

"Yes . . . but they got rough instead. Our only chance is catching the sons-o'-bitches red handed. We do that, we might have a tie to somebody back east."

"Doesn't sound like you've had much luck so far."

"Plenty of luck Morgan . . . all bad. I've got a few gunnys working for me . . . mostly trying to protect my own place. So do some of the others, but we've got no one who can stand against these marauders. They hit and run. They're good. Nobody wants to go up against them."

"Well," Morgan said, getting to his feet, "the marshal told me it was a hell of a bad time to come home. I guess he was right."

The judge frowned. "You walking away from it?"

"It's not my fight, Judge. I didn't come back to fight and there's nothing left to buy . . . at least for me."

"That's not the kind of thing your daddy would have said."

"I'm *not* Frank Leslie, Judge. Oh I thought about it. When I saw the Bit . . . walked up to my dad's hole in the ground . . . I thought about it. I was mad. I also thought it was just somebody had something against the Bit. Sorry, Judge. This is not for me."

"Morgan . . . do me one favor."

"If I can, Judge . . . I will."

"I've hired one man . . . one *damned good* man. He'll be here in a few days, three at the most. Stay with me . . . wait 'til he gets here and then sit in a meeting with us. That's all I'm asking."

"Who's the man?"

"I'd sooner not say 'til you see him. How about it?"

"I owe you. Sounds like that might square us. No promises beyond that."

"Agreed."

"I'll pass staying, Judge. Thanks anyway but I've got an itch to ride to Boise. I'll be back. You've got my word."

"Good enough, Morgan."

* * *

Boise was probably Idaho's answer to Wichita, Dodge City or any of the plains country cow towns. The westward trek of humanity in the sixties and seventies had, finally, brought some law and order to those towns. By the mid to late eighties, men like Morgan's father, the Masterson types, the Earps, had weeded out most of the killers. North of the major trails however, towns like Boise were ten to fifteen years behind the times.

Morgan was amazed at how much Boise had grown but it still looked like a prairie twister had simply dsposited it where it sat. There was little rhyme nor reason to its layout and there were three blocks devoted solely to a man's basic needs. One gunsmith, twelve saloons and fifteen brothels. Morgan reined up in front of the most lavish of the pleasure palaces, The Four Queens.

It boasted a fine saloon, private baths, a client's personal tonsorial services and the best ladies money could buy. Morgan moved to the bar.

"You wantin' any upstairs service," the barkeep asked him.

"No."

"Then the prices for drinks are posted on the wall behind me. What'll you have?"

"Is Belle in?" The question brought raised eyebrows from the barkeep and the shuffling of feet off to Morgan's left. He glanced in the backbar's mirror and caught sight of a tall, well dressed, menacing type. He was standing in front of a door which said *Office* on it.

"Who wants to know?"

"Lee Morgan." The barkeep's eyes shifted over Morgan's left shoulder. Morgan glanced into the mirror again and the tall man was walking toward the bar. Morgan did a half turn.

"I don't recall Miss Moran mentioning any appointments this morning."

"I don't have an appointment, but if you'll tell her the name, I will have."

"You seem damned sure of that, Mister Morgan."

"Why don't you try it?"

"After you tell me the reason I'll consider it."

"The reason is my business," Morgan said, "all you have to do is tote a message."

"I don't like you, Mister Morgan."

"Then by all means, let's keep our business as brief as possible."

The man's left hand slipped from the bar and moved toward his left hip. The barkeep had just bent forward, his hands disappearing beneath the bar. Morgan made one step backwards and both men found themselves staring at the business end of his Bisley Colt's. "Don't even *think* about it," Morgan said. "I want to see two sets of hands up on that bar . . . palms down . . . right *now*!" He punctuated the request with the click of the Bisley's hammer. The men complied.

"I repeat," Morgan said, "is Belle in?" The tall man nodded. "Office?" He nodded again. Morgan smiled. "Now tell the son-of-a-bitch up on the balcony to put down the scatter-gun and back off. Then you walk right straight to that office ahead of me and remember, you'll be the first to go."

"Back off Charlie . . . it's . . . it's okay. Put the shotgun down." The man complied. The tall man glanced at the barkeep and then turned and walked toward the office. Morgan fell in behind him.

He knocked. "Miss Moran . . . a gent to see you. Says his name is Lee Morgan."

A muffled voice responded. "Lee Morgan! Kee-

rist!'' The door flew open. The tall man stepped
aside. Belle Moran eyed the Colt's. Morgan holstered it. She gave the tall man a look of disgust and
then threw both arms around Morgan's neck.

Belle Morgan was, in fact, Mary Elizabeth
Cochran Moran, late of Seattle, Washington. She
was a year or two on the wrong side of thirty-five
and called herself, facetiously, a grass widow. Her
late husband was reposing beneath it, victim of a
fifth ace in a winning poker pot. She bedded the
man who shot him, dragged him back to Boise and
they jointly opened the brothel with two other
ladies. He christened it the *King & 3 Queens*. His
unwanted advances, a year later, against a fourth
girl resulted in his demise—and a new name. Belle
simply figured the new girl had done what she would
have eventually had to do anyway.

Belle had added an inch or two here and there, but
Morgan supposed she could make as good a use of
those as she did the rest. She had firm, large breasts
of which plenty was always visible. Her face was
full, round and displayed a perpetual smile. Her lips,
generously painted, were wide and sensuous and
Morgan knew what she could do with them.

"You've grown,'' she said, eyeing him. Her eyes
found his crotch. "Everywhere?''

"Why don't *you* be the judge of that,'' he said.

"Yeah Lee . . . why don't I?'' She moved over and
locked the door. Morgan had already removed his
rig, shirt and belt. Belle Moran did the rest. Morgan
poured himself a drink, slipped onto the bed and
rested against its headboard. Belle stripped . . .
slowly.

He got hard just watching her. How long had it
been? He thought back. God! Cheyenne . . . five
weeks ago.

Belle didn't bed anyone unless *she* made the choice. When she did there was nothing better. Morgan, of course, had long since concluded that there was no such thing as a bad screw, only good, better, best and by God, fantastic! Belle Moran was at the head of the class.

She worked her tongue along the inside of his legs, alternating every few inches. Where they came together, she excelled. She traced invisible paths around, along and beneath his shaft. At the same time, the light touch of her fingers caressed below it and paused at the most sensitive junctures.

Morgan's eyes closed and the empty glass slipped from his hands. He moaned softly as she increased the speed and intensity of her ministrations. "It's been a hell of a while," he said. It was a warning that he might react too soon. Belle knew what to do. She climbed onto the bed, straddled Morgan about waist level and leaned forward. She moved from side to side, her breasts brushing his cheeks, the nipples bouncing off his nose or darting across his lips before he could catch one of them.

He finally reached up, his hands closed around them and his fingers pressed on their swollen tips. Belle stiffened, her head went back and goose bumps popped up and ran the length of her body like a sudden rash. As he continued caressing, she eased forward until her own, damp womanhood rested over his face. He licked. She groaned and then steeled herself for what was to come.

Wave after wave of delight surged through her body. Suddenly, she reversed herself and the two of them shared oral delight. At the very peak of pleasure, she reversed herself again, slipped his shaft inside herself and they fell to a steady but mounting rhythm.

"God . . . yes . . . yes Lee," she said. "Oh . . . faster
. . . do it faster." Together, they ascended passion's
peak and the summit was conquered in a wild,
sweaty, moaning instant. Lee Morgan's body
arched upwards and Belle Moran's lifted for just a
moment. They hung, suspended in pleasure, came
together for a final, crushing embrace and collapsed
in delighted exhaustion.

Morgan poured himself a drink and opted to try
one of Belle's store bought, pre-rolled smokes. That
done, he began to dress. Belle finally stirred and sat
up.

"Would you pour me a drink, honey?" Morgan
did. He handed it to her. She smiled. "You're better
than ever . . . but what brought you back?"

"The thought of staying put . . . maybe having
something besides a horse, a rifle and a reputation."

"I heard about the Bit."

"Yeah," Morgan said, scathingly, "so much for
staying put."

"It isn't the only spread in Idaho."

"It was the only one I might have dealt on . . . besides, there's trouble here . . . big trouble from the
way Judge Barr tells it."

Morgan turned and looked straight at Belle. "You
know anything about it?"

She downed the last of her drink, slipped from the
bed and put on a dressing gown. "Just enough to
want to stay out."

"Yeah Belle . . . me too."

"You driftin' again then?"

"Prob'ly. I promised the judge I'd stop back at
his place in a couple of days . . . after that, well, I
don't know."

"You can come to work for me," she said. She
moved close to him and even after what they had

just done, he could feel a stirring in his groin. "How about it?"

"I don't do well working for somebody Belle . . . never have."

"It wouldn't be the same here . . . you *know* that Lee."

"I'll think on it," he said. "My poke tells me I'll have to do *something* . . . and pretty damned quick."

"You need a touch Lee . . . you know where to come."

A ruckus in the street got both their attentions. Belle stepped to the window and pulled back the curtain. Morgan saw a hulk of a man with a woman in his arms. Tears streamed down his face and two kids, a boy and a girl, trailed behind him. Both were crying.

"That's Ole' Thomassen," Belle said.

"Customer of yours."

"Not Ole'. God! That's his wife. He's takin' her into the Doc's office." She let the curtain drop and began to dress. She caught Morgan's quizzical expression. "Ole' had a bad crop two years back. I put him out front . . . bouncin' for me."

"A married man? With a family?"

"One o' my girls got carried off one time, beat up bad. The men dumped her about a half a mile from Ole's place. They took her in. His missus saved her life."

Morgan strapped on the Colt's and followed Belle through the Four Queens and across the street. Inside Doc Loudon's office, big Ole' sat in a chair, his face buried in his hands. His kids sat at his feet. They were all crying. Morgan walked into the doc's back room.

"Get out," the doc said, without looking up. "I don't need an audience. This will be difficult enough as it is." Morgan didn't push it. Back outside, Belle was just straightening up. She'd been talking to Ole' and trying to comfort the children. She looked solemn.

"The marauders hit his place, just before sunup. He was on his way to town. The kids hid in the storm cellar. His wife didn't make it."

"Burn him out?" She nodded. "He know who?"

"He didn't say, but I got a hunch he knows more than he's lettin' out."

The front door opened and Belle and Morgan looked up into the face of Tate Bosley, Boise's sheriff. Belle filled him in but she was cut short when Doc Loudon stepped out of his back room. Everyone looked up. His teeth were clenched, his hands still bloody. He shook his head. Ole' Thomassen leaned back in the chair and let out a pain-filled cry.

3

Morgan walked into Tate Bosley's office and found the sheriff filling out papers. Bosley looked up.

"Belle arranged for the Thomassen kids to have bed and board over at Miller's Boarding House. Ole' highttailed out of town. Nobody's sure where. Three or four gunnys have ridden in since morning and you're doing paper work. Why?"

Bosley wasn't ruffled. " 'Cause that's my job son . . . part of it anyways."

"What the hell happened to getting a posse up?" Bosley finished what he was doing and signed it. He slipped the sheet into a metal basket which held a dozen or more similar reports and then he got to his feet.

"You're Lee Morgan aren't you?" Morgan nodded. "You want to be deputized?"

"No."

"Well neither did fifteen or twenty others I asked . . . so, no posse. That paper I was working on is a report of what happened. I'll mail that off to the territorial marshal and ask for help. Should have an answer in a week . . . ten days maybe. Might even get the army stirred up if this keeps happenin'."

"Jesus Christ, Sheriff . . . what the hell are you saying? Shit! Men like my daddy would have had those bastards run down and strung up by now."

"Prob'ly Morgan. Old Frank Leslie was quite a fella." Now, Bosley's tone hardened along with his demeanor. "But this ain't eighteen and seventy five an' I'm no goddam Buckskin Frank or Bill Hickok." He pointed a gnarled finger at Morgan. "An' neither are you boy . . . so don't try to be. We got law. I grant you it ain't caught up with the country we're in yet, but if you don't start somewhere, you end up with no law at all."

"And none of these spineless bastards will ride posse?"

Bosley grinned. "They're not gunmen. They're storekeepers. Hell, half of 'em don't know one end of a Winchester from another. If you came in here lookin' for fast answers, son, you've wasted your time. I would have put a posse out . . . if I could have got one . . . but it wouldn't have done any good. Since I couldn't the only thing left is the paperwork."

"What do you carry that goddamn thing for?" Morgan asked, pointing to Bosley's hip.

"Because it's still legal."

"But you've never *used* it?"

Bosley grinned. "*This* end," he said, touching the butt. "Prob'ly put eight or ten notches on it. Drunks, a tinhorn or two. Puts 'em to sleep. Then I can usually get one o' the upstandin' citizens of Boise to help me tote 'em over here so's they can sleep it off."

Morgan's face flushed. He turned on his heels and jerked the door open.

"Morgan." Lee turned. "Don't use the Bisley . . . less'n somebody tries to kill you . . . and you'd best have a witness or two. Use it any other way . . . I'll come after you . . . unless you want *this*." He held out a badge. Morgan slammed the door.

Morgan had no more than walked through the

front door of the Four Queens when he was confronted by Belle.

"Ole' Thomassen just left here." Morgan looked past Belle and saw the tall, menacing looking man in a heap on the floor. "I think he busted Steve's jaw. He wanted a shotgun. He's headed for the Boise Hotel."

"Did he get the shotgun?" She nodded. Morgan wheeled and hurried to his horse. The Boise was two blocks away. He didn't tether his mount, he just let the reins drop. He could hear screams from inside the hotel's lobby and he moved quickly to where he could see in the window.

Ole' Thomassen had scattered about everybody. Eight or nine people, mostly well dressed, were kneeling, crouching or otherwise trying to stay out of the way. Ole' was looking up. So did Morgan.

Two men stood at the head of the stairway. Both wore store bought suits. Morgan could see the telltale bulges of shoulder holsters. He also caught sight of a third man . . . far to Ole's right. He also had a shotgun.

Morgan opened the door, carefully and stepped just inside.

"Ay know who done it . . . ay know he's up there. Ay, by golly, will kill him."

"Go home old man . . . you've come sniffing around the wrong tree."

"Ay'm comin' up . . . an' nobody, by golly, better get in Ole's way."

Ole' started up the stairway. Eight steps went to a landing and then it turned right and went up six more to the balcony. Morgan watched the two men at the top of the stairs. When Ole' Thomassen reached the landing, one of them nodded. Morgan stepped out of the foyer, whirled to his right, drew and fired.

"Shoot, Ole'," he yelled. Morgan's shot killed the man with the shotgun instantly. Reflexes fired his weapon and it tore a bucket sized hole in the ceiling. Morgan turned back in time to see a wide-eyed Ole' Thomassen take two .38 slugs high in his chest. Morgan took out the man nearest his own position and the man's body tumbled toward Ole'. The action prevented the second man from firing. Morgan was shocked by what happened next.

Ole' dropped his shotgun, grabbed his chest and staggered back a step. Then, shaking his head as though he was recovering from a surprise fist to his jaw, he lowered his head and charged up the remaining steps. The second man in the fancy suit lost his weapon. Ole' had him around the waist.

"Ole' . . . let him go, drop him, Ole'," Morgan shouted. "This is no good." His words were futile. Ole' tightened his grip. He was lifting the man from the floor, slamming him down again and with each movement, increasing his bear hug. Soon, only Ole's labored breathing could be heard. The man let go a moan or two and tried to put his hands up to Ole's face and neck to free himself. A moment later, there was a series of barely audible, snapping sounds. Ribs gave way. Lungs were punctured. The man coughed blood. His head drooped to one side. Ole' Thomassen turned him loose.

Ole's own exertion had merely shortened the time he had left. Even his brute strength was no match for two .38 caliber bullets. The door opened behind Morgan. Tate Bosley burst through it. He saw Morgan and looked up. Ole' staggered, tried to regain his balance and then crashed through the bannister and fell thirty feet to the marble floor. It broke his neck.

Even as the scene unfolded, two men had slipped from the room at the end of the hall, hurried down an iron fire escape and were already riding, hard, out of town.

"I'll have your gun, Morgan." Lee was crouched over Ole's body.

"He broke his neck. He's dead."

"I said . . . I'll have your gun." Morgan's hand was like lightening. He slipped Bosley's own pistol from the holter, let it slide into his palm until he could grip the barrel and brought the butt down on Bosley's skull. The sheriff collapsed. Morgan rolled him over, replaced the pistol and hurried outside. A few minutes later, he was riding the trail back to the northeast . . . back toward the Rocky Barr Ranch.

"That's a rotten damned shame," Judge Barr said, after hearing Morgan's story. "Ole' Thomassen worked for me once . . . eight, mebbe nine years back. Worked like an ox. Saved every penny." The judge shook his head. "An' two fine youngsters orphaned." He turned and looked Lee Morgan straight in the eye. "You see what we're up against. Can you ride away from *that*?"

"You told me you had hired a man . . . *one* man. Who the hell is he, Judge, Hickok's ghost?"

"He rode in late last night. You'll meet him at dinner. He's already got a plan. Right now, there's someone else I want you to meet . . . just back from a trip to San Francisco."

In the Rocky Barr's parlor, Lee Morgan found himself face-to-face with one of the most strikingly beautiful women he'd ever seen. She was very fair and her hair, a golden blonde, was swept up at her neck and piled in orderly curls upon her head. Her features appeared almost sculptured, slim nose, small but perfectly formed lips and closely set, hazel eyes.

Her throat was creamy white, long and tapered into a chest which supported two, perfectly rounded, firm breasts. The turquoise gown exposed much of both of them. Her waist was wasp-like and hips flared into long legs which Morgan could only suppose were as perfect as the rest he could see.

"This is Lee Morgan," Judge Barr said. He moved over and put his arm around the woman's waist and moved her toward Morgan. She held out her hand. "You two have something . . . almost in common." Morgan looked quizzical.

"Our names," she said, smiling. "Mine's Morgana . . . Morgana Barr."

"She's my daughter."

"My pleasure," Morgan said. He struggled to keep his eyes from drifting downward again. She smiled and held his hand for what seemed a somewhat inappropriate length of time.

The dining room was crowded. Over a dozen, well dressed men milled about chattering. Most looked stern. Morgan, hardly dressed for the occasion, found himself a somewhat out of the way corner. He sipped bourbon. Judge Barr finally appeared. On his arm, Morgana Barr looking more ravishing than before. He introduced her to the few who did not already know her and then asked that everyone be seated. A minute later, he reappeared.

"Gentlemen," he glanced at his daughter and smiled, "and *lady,* our guest of honor." He stepped aside and Lee Morgan looked up . . . astonished. There stood one of the most notorious man hunters in the west. A man who rivalled the likes of Hickok, Holliday, Earp—even Kit Carson. "Meet, if you please, Mister Tom Horn."

Small talk consumed much of the meal. Morgan entering into only a minor exchange.

"I'd heard you were dead, Mister Horn." Horn looked across the table, smiled and nodded. He finished chewing, swallowed and then took a swallow of wine.

"I heard the same damned thing 'bout a week back as I recollect. Can't be though. Not a word in the papers about it." Everyone laughed.

Horn was not a big man. Maybe five feet, eight or nine inches and 165 pounds. His hair was cut short and he wore a well groomed moustache. His face appeared somewhat leathery, years, Morgan supposed, of exposure to the elements. Big or not, Tom Horn's reputation was as big as Sawtooth Mountains. He was the last of a breed of men being devoured by the undertow of advancing civilization.

Horn was not a shootist in the sense of Frank Leslie or Hickok, though his skill with a handgun was considerable. It was storied that he had once won a shooting match down in Omaha. The first half of it lasted until noon. Twenty-two competitors were eliminated. It was near dark before it ended—Horn against William F. Cody. True or not, few men could rival Horn's skill with a rifle and he was reported to be as icy cold as a Bowie blade when it came to killing a man.

"Mister Horn," Judge Barr finally said, "everyone in this room knows why they're here and why I sent for you. You told me you had a plan. Would you share it with us?"

"Put a man on the inside," Horn said. "Best way . . . and by far the safest . . . to kill a Grizzly is to track 'im home. Next time he goes out, stay put and catch 'im comin' back."

"The only man who could do that, sir, would be

yourself." Horn shook his head. "Too many folks know me. A passle that I've never laid eyes on. Nope. Has to be somebody who can show cause for wantin' to join up and a reputation to back it." Horn sat back, picked up a table knife and pointed it at Lee Morgan. "Frank Leslie's boy. Sure got the reputation and there's enough old tales about Leslie's rivalries to make it work . . . mebbe."

"I'm here as a favor to the judge . . . to listen."

"Funny . . . Judge tol' me he reckoned you'd help out after what happened over in Boise."

"I'm not your man. I've got a score to settle . . . and I'll settle it, by myself."

"Lee . . ." Judge Barr said. It was as far as he got. Tom Horn stopped him cold.

"You've got a problem young feller. See, if you're runnin' around out there settlin' accounts . . . an' me, I'm working for the ranchers . . . settlin' accounts, well . . . it occurs to me our trails would have to cross."

"Likely, Mister Horn."

"Then . . . I'd have to kill you. I get a mite edgy man huntin'. Judgment's not what it was twenty years ago. I'd feel bad . . . real bad. I'd even say so at your buryin'."

"I don't like threats, Mister Horn," Morgan said.

"Oh now don't take me wrong, son. I'm not threatenin' you. No sir. What I related, that there's just the way it is. Seems to me we'd do better by one another—an' for these folks here—if we'd work together."

Morgan couldn't disregard the man but he was not without a reputation of his own. "You seem pretty certain of the outcome of any meeting we might have, Mister Horn."

"I'm downright positive," Horn said. "I've heard

about your gun hand. I'd guess you probably would give your own daddy a fair run . . . an' that makes me appreciate you 'cause I *saw* him." Horn scratched the back of his head and cocked it sideways as he finished his conversation. "Thing is, I'd prob'ly kill you from half a mile away. Fast gun don't do a man good at that distance."

"Seems like a good plan to me," one of the other men said. "Morgan there on the inside and Mister Horn on the outside. Sounds like we'd find out what we need to know." Others nodded and mumbled agreement but there was a tension in the air. Morgan finally dispelled it.

"I'll sleep on it," he said.

Morgan was awakened by the sound of what he thought was thunder. It proved to be a dozen riders in the front yard of the Rocky Barr. His first thought was a raid but the voices he heard soon relieved that fear. He slipped on his britches and shirt, stuffed the Bisley into his waistband and headed downstairs. Tom Horn was just ahead of him.

"What's the ruckus?" Morgan asked. Horn shrugged. They found Judge Barr on the front porch along with Morgana and one or two of the ranch owners who'd opted to stay the night. One of them was a man named Ben Strada.

Strada's spread was half again the size of the Rocky Barr. It was named for the area in which it was located, the Lost River. Strada had four sons, two nephews and a niece living with him. His own wife, her brother and his wife had all perished when a bridge gave way during a treacherous storm five years earlier. They were swept to their deaths in the Lost River.

The riders who had come so late were some of
Strada's men.

"Boss . . . they hit us. Same night you pulled out."

"My God! The family . . . what of . . ."

"Your niece boss . . . they took your niece. They
burned one o' the bunk houses and a toolshed but
nothin' else. It was almost like . . ."

"Like *what*, man, spit it out."

"Like they come after her." Strada turned to his
host. Judge Barr had never seen Strada look so pitiful, so helpless.

"You've got my payment . . . more if the others
won't join us. Do what has to be done. I want my
niece alive . . . safe and I want those bastards strung
up." The judge only nodded.

"Your niece, Mister Strada . . . how old is she?"
Strada turned and was looking into the face of Lee
Morgan. "I've changed my mind. I'll work with you.
I'll get inside their gang . . . if I can."

"God Bless you, Mister Morgan. She's twenty-
five . . . just three months ago. Her name is Lileth."

Tom Horn had walked into the yard and was
talking with Strada's men. A few minutes later,
Strada came back out of the house, fully clothed.
His horse was waiting. He mounted up and then
turned to the men on the porch.

"I'm going to start hiring men . . . any kind I can
get, at any price. When you get inside, when you
hear something, I want to know. Then, I'll be
ready." Strada spurred his horse and the thunder of
hoofbeats echoed again at the Rocky Barr and then
faded.

Back inside, Judge Barr, Horn and Morgan gathered in the study. Soon, Morgana served coffee.

"Strada's upset," Horn observed, "but he's
making a mistake hiring outside guns."

"I'm not sure I follow you," the Judge replied, "after all, Mister Horn, *you're* an outside gun."

"A professional. I won't sell out on you to the next man who offers me more. I'll finish the job I'm hired to do and if I don't, you don't pay."

"I agree, Judge," Morgan said. "We could end up having to face in both directions. The kind of men Strada's likely to get won't give a damn about who's who. If they can collect on one of your men . . . or Killerman's . . . they will."

"I'll try to talk to Ben later. He's usually got a cool head." Horn turned to Morgan. "Where do you start? Boise?"

"Uh uh. I had a run in with the law in Boise . . . Grover too."

"You've been a busy man, Mister Morgan."

"But it might come in handy. Let the word get back to both places about me. Tell 'em I came lookin' for work . . . you offered it and I turned it down."

Horn grinned. "Just ridin' in to get a look at the place."

"Maybe somebody will think so." Morgan turned to the judge. "I'll have to describe your place in detail . . . the whole layout. There's a helluva risk in it, Judge."

"What have I got to lose? I'm only biding time now. Do what you have to do, Morgan."

"What about you, Mister Horn?"

"Figure it's time you start callin' me Tom. What's your likin'?"

"Morgan will do just fine."

"Well," Horn said, "I figure there's two groups o' these bastids. They've hit ranches too far apart in two short a time just to have one outfit."

"I'll go along with that," Judge Barr said,

shaking his head, "but where in God's name do you start looking? It's a big country Horn."

"I was talkin' with Strada's foreman. That outfit hit the ranch from the northeast. There's a dozen or so smaller ranches in that area and then Killerman's place. I figure one batch o' these buzzards is holin' up along the Bitterroots."

"You know that country?" Morgan asked.

"Not real thorough."

"I used to hunt some of it as a kid. Lived close by for awhile. Use Taylor Mountain for a landmark. Follow the Salmon to its confluence with the Lemhi. That'll take you into one of the most remote regions of Idaho. Goes on for miles. Hunters used to go back fifteen, twenty miles. Never talked to anybody went back all the way. There's a cut . . . solid rock on both sides and the farther you go . . . the deeper it gets. They call it Gunsmoke Gorge."

"Sounds likely Morgan. What about you?"

"I agree, Tom, that there's likely two batches of raiders. I'll mosey over to Picabo. It's a meeting point for about every gunny riding through the territory. If I get anywhere I'll have a good chance there."

4

A cold, drenching rain had been falling for the last three hours. Morgan had the collar of his oil cloth slicker pulled up around his neck, his hat pulled well down on his head and he hunkered low in the saddle.

Mostly his thoughts had been with big Ole' Thomassen. The old Swede either knew *something* or saw *someone*. In all of the previous raids, there had been no reports of any of the victims searching out possible perpetrators. Ole' seemed to know where to go and who to look for. Not that it did anyone any good now.

Pacer, Morgan's big dappled gray, snorted. Morgan looked up. Light! Picabo. He rode in, eyeing buildings on both sides of the single street. There were fourteen buildings in Picabo. Six of them were empty. The decent folk had long since departed. There was a mercantile, a smithy and livery stable and an assay office. Their existence did not necessarily reflect the honesty of their proprietors. The balance of Picabo's business district consisted of four saloons and the Acey-Duecey. It was a hotel, brothel and saloon combined.

Morgan stabled Pacer, threw his bedroll and possibles over his shoulder and toted his Winchester in his free hand. The outside doors of the Acey-

Duecey were closed . . . the bat wings tied open,
against the chill. Morgan entered and looked
around. A dozen or so men were scattered throughout the saloon. Some drank and talked, four were
busy with poker, others mingled with the girls . . .
three of them.

There was no registration desk so Morgan walked
to the bar. He dropped his gear to the floor and
slipped out of his slicker.

"Got an empty?"

"Two dollars a night or eight fifty a week. Food's
separate. Eat down here. We got no room service."
The grimy looking barkeep grinned. "Least ways for
food."

"I'll start with two nights," Morgan said. He
payed, took his key and went straight to his room.
The furnishings were sparse. A bed with a lumpy,
straw filled matress, a three drawer dresser, a wash-
bowl and pitcher and a chamber pot. There was a
single window which gave the occupant a view of the
roof of the building next door.

Morgan pulled back the bed covers and saw no
signs of life. He didn't like bedbugs and had learned
to tote his bedroom with him . . . just in case. He
slipped his knife out, slit a footlong gash into the
end of the mattress and slipped the winchester into
the slot. He was using the chamber pot when he
heard the knock at the door. It came a second time
before he'd finished. He slipped the pot back under
the bed and opened the door, stepping back as he did
so.

"Water señor and towels." Morgan eyed the
Mexican boy and then looked passed him into the
hallway. Morgan nodded and the boy came in. He
filled the water pitcher from a bucket. "I am Jose,
señor." He turned and smiled. "Jose Delgado

Manuel Ruiz Esteban. If I can do anything for you, señor. Just call me."

"I'll do that," Morgan said, "but I think I'll stick with Pancho. You mind being called Pancho?"

"No, no, señor. That was my padre's name. Pancho Aguilar Esperanza . . ."

"Okay, Pancho," Morgan said, holding up his hands. "There is something you can do for me." Morgan held up a silver dollar. "Are there any . . . uh, *gringos* in Picabo? I don't mean like me . . . gun men. I mean rich type, *Yanqui gringos?*"

"No señor."

"You're sure?"

"Si. Jose," he grinned. "I mean . . . Pancho, he would know."

"Have there been any such men . . . recently?"

"No señor . . . no such men come to Picabo." Morgan nodded and flipped the silver dollar to the boy. "*Gracias amigo.*" Morgan held the door and Pancho took his leave. He had his doubts about Pancho's credibility but he also thought it likely that the best he'd get in Picabo was contact with a hired gun . . . no one really important.

Morgan made his way to the bar. He noted as few additional customers but none of them appeared to be much more than second rate gunnys and a grifter or two.

"Whiskey," Morgan said. The barkeep poured. Morgan downed the shot and nearly gagged. "That's the most god-awful whiskey I ever drank. You got better?"

"Nope."

"Beer?"

"It's green."

"I'll take it." The barkeep shrugged. Morgan heard the door and did a half turn to see who came in. It was a man. A pinch-faced little fellow in an ill-fitting suit and a derby. He was carrying a large, fancy leather case. He looked around the room and finally found Morgan. His eyes dropped to Morgan's rig. He smiled and walked toward the bar.

The barkeep brought Morgan's beer. He took a long swallow. It was green. It was still better than the whiskey.

"Good evening to you, sir." Morgan nodded. "My name is Mason sir, Andrew Jennings Mason. If you have a few minutes, I'd very much like to show you my wares." He held up the leather case.

"Not interested," Morgan said.

"Ahh sir . . . that is where you are mistaken. I assure you, just take a look and give me a few minutes and you will be."

"Why'd you pick on me . . . uh . . . ?"

"Mason, sir."

"Uh huh. So why?"

"By my reckoning, sir, after years of experience I might add, I'd wager you earned your keep with that Bisley Colt's. Not another man in here is wearing as fine a pistol."

"You're a gun drummer?"

"I am sir . . . with the finest manufacturer in the country . . . Smith and Wesson."

"I've never owned anything but a Colt's."

"And a fine weapon they were too, yes sir, fine weapons," he smiled, "in their day."

"But you've got one better?"

"I have, sir, I have indeed." He pointed to the case. "In there reposes the beginning of a line of firearms which will take this nation into its new century. It is the pistol of civilized man. A weapon which will maintain the law which Mister Colt established with his legendary Peacemaker."

"You want a beer, Mister Mason?"

"Why yes, sir, that would be fine."

"You get us a table," Morgan said, "and I'll get us a beer. I'll take a look see at your fancy piece."

If the pistol handled and fired the way it looked, Morgan would have to concede to the drummer's sales pitch. Nickled, beautifully hand tooled engraving and gutta-percha grips.

"Double action, six shot, five inch barrel, .38 caliber."

"I prefer something a little heavier," Morgan said, hefting the pistol. "Heavier caliber too."

"Look here, sir." Mason handed Morgan a metallic cartridge with a somewhat bulbous shell. "When that missile strikes its target, it flattens out. It will, putting it bluntly sir, tear a hole as big as a man's fist upon exiting."

"Well Mister Mason, I won't say I'm not impressed but I'm just not in the market for a new gun right now."

"Nor are most men of your ilk," Mason said, smiling. "You are my most difficult sale because you demand much and are loyal to a fault. Therefore, sir, if you will but sign this simple form, I will present this weapon to you along with holster and ample ammunition. I'd like nothing better than to place it in your hands for what my employers refer to as a field test."

"You want to *give* me that pistol?"

"In a manner of speaking, yes sir. I live in Boise, Mister Morgan. After using it, I'd like you to look me up and let me know, honestly, what you think. Anything we discuss thereafter will be determined by your interest."

Morgan frowned. "You know my name?"

"Oh yes," Mason said, standing up and folding up

his case. "By now, most everybody in Boise knows your name and what you look like." Mason pushed the pistol and ammunition boxes across the table. "Good day, Mister Morgan, and good luck to you."

Mason went upstairs and Morgan was puzzled. He got the answers to his questions when, later that evening, he opened the first box of ammunition to load up the new pistol. There was a handwritten note inside the box.

> Mason is a friend. He stopped by the ranch and I asked him to help. I told him where you were and what to do. Good luck.
>
>   Judge Barr

The rain had stopped. The clouds still hung low and the wind gnawed its way through a man's clothing and chilled his bones. Morgan hurried out of the Acey Duecey following his breakfast and over to the mercantile. He'd gone to see Mason early that morning but the drummer had already checked out.

Morgan was wearing the new Smith and Wesson. He'd pulled it a couple of dozen times in the privacy of his room. It seemed to increase his speed but he had an empty feeling without the weight of the big Bisley.

Inside the store, he lingered by the pot-belly, warmed himself and took stock of his cash. He had about fifty-five dollars. He spent just under fifteen of it on a new, sheepskin coat. He was not in New Mexico now.

"You're Lee Morgan aren't you?" Morgan had just pocketed his change from a twenty dollar bill. He looked up at the man behind the counter.

"Who wants to know?"

"A friend of mine," the man said. He motioned with his head and indicated a doorway to the back of the store.

"I'm staying across the street. If your friend is interested, that's where I'll be."

"I'm interested." Morgan looked up and found himself staring into the business end of a scatter-gun. "Why don't you step this way, Mister Morgan?" Morgan shrugged.

In the backroom, Morgan found himself in company with four men. One continued to hold a shotgun on him. The others were seated. Two of them were well dressed but they all wore either shoulder holsters or hip rigs.

"What brings you to Picabo?" The man who asked the question had his chair leaning back against the far wall. Morgan could see the shoulder holster. Morgan thought the man looked like a Pinkerton agent.

"Passing through," Morgan said.

"To where?"

"East."

"Where east?"

"That's *my* business."

"You shot up two of my men, Mister Morgan . . . in Boise. I don't like things that cost me money. They did. A lot of it."

"My mistake," Morgan said.

"That's hardly restitution. Why were you so inter-ested in defending an old Swede sod-buster?"

"A friend of a friend. Nothing personal."

"What friend?"

"Belle Moran."

"Are you usually that impetuous?"

"They hardly gave me a chance to get their side of

the story," Morgan said. He unbuttoned the heavy coat. One of the other men moved forward in his chair and Morgan detected a shifting movement by the man holding the shotgun.

"What's your game, Morgan? You pistol whipped the sheriff and already crossed swords with the territorial marshal. Or so I've heard. Then you try to save some farmer as a favor to a Boise whore." The man smiled. "You are an enigma, Mister Morgan."

"I'm a man who keeps his business to himself and appreciates it when everybody else does the same."

"But you *didn't*," the man replied, standing up now. "You stuck your nose in *my* business. You owe me Morgan . . . at least an explanation."

"After which you nod at shotgun over there and I get my nice new sheepskin coat all pocked up with bird pellets."

The man pulled a cigarette case from his inside pocket, opened it, removed a cigarette, offered one to Morgan, who declined, closed the case and replaced it in his pocket. He lit the cigarette, took a long drag, savoring the smoke, exhaled and then said, "I could have ordered you shot anytime. Why do you suppose I didn't?"

"I've got something you want . . . or you think I do."

"Are you on Judge Barr's payroll?"

"I'm not on anybody's payroll."

"But you do want to find out who burned out the Spade Bit, don't you?"

"Why should I?"

"Because it was your home . . . or what passed for it." The man smiled. "If you tell me you're not that old shootist's son . . . old Leslie, well then Morgan, our little talk is over."

"Yes," Morgan said, "I'm Leslie's son and I did

live at the Spade Bit ranch once and, yeah, I'd like to find out who burned it down." Morgan smiled. "I'd buy the son-of-a-bitch a drink."

"That so? Why is that?"

"I rode back up here to settle accounts with the folks who lived there. Somebody saved me the trouble."

"What account did you have to settle. They owned it legal and proper, didn't they?"

"They did. It's *how* they got it that bothered me."

"I don't follow."

"Easy enough. A retired gun fighter moves in. Got a son who doesn't exactly stay within the law. Not neighbors you'd invite to Sunday dinner. On top of that, the law was never quite able to pin old Frank Leslie down . . . or his son. Judge Barr sure tried enough times. Anyway, when old Leslie finally got his, the son stood to inherit the place. A simple change in a deed here, a little shuffling of papers there and pretty soon, Leslie didn't own the place anymore and his son has got nothing to inherit but a lousy reputation."

"You sound . . . shall we say, bitter."

"Not as bad as it was. Not after I saw the Spade Bit. The thing with the old Swede was just like I said. Fact is, I thought the old bastard might have some information for me. He used to work for Judge Barr."

"So," the man said, grinding out his cigarette beneath his boot heel, "you'd like to see the same thing happen at the Rocky Barr as happened at the Spade Bit?"

"Yeah . . . only I'd like to do it personal."

"Can you prove that," the man said, whirling to face Morgan, "or are you really not what you seem?"

"I don't have to prove a damned thing to anybody." Morgan had carefully eased back the hem of the skeepskin coat. The new pistol was at the ready.

"Prove it to me, Morgan, and I'd make it worth your while. You'd get that chance at the Rocky Barr. You could ride out of Idaho a lot wealthier than when you rode in."

"So you're the fella that engineered the destruction of the Spade Bit?" Morgan smirked. "The other ranches too, huh?" He smirked again. "Real nice work, yes sir. Rocky Barr still stands, Josh Killerman's Rocking K still stands and Ben Strada's place."

"They're big spreads . . . hard to get at but . . ." Morgan had hit a nerve. The man's response was quick, defensive. Obviously he wasn't the biggest fish in the stagnant pond and he was getting some pressure from someone. Morgan decided to push . . . hard.

"But you figure they'll all buckle under now because some dumb son-of-a-bitch stole Strada's niece." Morgan forced a laugh. "That . . . when they could have had old Judge Barr's daughter for Chrissake!"

"Daughter?" Morgan's play got the desired reaction. "Judge Barr's daughter is in . . ."

"San Francisco? Jeezus," Morgan said, sneering, "who the hell you got workin' for you, blind men? Morgana Barr is out at her daddy's ranch right now. Oh you may get some folks stirred up with your move against Strada, but you move against Judge Barr and you'll get action." Morgan moved his right arm so quickly no one in the room had any warning of his intent.

Morgan himself was astonished at his own

increased speed. The lighter, short barreled, Smith and Wesson was pointed right at Morgan's target. He smiled.

"You won't ride out of Picabo alive."

"Neither will you," Morgan said. "Now get that scatter gun off of me and clear these half assed slingers out of here. Maybe then," he continued, giving his most sinister grin, "just maybe, you and I might do some business."

Moments later, Morgan and the man were alone. "I'm Jake Lambert," the man volunteered.

"I want ten thousand dollars, Mister Lambert, and that's just for what I know. How to get into the Rocky Barr and how to get hold of the judge's daughter. I can supply the same information at Killerman's place. When it's all over . . . when your people have control, I want the rest."

"The rest?"

"Ten percent."

"You're crazy."

"Who says so . . . you? That might irritate me a little Lambert except I know you're not the top man."

"And how do you know?"

"You didn't engineer the Strada kidnapping and you people can't be in two places at once. Besides Lambert, your end of things isn't going too well right now. The biggest thing you've managed is the Spade Bit. . . which is nothing as long as the Rocky Barr is standing."

The man turned. Morgan saw a look which displayed both concern and embarrassment. "I can tell you now, Morgan, ten percent is out of the question. You may have information of value but we'd still have to act on it . . . you couldn't do it alone. That's why you're in Picabo."

Morgan sat down. He pondered Lambert's observation. In fact, he was killing time until he could
play the ace he held. He looked up. "That ten
percent bother you 'cause it's more than you're
getting?"

Lambert was caught short. Here was a man who
was more than the two bit, fast handed son of an old
time killer. "No . . . no it *isn't* more than I'm
getting."

"You don't think it would be worth another ten
percent to your boss to get this thing over with in a
hurry . . . and before you start losing riders."

"We haven't lost a man yet, except for the two
you got. That won't happen again."

"It damned near happened tonight right here in
this room, Lambert. I can assure you, it'll start hap-
pening in a big way shortly." Morgan could almost
read Lambert's thoughts. "You can backshoot me . .
. it won't stop what I just told you. What I know has
already happened . . . all hell's about to bust loose in
Idaho." Lambert was whipped and Morgan knew
it.

"I've got to . . . to talk to my people."

"Why? You and I can deal. We make some moves
on our own, get them done and then you talk to your
people. By then they'll have felt the sting and will be
ready to deal. There's more here than ten percent—
for both of us."

"You're talking a double-cross Morgan. You don't
know who I'm dealing with . . . you . . . you don't
understand."

Morgan had him on the run. No double-cross?
Then the action wasn't all local. Morgan moved to
play along.

"Okay . . . then let's just make ourselves look too
good to be ignored. As much as there is at stake,

I've got to figure somebody would be willing to pay plenty. It's heating up. The army will be in on it eventually. Right now, it's a civil matter with a handful of lawmen to deal with it. Most o' them can't catch cold.''

"All right. . . what's your plan?''

"You sleep on what I told you, Lambert. Think on it hard. We meet again. I want a deal . . . a solid deal. Give it to me and I'll deliver.'' Morgan got to his feet. "Fuck with me, Lambert . . . and I'll kill you.''

5

Lee Morgan's plans were pretty simple—if they worked. They were dangerous as hell if they didn't. When the time was right, he'd produce Judge Barr's daughter and suggest that she be taken to the same spot where Strada's niece was being held. That, he figured, would lead him to the top man. If he got that far, he'd reveal the presence of Tom Horn. The combined information ought to solidify his position.

He had plenty of time to ponder the possible outcomes. Some of them, he thought, were none too pleasant. Neither was the ride from Picabo back to Grover. The rain of four days had turned to snow. The wind, down from the Sawtooth, piled it up against every break. Morgan couldn't remember the last time he was so glad to see the lights of Grover.

He stabled Pacer and payed extra for a rubdown and top quality feed. He walked toward the Sawtooth saloon, hoping he wouldn't be seen by any old acquaintances and hoping the gun drummer, Mason, had managed a message to Judge Barr. He knew he didn't dare ride to the ranch again but he would have to try to make contact with either the judge or Tom Horn.

"Whiskey," Morgan said to the bartender. He wasn't the same man Morgan had seen on his first

50

day in town. "Leave the bottle. I've got some warmin' up to do."

"Which way'd you ride in?"

"West," Morgan lied. He was also wondering about the marshal. "You got law here?"

"Marshal's got an office but he's not in it most o' the time. Rode out two days ago for Boise. Doubt he'll be back too soon with the kind o' weather we got." Morgan nodded. He was relieved.

After another drink, Morgan shed the sheepskin coat and found an empty table. He'd been seated for only a few minutes when two men entered the Sawtooth. Morgan knew they spelled trouble for him. They were the two riders he'd used the Black snake on, the day he'd ridden up to the Rocky Barr. They glanced around but missed seeing him. Both were stomping their feet, knocking off snow and blowing on their hands to warm up. A moment later, they walked to the bar.

Morgan had learned from Judge Barr that the taller of the two was Milt Ryker. He was a drifter, better than average with a six-gun and a shade too hot-tempered to hold any position of responsibility. His saddle compadre was Billy Creek, a nonentity whose sole claim to fame rested on his dubious reputation with a pistol.

"What brings you boys all the way down to Grover from the Barr?" Ryker responded. "Lookin' to hire some hands. Figgered they might be a few loafin' around after what happened down at the Spade Bit. Seen any?"

"Few. Fact is, a fella rode in tonight," the barkeep said. He leaned to one side so that he could see around Ryker. He frowned. "Hell . . . he was settin' right over there." The barkeep pointed, Ryker and Creek both turned but they never got all the way around. Both spotted Morgan just as he reached the door.

"That's the son-of-a-bitch with the bullwhip," Creek shouted. Creek and Ryker both were wearing long, heavy coats. Ryker had his clear of his hip first, but Creek was in his line of fire. He pushed Creek to one side, planning only to get the drop on Morgan. Too much happened too fast.

Morgan whirled, in a crouch. The Smith and Wesson again proved its worth. Ryker took a slug in the chest which shattered his sternum and distributed the bone fragments into both lungs and his heart. The bar held him up for a moment, then he slid down, slowly, dead by the time he'd attained a sitting position.

The bartender dived for cover almost at the same instant Billy Creek made his move. He'd cleared his coat and made his draw but he never got to fire. Morgan turned the little S & W on a flick of his wrist and Creek took the .38 through the head. Just then, the door opened behind Morgan. He turned and found himself face to face with one of Lambert's men. He'd been reasonably certain he was being followed from Picabo. If what had just happened was inevitable, it couldn't have happened at a better time.

Morgan turned back, addressing himself to no one in particular. "Anybody asks questions . . . just tell the truth. It'll save me looking for you later." He holstered his gun, turned, stared for a moment at Lambert's man, half smiled and walked out. He made his way, quickly, to Sarah Browning's boarding house.

Sarah was a fine looking woman. Solid, tall but not lacking feminine attributes. She had once cooked out at the Spade Bit and had nursed

· Morgan's father through more than one bout with ailments.

Morgan's thrice failed efforts to settle down had been highlighted by an association with Sarah. They'd gone to town dances and picnics together and she'd even managed to get him into church. He'd never managed to get her into bed. He'd often wondered if that had finally driven him back to the wild life—a conquest he couldn't claim.

"Hello Sarah." It was dark. She squinted.

"Lee? My goodness! Lee Morgan?" He nodded. "Come in out of the cold." He did. She took his coat and he sat down and tugged off his boots. He remembered Sarah's fetish about clean rugs.

"I need a room."

"I have one. How long . . . *this* time?"

He stood up. "It's good to see you again," he said. She didn't pursue her question. "Am I too late to get something to eat?"

"Of course you are," she said, then she smiled. "Bacon and eggs do?"

"And a little coffee."

Lee took a seat at the kitchen table while Sarah flitted about preparing his food. "When did you get back?"

"A while ago."

"I suppose you heard about the Bit?"

"I did. I shot two men at the Sawtooth," he blurted out. "Just before I came over here. It was self defense."

She turned and gave him a pitiful look. She shook her head. "Isn't it always?"

"It is with me," he said.

She smirked. "Your father too . . . as I remember him talking about it. They're no less dead . . . are they?"

"I wanted you to know. Nobody will come looking for me . . . unless it's the marshal. I figure to be gone before he gets back from Boise." She didn't respond but rather returned to preparing his food. When it was ready, she put it before him, poured two cups of coffee and took the chair kitty-cornered from him.

"Smells damn good," Morgan said, smiling.

"You know Lee, they've got horseless carriages back east. Electric lights and trolley cars and inside water closets. You carry a gun and ride a horse and shoot men down in barrooms like some pulp novel villain."

"Good," he said, between bites. He washed them down with a swallow or two of coffee. He wiped the corners of his mouth. "If I was going blind . . . would you want me to cover my eyes up right now . . . tonight . . . or let it happen when it happened?"

"You're such a damned child," she said, angrily. "It's the kind of answer I would expect. My God! Take off that damned gun and settle down. *I* live in this country. The people who board with me live in this country . . . we don't go around shooting people . . . self defense or not."

Lee mopped up the egg yoke with his last crust of bread, folded it and slipped it into his mouth. He washed it down with the last of the coffee and then slid the cup toward Sarah. She refilled it.

"No disrespect intended," he said, "but you don't live civilized because there is civilization. You just ignore what's going on around you . . . let somebody else make it right. I came back to see about buying back the ranch. You know what I found. It didn't happen just here. There are violent men out there and Mister Edison's lights and a few noisy street machines aren't going to stop them."

"Men like you . . . like your father . . . you won't give up, will you? You won't admit that your time is over. Somehow you seem to think you'd be less a man if you ran a general store or taught school. They have violent men back east too but citizens don't go about gunning them down. There are laws, law men, courts and judges. It's a requirement of a civilized social order."

"And someday it'll get here to Idaho. West too. It will happen when those greedy men who take what someone else has worked for, are made to understand they can't do it out here anymore than they can back east."

"I don't want trouble under my roof," Sarah Browning said. "You can stay the night." She got up, hastily cleared the table and started for the upstairs. Morgan caught her arm.

"I'm sorry about your husband. I heard."

"It changes nothing between us," she said. "I don't want anymore hurt."

She pulled free of him. "Please . . . don't make me ask you to leave." Morgan looked into her eyes and nodded.

Lee Morgan woke himself up . . . a habit he'd long since mastered . . . about 2:30 the following morning. By now, he concluded, the Sawtooth was closed and Lambert's man would be fast asleep. It was the one opportunity he might have to get a message out of Grover and into Judge Barr's hands.

He dressed, slipped quietly downstairs and eased out the front door. The snow and wind had increased and struck him like the slap of a hand. He sucked in his breath and tucked his chin against the thick, wool collar of his coat.

At the livery stable, Morgan had a hard time rousing old Ben Grafton. Grafton was none too pleasant when he finally responded to the incessant pounding at his door.

"You got 'ny idea what the fuck time it is?"

Morgan handed Ben a sealed envelope. "Your boy takes that up to Judge Barr for me *now* and brings me back an answer. There's a hundred dollars in it."

Ben stepped back and invited Morgan inside with a toss of his head.

"Must be goddamn important."

"A hundred . . . by the end of the week."

"Fifty now," Grafton said, "fifty when he gets back."

"You've got my horse. I won't be leaving. Hold him 'til you get your money."

Grafton grinned, exposing short, dingy teeth. "Bullshit! You can steal a goddam horse Morgan . . . you've done it before . . . and worse."

"Then hang onto my saddle . . . it's worth fifty."

"Like I said . . . must be awful important. How's come you don't ride it in?"

"I've got a man to meet. I miss 'im and neither one of us will get payed."

"Sattidy," Grafton said, "by noon . . . or I got a saddle *an'* your horse."

"You get the money when I get Judge Barr's answer. Faster Luke rides the faster he gets back." Grafton nodded and Morgan returned to Sarah Browning's.

Dawn came to the Bitterroots as brittle as dry bread. The sky was clear and the air seemed frozen in place. Tom Horn snuffed out the last of the coals from his fire and scooped cow dung over it. The dung had been fresh a few minutes earlier. Now it was cold. In ten minutes, it would be frozen solid. It stopped the smoke from trailing too high.

Horn saddled his mount, double checked the tie downs on his pack mule, checked the loads in his Sharps and his Henry and mounted up. He rode back down the slope and onto a rolling meadow. He reached the Lemhi River and turned to follow it . . . south.

By mid-morning, he'd reached the spot where the river took a sharp bend back to the west. Here is where he'd leave it. He turned east and began the slow climb that would take him to the tops of Medicine Ridge. The spiny outcropping tailed off to the southeast and eventually ran headlong into the granite wall of the Continental Divide.

Somewhere in between, he'd find the entryway into the area known as Gunsmoke Gorge. Horse and mule were at a walk. Tom Horn had just bit off a chew. He'd been obliged to slip the tobacco under his armpit for twenty minutes to soften it up. He tucked the chunk back into his coat pocket. It was then he heard the shots! There were three but just exactly their point of origin was tricky to discern. Horn reined up and cocked his head. The reverberations continued. His mount snorted. He patted the mare's neck. The mule balked. Horn nudged his horse ahead, taking up the slack in the tether line.

Another shot! Straight ahead . . . no doubt. Horn raised up in his stirrups, shoved his hat back, shaded his eyes with his free hand and scanned a hundred and eighty degrees. Off to the left, he saw what he wanted . . . a stand of trees. He rode toward them.

A small stream, ice forming along its banks, meandered through the grove. It left his animals with both grazing and water. He tied them short . . . about twenty feet and hobbled both. He removed his heavy coat, rolled it up and slipped it between the

ties on his pack mule. He undid a bundle and
removed a shortwaisted, wool and cotton wind-
breaker.

Working at a slow but carefully practiced routine,
Tom Horn removed a leather case from his pack
mule. He pulled a box of ammunition from his
saddlebags, checked his pistol load and then opened
the leather case.

Inside was Horn's magnificent, customized man
killer. A Remington Creedmoor, .44-90. The rifle had
been manufactured for quick dismantling or
assembly. Its 32 inch, octagonal barrel, machine
threaded for a fitting to a pistol grip stock.

Horn wiped the light moisture from the weapon,
assembled and loaded it. He replaced the case,
shoved his hat down more snugly against his head
and set off along the creek.

About a quarter of a mile away, he crossed the
creek and climbed a razorback ridge which he
followed for another mile. Soon, he had a view of the
open valley below. He'd found what he'd wanted. A
line shack used for summer round-ups . . . now
presumably abandoned. This one was not.

There were three horses tied outside and he could
see a deer laying near the front door. He guessed the
animal was the victim of one or more of the shots
he'd heard earlier. Horn guessed that the line shack
either belonged to the Strada spread or the
Killerman ranch. Either way, it was remote from
both and afforded the marauders a place to hole up .
. . or, he mused, a place to stash a kidnap victim.

The door opened, Horn tensed. He shifted his
weight and hefted the Creedmoor to his shoulder.
He steeled himself against the recoil, positioned the
barrel and took aim. A man—then two—stepped
outside. One of them knelt beside the deer. They

were talking.

Suddenly, a third man appeared. Horn lowered the rifle and rubbed his eyes to remove the excess moisture. He squinted. Yes, he thought, it is . . . it's Ben Strada. The three men talked for several more minutes. Finally, Strada disappeared back inside. The others strung up the deer. Strada reappeared and was carrying a woman's hat. He and the first man mounted up, exchanged conversation with the third man and then rode off to the south. The remaining man began gutting the buck.

Tom Horn pondered what he had seen as he made his way back to his horse. Had Strada's men found the girl? Had they stumbled into the marauders? or had Strada received a message and made a deal?

Horn didn't repack the Creedmoor. He mounted up and started toward the line shack, cradling the weapon in his arms. Horn began to think back on the incidents which had led him to the remote area. Strada's men suddenly appearing. The story of a raid and the kidnapping of his niece . . . but no serious destruction to his place. Thus far, according to Judge Barr, no ranch had escaped the fury of the raiding band. Why, he wondered, had Strada's? How did the gang know exactly when and where to hit? Strada had more than fifty good men working for him.

The line shack was in view. A ribbon of white smoke curled up from the single chimney. The deer was gutted and all but stripped of hide. The man was not in sight. Horn dismounted, tethered his horse to a fallen log, made a quick survey of the terrain and began walking down the hill.

Horn had halved the distance to the shack. The snow had deepened and the going was tougher. Suddenly, the man appeared from the opposite side of the building. He spotted Horn at once. Perhaps a hundred and seventy-five yards separated the two, but the man obviously didn't want company. He drew and fired his pistol!

"It's Tom Horn." Tom stopped. The man darted inside. The old man hunter waited, once again positioning the Creedmoor. There was no window on his side of the shack. The man reappeared, rifle in hand.

The first shot was fifteen or so feet in front of Horn. The second, closer but off to the right. The man wasn't taking his time. Tom Horn did. He sighted the Creedmoor until its barrel levelled out on the man's chest. The third shot struck a log just three feet from Horn's legs. Horn squeezed the trigger.

The .44-90 barked and Horn's whole torso rocked from the recoil. The shot itself was sharp and clear but it boomed against the nearby ridge, bounced off and spread out over the snow. Even before the sound had faded, the man in front of the shack was hit. The force lifted him from his feet and hurled him backward, spreadeagled, into the snow. His rifle burrowed into a nearby drift, barrel first. The man didn't move.

Horn heard the whinny of the man's horse, now tied on the opposite side of the shack. The horse settled down. Horn waited. He could hear nothing else. He moved cautiously toward the shack.

The shack was empty but there were ropes—or pieces of ropes—around the rungs of the back of a wooden chair. They had been cut. Someone had been tied to it. Horn moved outside and examined the man. Most of his chest and back was pulp. Horn went through his pockets.

A kerchief, two expended rifle shells, a piece of

chaw and half a sack of makings. There was no indication of who the man was and Tom knew he hadn't been among Strada's riders.

Nearly three miles away, Ben Strada pulled his mount up short. "That was a rifle!"

"Yeah," the other man said, "sounded like a Sharps." Strada frowned. "Get back to the shack . . . check on Owens and look for tracks. I'm going on over to the Killerman place." The man nodded. He'd ridden only a few yards when Strada hollered at him.

"Yeah?"

"You see anybody you don't know," Strada said, "don't take any chances. Kill 'em!" The man nodded.

6

Sarah Browning changed her mind. Lee Morgan could stay with her as long as there was no trouble. By late morning on his third day in Grover, there hadn't been.

That aside, Morgan was getting edgy. Today was the deadline for the deal he'd made with Ben Grafton. Morgan hadn't seen anything of Grafton, his son or Lambert's hired gun. No news wasn't good news. On top of that, Morgan knew the marshal was due back almost anytime.

When he answered the door, he found Sarah Browning holding out an envelope. Somebody had come through. "I'll be movin' out today," he said, "one way or another."

"It's just as well. I don't like old ashes stirred up." Morgan smiled. "If there are no coals," he said, "what difference does it make?" She walked away without responding. He watched her descend the stairs, then he opened the envelope.

Sawtooth saloon. Upstairs.
1:30 today.

Lambert

Morgan rolled the makings, lit up, set fire to the

note and watched it burn itself away in the wash-bowl. The shot spider-webbed the mirror above the chiffonier and Morgan dived for the wall just below the window. Behind him, downstairs, Sarah screamed.

Another shot smashed through the window. By the angle of the shot, the shooter was in the house next door . . . or on its roof. Morgan heard the creak of a board in the hallway. He fired two blind shots out the window, tucked his body into a ball and rolled toward the bed. The door flew open and Morgan fired.

The man's reflexes managed to pull one of the triggers on the shotgun. The blast tore out a chunk of the ceiling a foot across. Morgan's shot was fatal. Instantly, he was on his feet, propelled himself over the man's body and down the stairs.

"Are you all right?" he yelled. Sarah was standing in the archway between the hall and the parlor, hands cupped to her mouth. She just nodded.

Morgan went out the front door, took a sharp right turn and saw a man darting around the corner of the house next door. He cut between the houses and made for the protection of a huge elm tree. A shot tore bark from it. Morgan wheeled and fired. It was the first good look he'd had of his antagonist. The man pumped another round out of the Henry and then turned and disappeared into an alleyway. Morgan backed against the tree and reloaded.

Morgan kicked down the door of the room above the Sawtooth saloon. Lambert was sitting on the edge of the bed. Another man leaped to his feet from a chair. Morgan slammed his fist into the man's jaw and sent him reeling. Then, he leveled the pistol at Lambert's head.

"What the hell is this all about?" Lambert's question carried audible concern and a fearful expression.

"I warned you in Picabo," Morgan said. He eyed the man he'd hit, just now shaking off the blow and trying to get to his feet. "He makes a move, you're my target, Lambert."

"I want to deal, Morgan. That's why I'm here. That's why I sent you the message."

"Followed with two gunnys . . . only they came up short."

"I swear to Christ, Morgan, they aren't my men."

"How about the man you work for, Lambert, can you speak for him too?"

"I can. I mean . . . he doesn't know anything about you. I simply told him that I had a plan that was worth more to him than Strada's niece. He gave me five days, Morgan . . . five days to deliver. Jesus! There are gunnys riding into Idaho from every direction. Those men could have worked for anybody—even the law."

"You going to deny you had me trailed?"

"Hell no . . . but my man saw what happened at the Sawtooth . . . you forget that? I know those men worked for Judge Barr. That's what convinced me that you were telling the truth."

Morgan considered Lambert's position and his words. They made sense. He looked at the man on the floor. He put both hands out and shrugged. Morgan stepped back and slowly holstered his weapon.

"Sit tight, Lambert, and tell me your deal."

"You produce Barr's daughter and bring her to Ketchum. You've got four days to do it . . . all of it. I'll have a man waiting for you. His name's Pete Walker. He'll lead you from there."

Lambert moved his hand toward his coat. Morgan drew. "Easy . . . I've got your money. All of it . . . ten thousand." He pulled a thick envelope from his inside coat pocket. He smiled. "See . . . I trust you."

Morgan took the envelope and slipped it into his pocket. Again, he holstered the S and W. "The only thing I don't like so far, Lambert, is your man. I meet *you*. *We* do the dealing."

"You didn't count the money. I figured you trusted me."

"You figured wrong. If it's not all there I'll come looking for you and I won't be so damned accomodating the next time."

"Damn it! I've got things to do . . . preparations to make so that we . . . you and I . . . get the most out of this that is possible."

"Then," Morgan said, smiling as he backed out the door, "you'd best get started. You've only got four days."

Big Ben Grafton was hauling horse feed when Morgan showed up at the livery. He jammed a pitchfork into a bale . . . hard. "I was just thinkin' about you son. You begun to be a worry to me."

"You got my answer?"

"Depends."

Morgan pulled the envelope from his pocket, rifled the bills and withdrew two one hundred dollar notes. "Your boy's money and a hundred for taking care of my horse and forgetting that you saw me today."

Grafton snatched the money from Morgan's hand. He smiled. "Don't push your luck, Grafton."

"You don't scare me none, gun man. That pistol won't help you none while I'm bustin' your ribs." He smiled again. "I figure mebbe that there message was worth a whole heap more'n a hundred."

"Don't try to run a bluff with me," Morgan said. "I picked you and your boy for the job because neither of you can read." Grafton frowned and then assumed a surly expression.

"You callin' me and mine dummies?"

"On the contrary, I knew you'd be smart enough to keep the deal to yourself. Why take a chance on losing it all?" Once again, Morgan's lightning-like right hand produced the pistol. He pointed it at Grafton's head. "The answer," Morgan said, "right now!" Then he smiled. "And tell your boy to come down out of the loft . . . real slow and careful. If he gets careless . . . you'll be the first to pay for it." Grafton's jaw dropped. "Tell him . . . *now.*"

Morgan had Grafton's son ready his gear and saddle Pacer. Then, he sent the youth to Sarah's house to fetch the rest of his belongings. Ben Grafton produced an envelope and handed it over to Morgan.

> I've left the appropriate orders with my men. You won't have any trouble on the RB and Morgana will be waiting. Nothing yet from TH. May God ride with you.
>   Isaac Barr

It was snowing again by the time Lee Morgan and Morgana Barr reached the eastern boundary of the Rocky Barr ranch. It had taken Morgan three full days to ride up from Grover, make his way to the area on the ranch where Morgana took her daily ride and pull off the bogus kidnapping. By midnight of that third day, they had reached the last of the Barr's line shacks.

"We'll get out of the cold, eat and spend the night," Morgan said. "We should get to Ketchum by noon, if we get an early start.''

Morgana prepared rabbit stew and even baked biscuits once they had warmed up. Morgan made certain the mounts were out of the weather and then the couple ate . . . mostly in silence. Afterward, with a cup of hot coffee, Morgan rolled a smoke.

"Would you do me one of those?" He looked up, surprised. She smiled. "It's quite common in San Francisco. At least among the young women. Do you find it that shocking?"

He considered her. She was strikingly beautiful and there was nothing artificial about her. He couldn't help but let his eyes roam the form beneath the buckskin, low cut top and the shapeliness of legs, emphasized by the form fitting riding breeches.

"Takes quite a lot to shock me," Morgan said.

"But that doesn't answer my question."

"No . . . I don't find it shocking." He handed her the cigarette and then held out a match. She took a long drag, leaned her head back and let the smoke seep from pursed lips. It hung in a blue haze just above her face.

"My father would," she said, looking again at Lee. He didn't get her meaning. "Find it shocking, I mean."

"Yeah . . . I'd guess he would."

"He'd find a lot of things shocking about me. San Francisco isn't Idaho. It isn't folksy little dances on Saturday nights at the local Grange hall." She sipped her coffee and then licked her lips, slowly, provocatively. "Have you ever been there?" Morgan shook his head. "You'd like it."

"Mebbe . . . but I don't like feeling cooped up . . . hemmed in. I think that's what I'd feel."

"Not if you were with the right person." Morgana suddenly slid far down on her chair and thrust out her right leg. She held it up. "Would you mind," she said "my boots?" Morgan ground out his cigarette, eyed her and then took hold of the tall, black riding boot. It came off . . . hard. The left was worse and he ended up on his ass on the floor. Morgana laughed. Morgan just grinned, sheepishly.

It might have been the horses stirring or the howl of a wolf. Either way, Morgan was awake instantly and holding the little Smith and Wesson. The fire had nearly died out and the cold was invading the shack. Morgan sat quietly on the edge of his bed just listening. Now, there was nothing but the wind off the Sawtooth and his own breathing.

He'd been staring at the floor. He looked up. There before him, silhouetted by the remaining glow of the fire, was the upside down "V" of Morgana Barr's legs. She reached out and took his face in her hands. She bent from the waist and kissed him. Her tongue darted between his lips and she lowered one hand, found one of his and lifted it to a bare breast. The nipple hardened under his touch. She stood straight again.

"Why," Morgan asked.

"Why not?" she replied. She had spread a buffalo robe on the floor near the fire. She moved to it, dropped to her knees and then slowly lowered herself down. She took the poker and stabbed at the coals. They sparked, popped and briefly flared into a small flame.

The light played across the creaminess of her stomach and the dark patch below it glistened. Lee Morgan was in no mood to question her further. He slipped out of his britches and long-johns and walked to her. He looked down.

"I like to see the man who's making love to me," she said. He shoved a large log into the fireplace and prodded it into position. Soon, it caught and the flames swelled up around it. Morgan knelt between Morgana's legs, lowered his torso and began licking her breasts.

Morgana's breath was soon coming in short, rapid gasps. Her fingers dug into the robe and she undulated her hips beneath Morgan's groin. He continued to lick, pausing, alternately, at the pink tipped summits of soft flesh.

"Gawd . . . it's been so long . . . so very, very long," she cooed. Her hands found her own thighs and rubbed their insides. Her body stiffened with the delight of it. Morgan went lower . . . lower still.

Morgana Barr climaxed almost instantly . . . but she showed no signs of wanting Morgan to stop. He didn't. His tongue worked in and out of her most intimate recesses, pausing only at the most sensitive junctures or in response to the girl's reaction.

He glanced up. She was fingering her nipples and even thrust the tips of her fingers into her mouth to moisten them . . . transferring it to the sensitive buds. His own passions had built to their peak and he now covered her with himself and carefully guided his swollen shaft, inch by inch, inside her.

"Slowly," she said in a whisper, "do it slowly . . . make it last." Morgan complied, pumping with a controlled rhythm on which he had to concentrate. He licked at her ears, nibbled at her neck and then raised up enough to slip his hands over her breasts.

Suddenly, she began to respond. It wasn't slow. It wasn't controlled. It was a frenzy of unleashed emotion. She moaned, cried out and thrust her hips so hard against his own that there were even moments of pain. He raised up so that he could take total control of the depth and speed of the activity.

"I'm . . . I'm . . . oooh . . . Jeezus," she cried.

Morgan now thrust against her and they were
pumping together. It was, finally, together that
they reached the ultimate moment, the blending of
man and woman, body and soul. Their nakedness
crashed against the buffalo robe in a final burst of
lust and then they lay, quiet, content—spent.

Ketchum, Idaho was a barely organized pile of
kindling wood in a valley of the Sawtooth
Mountains. Between Picabo to the south and
Stanley to the north, it was the only respite from
untold acres of wilderness.

It was a winter haven for the permanent
employees of two score of small ranches. There were
three saloons which doubled as bawdy houses, a
livery, general store, stage station and, of all things,
a church! The latter was the domain of one Ephram
Gregory Culpepper. He was a hell-fire and
damnation bible thumper who claimed to be a
prophet of the first order. He'd been known to shoot
a man or two who'd questioned his dubious
credentials.

It was to Parson Culpepper's church that Morgan
rode when, just after noon, he and Morgana rode
into Ketchum.

"Stay mounted," Morgan told her. He trudged
through the two feet of snow and pounded on the
door. A woman opened it. Her hair was stringy,
much of it pulled back, tight, against her head. She
wore a long, high-necked, black dress. There was no
sign of cosmetics on her face and she displayed a
perpetual frown.

"Who dost thou seek?"

"The parson," Morgan said. "Mister Culpepper."
The woman stepped back and Morgan entered. She
closed the door behind him and he followed her into

a small room, obviously the parson's study.

"Sit thee here . . . and wait," the woman said. She exited the room, closing it off behind her. Morgan peered out. Morgana remained on her horse. He felt a little guilty. It was cold and beginning to snow again.

Morgan's head turned to the sound of the sliding doors and he couldn't hide his reaction to Ephram Culpepper. The preacher could have passed for kin to Abe Lincoln. Tall, gangly, gaunt of features. His face was framed in an inch wide, inch long, black beard . . . a horseshoe shape which was trimmed to a fault. Only one feature of the man set him apart from the likes of Lincoln or any man of God Morgan had ever seen. Tied down low on his left thigh was a black holster. In it reposed a Colt's .45 Peacemaker. Culpepper smiled when he saw Morgan's eyes fall upon it.

"It's my proof to the doubters and the sinners of the world," Culpepper said. "It is spoken of in the Good Book."

"A gun?" Morgan frowned. He was no Bible scholar but he'd read some and heard aplenty.

Culpepper grinned, perhaps at his own interpretation. "Blessed are the peacemakers," he quoted. "For they shall be called the children of God."

In a flash, Culpepper's long, slim fingers curled around the butt. He moved with the precision only practice can bring. He displayed the Curly Bill spin, the border shift, three fast draws and ended by flipping the weapon into the air, catching it after a two and a half twist and holstering it. "I can shoot with the same precision," he said dryly. "If I salvage no souls, I am at least assured of their undivided attention and I am free of hecklers."

"I'll remember that," Morgan said, clearly

impressed. He glanced again out of the window at Morgana. Then he said, "I am given to understand that you know why I'm here." Culpepper nodded. "You'll take the woman in?"

"I will . . . and you can feel safe about her."

"Yeah . . . I feel a hell of a lot better about leaving her here than I did before."

Culpepper reached into his inside coat pocket and withdrew an envelope. "I've written the letter as the good judge asked. It will verify Miss Barr's presence and states that she will be released upon receipt of the appropriate sum. Also in the envelope is Judge Barr's own letter to me . . . for your own verification."

Morgan read both, looked up and nodded. "If I get what I want . . . a meeting with the top man, I'll get word to you."

"And if you don't?"

"No plan, friend," Morgan said. "Use your own discretion."

"Mister Lambert *is* in Ketchum . . . Addie Terhune's place."

"You know for sure?"

Culpepper nodded. "I know. I know Lambert. Shot up two of his men one time."

Morgan smiled. "Wouldn't attend services?"

Culpepper wasn't smiling. "Beat up one of Addie's girls . . . real bad. Didn't want to crawl back on their hands and knees and apologize and then ask for Divine forgiveness. I saw to it they got another chance . . . face-to-face with their Creator."

"You a friend of Adele Terhune's?"

"Am now," Culpepper said. "Used to be her husband . . . twenty years ago. She is what she is because of me. I left her destitute. Now . . . I'm working off the debt."

"A Bible-thumping gun slinger," Morgan said, shaking his head in wonderment, "you really believe Jesus would have done the same?"

"Don't know," Culpepper replied, scratching at his beard thoughtfully. Then he smiled, "But he had a dozen men working for him that I figure would have."

"You're my kind of preacher, *Reverend* Culpepper," Morgan said. "I'll be in touch."

The ride to Addie Terhune's saloon and whorehouse was a short one but Morgan felt better than he had in several days. He knew now that Morgana would be safe and he was in a position to make demands which would, almost certainly, get him on the inside.

Culpepper knew whereof he spoke. Lambert and two gunnys were ensconced in Addie's best room. Morgan eyed the two men with disdain and Lambert dismissed them with but a nod of his head.

"Where's the girl?"

"Safe."

"We had a deal Morgan."

"Had is right," Morgan replied. "Things have changed." Lambert was livid. "I can offer more than just the girl . . . and I want in on the action against the Rocky Barr . . . direct!"

"You son-of-a-bitch! I stuck my fuckin' neck out a long ways for you." Lambert was on the verge of trying Morgan. Morgan knew it. He shoved the sheepskin coat away from his hip. Lambert's fingers were flexing. Morgan smiled. "I don't deliver . . . we're *both* dead men."

"Uh uh," Morgan said, pointing with his left hand at himself, "not me. I can deliver . . . and right now Lambert . . . what I can deliver is a helluva lot more important to your boss than you are."

"Look," Lambert said, relaxing his fingers and sounding more pleading than angry, "I told . . . uh . . . my people that I'd deliver a bigger fish than Strada's niece tomorrow. Hell . . . even if I *wanted* to deal with you there isn't time."

"There's time. You're less than a day's ride from your people." Morgan took off his coat, sat down and began to roll a smoke. "I can deliver Morgana Barr within six hours. I want in for the raid on Barr's ranch . . . another ten thousand for the additional information I've got and the ten percent we talked about."

Morgan spit out a loose piece of tobacco, wet his lips and lit the cigarette. He looked up at an astonished Jake Lambert and added, "And I want to meet the top men . . . here."

"You're fucking crazy Morgan. I've got enough men to handle you. You might get some of 'em . . . but you can't get 'em all. The answer is *no*!"

"And what's your boss gonna say about that?"

"Nothing," Lambert replied, grinning. "He'll never know anything except what I tell him. That'll be that you tried a double-cross and I had you killed."

"And when he finds out the truth?"

"He won't."

"The hell he won't. Damn near any man you've got working for you would sell you out in a heartbeat for the right money and I've got the *right* money. Ten thousand, Lambert. You gave it to me yourself."

"You rotten bastard!"

"Relax, Lambert. I'm not crossing you. I'm just sweetening up the pot for both of us. Play the hand," Morgan said, "you've got a sure draw to an inside straight and you're in too deep to fold."

Jake Lambert made one, final, pathetic plea to Lee Morgan. "Damn it Morgan . . . there just isn't time. I'm most of a day's ride from my contact. He expects me to ride in there with the girl late tomorrow. I can't ride in without her."

"You could if you rode in early . . . like tomorrow morning."

"Now how in the hell am I going . . . to . . . do . . ." Bullshit! It's snowin' like a son-of-a-bitch out there . . . and cold. Goddam it . . . I'm not leavin' tonight. Tomorrow's ride is bad enough."

Morgan shrugged. "It's up to you," he said.

Morgan stood up, butted his cigarette and slipped on the sheepskin coat. He walked to the door, opened it and then turned around. "I'll be downstairs . . . at least 'til midnight. If you change your mind, let me know. If not I'll do the next best thing."

Morgan was half way through the saloon, wondering if he had pushed too hard. A man . . . any man, could only be pushed so far. Jake Lambert had been pushed since the day they first met and Lee Morgan had done all the pushing. He'd learned first from his father and then from first hand experience, that being surprised in a fight could be fatal. He thought he'd gauged Lambert correctly. But what if he hadn't.

He looked up at the poker table to which he was headed. The man on the far side of the table glanced at Morgan and then his eyes shifted to a spot just above Morgan's head and behind him. The man started a movement to his right, off his chair.

"Jeezus!" the man shouted. Morgan's right hand moved like the bull whip and came up with the S and W. He crouched, spun to his left and fired. He was only shooting from the memory he had of the stairway. He fired a little low.

His shot struck Jake's gunny in the groin,
traveled upward, obliquely, and severed his spine.
He fell forward, over the bannister and somer-
saulted through the air, landing on the end of the
bar . . . dead! A half a dozen pellets from the shotgun ripped into Morgan's left coat sleeve. Two of
them pierced coat and shirt and longjohns. Morgan
felt the sting against his flesh.

The second man's shot took Morgan's hat off.
Morgan killed him. The .38 smashed into his chest,
dead center. The door opened and Ephram
Culpepper stepped inside, ducking a little to do it.
Morgan saw him draw and fire just left of Morgan's
position. There was grunt and then a body toppling
over chairs and crashing to the floor. Culpepper
holstered the Peacemaker.

"Let he that thinketh he standeth take heed lest
he fall." Morgan turned. One of Lambert's gunnys
lay dying. A man Morgan had never seen. "Addie
overheard the gentlemen upstairs planning your
untimely end," Culpepper said. "One of her girls
came by to let me know about it."

"I owe you," Morgan said.

"A small contribution to my humble ministry will
suffice." Culpepper's eyes then shifted to the
balcony. Addie Terhune was standing there and
pointing down the corridor. Morgan holstered his
gun and went upstairs.

"You're all alone, Lambert. I told you to play out
the hand. Too bad. Now you're out of the game."
The door opened and Lambert stepped into the
hallway. He had both hands in the air.

"We can still deal," he said. "I . . . I got scared.
I'm dealing with powerful people. You'd understand
if you knew them. Jeezus Morgan . . . please . . . I

know I can't take you . . . I know it. Just give me a
chance to ride out. I can still make the deal . . . just
let me ride out."

Lee Morgan had been in the spot before. He knew
the outcome already. He even knew how it would
come about. He backed up to the stairway, turned
and started down. Jake Lambert made his move. He
was pretty good. He was also scared and he was
much too fast to be accurate. Morgan killed him.

7

Tom Horn had decided to get himself warm and have a cup of coffee. Why waste a perfectly good line shack and a hot stove? Besides, he had some figuring to do. Strada's niece had obviously been held in that shack. Strada had been there only minutes ago. Horn was deeply disturbed by that turn of events. He'd seen it before. The big land company . . . or the railroad . . . or whoever . . . finally gets to someone inside the ranch owner's association. Was it Strada?

Then again, Horn knew it could be almost anyone in the group. Nearly every man would have the opportunity to get onto Strada's ranch and kidnap his relative. It would certainly keep the attention off of them . . . or at least most men wouldn't look for an inside connection. But Tom Horn wasn't most men. He had the distinct feeling that Lee Morgan wasn't either.

He heard the horse snort. Someone was back. He grabbed the Creedmoor, leaned his chair back against the wall for support and waited. The door latch lifted. He heard the man outside shift his weight and cock his pistol. He'd shoot first, Horn thought, and worry about whom he'd shot later. Horn pulled the Creedmoor back until the butt plate rested against the wall. Then he pulled the trigger.

The .44-90 took out a chunk of the door the size of a dinner plate. The old, rotting wood just splintered. Most of it was driven into the man's chest and abdomen. The slug from the Creedmoor did the rest.

Horn sat in the silence after the reverberations of the shot had died away. He listened. There was no sound. He opened the door, moving slowly, carefully. The snow in front of the shack was a dirty pink. The man's face was frozen into a quizzical expression. Horn stepped over his body and found the tracks where he'd ridden in. Two sets of tracks headed south . . . only one set coming back.

He returned, knelt down and removed the man's hat. It had partially covered his face. "I'll be goddamned," Horn said, aloud. "Toby Summers." Horn studied the man's face . . . a confirmation of his first belief and then he looked south. "There's suthin' *big* afoot," he said.

He pushed himself to his feet with the Creedmoor as a crutch. He stood it against the wall of the shack and commenced to bring the men's bodies inside. That done, Tom Horn headed for his mount. Whatever was going on . . . it was south of where he was and he intended to find out.

Of all the puzzlements to date, the appearance of Toby Summers was the most disturbing to Horn. Summers had a reputation as one of the best bounty hunters still alive. He didn't work cheap when he worked at all. In recent years, that had become more common. Many states now outlawed bounty men and rewards being payed were far below what they had been in the mid eighties. Mostly though, Summers had made a habit of never working for an organization . . . only a man . . . one man and Summers had to be certain that his employer was

the top man. Either he'd softened with age and
grown careless or he was working for Ben Strada.

The break in the trail was clear enough for a blind
man to follow. A single set of hoof prints trailed off
to the southwest. That would be Ben Strada. Tom
Horn studied his map of the country. About eight
miles distant was the Killerman Ranch, the Rocking
K. The other set of tracks veered east and a little
north. A wagon . . . not heavily loaded and pulled by
only one animal . . . and a rider on horseback.

Horn stood up in the stirrups and took a slow, half
turn of the horizon. Nothing unusual. He sat back
down, took a final glance toward the Killerman place
and then turned east. First things first and he was
looking for Gunsmoke Gorge . . . not Ben Strada.

Tom Horn's eyes scanned ahead constantly. He
was riding in the open. He didn't like it. He stopped
several times to get his bearings. He was grateful,
finally, when he saw the stream called Leadore.
Once he crossed it, a stand of trees paralleled the
tracks he was following. He'd have some cover.

The pack mule bellowed, the tether line grew taut
and Horn's mount dug in, whinnied and then
balked. Horn still cradled the Creedmoor and as he
slipped from his horse, he freed up the Winchester.
The sickening sound of an arrow burying itself in
flesh now reached his ears. The mule toppled over. A
second arrow already protruded from the animal's
side.

"*Whhewt . . . thunk!*" His horse reared. Horn
could see the arrow in the animal's neck. In a crouch,
Tom Horn darted for the opposite bank of the creek.
The skimpy shelter it provided was limited to a
boulder or two.

Two more arrows assured that Tom Horn would
walk from this place, if he got away from it at all.

The water was icy cold . . . knee deep. He would not long be able to stay in the water. Far across the creek in the tree line where he'd hoped to find some cover, he saw movement. One man . . . two. For sure . . . two.

"Horn," he whispered to himself, "b'lieve you got yourself in a tight." He looked in both directions. Behind him there was a creek wash. It led back northwest and into some trees. Thing was . . . it was better than 150 yards to the wash . . . all open ground.

The ricochet of the rifle bullet off the boulder just inches above Tom's head, answered the question he'd been asking himself. Did his pursuer . . . or pursuers, have anything other than bows and arrows? Another shot was closer. A third spattered rock chips against his coat. It had come from a different angle.

"Two it is, Tom," he said, "an' in a minute, them fellas is goin' to have you in a crossfire." A few feet from him, he spotted a snagged tree limb. He eased toward it. Another shot was way off the mark. Both men were re-positioning. Tom freed up his Bowie, slit a hole in his denims at about calf height. He slipped a sturdy part of the snag through the hole. He let his weight fall back . . . pulling on it. The denim ripped a little more . . . then held.

A rifle shot hit the water in front of him and he heard the bullet beneath its surface. He wedged the Creedmoor down beside him and then pumped a round into the Winchester's chamber. Another shot from his front side struck the rock, chipping it. He felt grains of sand strike his cheek.

Now, Horn slipped the Winchester between his knees, tested the water's depth, nodded, smiling and picked up the Creedmoor. A shot came from behind

him. It was close . . . too close. He turned, hefted the
Creedmoor and fired a round at nothing. He ducked
down. None too soon. Another shot struck the
boulder which, a moment before, had been hidden by
his head!

Tom pushed with all his strength against the
creek bottom. He went staight up and then
backward. The Creedmoor flew from his hand and
landed, ten feet away, in the water. It gurgled out of
sight. Tom landed on his back and disappeared. The
current tugged at him but the snag and the denim
britches held. His upper body floated to the top
until his face was out of the water. The only other
thing above the surface was about two inches of the
Winchester's barrel.

"Sure givin' that water proofin' elixir o' your'n a
test, Mister Winchester," Tom said to himself. A
moment later, he heard legs splashing into the water
from in front of him.

"I think I got him," the man yelled.

"You'd better make sure." The splashing stopped
. . . thirty to forty yards. Tom tilted his head
forward slightly. He could see a man. He was
dressed in buckskins and a buffalo coat. He was
raising a rifle to his shoulder. Tom Horn pulled with
all his strength against the snag. He submerged.
The shot, deflected by the water, ripped into his coat
just at the collar. He could feel the pull but no pain.

"I just made sure," the man yelled.

There was splashing in the water behind him. His
lungs were tightening. The rifle was totally submerged. He couldn't risk the shot. He pulled again
with his leg and struggled, underwater, to free
himself from the snag. The splashing in front of him
was very near. Tom Horn opened his eyes. He could
see leather boots.

The man was upon him. Tom stood straight up,
coming out of the water with an old Indian yell and
sounding like a banshee. He swung the Winchester
like a sledge-hammer, full from behind him. The
stock cracked and so did the man's skull. Tom went
forward . . . back into the water, face down.

"Son-of-a-bitch!" The voice was behind him. Tom
grabbed the man's rifle as it entered the water and
then rolled to his left, struggling to regain his
footing. He struck a rock and felt a sharp pain on the
back of his head. He pulled his knees up to his chest
and pushed.

Two shots entered the water where Tom had been.
He reasoned that one or both of them must have
struck the body of the other man. Tom came out of
the water and fired three shots from the Henry in
rapid succession. Two of them struck their intended
target. One in the shoulder, the other in the side.
The man went down.

Tom Horn dragged the wounded man from the
creek, hog-tied him and then went back to the water.
He retrieved his weapons and then dragged the first
man's body from the water. He knew he'd have to
move fast if he was to keep from freezing to death.

The wounded man was white. His companion had
been an Indian or at least a half-breed. Horn was
lucky to be alive. The man was now howling for help.
Horn ignored him. The wounds would freeze shut so
the man wouldn't bleed to death. At least he'd live
long enough to tell Horn a few things.

Horn unpacked his gear, lugged it to a clearing
about forty yards into the trees. He knew it was
risky, but he had to build a fire. He did. He stripped
out of his half frozen clothing, got himself dry and
put on plenty of dry, warm clothing. He unloaded all
his weapons and broke them down to dry their

working parts.

Those things done, he went back and carried the wounded man over by the fire. "You're a dead man, son, so you might as well tell me what I want to know. You an' your friend have horses."

"God mister . . . please . . . please. There's a doc. He can save me. *Please*."

"A doc?"

"In the camp. Six, seven miles." The man coughed. He'd warmed some and the bleeding had started again. "Our horses are tied south—about half a mile back. Jesus! You can't just let me die."

"This camp," Horn said. "Is it called Gunsmoke Gorge?" The man nodded. "Who do you work for?"

"Oh God . . . please mister . . . help me."

"Talk to me, son . . . if you want relief."

The man nodded. "I don't know the big boss . . . just the ramrod. Name's Brock." The man coughed and winced. The bleeding in his side was profuse. "That's . . ." he coughed . . . "that's all I know, Mister."

Tom Horn looked up at the sky. It would be dark in less than an hour. He still had the horses to find. He knelt beside the man, cut open his shirt and examined the wound in his side. It was bad. If he could get quick medical attention, he would live. Otherwise, he'd bleed to death.

"I can't take you to that camp," Horn said, standing up. "I'd get killed. You wouldn't make it on your own and it's too damned far to the Killerman spread. I got no doctorin' supplies with me for anything that bad." Horn turned, picked up the Henry the other man had been carrying and walked back to his prisoner.

"Mister," the man coughed, "God . . . what . . . what are you gonna do?"

"Recognize that I can't help you and try to remember that you tried to kill me . . . you no good bastard." Tom Horn pulled the trigger.

Addie Terhune kicked on Morgan's door. "Got some breakfast for you," she shouted. A moment later, Morgan opened the door. While he washed his face and finished dressing, Addie prepared a place to eat. "You didn't fare so well last night, did you?"

" 'Bout three hundred . . . give or take twenty dollars one way or the other."

"You usually that bad at poker?"

"If I was," he said, smiling, "I'd damned well quit."

"Well, better luck next time." She started for the door.

"I don't like eatin' alone . . . I get plenty o' that."

"I've had breakfast . . . two hours ago."

"How about some coffee?"

"And some *answers,*" she asked, smiling.

"You got'ny?"

"I doubt it."

"You mind bein' asked?" She shrugged. Morgan ate his eggs and a slice of toast washed down with two swallows of coffee. Then he looked up. "What do you know about what's going on in Idaho?"

"It's bad for business . . . sometimes anyhow. I get plenty of customers . . . from both sides . . . but mostly . . . I get trouble just like ever'body else."

"That it?"

"That's enough. I'm not buyin' more trouble than I already got, Mister Morgan."

"You got as big a stake in this as most ranchers. Why not?"

" 'Cause I'm not rooted like them ranchers. I can move on to any two-bit cow town around. Minin' camps too . . . or lumberin'." She smiled. "Men are the same no matter what they do for a livin'."

"No names . . . no faces . . . no locations?" Morgan considered her. He went back to eating and waited for a reply. He got it.

"Nope."

"Then tell me about the preacher."

She laughed. "The Reverend Mister Culpepper. Reason he's a preacher is 'cause o' the fact he's already been damn near ever'thing else. Not worth a tinker's damn at any of 'em . . . 'ceptin' for shootin'. Now at *that* . . . there's not too many better."

Morgan finished his breakfast and poured more coffee.

"You want that coffee spiced up a bit?" He nodded. She slipped a hand under her dress, lifted it to her thigh and revealed a small, silver flask. It was held in place by a garter. She took off the lid and poured half the contents into Morgan's coffee and the other half into hers.

"I thought women like you carried a knife or a Deringer in that spot." She raised the dress again, lifted up her other leg and Morgan saw the Deringer. His eyes trailed above the gun. She grinned.

"That's not for sale anymore."

"What kind of a man does it take to get it?"

"One I like," Addie replied, "an' it takes me longer to figure out if I like somebody than it used to."

"Anything special you look for?"

"Yeah . . . one that don't ask too many questions."

"You helped the other night. Was that for Culpepper?"

"That was for Addie Terhune. I don't like Lambert . . . that is . . . I didn't. I don't like anybody gettin' backshot . . . an' I don't like others gettin' the idea that this place can be used for their personal business . . . good, bad or otherwise.''

"Can you trust the preacher?"

"If he likes you . . . yes."

"He don't know me that well."

"He's not doing it for you . . . he's doing it for the judge."

"Then you *do* know."

"I know he's helpin' Judge Barr. I don't want to know anything else." She got up. "I've got work to do."

"I'm obliged for the breakfast."

"Don't be . . . it'll be on your bill."

It had been three days since Morgan's confrontation with Jake Lambert. He'd concluded that someone would come looking. Now he was beginning to wonder. He was also wondering about Morgana Barr but he didn't expose the connection with Culpepper more than it had been. Just after noon, another knock came at his door.

"Yeah." Morgan had his pistol leveled at one of the panels, about belly high.

"Miss Addie says to tell you there's a man in her office who wants to see you . . . a gun drummer."

Addie let Morgan in and then took her leave. "Mason," Morgan said, smiling, "before anything else, I'll tell you now that your Smith and Wesson is a fine piece."

"I knew you'd find it so, Mister Morgan. Later . . . we'll settle accounts." Morgan nodded. "I've a message for you." He handed Morgan an envelope and then walked to the door.

"Hold it, Mason. You been to the ranch?"

"Good afternoon, Mister Morgan." Mason walked out. Morgan was angry. He opened the door to yell at Mason but thought better of it. After all, he

didn't know who else might be in Addie's place. He
closed the door, ripped open the envelope and read.

> I appreciate what you and others have
> tried to do. I really believed if we banded
> together we could stand against these
> men. I know now that we cannot . . . and
> the risks are too great. Please return at
> once with my *property*.

>   Isaac Barr

Judge Barr buckling under! Morgan couldn't
believe it. No man he'd known, save for his father,
had been stronger and more principled then Judge
Isaac Barr. He read the note again. He sat down.
Perhaps Tom Horn had learned something, he
thought. Or perhaps the judge was just too
concerned for Morgana's life.

"Damn!" Morgan was up against something he
hadn't often had to face. He didn't know what to do.
The door opened. It was Addie Terhune and she
looked scared!

"Addie?" Suddenly, she was shoved inside the
office. Behind her, two men appeared from either
side of the door. Both were leveling shotguns at
Morgan. He started to get up.

"Stay put," the first man said. He stepped inside,
looked around quickly and then re-focused on
Morgan. The second man was whispering to a third.
In a moment, he entered the office as well and shut
the door behind him.

"We've got a bit of a wait," the first man said, "so
the lady here can pour us all a drink." The second
man moved to Morgan's side and relieved him of the
S and W pistol. Two minutes later, the door opened

again and Mason stumbled through it. Behind him, a third man.

Before anyone could say anymore, a fourth man came into the office. He was well dressed but armed with a cross-draw style, waist belt holster.

"Morgan, I'm Harv Jessup. You killed four men who worked for me. Jake Lambert was one of them. That was very costly, very costly indeed. Nonetheless, I was told you could do something for me. If what I heard was true," he smiled, "then I would be of a mind to forget all about the cost. I'll ask you just once. Is it true?"

"I talk to the top man." One of the men holding a shotgun slammed the stock into Morgan's back between the shoulder blades. He groaned and went to his knees.

"I'll tell you now, Morgan, the next time I want him to use that shotgun, he'll use the other end. You're as high as you're going to get . . . at least for now."

Morgan got to his feet. He pulled his shoulders back and flexed his back muscles to ease the pain. "It's true," he said.

"You've got the girl?"

"I've got her."

"Where?"

"Now, Mister Jessup, you've gone as high as you go." Morgan smiled. "At least for now."

"Don't make the mistake of pushing me, Morgan. I'm not Jake Lambert."

"Exactly," Morgan said, "and that makes the difference between the real value of my participation and the double-cross that Lambert planned."

"Double-cross?" Jessup considered Morgan. "You telling me that Jake Lambert double-crossed you?''

"Not me . . . you, Mister Jessup. And whoever else is involved. I've got brains enough to figure out that I'm not up against a few cheap guns . . . and I'm not that greedy." Morgan sat back down, leaned back and feigned complete relaxation. "Why don't I tell you everything and then you tell me what it's worth?"

"Yes, Mister Morgan, why don't you?"

"The rancher's association hired a man killer—a professional. I'm not talking about a gunny. I'm talking about a *hunter*. A man who stalks his prey and kills him and moves on. He'll chip away at you." Morgan grinned. "My guess is that he's already started."

"And you know who this man is?"

"I do . . . and pretty much where to find him."

"How?"

"Mister Mason here. He's my contact with the ranchers." Morgan eyed Mason. He could see Mason's fear, but all he could do was hope that Mason would play along. "That's why he came to see me this morning . . . to let me know the whereabouts of the man the association hired . . . and to collect."

"Collect?"

"His pay. Five thousand."

Jessup looked doubtful. "That's a lot of money, Morgan. Just who was going to pay him?"

"*I pay him,*" Morgan replied, "it's . . . well, call it an investment. I'll get it back."

"From where . . . or should I say . . . from *who*?"

"Either from you and your people or directly from Judge Barr."

"All right, Morgan. Who's this man killer?"

"Tom Horn."

Jessup was incredulous. "That's just a name," Jessup finally said. Morgan knew the man was fishing and trying to maintain a composure he didn't feel. "Can you prove that?"

Morgan chuckled. "Everyone of you damned people ask the same question. Lambert asked me what I could prove too." Morgan got to his feet.

The man behind him, holding the shotgun, stepped forward. Jessup held up his hand. Morgan glanced back at the shotgun man. He grinned. He turned back to Jessup. "I've got Judge Barr's daughter . . . you've got Ben Strada's niece and I know where Tom Horn is looking. Which of those things do you think will bring the most results, Jessup?"

"Where's he looking?"

"You want it *all* from me, don't you?"

"You've got the girl. She's your security." Jessup smiled now. "Unless you're lying."

"But you already know I'm not," Morgan said. "That's the reason it took you three days to contact me. I've got her and Tom Horn is snooping around up in the Bitterroots." Morgan could see the slightest change in Jessup's demeanor. Although he hated to run the risk of Horn being found, he'd have to play out the charade.

"A well hidden gorge, Jessup. Folks hereabouts call it Gunsmoke Gorge."

"You're guessing."

Morgan laughed. "That's a marked improvement, Mister Jessup. A few minutes ago I was a liar. Now I'm a guesser. You forget," Morgan said, "I was raised in these parts. I expect I know the country about as well as any man . . . better'n most . . . sure as hell better'n Horn. Now eventually, he'll sniff you out. Whole thing is for somebody to find Horn before he finds you.''

"And that somebody is you. Am I right?''

"I want three things," Morgan said. "I want the chance to ride with you when the Rocky Barr is taken out. By my reckoning, the judge will buckle under to save his daughter. I want a third of the ransom money.''

"And what do you want for taking out Tom Horn?''

"Whatever the rancher's association was paying him . . . and the reputation for the job . . . whether I do it alone or not.''

"That's all?''

"That's two. The Rocky Barr and the ransom go together, Jessup.''

"All right, Morgan . . . what's the big payoff?''

"A job with the *top* man in your organization . . . permanent and with all the benefits.''

"What makes you think there is such a man or such a job?''

"Because you don't have the stock for taking over half of Idaho. That will take a big cattle or railroad operation." Morgan smiled. "As for the job, yours will do fine." He added, hastily, "or one just like it.'' Jessup found no humor in Morgan's latter comments but he obviously had come to Ketchum to deal.

"I can deliver on all of those things, Morgan, except possibly one. You said you wanted in when the Rocky Barr is wiped out. If the judge agrees to get out that will be the ransom. If he's out, there's no need to destroy it.''

"Bullshit! Your people want land . . . not buildings. I want to see it burn.''

"Why?''

"That's my business and it's going to stay that

way, Jessup. As to the ransom. . . your people can pay me a third of what it's worth to them to acquire it.''

"You deliver the girl to me today . . . here. I'll get back to you about Horn.''

"Uh uh. I ride back with you. I talk to the top man with you. If everything is like you tell me it is, Mason here will deliver the girl. We can pick a spot later and I'll get word back to him. When the exchange is made I'll go after Horn.''

"I told you, Morgan . . . you're as high as you go . . . for now.''

"You told me that when we started this, Jessup. Now we're finished. Take it or leave it.''

"I told you, Morgan . . . don't push me.''

"And I'm telling you Jessup . . . we do it that way or I'll take what I can get for Morgana Barr and ride out.''

"You're a smarter man than I gave you credit for,'' Jessup said, smiling. "All right, Morgan, we'll do it your way.'' He turned to his men. "Get the horses and get ready to ride out. Zeke . . . you stay here with Mister Morgan and our hostess. If things don't go well you know what to do.'' He turned and smiled at Morgan. "My insurance . . . Mister Morgan.''

8

Lee Morgan was on the inside. The young, steely-eyed gunman found himself the object of considerable attention as he and Harv Jessup rode into the very bowels of Gunsmoke Gorge. Plenty of money had been spent to establish the base camp. Mogan could only guess of course, but he estimated facilities for about a hundred men.

Futher, Morgan figured it was about five miles from the entrance, well hidden and well guarded, to the lone, wooden building in the camp.

"All the comforts," Morgan observed as he and Jessup dismounted. "At least for the ramrods." It was cold. Morgan glanced back at the rows of tents pitched on either side of the rocky gorge. They housed the riders.

"They're all equipped with coal oil stoves," Jessup said. "Besides, it's perfectly safe to build fires down in here." He pointed to the sheer rock walls on either side. "There's a constant wind at the top. Flattens the smoke out and disperses it before it ever carries too high. You'd have to be within a mile to see it." He grinned. "Even then, Morgan, what the hell good would it do you?"

"None," Morgan said, "from what I could see when we were riding in. I'm impressed."

He was even more impressed inside the two room

shack. The raiders were listed in varying unit strengths with military precision. On the wall, behind the only desk, a topographical map indicated Idaho ranches. Marked in red were those which had been destroyed. Green indicated those still in operation. Yellow marked ranches which had simply been abandoned by frightened families.

Morgan turned to his left at the sound of footsteps. Emerging from the small bedroom was a tall, distinguished looking, well dressed man. he was attired in a suit but Morgan could see the telltale bulge of a shoulder holster.

"This is Lee Morgan," Jessup said. "He wants in. He looks and sounds as though he'd fit and he's got a head start on contributing to our cause."

The man nodded at Jessup and gave Morgan a studied going over.

"I'm Brock," he said. "That's name enough." He moved over behind the desk. "A drink, Mister Morgan?"

"Yeah . . . fine."

Brock poured three. Morgan noted the small quantity. "Welcome," Brock said. They all drank. Brock nodded for Jessup and Morgan to sit. They did. "One of Harv's men rode in late last night. He told me what you've done. . . who you've got and what you want. I know something of your background, Mister Morgan, so I'll ask the question. *Why?*"

"Because Judge Isaac Barr was responsible for my father's death," Morgan lied. "Indirectly, anyhow."

"I'm not in this to aid men in carrying out personal vendettas, Mister Morgan. There is too much at stake."

"I know what's at stake . . . at least enough to

know I want in." Morgan was cool, relaxed and felt on sure footing. "Old man Barr is just a bonus I'll get out of it."

"Your demands are . . . shall we say . . . quite ambitious."

"Yeah . . . but what I can deliver is more than you've been able to accomplish. Eventually, the army will get dragged into this unless you do the job quick and clean. I don't think even what you've got here is adequate if that happens."

"Of course, sir, you are correct. That's why you've been permitted to live this long." Brock leaned back and put his fingertips together. "But make no mistake, Mister Morgan, you'll be expected to deliver your end, in full, before I'm convinced."

"I don't have a problem with that Brock . . . just with bastards that try to double-cross me."

"Yes. . . I can appreciate that and, frankly, I don't understand what happened to Mister Lambert. If, in fact, he did try such a thing, you only did what I would have had to order done anyway. You see if we allow that kind of thing, we'll soon have no trust from those men outside. It is them upon whom we rely to get the job done."

"You doubting my word about Lambert?"

"It's academic isn't it? He's certainly in no position to defend himself against your accusations. Let's just say that I'll be both happy and convinced if you can deliver on your claims. If not, I'll have you killed, Mister Morgan. It's really just that simple."

"And if I *do* deliver?"

"Your demands . . . or shall we call them requests . . . will be met. No questions asked."

"What's your reaction to Morgan's claim about Tom Horn?" Jessup asked. He looked at Morgan as he posed the question.

"Someone is out there. We've already taken losses," Brock said. "One man . . . particularly one with Horn's reputation, can be more damaging to us than a cavalry company. He *must* be stopped." Brock leaned forward. "Whether or not it's Tom Horn really doesn't matter, does it, Jessup?"

"I guess not."

"Morgan," Brock said, getting to his feet, "you write up the necessary message to get the Barr woman up here. Once that's done, Tom Horn is all yours." Brock smiled. "Make certain you live to collect, Mister Morgan."

"If I don't, you're the winner again aren't you?"

"I'd say so. Not even Tom Horn can take all my men out. Now then, Jessup will arrange quarters for you."

"I want to see Strada's neice." Jessup's head jerked toward Morgan. Brock frowned. "I don't want Morgana Barr killed no matter what happens. If Strada's niece is actually up here . . . still alive . . . then I want to know it for certain."

"You have other plans for Miss Barr," Brock asked, grinning.

"Let's just say I want her breathing and leave it at that."

"You've got iron, Mister Morgan. A lot of iron. If you're what you seem, we'll get along just fine. Very well then, Jessup will take you to the girl. One more thing, Mister Morgan."

"Yeah?"

"There are two small ranches just this side of Killerman's place. Joe Galbraith and Todd Blaisdell. They've given us some trouble."

"What about it?'

"We're taking them out—in the morning," Brock

said, smiling. "I'd like you to lead one of the raiding parties. You can have your choice. It's just that everyone in the Gorge has to earn their keep. In your case . . . until you've done for us what you say you can . . . this will be, uh, a token gesture of good faith. Any problems with that, Mister Morgan?"

There were plenty and Morgan knew it but there wasn't a damned thing he could do about it. He didn't dare even hesitate. "None at all, Brock. I'll take the Blaisdell place. I met Galbraith once . . . a long time back but there's no use taking chances."

"Very good Mister Morgan . . . yes . . . very good indeed. The men will form up at dawn."

"I'll be ready."

Harv Jessup led Morgan to an isolated tent behind the house. Two men guarded it. "The girl's in there," Jessup said. Morgan nodded, ducked low and entered. Instantly, he put his index finger to his lips. The girl frowned. She was tied but not gagged. He knelt by her.

"You're about to have company," he said, loudly. "Morgana Barr. I imagine you know her . . . don't you?" The girl's eyes showed fear but she nodded.

Morgan leaned down and pulled her head close to him. "Don't make a sound," he whispered. "I'm here to get you out. It won't happen right away . . . but you'll be safe." He got up and looked into her face. Such a tactic was always risky. She blinked. He could see the moisture in her eyes. She nodded.

Morgan left the tent. Jessup was standing nearby talking to one of the guards. He turned. "You satisfied?" Morgan nodded. "Then let's get you bedded down. Sounds like you've got some riding to do in the morning." Morgan knew Jessup was particularly pleased that Brock had ordered the rails and collared Morgan to lead one of them. As for Lee

. . . he didn't know what the hell he was going to do.

Tom Horn, by contrast, knew exactly what he was going to do. He found a cutaway in a craggy, rock wall and made camp. There was a light snow beginning to fall again but inside the cutaway, he could build a fire. It also provided a good vantage point from which to view the valley below. Just half an hour earlier, he'd spotted a lone rider headed west. He assumed it to be one of the raiders and decided to gamble that, eventually, the man would return. At that point, Tom would trail him to Gunsmoke Gorge. In fact, the man Horn had seen was the messenger riding out to fetch back Judge Barr's daughter.

During the three days that Morgan had cooled his heels in Ketchum, Horn had followed several trails. Thus far, all of them had been dead ends.

After his encounter with his would-be killers, Horn doubled back to the Killerman ranch. There, he spent the night and learned that Ben Strada had not been at the ranch. It puzzled him, given the trail he followed which he believed was Strada's. Killerman himself was none too receptive to Horn. He'd voted against Horn's hiring. Josh Killerman was a man who believed negotiation was the best settlement of dispute.

On the second day out, Tom had hoped to pick up Strada's trail again but a new snowfall stifled the effort. Instead, he stopped by several small ranches and visited with their owners. He did his best to bolster their spirits. Most of them had heard about Strada's niece and they were certain Strada would knuckle under. If he went Killerman would follow. Soon, the small ranch owners would be on their own. That, Horn knew, would finish them.

He spent most of the third day swinging far to the southeast. If he was going to approach the Gunsmoke Gorge area again, it would have to be from a direction much less obvious than the one he tried earlier. His trail brought him to the rocky cutaway and his present campsite.

Dawn brought a familiar sound to Tom Horn's ears. The rumble of distant hoofbeats . . . a lot of them. He grabbed the Creedmoor and moved outside the cutaway.

"Movin' out fer a raid," he said to himself, aloud. He counted more than thirty riders. They were following about the same trail that the lone rider he'd seen the day before taking. "Well, sir . . . they hired me. Guess I'd best earn my keep." He hurried back to the cave and picked up both his Winchester and the Henry he'd taken from one of his two assailants. He dug into his gear and produced two boxes of ammunition.

By the time he got back to his vantage point, the lead riders were almost parallel with him. He'd wait a moment more. The Creedmoor would furnish his introduction. He figured he could take at least two men out before the riders would react. After that, he'd use the repeaters and go after some of the mounts. As for himself, he was in the best possible position. Completely out of reach of his enemies. The only way up was the way he'd come and those riders were nearly three miles away from the trail.

He line sighted the fifth man from the end and fired. The Creedmoor sounded like a Napoleon gun among the rocks. The man dropped. Two riders behind him pulled up short. He slammed another .44-90 into the chamber and fired again. Another man dropped. He hefted the Henry.

"Where the fuck is he?" one of the men screamed. Several dismounted and found the best cover they could. The lead riders turned and stopped. Even at horses, the distance provided a real challenge for a marksman. Tom Horn met the challenge. One . . . two . . . three mounts went down. One man was struggling to get to his feet. Horn went back to the Creedmoor.

A man named Lyle Buford had been picked to lead the second raid. He was riding up front with Morgan. Morgan knew almost at once that Tom Horn was doing his job. He finally turned to Buford.

"That son-of-a-bitch will take out a dozen men if we don't stop him. That's what I'm here for and I'm not missing the chance. Get the men back to camp. We'll have to hit the ranches another time. I'm going after Horn."

"That ain't part o' the orders."

"Those are my orders," Morgan said, spurring Pacer and shouting back as he rode off. "Do as you goddam please, Buford, but that son-of-a-bitch will kill you if you stay where you are."

Harv Jessup ran half the length of the camp to be first at Brock's cabin. Brock was just sitting down with a cup of coffee.

"The men are back . . . that is . . . some of 'em." Brock looked up, quizzically. "Somethin's wrong."

"Morgan?"

"Don't know. So far . . . all I've seen is Lyle. He's ridin' up now."

Buford told the men what had happened. All totalled, Tom Horn had taken out four men and seven animals. Only the men's retreat had kept him from a higher toll.

"And you say Morgan claimed it was Tom

Horn?''

"That's what he said . . . and that he was goin'
after him." Brock assumed a studied expression.
Finally, he shook his head.

"He couldn't have known," Brock said. "I didn't
really plan those raids until he got here."

"And I had a man ridin' drag—trailed us all the
way from Ketchum," Jessup said. "Nobody
followed *us*."

Brock got to his feet. "Lyle . . . you were out there.
What do you think?"

Buford smiled. "I think Mogan's all right," he
answered, "but I put Joe Banks on him anyways.
Banks is about the best tracker we got. Morgan
won't lose 'im and Banks can handle himself if
there's trouble."

"Good thinking," Brock said. "Now . . . with
Morgan preoccupied and Horn . . . or whoever it was
that shot us up . . . figuring he stopped us, we'll try
it again. Harv . . . you lead it. Take thirty men and
hit those ranches . . . hit them hard. We don't want
any of them getting the idea that there's hope riding
around out there."

Lee Morgan hadn't been in the Bitterroot country
for some time but he knew that the man who'd shot
up the raiders could only be in one or two spots. He
picked the right one on the first try. Half way up the
trail to where Horn was located, Morgan knew he
was being trailed. He opted for the easy way out.

He dismounted, let Pacer have his head, up trail,
slipped into the confines of some nearby trees and
waited. A few minutes later, a rider came into view.
Morgan smiled, pointed the Winchester into the air
and fired twice.

The rider, Joe Banks, reacted predictably. Since

neither shot came anywhere near him, he assumed Morgan had found a target . . . or someone was using Morgan for a target. There was a bend in the trail about fifty yards beyond Morgan's hiding place. Banks spurred his mount and rode past Morgan at a gallop. He reached the bend, reined up and dismounted. Morgan came out of the trees, raised the Winchester and waited. If he was right . . . if Tom Horn was up trail, Morgan would know it in a moment. If not he'd take Banks out.

The Creedmoor's roar answered Morgan's question. Joe Banks died instantly. When the shot's echo died away, Morgan hollered.

"Horn . . . it's Lee Morgan." There was no reply. A moment later, Morgan heard a noise above and slightly behind him. He crouched and spun around, looking up. Tom Horn was smiling down . . . Creedmoor at the ready. "You're one up on me," Morgan said.

"Well," Horn replied with his slow drawl, "that's just about right. I don't much like bein' even up with a man . . . an' I plumb hate losin'." Horn motioned off to his right. "Camp's back up there, ride in."

Horn and Morgan rounded up Banks' horse, wrapped Banks' body in his own bedroll and then sat down and exchanged information. Horn talked first. He was just finishing up by expressing his puzzlement about Ben Strada when the two men heard the riders. They moved to Horn's lookout position.

"Shit," Morgan exclaimed. "They're moving right out again . . . going after the Galbraith place and the Blaisdell spread."

"That where you were headed?" Morgan nodded. "Well . . . they can burn 'em out but they won't find no people. Ever'body's meetin' at Killerman's ranch today. S'posed to be gettin' some word down from the Guv'nor's office." They watched the riders until they were out of sight. They returned to Horn's camp and Morgan then told his story. He got a distinct reaction from Tom Horn when, toward the conclusion of his story, he mentioned Brock's name.

"This fella Brock . . . what's he look like?"

"Tall . . . clean shaven . . . graying a little. Dresses nice. Wears a shoulder rig."

"Got a little twitch in his left eye?" Morgan looked up. He was clearly surprised.

"Yeah Tom . . . matter of fact, he does."

"I'll be damned. That there would be Riley Brock."

"You know 'im?"

"Did once'st. Rode a posse with 'im . . . down in Texas. We was lookin' for Big Ben Kilcannon an' his cattle thievin' bunch."

"Brock was a lawman?"

"Pinkerton agent . . . one o' the best. Faster'n hell an' got a head fer figgerin' things out." Horn shoved his hat back on his head, rubbed the end of his nose and then continued. "Dedicated too. Too young fer the war but figgered ever' man owed his country. He was doin' his time in *gummint* service by workin' fer the President."

"You sound surprised that he'd go bad."

"I am. Not that kind o' man. I ain't sayin' he's not givin' the orders down there, Morgan . . . but if'n he is my guess would be that he's workin' fer somebody bigger. Railroad mebbe . . . but somebody he respects. He was a mighty set fella . . . always figgered that whatever was best fer the country was the best thing to do . . . no matter how many little fellas got hurt along the way."

"Then what you're saying doesn't make him the top man . . . if you're right."

"I'd wager on it. He might be the ramrod out there, but they's bigger fish he's answerin' to."

"That's an edge that'll come in damned handy," Morgan said. "I think he trusts me more than not."

"How you figgerin' to explain that," Horn asked, pointing to Banks' body, "an' not gettin' me?"

Morgan grinned. "I've been pondering that Tom. Banks can take the blame. He won't complain about it." Horn snickered. "You mind giving up the Creedmoor?" Horn frowned. "It may convince Brock that I was close . . . damned close. Close enough you had to ride out kinda sudden like. The Creedmoor isn't something you'd likely give up easy. I'll just tell him I'd have had you except Banks there got in the road."

Horn got to his feet. "You're the only son-of-a-bitch I ever rode with what could get that piece without killin' me fer it."

"It's the only way I'd want to try," Morgan said.

"Well . . . since you're on the inside and I know what I need to know . . . think I'll ride on back to Killerman's place . . . see how their meetin' went. I'll do some snoopin'," Horn continued, "smell out what I can about Brock."

"We need a way to get word back and forth to each other," Morgan said. "There's an abandoned mine shack about fifteen miles from here . . . southwest. Follow Leadore creek where it angles off toward Flintiron Mountain."

"That's the big 'un ain't it?"

"Yeah. The shack's easy to spot. Almost at the base of the mountain. Anything important . . . leave it there. Let's try to meet there in a week." Horn nodded and the two men shook hands. Horn waited until Morgan was back down in the valley and then he packed his gear and broke camp. He was almost ready to ride out when he heard hoofbeats again. He checked. The marauders were returning from their raids. They were riding hard and he figured they'd overtake Morgan before he got back to Gunsmoke Gorge.

"Watch yourself, boy," he said, aloud. As he turned to head back to his animals, he spotted two more riders. Just behind them, rode gun drummer Mason and Morgana Barr. "Things is shapin' up in a hurry," he mumbled.

9

Morgan too had heard the returning riders coming up on him. He broke his trail and stayed out of sight. Similarly, he spotted men bringing in Morgana Barr. He decided to stay out until nightfall. It was risky but he was betting that whoever was standing guard would let him through when they saw Banks' body. He was right. He rode up to Brock's shack just before midnight.

"You're a puzzlement to me," Brock said, "a disturbing one. I don't like to be disturbed, Morgan."

"Barr's daughter is here like I said. You lost men to Tom Horn. Like I said and you burned out a couple of insignificant ranches without accomplishing a damned thing. Frankly," Morgan said, leaning back against the wall and folding his arms, "it's *me* that ought to be *disturbed*. I had Horn dead to rights and your man Banks fucked it up."

"All I've got is your word." Morgan turned suddenly, exited the shack and returned a moment later with the Creedmoor. He tossed it to Brock—hard. Its weight stung Brock's hands when he caught it. He winced. He looked down at it.

"You think Horn would give *that* up. I was that close Brock . . . close enough to force him out. Banks goddam near got us both killed. That won't happen again, Mister Brock."

107

"You telling me this is Tom Horn's Creedmoor?"

"I don't have to tell you that, Brock," Morgan said, scathingly. "Look at the goddam initials on it . . . and the date. Before the Creedmoor I heard that Horn used to use a .50 caliber Sharps. That right?"

"How the hell would I know?"

"Because you rode posse with him . . . once anyway . . . down in Texas, wasn't it?" Morgan's cool headed use of the information he possessed now payed handsome dividends. Brock visibly displayed his surprise.

"You figure me a two bit gunny with a greedy heart and Harv Jessup's mind . . . or maybe Lambert's . . . or Banks' out there. I'm not and the sooner you believe that, the better chance you got of stayin' alive." Morgan had played out the whole hand . . . at least all the cards he held at the present time. He leaned back again smiling.

Brock considered him. He stood the Creedmoor in the corner and then sat down at his desk. "You're clever all right," Brock finally said. "That's the part that bothers me most. Maybe you're just clever enough to pull off what nobody else could."

"That the Pinkerton in you Brock?"

"Seems you've got all the answers, Morgan."

"Not quite."

"Really? What's missing?"

"The top man," Morgan replied. He straightened, walked to Brock's desk, rested his weight on his hands and leaned down . . . close to Brock's face. "Who do you work for," he asked.

"Morgan . . . you're pushing too hard . . . too fast."

"Then you're not denying there *is* somebody higher."

"I'm not denying . . or *confirming* a damned thing for you."

"Have it your way, Brock," Morgan said, smiling. "The one thing I've got that you don't is time . . . plenty of time." He straightened, walked over and picked up the Creedmoor, walked to the door, turned back and flicked the brim of his hat in a somewhat contemptuous gesture of goodbye and walked out.

Morgan stashed the rifle with his gear and then went over to the tent where Strada's niece was being held. The guards showed signs of wanting to stop him but his steely-eyed stares backed them down. He went in and found, as he'd expected, Morgana Barr. Again, he gestured for silence. He waited, quietly, for a moment and then stepped back outside.

"You boys go for a little walk." He was grinning. "Half of that in there," he said, smiling, "is my property. I am to do a little inspecting." The two men looked at each other and finally one of them shrugged. They walked off to some nearby trees and rolled themselves some smokes.

"You can talk now," Morgan said, "if you keep it low."

"I didn't think you would let it go this far," Morgana said. Her tone belied her calm appearance.

"You'll be safe. Don't worry." He turned to Strada's niece. "Your name?"

"Lileth Joy Johnson," she said. "My mother is Ben Strada's sister."

Morgan nodded. "Sorry . . . but I didn't remember the name . . . Lileth. What do folks call you?"

"Lil . . . mostly."

Morgan recalled that she was twenty-five. She looked older. She had long copper hair. Her face was small . . . mostly like the rest of her . . . except, Morgan noted, her breasts. She was only about five feet, two inches tall but she had large, pendulous breasts. His eyeing of them did not go unnoticed by either woman.

"We're going to get you both out of here," Morgan said, "and safely. You'll just have to be patient until I can make my move."

"My uncle may have me out before that," the girl said. Her tone was somewhat disrespectful of Morgan's claim. "He knows the right people . . . the people to talk to . . . the people who will take action at once."

"If you mean the Governor," Morgan said, "forget it." Morgan turned to her. "What do you mean?"

"My father helped to elect that man . . . if the Governor is obligated to anyone . . . it's my father. He turned my father down. I fail to see how this . . . this girl's uncle is going to help."

"Your father is not the man he once was," Lil said. "Ben Strada gets things done in Idaho today with action—not on a worn out reputation." Morgana Barr jerked toward the girl. She couldn't reach her. Morgan slipped between them.

"You keep this up and you'll get us all killed. Get along," he said. He got up. "After it's over . . . you can scratch each other's eyes out . . . I don't give a damn. For now . . . get along."

Morgan lay in his tent wide awake. He had mixed emotions. He was glad both women were safe but he was troubled by their petty jealousy and concerned about Ben Strada. Horn suspected Strada could be on the wrong side in the fight and yet Strada's niece was certain he'd use all his power to negotiate her release. Strada might have more answers to questions than Morgan realized. He decided that finding Strada was his next move.

The new day brought the news that Brock had

ordered another raid. This time on the Elk Horn Ranch about twenty miles due south. The marauders struck paydirt there. The ranch's owner, Silas Freeborn, was killed. So were ten ranch hands and Freeborn's brother. All the buildings were burned out. By Brock's accounting, it was a complete success.

"One more down," he said, marking the big wall map. He turned back to Morgan, whom he'd summoned just after sunup. "I was kept up most of the night," he said smiling. He seemed to Morgan . . . almost congenial. "I was thinking about you. You're a good man, Morgan, a good man to have on my side. I'm through doubting. You're in. No more raids, no more . . . well, *proof.* Get me Tom Horn. In the meantime, I'll begin contacts to negotiate with Strada and Judge Barr. You'll be well taken care of. You have my word on it."

Morgan was wary but now it was Brock who was holding cards and he proved himself a worthy player. Enticing Morgan with things that, right now, Morgan couldn't prove one way or the other. He had to play along. "When the time comes . . . soon it will be too . . . you'll meet the *right* people. I promise you that, Morgan." He walked up and offered his hand. "Deal?"

Morgan continued to study Brock's eyes for a few moments. The information had come fast. Brock had all but admitted that there were higher-ups. If the land war in Idaho was ever to be ended, it was these men . . . these right people to whom Brock alluded, that would have to be brought down.

"Deal," Morgan finally said. They shook hands. "I saw the women last night. I want . . . uh, some time with them before they're turned back to their relatives." Morgan grinned.

"Fine," Brock said. He wasn't grinning. Lee was about to learn that Brock's icy exterior was not just a facade. "You can have them first. A few of the other men have earned some rewards as well. Oh . . . by the way," Brock said, reaching beneath his desk, "you might want this. After all . . . to the victor as they say." He handed Morgan the guncase which had belonged to Mason. Morgan frowned.

"I know he was your man but he was an outsider. Besides, you've got run of camp and anything else you need now. I didn't figure you'd care."

"Care? About *what?*"

"Why Mason, of course. I had him shot."

Tom Horn rode into the middle of one hell of a fight. It was the worst possible kind . . . at least as far as Tom was concerned. Neighbor fighting neighbor . . . or arguing loudly, at least. The ranchers were split about down the middle over the latest incidents. One of those incidents shocked even Tom Horn.

Tom knew that Josh Killerman didn't have a lot of use for him but the expression on Killerman's face when he answered Tom's knock at the door was one of hatred.

"You're a nervy son-of-a-bitch," Killerman said. "I'll give you that much." He grabbed Tom's coat collars and pulled him inside. The aging manhunter tried to defend himself but two more men jumped him. He took some hard blows to the solar plexis and finally to the jaw. He went down. Someone kicked him.

"That's enough!"

"Not near enough, Marshal."

"Don't make me draw a gun in your house Josh . . . now damn it, back off." The men moved back and Marshal Seth Rawlings got Tom Horn back on his feet.

"You plannin' on takin' him out o' here, Marshal?" Rawlings didn't like the question. He scowled at the man who'd asked it. He moved Tom to the dining room and sat him down in a chair.

"Now," he said, turning to the men . . . about a dozen of them, "I want to hear what Mister Horn has to say. If I don't like it or I don't believe it or it can't be verified, then he goes back to Boise with me. Anybody tries to make it different is bustin' the same law."

"He's a murderin' bastard, Marshal. You already know that. You don't need no evidence . . . and neither do we . . . none we ain't already got."

"I'm warning you, Parsons. I'll kill any man interfering with my job." The men present were obviously angry to the point of revenge. One of them, Tom noted, had a rope. Nonetheless, they knew Seth Rawlings and, for the time being at least, backed off.

"Horn," the marshal said, looking into Tom's face. "Ben Strada is dead. Shot from ambush. Most here figure you did it. Whether by mistake or design they don't know. Right now they don't care."

"Seems to me you don't much care either, Marshal."

"I got a job, Horn. I'll do it. Like it or not."

"I didn't shoot Strada. Ain't seen 'im."

"You killed his man," Rawlings said, "Toby Summers. Lyin' about it won't help you none either. Found Summers blowed apart by a heavy caliber rifle . . . no scatter gun. You carry a Creedmoor don't you?"

Tom looked into Rawlings' eyes and then around the room. He half smiled. "I killed Summers right enough 'cause if I hadn't, he'd uh killed me. An' yeah . . . I got me a Creedmoor, or I did anyways.''

"You *did?*"

"I lost it durin' a run-in with some marauders. Anyways . . . I didn't kill Strada.''

"But you admit killing Summers?'' Horn nodded. "They were together.''

"They weren't the last time I saw 'em.''

"You just told us you hadn't seen Ben Strada.''

"Marshal, I can tell you a whole heap o' things, but this ain't the time,'' he looked around again, "an' it sure as hell ain't the place.''

"I'll decide that,'' Rawlings shot back, "not you. Anything you got to say, you say it here and now. I'll stick by you because it's my job, but these people deserve to know the truth.''

"We won't be gettin' any o' that from Tom Horn. He's a lyin', payed for killin' bastard. Ben was shot with the same gun what killed Summers . . . an' the rest o' them at the shack too.''

"An' two men that tried to bushwhack me later and four o' the raiders and a half a dozen o' their mounts,'' Horn said. "I had my suspects about Strada but I didn't kill 'em. I been up in the Bitterroots for near a week.''

Rawlings frowned. "Where was Strada killed?''

"Between Boise and the Rocky Barr ranch. Found him down along the Middle Fork after we tracked his mount back. The horse was one he'd taken from Judge Barr's place. He just went on home.''

"Horn said he was out a week . . . been all o' that an' more. He had plenty o' time to get Ben.''

"But I didn't . . . an' how you know he was done in with a Creedmoor?''

"Because the bullet was still in him,'' Rawlings said. "He was shot from one helluva distance. It's

not the kind of a shot many men can make. At least
. . . none from around here.''

Tom Horn grinned. ''There must be two hunnert
gunmen in this valley right now . . . on both sides o'
the law. Out o' that many . . . a few are good. Hell
fire . . . Toby Summers could o' made a shot like
that.''

''I told you Horn . . . if I didn't like your answers
or I didn't believe you . . . we'd head for Boise.''

Rawlings stepped back, drew his pistol and said,
''Let's go.''

Tom stood up. ''Which is it, Marshal? You don't
believe me or you just don't like what you hear?''

''No matter . . . we're goin' to Boise either way.''

''He done it, Marshal an' he's gonna pay for it.''
One of the men bulled their way through the others
but Rawlings whirled and caught the man on the
jaw with the barrel of the Colt's. He and Tom then
backed out of the ranch house to their horses.

''It's a long way to Boise,'' one man yelled.

''You'd best keep these men in line, Josh,''
Rawlings warned.

''You did your job, Marshal . . . none of 'em would
be here.''

''And if your association didn't hire on mankillers
. . . I'd be out tryin' to do that job.'' The marshal
mounted and then turned to Tom. ''I want your
word you'll ride with me clean.''

''You got it,'' Tom said. ''Time we get to Boise . . .
you'll be thinkin' differ'nt.''

Lee Morgan had planned to ride out of the Gorge
that very day. The news about Mason and Brock's
change of mind . . . if not heart . . . held him back.
Now, he figured, he'd have a chance at finding out
when and where Brock planned his next raid.

Perhaps he could warn the would-be victims or, at worst, somehow foil the attempt.

On the pretext of giving Tom Horn a day or two in which to re-position himself, Morgan payed Brock a visit that evening. Brock was out of the shack. Morgan was tempted to try a quick search but he considered the risk too great. He was firmly ensconced with Brock now and whatever he might find in the shack would be of little value if he got caught.

He simply took a bottle of whiskey off a shelf, opened it and sat down at Brock's desk to wait. When he started to pour himself a second drink, he noticed a single name, hastily scratched on a piece of paper. *Belle.* Belle Moran? Boise? He wondered. Why would Brock have jotted down so unlikely as name as hers? The door opened.

"Well now," Brock said, "I rather hoped you'd be out hunting Tom Horn." The door closed. Morgan twisted around and hefted his glass in a gesture of greeting.

"Horn will need a day or two to find another roosting place. There are one or two likely spots. Tomorrow, I'll start checking them out."

Brock moved to the other side of the desk. Morgan noted that he made a hasty check of its order. He would have noticed almost anything that was out of place. There was nothing to notice.

"I've sent a rider to the Rocky Barr. I've decided to put some double pressure on the good judge. I informed him we had both his daughter and Strada's niece. I'll let him worry about handling that end."

"You planning to strengthen your position a little more?" Morgan sipped the whiskey and smiled, displaying an off-handed attitude.

"You mean another raid in conjunction with the notes?"

"Yeah . . . mebbe."

"Is that what you'd do?"

"Prob'ly. I'd like the judge to know we're still out here—that nothing's changed."

"We are Morgan . . . and it hasn't. As a matter of fact, I have something very close to that in mind." Brock smiled. "A little more ambitious perhaps . . . but similar. I'll be riding out myself tomorrow. Gone a week or more. When I get back I should have an answer from the judge. No matter what it is we're going to bring the rest of the ranchers in line once and for all."

"Sounds impressive," Morgan said. He felt a tension. Something big was in the making. He looked at Brock . . . hoping.

"Now what can I do for you?" Morgan realized that Brock would say no more. He didn't care to push the issue. He smiled, put the bottle on Brock's desk and got to his feet.

"You just did it, Brock. Thanks for the whiskey." Brock smiled.

10

The snow was wet and heavy and getting worse. The
ride from the Rocking K had taken its toll on men
and mounts. Seth Rawlings wanted no more.

"We're gonna hole up in Ketchum," he said. Tom
Horn just nodded. The two men had hardly spoken a
word since they left the Killerman spread. It was a
long trip to Boise and Tom figured he'd have plenty
of time to tell his tale.

Rawlings knew exactly where he wanted to go and
it wasn't to any of the saloons. The last thing he
needed was trouble. He rode straight to the parson-
age. A few minutes later, he and Tom Horn were
warming themselves by a cozy fire.

Ephram Culpepper walked in. He eyed both men
and grinned. "Who's got who?" he asked.

"Howdy, Ephram," Rawlings said. They shook
hands. Rawlings did a half turn. "This is Tom
Horn."

"Yeah . . . I had that much figured out. Howdy,
Mister Horn. I'm Culpepper . . . God's man in these
here parts." Tom moved toward him, smiled and
shook his hand.

"I've heard about you. Like what I heard too.
Always kinda figured the Lord needed a hand in
this country. Man like you gives Him a strong one."

"Some wouldn't agree."

"Some wouldn't agree with anythin'," Horn said. He glanced at the marshal. "By the way . . . he's takin' me in . . . to Boise."

"For *what*? I heard the ranchers hired you, Horn."

"You heard right," Seth Rawlings said, scowling. "A damned bad idea. Now . . . seems like Ben Strada's been shot . . . from ambush. Ranchers think Horn here did it . . . by accident maybe . . . but did it, just the same."

"What do you think, Seth?"

"I think the judge'll decide."

"How long you been out lookin'," Culpepper asked the marshal.

"Not long. I was up at the Rocky Barr when I heard. I got a message to ride over to Josh Killerman's place and I did. Horn here," Rawlings continued, gesturing, "rode in as big as you please."

"Not too smart for a guilty man is it?"

"Mebbe not . . . then again . . . mebbe it's the smartest thing a guilty man could do."

Culpepper's woman brought coffee and fresh baked pie. The three men ate and chatted about nothing in particular. Rawlings finished first. "Horn, I'd like to hear your side of the story. All of it."

"Me too," Culpepper said, grinning. "Then, Marshal, you can mosey on over to Addie's place and arrest the man who *did* gun down Ben Strada." Both Rawlings and Horn were shocked. Culpepper, still grinning, just nodded. "Been holed up there for three days . . . roarin' drunk, braggin' about it. Says nobody will do anythin' since he's workin' for the *right* people."

Marshal Seth Rawlings listened closely, eyed Culpepper with considerable suspicion and then said, "How's come you didn't go take 'im out Ephram? I was given to understand you, more or less, keep the law in Ketchum. Particularly where Addie is involved."

"Real easy answer, Seth. They's five more of 'em over there. Ever' one a gunny. Tried to weasel in on Idaho's troubles. Seems neither side wanted 'em, but from what I can gather, Ben Strada run 'em clean off 'n his spread. Fella what shot Ben didn't take kindly to that an' he's got a long memory."

"You speak like you know 'im," Tom said.

"I do. So do you an' the marshal here too. Jess Blanchard."

"Shit!"

"Yeah . . . an' his two brothers."

"You know the other two?"

"Only one of 'em. Sam Beecher. I figure it was big Sam's gun what Jess used to kill Ben Strada."

"It was," Tom said. "And it is a Creedmoor .44-90 just like mine, or the one I had."

"Speakin' of that," Seth said, frowning, "you're not a man that loses his gun. That made me itchier than anythin' else you said."

"I didn't lose it. I gave it to young Lee Morgan. He's on the inside now . . . ridin' with the marauders. He had reason to want my gun. A damn good reason. He's got it. He's got Morgana Barr too an' by now, I'd wager, he knows the whereabouts of Strada's niece."

"Why the hell didn't you tell me that back at Killerman's place?"

"*You* know who you can trust out o' that bunch, Marshal?" Tom Horn shook his head. "I damn well don't, an' I didn't live this many years by gettin' careless." Rawlings nodded. Tom Horn was right and he knew it.

"Well, Marshal, what'll it be? Jess Blanchard gonna ride out?"

"He won't come in without a fight," Seth said, "an' you know it."

"I'll stand with you, Marshal. Two or three o' them fellas got prices on their hats . . ." Culpepper grinned, "Muh church here could use the money." Both he and Seth turned to Tom Horn.

"Seems about the only way I'll ever convince them fellas back at Killerman's place that I didn't do it."

"The odds aren't exactly on our side," Seth said. "Horn . . . you're not a gun hand . . . that is with a pistol."

Tom took his hat off, held it just above the top of his head and then scratched with his little finger. "Nope . . . but I'm pretty handy at evenin' up them odds you mentioned."

"You'll be wearing a badge, Horn . . . or you won't be going. When you got a star on you give a man a chance."

"Yep . . . I figgered on that, Marshal. I'll give 'em as much as I can . . . an' still keep breathin. That there is about the best offer I can make you."

"I'll get the badges," Seth said.

"I got me a brand new Remington shotgun," Culpepper said to Tom. "I'd be mighty proud if'n Tom Horn was the first man to use it."

"Obliged," Tom said, smiling. "I'll be glad to."

Marshal Seth Rawlings returned a few minutes later with two tin stars. He pinned one on each man's coat and then turned to face them.

"Raise your right hands," he said. They did. "You're swore," he said. "We'll go in an' get 'em at first light. Mebbe they'll be liquored up . . . or still

asleep. For now . . . that's what I plan on doin' . . .
gettin' some sleep.''

Marshal Rawlings, Tom Horn and Ephram
Culpepper all came out of their beds in the small
hours of the morning. A loud and persistent knocking had aroused them. They converged in the
hallway just after Culpepper's woman had opened
the door. The question as to whom was the most
surprised remained unanswered. Four men stood
staring at each other. Rawlings, Culpepper, Horn
and Lee Morgan!

The clouds were gone . . . with them, that heavy,
wet snow. The sky was the purplish-blue it becomes,
just before full daylight on an icy morning. Lee
Morgan's internal alarm clock brought him out of
bed at 5:15. It was a quarter hour before he'd
planned but Tom Horn's moving about had
awakened him.

"I didn't git a chanc'st to ask you, Morgan," Tom
Horn said, "but did you bring my rifle?"

"I did. You planning on using it today?"

"Not likely. The Winchester prob'ly."

"And Culpepper's new scatter-gun."

"Yeah . . . that too."

Lee had ridden hard, even with the deep, high
country snow, to reach Ketchum by the night
before. He could still scarcely believe the dumb luck
of running into Tom Horn and the marshal. He'd
ridden from Gunsmoke Gorge with only two goals in
mind. Find Horn and give him its location and then
find Ben Strada. He intended to solicit Culpepper's
aid. He had already achieved all his goals—and then
some. Now, he pondered the price he might have to
pay for them.

"Seth pin a tin star on your coat yet?" Horn

asked, grinning.

"No . . . but he will, Tom."

"You mind?"

"I mind . . . but less than I used to. Anyway, for this job it seems right."

Tom Horn smiled and nodded. "The damned things always seem right when you're behind one."

Morgan pulled on his boots and stood up, stuffing in his shirt tail.

"Maybe . . . but I don't plan on making it permanent." The door opened and Ephram Culpepper stuck his head around it.

"Mornin' gents. The marshal says he's ready. Says to tell you *he'll* ask 'em to give it up . . . then he'll wait."

"An' if one of us gets shot he'll have his answer." Morgan strapped on his rig. Tom Horn smirked. They went downstairs.

"Horn . . . cover the back way out over at Addie's. Anybody comes through here is yours."

"Do *I* have to ask 'em anything, Marshal?" Tom was grinning.

"No, Horn, you goddam well don't, and I don't like it that way." Seth Rawlings wasn't grinning.

The four men stepped into the morning air. Each took a short gasp as the cold invaded their lungs. Breath exhaled in steamy clouds, quickly enveloped whiskers and froze in place. Only Lee Morgan was exempt.

The quartet of men reached the corner, moved to the middle of the street, their boots squeaking in the virgin snow. At the end of that street, they paused. Half a block away was Addie Terhune's place. A ribbon of white smoke curled up from the roof, itself appearing amost frozen in place. Seth Rawlings reached out and slapped Tom Horn on the shoulder,

Horn nodded, stuck one arm up and waved and
trudged off toward the back of the saloon.

The remaining three men started across the
street, diagonally. At the center of the main street,
Morgan stopped.

"Somebody rode out . . . recent." The others
looked at Morgan's finger, pointing to the ground. A
single set of hoof prints had marred the newly fallen
snow. "The prints were headed west."

"How recent you figure?" Rawlings asked.
Ephram knelt down and then dropped to all fours to
get a closer look. He studied two of the prints, stood
up and brushed himself off.

"Hard to say fer sure, Marshal. Always is in the
snow but I'd guess not more'n a couple o' hours.
Now new snow in them prints an' no sign o' much
bustin' at the edges. Horse made 'em after the snow
froze."

"Who in hell would ride outa here that early?"

"A man with a mission," Lee Morgan replied,
looking west.

"What are you thinkin', Morgan?"

"These boys aren't particular who they work for . .
. highest wage'll buy what they got to sell. Couldn't
sell it to Strada . . . so they killed him. I'm sure he
spoke for the association. They been layin' around
. . . lettin' the word out that they're available."

"An' Tom Horn took out a few o' that fella
Brock's riders?"

"Yeah, Marshal. That's what I'm thinking."

"Well let's see to it Brock don't get no more'n one
of 'em." Rawlings and Morgan both looked at Culpepper. The wily old gunman turned Bible thumper
was looking off to the west deep in thought.

"What's on your mind?" the marshal asked.
Culpepper didn't answer. "Ephram?" Culpepper's

head jerked around. He smiled weakly and shrugged.

The rifle shot tore into Seth Rawlings' right leg, just above the knee. He'd dropped his hat and stooped to pick it up. He'd moved a little faster than his would-be killer had figured. Had he not done so, the shot would have been through his temple. As it was, Seth howled and fell forward.

Both Morgan and Culpepper were blasting away in the direction of the shot, high up, probably on the roof of Addie's place. They found no target but the fusillade drove off the rifleman and gave them a chance to pull Marshal Rawlings to cover.

"Goddam it!"

"You're out of it, Seth. You leg's broke."

"I'll be damned if I am. Get me a rifle." Seth, wincing in pain, twisted his body so that he could see Lee Morgan working his way along the building fronts. "Morgan, damn you, get back here."

"Sorry, Seth," Ephram said, "but unless one o' those gunnys busts out an' runs this way . . . looks like you'll have to sit this one out."

"Ephram! Goddamn you, Ephram. Get me a rifle. You're a damn deputy . . . you do as I tell you. Ephram!"

Behind Addie's place, Tom Horn had heard the shot. He'd pushed himself into a doorway opposite the back stairs leading from Addie Terhune's room. Then, there was only the silence of the morning. A moment later, he heard the crunching of snow above him. In another second, a man came into view. He was carrying a rifle. He jumped from the roof to the stairway balcony, ran down the stairs, turned and saw Tom Horn. His mouth flew open. It would remain open, frozen in place. Horn let go with the shotgun.

Instantly, Tom moved out of the doorway, cut, catty-corner across the narrow alley way and pressed himself against the wall of the saloon. He slammed another shell into the shotgun. He eased himself along the wall toward the back door.

Out front, Morgan had reached the main entrance. The outside doors were closed but the bat wings were tied open. Morgan couldn't see a damned thing for the half inch of ice on the windows. He hugged the wall. Ephram Culpepper had crossed the street and slipped into a doorway. Morgan looked over, nodded and then pointed to a rocker which sat just a few feet away on the opposite side of the big window in the front of Addie's saloon. Culpepper nodded.

Ephram Culpepper pumped three rounds into the plate glass widow. The first two simply pierced it. The third spider-webbed the center of the glass and the cracks in it converged on its center. The window seemed to explode.

Morgan dashed from his position, swung himself around the solid backed rocker, lifted and leaped forward, through the opening where the window had been. Culpepper, himself changing positions, heard three shots. Two were pistol shots, the third a rifle. The latter struck the wood just above his head. Culpepper stopped, turned to his right, looked toward the roof and let go two more shots. There was a grunt, a man's body teetered on the roof's edge and then fell backward. Culpepper darted into another doorway and commenced reloading.

Inside the saloon, Lee Morgan was crouched behind the street-side end of the bar. The rocker had provided good cover although the second shot had pierced the pack, splintered the wood and sent a sliver of it into Morgan's left hand. He yanked it out, tearing the skin in the process. He cursed underneath his breath.

"Addie," Morgan shouted, "it's Lee Morgan. You okay?" No reply. "Addie!" No reply. Morgan reloaded the Smith and Wesson. Inside the heavy pocket of the skeepskin coat, Morgan had tucked the old Bisley Colt's. "Addie," he shouted, trying again. No answer. He heard the squeaking of a door hinge upstairs. He stayed in a crouch but scurried along to the opposite end of the bar.

"Your woman's right up here," a man's voice hollered. Morgan stayed put. He caught a glimpse of a shadow just to his right. He turned. He heard the door open. Two shots rang out. Both were from outside. Culpepper? Morgan thought so. He took advantage of the distraction and he took a chance. He moved three feet to his right, removed his hat and tossed it onto the end of the bar, just above where he'd been and then he stood up.

Morgan's hat flew from the bar. Morgan saw the gunman, Louie Blanchard, one of Jess Blanchard's brothers. Morgan shot him between the eyes. Instantly, he went down again, this time twisting so that he was on his back. A figure appeared at the street end of the bar, silhouetted against the outside light. Morgan fired, the figure fired, Ephram Culpepper, just coming through the window opening, fired.

The man's shot missed Morgan's head by little more than the width of a razor. Morgan's shot struck the figure in the groin. Culpepper's shot smashed into the man's back and severed his spine. Ephram grunted and went down, face first.

"Ephram," Morgan shouted.

"I'm hit!" A woman screamed. There was the sickening series of thuds and bumps as a body bounced down the stairs. Two shots smashed into

the wall above Morgan's position . . . holding him
down. A shotgun roared and there was silence.

The first man to die in the fight had been Willy
Keene. He was a twenty-two year old, pock-faced
gunny with a bloated view of his own worth. Tom
Horn had killed him out back. The man on the
roof, dead by two shots from Jake Culpepper's gun,
was Sam Beecher. Morgan's victim, inside the
saloon, was Louie Blanchard and the one he and Culpepper had shared, at the end of the bar, was Rick
Blanchard. Morgan sat up.

"How bad you hit?" he asked Ephram.

"I'll live."

"*Horn!*"

"Yep . . . I'm here. Took out a fella up on the
balcony."

"That's five," Morgan said. "There was only
supposed to be six and one rode out."

"Stay put," Horn shouted back. "Jess Blanchard
had another brother . . . a kid name o' Eustis. Was
either him or Jess what rode out . . . but they's one
of 'em still here . . . upstairs."

"You sure?"

"Yep. One o' the girls is laying at the bottom o'
the stairs. Looks like she's got a breathin' problem
. . . throat's been cut."

"Addie?"

"Nope."

"What makes you think there's still one up
there?"

"Showed himself at the window o' Addie's room.
Spotted him and I come through the back door . . .
took out the fella on the balcony. Man I saw didn't
have time to get that far."

Ephram Culpepper sat up. His right arm, high up
near his shoulder, was bleeding profusely. He

winced as he tried to move it. Upstairs, a door opened. Morgan stood up.

"I'm comin' out," a voice shouted. Morgan looked up. He could see a man . . . rather more a boy. He was holding a sawed-off shotgun in his right hand. The barrel was resting beneath Addie Terhune's chin. His left hand was around her waist and in it, he held an old Colt's Dragoon. "Anybody even breathes, her head comes off."

Addie was naked. Her arms were pulled behind her and obviously tied. Her mouth was bleeding, her eyes were big and round and her body was covered with goose bumps. Even under the circumstances, Morgan couldn't help but look at her breasts. They were big, round and jiggling with every movement. The brown ends were protruding, hardened by the chilly air. The dark patch between her legs was bigger than on most women Morgan had seen.

"You won't make it," Morgan said.

"I'll make it." The Dragoon barked. The shot was nowhere near Morgan. He didn't move. Still, he knew that Eustis Blanchard would kill Addie . . . probably out of panic more than desire. It was Jess then who had ridden out of Ketchum. Morgan was now certain he knew why.

Eustis and Addie reached the bottom of the stairs. Eustis pushed Addie in front of him and began backing, slowly, toward the front door. Again, he fired. A shot in Tom Horn's direction and another at Morgan. Neither was close. He dropped the Dragoon, reached behind him and felt for the doorknob. He found it, turned, pulled and moved forward. The icy air rushed in, Addie stiffened as it engulfed her nakedness. Eustis Blanchard tightened his grip on her waist and pulled hard. She backed. He stepped outside. His eyes got big, blinked and went closed. The shotgun clattered to the wooden sidewalk and Eustis Blanchard crumpled into a heap. Addie moaned and dropped to her knees. Marshal Rawlings, delicately balancing himself with his left hand on the door jam, stepped into view. He was holding his pistol by the barrel.

"We got one of 'em alive anyway," he said.

11

None of the others had seen or heard Tom Horn
leave Addie's saloon . . . but leave he did. No one
could be sure just what Jess Blanchard was up to or
what he knew, but they couldn't risk letting him
reach Gunsmoke Gorge.

He had a two to three hour head start but Tom
Horn had dogged many a man with far more than
that. Besides, Blanchard couldn't know he was
being trailed. Horn pushed his horse hard through
the snow. The trail was clean and clear and by noon,
Tom had narrowed the lead to no more than a
quarter of an hour.

He swung off the trail and moved into a stand of
trees along a ridge. The going would be tougher but
he reasoned that Blanchard would, at some point
soon, stop to rest. He was right. Jess Blanchard was
at the crest of a hillock and looking down on the
inviting sight of smoke from a house.

It was the small ranch home of Jude Bailey and
his family. Bailey had missed being wiped out on
three different raids but he knew—as did Tom Horn
—that it was only a matter of time. Now Blanchard
could do the job almost by himself. Tom didn't
intend to let that happen.

He tethered his mount by a tree, slipped the
Creedmoor out of its case, assembled it, loaded and

then strolled, casually, to the spot where Blanchard
had stopped. He looked toward the cabin. Blanchard
was half way there . . . Horn estimated about 590
yards . . . a third of a mile. There was no wind. Tom
knelt in the snow, resting his right elbow on a tree
stump.

A woman exited the cabin. A man stepped out
behind her.

"Damn," Tom Horn said, aloud. Jess Blanchard
reined up and slipped a rifle from the saddle scabbard. Tom lowered the Creedmoor's barrel brace
into his left hand, wiggled his torso until the butt
was tight against his shoulder. He sighted.
Blanchard raised his own rifle. The woman, bent
over, now straightened up. She was looking right at
Jess Blanchard. She screamed but the sound never
reached Tom's ears. It might have had it not been
drowned out. He squeezed the trigger and the huge
gun recoiled, its barrel jumping up and the stock
slamming into Tom's shoulder pad. Jess Blanchard
was still sighting in on his own target when the
.44-90 slammed into his back. He flew from the
horse as though pulled by a rope.

The Baileys could not seem to thank Tom Horn
enough. He learned that Bailey's men . . . only four
of them, had long since abandoned him. Horn
warned them to pack up and ride to Ketchum until
the trouble was over. Tom then went through
Blanchard's gear. He found only one thing of
interest . . . a letter with a Boise postmark.

> Blanchard,
>   If you and your men can't get on at
> Strada's place, ride, alone, to the shack
> marked on the enclosed map. You'll find
> work waiting. *Don't* under any circum-

stances try the RB. We have it. Your
money will be at FQ.

TY

Morgan was about the calmest man in Ketchum.
He knew why Tom Horn had ridden out but the fact
didn't impress Marshal Rawlings. Rawlings and
Culpepper both got treatment for their wounds and
Morgan spent a couple of hours with Addie
Terhune. Those things done, Culpepper and Morgan
brought young Eustis Blanchard to the marshal.

"Best I can figure, boy; you've done nothing too
bad yet. Leastways . . . not here," Rawlings continued, "and *here* is where you are and all I'm
interested in. Now what were you boys up to?"

"You can't scare me, Marshal," the boy said, his
voice quivering.

"Good," Rawlings said calmly. "Then it won't
scare you none to know you'll *hang* for what
happened here."

The boy's eyes got big. "You just said . . . I didn't
do nothin'."

"But you're all I've got." Rawlings eyed both
Morgan and Culpepper. He could read in their faces
that they knew what he was doing. "I think them
fancy lawyers got a name for it . . . guilt by association. No jury'll give a tinker's damn whether you
gunned somebody or not. They'll sentence you to
hang . . . an' I'll see to it you do . . . unless you want
to tell me what your brother is up to."

"I . . . I don't know." Rawlings smirked. "I *swear*
to you, Marshal, I *don't* know. I mean . . . Jess, he
was s'posed to have somethin' worked out . . . he . . .
he got a letter from Boise. He didn't tell me nothin'
. . . he never did . . . hardly."

"You mentioned a letter. From who?" Blanchard

shrugged. "Jess never mentioned anybody?"

"Just once . . . uh, he said he had contact with the *big* boss." Morgan frowned. "Brock?"

"He never mentioned no name . . . but, well, it couldn't o' been Brock. Now he was a fella we was s'posed to meet east o' here. But Jess knew that before he got the letter from Boise."

"Did you see that letter?" Morgan asked.

"Not to read it . . . but it come from Boise . . . that's sure. An' Jess, he was real happy about it."

"Because it came from the man he called the *big* boss . . . right?" Blanchard nodded.

"Take him over and lock him up," Rawlings said to Culpepper.

"Marshal," Eustis said, whining, "you gotta help me . . . you just gotta."

"Why? You tellin' me you wouldn't have killed Addie Terhune?"

"I was just usin' her to get out . . . that's all. I swear it." Rawlings just stared at the boy and Eustis was led away, tears in his eyes. Seth then turned and eyed Morgan.

"What's eatin' at you?"

"Boise . . . and maybe some answers."

"Then you believe that kid?"

"I saw a reference to Belle Moran's place in Boise . . . on Brock's desk over in the Gorge. That much of what Blanchard said ties in."

"So what do you plan to do about it?"

Morgan got to his feet. "Nothing . . . right now anyway. Things are moving too damned fast. There's a showdown coming . . . a big one. Right now . . . I'd best get those women out."

Seth looked quizzical. "Shit Morgan . . . *how?*"

"Brock is gone. Probably meeting Mister Big over in Boise. Told me he'd be gone a week . . . mebbe more. When he gets back it'll be too late to do anything."

"And now?"

"Nobody will question me if I tell them Brock sent me in to get the women. It's likely the only time I'll have a chance."

"And when he finds out what you've done?"

Morgan grinned. "He'll be mad as hell."

"What about Horn?"

"If he did what he went to do, Jess Blanchard is dead. Horn will be back here. When he gets here keep him here 'til I get back with the women."

"Goddam leg," Seth said. "I won't be much use."

"Keep that badge on Culpepper." Morgan took his own off. Seth frowned. "You want me to wear it into the Gorge?"

"No ... but I'd like to think you'll hang on to it 'til this is over."

"I'm no lawman," Morgan said,. He tossed the tin star on the table.

"An' you got no ranch to defend," Seth added. "Without the badge, that makes you a hired gun. That's wrong no matter who hires you."

"You hired me. Same man. Same gun."

"It's different, Morgan, an' you know it."

"It's different to you, Seth. Not to me."

"You're a dyin' breed, Morgan ... a damned poor shadow of your ol' daddy."

"Handy when the law needs me ... a scourge on humanity when I refuse to wear a piece of tin." Morgan shook his head. "That don't make much sense to me."

"But you want me to keep the badge on Ephram Culpepper."

"Yeah ... he's standing for you ... I'm riding for Judge Barr."

"Bullshit! You're riding for Lee Morgan."

Morgan walked to the door and then turned back. "If that's true, Marshal, it wouldn't change just because I pinned on that tin star." He opened the door. "I'll be back . . . with the women."

Ephram Culpepper watched Morgan ride out. Then he walked back to the room where Seth was waiting. "Where's Morgan off to?"

"To bring back Strada's niece and the Barr girl." Ephram glanced at the table and saw the badge.

"Looks like you're short one deputy."

"You quittin' too?"

"I'll stand for you, Seth, 'til your leg ain't hurtin'."

"This'll likely as not be over with before that happens." Ephram grinned. "Well . . . preachin' and keepin' the peace seem to go together pretty good. Leastways . . . I'll give a try at it for a spell."

Morgan passed within five miles of Jude Bailey's place . . . and Tom Horn. Horn finally yielded to the Bailey's request that he stay the night and escort them back to Ketchum. It hadn't been his plan but with Blanchard's letter in his possession it might prove the wisest thing anyway.

Morgan was cold, tired and hungry but he pushed on until Pacer needed rest. He nosed out a line shack along the foothills of the Bitterroots and spent about three hours. It was almost dawn before he set out again. As he neared his destination, he began to hear gunfire. The source, which he found about fifteen minutes later, was another raid. This time on Jimmy Caleb's place. He saw the smoke and felt a new anger welling up inside but he knew there was nothing he could do. In fact, he rode even harder. It would be to his advantage to get to the Gorge when even more men were away.

It was near noon the following day when he finally

passed the outer perimeter and entered the rocky fortress. He was surprised to find Harvey Jessup still in camp and still in charge.

"We've been wondering about you," Jessup said. "Thought maybe I misjudged you."

"You didn't."

"You get Horn?"

"No . . . seems like that's not so important anymore." Jessup frowned. "Ran into Brock on the trail. He ordered me back here to pick up the women."

Jessup's face went a bit white. Morgan caught it in spite of the fact that Jessup did his best to cover it. "That right? You s'posed to meet 'im are you?" Morgan smelled a rat. He nodded. "Where?"

"Boise." It was a guess but it caught Jessup off guard.

"When, Morgan?"

"Soon as I can get there."

"An' he told you to bring both women?" Morgan thought it an odd question. On top of that, Jessup shifted his position a little.

"Yeah," Morgan replied, "why?" Jessup reached. He was fast. Lee Morgan was simply faster. The shot sounded like a cannon. Morgan knew that the results would be. He acted first. He threw open the shack's door and shouted for the men guarding the women. Both responded.

"What the hell happened?" one of them asked. He was looking past Morgan and into the shack.

"Jessup tried to kill me," Morgan replied. He holstered his gun. "I confronted him about the ambush he set up to get the Blanchard brothers."

The revelation got response. Obviously, both men knew about the men in Ketchum. It had been a long shot but Morgan reckoned that anyone put to guarding the hostages would have to be close to

Brock.

"You tellin' us the Blanchards got bushwhacked?"

"They did . . . and Jessup there," Morgan said, gesturing behind him with his thumb, "was responsible. Brock doesn't know who else Jessup might have on the inside. He sent me back for the women."

Morgan's statement brought much the same reaction as he'd gotten from Jessup. Something was not right. He'd have to gamble.

"The women?"

"The one that's left," Morgan said, easing his hand toward his hip. Each time he'd mentioned women, he'd gotten a strange response. He'd concluded, correctly, that one of the women was with Brock.

"He never said nothin' about it when he rode out."

"Why in hell should he?" Morgan snapped. "He didn't know it. He didn't know that son-of-a-bitch was gonna set up the Blanchards either. You want to argue with me . . . fine. You can explain it all to Brock yourself when he rides back in."

"No . . . I . . . I didn't mean that." The man looked in the shack again. "Jessup . . . Jeezus! I figured him all wrong."

"Money's a pretty good incentive," Morgan said, off-handedly. "Some o' these ranchers got plenty of it. Nothing would be better for them than to have a man on the inside."

"Yeah," the man said, pointing, "there was some of us figured it might be you."

"You were supposed to figure that," Morgan said, smiling. "The Big Boss wanted it that way."

"You work for . . ." Morgan held his breath. The man held his tongue. "Shit!" Morgan couldn't push it.

"Get the woman." The men nodded and disappeared around the corner. Several others had gathered nearby but now seemed to drift off, convinced of Morgan's validity. Fortunately, most of those with any reason to question him further were out of the compound. He wanted to be gone before they rode back in.

A minute later, the two guards showed up with Lileth Joy Johnson, Strada's niece. "Untie her," Morgan said. The man frowned. "You don't figure I can handle her?" The man cut the ropes. "Get a horse saddled and out front."

"I don't like your tone, Morgan. Who in hell made you the ramrod?"

Morgan shot a glance at Lil Johnson . . . a sort of silent apology. "Fuck you then," Morgan said. "I'll do it myself and take it up with Brock later."

"Yeah . . . yeah . . . we'll get the goddam horse." The door slammed.

"We're riding out," Morgan said, softly. "You'll be safe in a couple of hours. We're going to Ketchum. Just do as I tell you."

"They took Miss Barr. I heard some men talking. They said she was supposed to be taken to Boise."

"Shit," Morgan said, under his breath. Brock had something up his sleeve or the Mister Big in Boise did. "You got a heavy coat?" The girl shook her head. Morgan looked around and spotted Harv Jessup's sheepskin. He took it. "It'll be too big but you'll stay warm."

"I . . . I don't understand."

"Don't try right now. There'll be plenty of time on the trail. There's not a lot of that right now." The door opened. Morgan motioned to the girl and they walked past the two men without exchanging a word. Minutes later they were riding toward the trail that led out of Gunsmoke Gorge.

12

An icy blast of air poured down from Canada, across
the northern Montana glacier country and fanned
out east and west. The wind from the Bitterroots
carried it into Salmon Valley and it froze everything
in its path. Tom Horn had managed to keep just a
couple of hours head of it but the temperature
hovered near zero when he finally rode back into
Ketchum.

"You get Blanchard?" They were Seth Rawlings'
first words. Horn smiled. "I got 'im."

"Glad you're back."

"I was wonderin'."

"Morgan rode out . . . east. Thought you might
cross trails." Horn huddled near the pot belly and
rubbed his hands together, briskly. "We might
have, 'cept I was in a house. Rancher's place . . .
Jude Bailey."

"They hit Jude?"

"Nope . . . but Blanchard was readyin' himself
to." Horn fished out the letter he'd found and
handed it to Seth. By then, Ephram Culpepper was
stirring. "Bailey family rode in with me. We was
plannin' on waitin' another day but the weather
didn't look too fit."

Horn gestured toward the door. "Good thing we
moved out. Norther'll freeze ever' thin'." Horn

140

scratched his head. "Hope Morgan an' them women gits out of it."

"He will," Culpepper said, "if he gits out o' that hole in one piece." Culpepper extended his hand. "Glad to see you, Horn." They shook hands and Culpepper set about to make some coffee.

Seth Rawlings read the letter . . . first to himself and then out loud.

"You make anythin' of it, Marshal?" Tom Horn asked.

"Some. Some's easy. The R B here . . . that's the Rocky Barr ranch."

"Yeah, I figured that part. What I couldn't figure was what he meant when he said . . . what is it . . ."

"*We have it*, is what he wrote," Seth looked up. "That don't figure. Judge Barr has been the toughest holdout in the valley."

"Unless he's buckled up since Morgan took his daughter in."

"Don't hardly seem possible," Marshal Rawlings replied. "Morgan told me that fella Brock was s'posed to be gone fer a week. Now by my reckonin' . . . that'd be a trip to Boise. Figured he'd likely find out what he's supposed to do an' then contact Judge Barr."

"Yeah," Horn agreed, "but Blanchard had this letter more'n two weeks ago . . . a'fore Morgan ever took Barr's daughter in." Seth looked down and scanned the letter again. "Well, this here F Q is easy enough," he looked up at Tom, "that'd be the Four Queens . . . Belle Moran's place."

"An' the feller what wrote it . . . that there T Y?"

"No ideas," Seth said. "Not even a good guess." Ephram Culpepper poured three cups of coffee, moved a chair up near the stove and sat down. "Looks like one of us got some ridin' to do, Horn . . .

to Boise.''

"Morgan said to sit tight 'til he come in with the women." Ephram grinned. "You takin' orders from Lee Morgan now, Seth?"

"No goddam it," Seth replied, irritably, "but maybe he'll know somethin' else from one o' the women . . . or from somebody up in the Gorge."

"That's if'n he gets back at all," Ephram said.

"He'll make it." Ephram looked up at Tom Horn. He smiled.

"I didn't mean if'n somebody took 'im out, Horn. I meant he might have to git out o' this weather."

"That he will," Seth agreed. "Especially with two gals fer saddle companions."

The door opened and all three men came up with weapons. The door closed, the man stomped his feet, pulled the neck scarf down and removed his hat. They were looking at Judge Isaac Barr.

Lil Johnson was shivering almost uncontrollably. She was curled into a ball, back against the outside wall of the dilapidated line shack. Lee Morgan struggled to clear the drifted snow from in front of the door.

"Can w . . . w . . . we build a fire?" she asked.

"If there's wood," Morgan said. He stopped digging and looked up at her. "I've got some coffee too." She smiled, weakly and nodded. The wind, sharp as a straight edge, was out of the northeast. Morgan tethered the animals on the southwest side of the shack. He wasn't certain of their exact location but he was guessing the shack was on Josh Killerman's Rocking K spread.

Morgan finally forced the door and the couple got inside. The furnishings were sparse. A tick mattress, without a bed frame, a small table with one broken chair and a #7 cook stove. Several 2 x 4 and 2 x 12 boards made up some cupboard space. It was empty, save for a coal oil lamp about a third full. Morgan pointed and smiled. "Light and firewood," he said.

Twenty minutes later, the shack, in spite of its flimsy construction, was warm and cozy. Lil set about to make coffee and warm two tins of beans. Morgan ventured into the cold again in search of more wood. They ate in silence with Morgan finally breaking it as he rolled a smoke.

"You hear anything else when Brock took Miss Barr away?" Lil shook her head. She sat, legs pulled beneath her, near the stove. Both hands were wrapped around the tin cup and she blew, gently, at the steaming contents. "You still cold?"

"Inside," she said, "with fear."

"You're safe now. We both are."

"We're out of that camp . . . yes . . . but *safe?* I wish I'd never come to this god-forsaken land." Morgan frowned. "Oh . . . I'm no pioneer woman . . . I haven't the stomach or the backbone for it. My parents are dead and gone. They . . . they burned to death. My mother was Ben Strada's sister. The only family on either side still alive. I was not yet of age so . . ."

"So here you are." She nodded. Morgan winced. How could he tell her that she no longer had an uncle either. "I hate to bring it up, but we'll have to ride out before daylight. I don't want to run the risk of being spotted."

"I understand. I just want to get home . . . that's all." They finished their coffee and Morgan put the last big log in the stove.

"That'll burn down in a couple of hours. There isn't anymore. I'll bust up the table and chair in the

morning. We'll at least get warm and have some
coffee before we ride out. You take the mattress and
both coats. I've got my bedroll.''

Morgan's whole body ached. He hadn't realized
how dog tired he really was and how much he ached
in every bone and joint. He stirred only when he felt
the press of weight atop him. Cold air rushed into
the gap in the bedroll and he blinked awake.

"I'm freezing," Lil Johnson said. She had opened
the gap and was slipping between the top cover and
Morgan's body. She was naked! He heard the
crackling of a fire and glanced at the stove. She had
started another fire with the chair. Half her lithe,
young body was visible in the dancing light from the
flames.

"You sure you want it this way?" She answered
with a kiss . . . a heavy, passionate kiss. Her tongue
darted into Morgan's mouth. He was surprised at
her expertise.

Her breasts were small but firm and the nipples,
hardened in the cold of the shack, seemed nearly as
big as the breasts themselves. She scooted down
and brushed them along Morgan's lips. He moaned
softly.

Lil slipped still farther into the bedroll and began
undoing Morgan's belt. By the time she had
stripped him, he had responded to her efforts and
his own desires. His mind was filled with contra-
dictions but Lil Johnson's mouth around his blood
gorged shaft quickly dulled his thinking processes.

"Love me," she whispered, "love me and I'll do
anything you ask." Morgan thought it almost
humorous. It was Lileth who was doing the love-
making . . . and in ways which Morgan would
probably not have had the courage to ask . . . at least
the first time around.

Her hands caressed his body, exploring, stroking, pausing at the most sensitive junctures. He found her breasts and stroked and pulled at them. Lil's hips were soon gyrating atop his groin . . . and she rubbed along his shaft . . . back and forth. He could feel the moisture of her arousal.

She was on her knees, her head was thrown back and her eyes closed in a delirium of ecstacy. Suddenly, she stopped. Her breathing was heavy, almost labored. She leaned foward. "I . . . I've *never* . . . not completely . . . not with . . . with a man . . . just . . . just a boy I knew. We just . . . touched."

"Jeezus," Lee whispered. He doubted that Lil even heard him. He nodded. He moved her from atop him, layed her down and began kissing her. He let his hands wander over her body while his tongue and lips worked along her neck, breasts, stomach and finally to the very center of her emerging womanhood.

"There'll be a little pain . . . a kind of sharp, burning pain . . . just for a second," he said. Their eyes met. She smiled and nodded. Morgan entered her with all the care and finesse he'd acquired. Even he was surprised at the minimal resistance her hymen offered. Lil's only reaction was a slight stiffening, a frown on her face and the gentle biting of her lower lip. A moment later . . . her face seemed radiant with a pleasure she had never known.

Morgan pumped with a measured rhythm . . . continuing his gentle caresses and kissing. He was about to burst and had to struggle againt the temptation of pleasing only himself. Slowly she began to respond. Her body joined his own in the age old, pleasure filled motion of male and female . . . once again a single entity of creation.

"Oh it's good . . . oh God . . . it's so good . . . oh

Morgan . . . God . . . oooh God . . . oh GOD!'' Lil's
climactic reaction came upon her so suddenly even
she wasn't ready. Morgan, caught unaware, quickly
recovered. They reached the peak of ecstacy
together, hovering for a moment and then collapsing
into each other's arms and the void which follows
the summit of human contact.

Morgan added a few final pieces of wood to the
dying fire and then rolled a smoke. He slipped into
the bedroll next to Lil. He thought she was asleep.
She turned on her side and kissed his cheek.

"Thank you," she said. "You were very gentle . . .
I . . . I somehow knew you would be."

"No regrets?"

"No regrets. I was a girl . . . now I'm a woman.
Only a man can make that possible . . . not a boy."

Judge Barr's sudden appearance in Ketchum
proved even more a surprise to Seth Rawlings than
he had, at first, imagined. Seth assumed that Barr
was looking for him and by sheer luck had found
him. Neither was the case. Rawlings quickly
brought Judge Barr up to date on events.

"I'm glad you're here, Horn," Barr said. "I've
brought money and tomorrow I'll pay you off."

"Haven't really don't the job yet," Horn said.

"You've done all there is to do . . . it's over. I'm
here because of this." Judge Barr produced a letter.
Seth Rawlings read it . . . aloud.

> Judge,
>   Your daughter and Ben Strada's
> niece will both be returned to you . . . un-
> harmed, when you comply with the
> instructions set down herein. Contact all
> the ranch owners. Gather them . . . with

yourself, in Ketchum. Be there no later
than Thursday night. My people will
meet with you Friday. If all goes well . . .
you will see the women safely returned.

Brock

The old marshal studied the page and then handed
it to Tom Horn. "That look familiar?" Horn glanced
at it and nodded. Judge Barr frowned.

"You mean you got a similar letter? That's why
you're all here?"

"A similar letter," Horn said, "same hand writin'
. . . not to us but to Jess Blanchard. Come out o'
Boise . . . an' come out at a time when this here fella
Brock couldn't o' wrote it." Horn handed Judge
Barr both his letter and the letter Horn had taken
from Jess Blanchard's body.

"I . . . I don't understand."

Ephram Culpepper now looked at both letters.
"Looks to me like you been dealt a crooked hand,
Judge." He glanced at Marshal Rawlings. Seth
nodded his agreement.

"They pull every ranch owner left all into one nice
little bunch."

"Move in from both directions," Tom said. "That
outfit out o' Picabo an' the main bunch from the
Gorge. Sounds like they figger to do in Ketchum the
same as ol' Quantrill did down Kansas way back in
sixty-four."

"An ambush?" Judge Barr looked down. He
paced, rubbed his forehead and then studied the
letters again. "You're saying that this man Brock
didn't write these?"

"Couldn't have . . . leastways not accordin' to Lee
Morgan. Brock was nowhere near Boise an' we've

got that kid locked up across the street. He confirms that there's somebody bigger'n Brock involved.''

"Then I've asked all these men to ride in here to their deaths . . . just to save my daughter and Ben Strada's niece. Now . . . God . . . even Ben is . . .''

"What did you tell them?" Seth asked. The judge looked up, quizzically. "The other owners? What did you tell them?''

"I . . . oh God . . . I *lied*. I didn't want to risk being turned down. I told them we had a plan . . . a good plan and . . . and *help* on the way.''

"Too late to do much about that," Ephram said. "Hell . . . they'll be here tomorrow. I figger them maraudin' bastards will hit Friday." He looked at Tom Horn. "How many you guess Tom?''

"Seventy . . . eighty mebbe . . . in both batches.''

Judge Barr leaped to his feet. "I've got to ride out . . . warn the others." He reached for his coat. Tom Horn caught his arm.

"Judge . . . hold on. Where you plannin' on startin'? East? West mebbe . . . or should you ride north first?" The judge quickly recognized the futility of his thought. He slumped into a chair.

"I'll have to order a complete evacuation of the town," Seth said, "at first light. I hope you two will help. Organize the town's folk an' git 'em out o' here. I'll stay behind and try to talk sense to the ranch owners as they ride in.''

"I'll stick, Marshal," Horn said. They both looked at Ephram. He nodded. "If'n I figger 'im right. . . Lee Morgan oughta be ridin' in sometime tomorrow . . . hopefully with them gals . . . your daughter should be safe, Judge.''

Judge Isaac Barr looked up. There were tears in his eyes and an expression on his face which took all three men by surprise. He got to his feet, walked to

the table and picked up the two letters. He read
them both, held them up and studied each with care.
His face paled.

"My God!" He put the letters down. His hand
was trembling. "I . . . I think I know who wrote
these," he said. His voice was soft now . . . he pushed
to get more volume. He was choked up. "The initial
. . . the T and the Y . . . they . . . they were short for a
ranch name a few years back. The Yellow. It was
called the Yellow. The whole name was the Yellow
Pine ranch." Marshal Seth Rawlings' jaw dropped.

"Tom Yeager's place?" Seth nodded in confirmation of his own question and its answer. "Jeezus . . .
it makes sense." He looked at Ephram and Tom.
"Thomas Seaton Yeager . . . United States Senator.
He's been fightin' for mineral rights in Idaho for
years. Struck some gold up on his place . . . got
hisself in some trouble last election time. Accused o'
sneakin' around other folk's property . . . checkin'
fer gold . . . silver . . . copper. He got out of it . . . got
re-elected but they was plenty o' noise about it."

"Jehosophat! A Yewnited States Senator? You
sure about this, Judge?" Judge Barr looked up,
slowly. Tears filled his eyes. He nodded.

Seth Rawlings worked his way over and sat down
next to Judge Isaac Barr. "Isaac . . . are you sure?"

"I should have recognized the hand sooner . . . I've
seen it enough times." He looked into Seth's eyes.
"He wanted me to recognize it . . . didn't he?"

"Prob'ly," Seth replied, weakly. He shook his
head and then looked up at the others.

"Tom Yeager has been comin' out to the Rocky
Barr fer a good long time now. Courtin' Morgana.
They planned on gettin' hitched up next spring."

"The girl . . . does she . . ."

"Know?" Tom nodded. "Can't be sure . . . but it'd

seem likely."

"If that's the case," Ephram said, "then Lee Morgan's a dead man."

Morgan was cold enough to be dead but there, the similiarity ended. He and Lil rode out of the line shack well before dawn. Their horses struggled with the off trail snow. Morgan couldn't risk running into the returning marauders. Brock or most anyone else. He ordered that they ride an hour . . . then walk a half hour to give the mounts a rest. They were not making the time he'd hoped for however and, after their latest stop, he decided to risk a return to the main trail.

Some six hours after they'd ridden from the line shack, Morgan and Lileth Johnson rounded a curve in the road and spotted a buggy. Morgan, throwing caution to the wind, fired a shot in the air. Moments later, they came face to face with Josh Killerman.

They exchanged information and Morgan was clearly concerned about the turn of events. Nonetheless, he felt the only option open to them was to reach Ketchum. He freed himself of the slow pace of his trip by leaving Lil with Killerman. Then, he gave Pacer his head.

Seth Rawlings had come to the conclusion that there was no end to the surprises he'd been getting. At just after four o'clock the door opened and Lee Morgan walked through it.

"I'll be damned," Seth said. "I figgered you was dead . . . sure."

"Not yet," Morgan said. He moved to the stove and poured himself some coffee. "Ran into Josh Killerman coming in. Strada's niece is with him now. They'll be here tonight. Killerman told me . . ."

"I know what he told you . . . an' why." Seth told

Morgan what had happened. Horn, Culpepper and Isaac Barr were even then rounding up Ketchum's populace and readying them to move out. They were getting plenty of resistance. Morgan had about decided to join them in the effort when Addie Terhune walked in. She looked straight at Morgan.

"I didn't know you were back but it's a good thing." She stepped aside and in walked Belle Moran from Boise. She looked stern.

"What the hell are you doing here?"

"Where's Judge Barr," she asked.

"Trying to round up some citizens, why?"

"You'd best get him," Belle said, "and anybody else that owns anything hereabouts. I rode in to warn you." Morgan nodded and left the office.

The decision was made to bring together the area's ranch owners and the citizens of Ketchem that night at Addie's place. Both Seth Rawling and Judge Barr protested the idea at the outset. They felt strongly that the families should clear out but Tom Horn found a solution to the disagreement. He suggested that the decision be left to those affected. The vote was to meet that night.

Belle found Lee Morgan at a corner table. He had a bottle and a glass and he had just rolled a smoke.

"You want company?"

"Why not?"

"Does the judge know *everything?*"

"All he needs to know, I'd guess. Is Morgana solid with Yeager?" Belle nodded. "Has been all along. That's why she agreed to come with you so easy."

"How come she didn't turn me in to Brock?"

"From what I could find out, Brock didn't know about her. Nobody did 'cept her an' the good senator. She finally told him but . . . well, by then you'd already got in an' out again with Strada's niece."

"You got any kind of a head count on their men?"

"More'n hundred," Belle said. "They'll burn this place to the ground an' kill anybody they find. Don't recall ever seein' a man with the gold fever as bad as Yeager's got it. He's crazy."

"I thought he was in pretty good shape."

"Ever'body did. That's 'cause he was . . . once. He stuck ever'thing into a railroad venture. He got conned. He used his office to get a lot of big cattlemen involved but he had to promise rail transport out of Idaho . . . same as it is down in Wyoming an' Kansas an' Nebraska. Hell . . . even Montana is in better shape. When that fell through . . . he was in big trouble."

"An' those cattlemen *still* don't know?"

Belle shook her head. "With his power, Yeager's been able to stall 'em but he needs cash. A lot of cash an' in a big hurry. A lot of mining rights are government owned. He can't do much with those but if he's got access to the land around them, he can come out of it."

"You mean sell the access rights to the big mineral outfits?"

"As best I can get the story . . . yeah." She smiled. "The son-of-a-bitch even had me boxed up and wrapped. I believed what he said."

"Which was?"

"Talk a woman likes to hear . . . particularly one like me. I fell for it like some little virgin farm girl."

"You didn't know about Morgana Barr?"

"Not then." Belle downed a drink. She winced and shivered. "How do you stop somethin' as big as Yeager?"

"I don't know for sure," Morgan said. He leaned forward. "Hell, maybe you *don't.*"

"Somebody's gotta *try*."

"Cemeteries are full o' folks that *tried*."

"You quittin'?"

"It's not up to me." Morgan gestured around the room. "It's up to the people that fill this place tonight. Idaho is theirs."

"An' what do you get out o' helpin' 'em, Morgan?"

"I'm here. The Spade Bit is gone. I guess I owe some'thin' to somebody for that."

"And then what?"

Morgan smiled. "Good question, Belle. According to Seth Rawlings, I'm an antique. A poor imitation of my daddy . . . lived past my time."

"Hell . . . you're not that old."

"No . . . but Seth is right. For *who* I am . . . *where* I come from and *what* I am . . . well, I guess I should be in some eastern museum or maybe old Bill Cody's *Wild West Show*."

"Bull! If the men comin' west now are all like Tom Yeager . . . this country needs you bad . . . you an' Tom Horn an' a thousand more like you."

"Maybe . . . but it won't happen. No, I'll end up hanging from a tree, or get shot on some dusty street, or bushwhacked on some back trail. Horn too."

"That's a poor way to go out."

Morgan looked up and smiled. "Not so bad maybe. Beats hell out of Cody's Wild West Show. Or Barnum's Dime Museum. I don't want to end up throwin' in my hand in some damned fancy, eastern boarding house."

"Why don't you come to work for me?"

"Pimpin' or shootin' people?"

"Goddam, Morgan, you're an ungrateful bastard."

"I don't mean anything by it, Belle. I appreciate it. Your heart's in the right place. It's just that what you're offerin' is no different really than back east."

"Well . . . mebbe we're both just spittin' into the wind. Might end right here . . . right in Ketchum, Idaho. Gunsmoke an' blood soaked snow. Make great writin' for Ned Buntline or somebody like 'im."

"Gun fighter and the whore," Morgan said, grinning, "that it, Belle?"

"I had something a little more refined in mind. The lady and the shootist maybe." Morgan laughed. Belle Moran poured them both a drink and they proposed a silent toast.

13

Dawn came to Ketchum like a fragile piece of crystal. Ice clung to the trees, telegraph wires, windows and anything made of metal which was exposed. The air was as still and cold as death itself. The only sign of life was a single curl of blue-black smoke belching from the chimney at Addie Terhune's palace of pleasure.

Brock stood in his stirrups and surveyed the scene below. Behind him, fifty-five men sat their mounts, cold, irritable and more than ready to raze the quiet, mountain town.

"I don't give a goddamn about anybody down there," he said, "except Lee Morgan. If he's there I want the son-of-a-bitch alive. I don't care that he's shot up first but I want the pleasure of finishing the job." He looked at the man next to him. "You got that?" The man nodded.

Opposite Brock's position, a little to the south and east of Ketchum, a gunman and bounty hunter named Jace Kileen headed up a band of forty men. Of the force at Tom Yeager's disposal, these two groups represented all but twenty-two men. A dozen of those had simply ridden out . . . either too good to participate in such a slaughter . . . or simply too yellow. The remaining ten stayed with Senator Thomas Yeager in Boise.

At Brock's signal—a single rifle shot—both hands would converge on Ketchum. Anything or anyone in their respective paths was subject to destruction. Their target was Addie's place and the people they believed were in it. All of the ranch owners from a hundred to a hundred fifty miles around.

Down along the main street, hidden from view inside second floor rooms or up on roof tops, were thirty-five ranch owners. Among them, acting as their leaders, was Judge Isaac Barr and Josh Killerman. These men, mostly pioneer stock who had fought Indians and outlaws most of their time in Idaho, were the cream of the crop available. Most were good rifle shots and none of them were strangers to fear.

Ketchum's main street ran north and south. At the south end, huddled in the blacksmith's shop, was Lee Morgan and a half a dozen of the town's men. They too were men who could use weapons . . . at least with some skill. On the opposite end of the street, Marshal Seth Rawling waited with five more such men. Lined up in front of Seth and his men were half a dozen plungers all wired to dynamite. There were four rows of it, about ten feet apart, stretching along the street from one side to the other. At the far end of the main street, Morgan had a similar set-up.

In between them, with the heaviest concentration of explosives placed right in the street's center, was Ephram Culpepper. He was heavily armed . . . alone save for his woman who would load for him. He had a single plunger in front of him. Between them, the set-up had taken to within an hour of dawn. Several things they wanted to do had to be abandoned. The lookouts returned with word that the marauders were riding in.

West of Ketchum, ready to move out—and with luck—catch the stragglers, were the bulk of Ketchum's citizenry. About sixty merchants, barbers, drovers and a few miners. Leading them was Tom Horn.

Everyone had gathered the night before at Addie Terhune's place. They drank and listened. They listened to Judge Isaac Barr and to Seth Rawlings. They listened even to Belle Moran and Tom Horn. Finally, Lee Morgan spoke to them. If they let others destroy Ketchum and drive them out, they were finished, he told them. If it must be destroyed . . . let them do it . . . destroy the plague which threatened it along with the town and then rebuild bigger, better and stronger.

By two o'clock—working in shifts and with the women keeping hot coffee and food ready—the men had rounded up dynamite, weapons and ammunition. They acted according to plans formulated by Rawlings, Horn and Morgan. The women and children were housed in Culpepper's church—the only building with a basement. Now . . . they were ready.

Brock slipped his rifle from the scabbard, raised it above his head, reached up and levered a shell into the chamber and pulled the trigger. The men moved out. Slowly at first . . . then their mounts broke into a trot, a gallop and finally . . . full-fledged run. Their timing was nearly perfect, both groups reaching their respective ends of town almost simultaneously. By now, the lead men had begun to shout and they were shooting into every building.

The din was deafening. Shots, the shattering glass, the old rebel yells, Indian war-whoops and plain old, cowpoke yah-hooing. Morgan and

Rawlings waited . . . waited . . . waited. The lead men
were nearing the center of the town. Others were
strung out behind them, all the way to the street's
end.

"Now," Morgan said. The men behind him pushed
down.

"Now," Seth Rawlings said. The men behind him
pushed down. There had been no time to bury the
explosives. Indeed, even had there been the time,
the ground was steel hard. Some of the dynamite
was pulled from its wiring by the horse's hooves. It
would not detonate for all of it was simply buried
beneath the snow. That aside, much of it did go up.

Horses and men alike were ripped to shreds.
Limbs were torn from bodies and men flew through
the air like so many rag dolls. There were screams as
huge holes were torn in the street and the snow
turned from a pure white to a pale pink and then to a
scarlet.

Fifteen to twenty riders reached the center of
town . . . escaping the explosives behind them. Three
or four—the most astute among them—dismounted
and rushed for the safety of nearby buildings. The
others milled about atop the last of the charges.
Ephram Culpepper shoved down the handle of his
plunger. Eight men died instantly.

The roar of the dynamite faded. Now, from either
side of the street, a fusillade of rifle fire poured down
upon the still breathing but hapless victims. Inside
Addie Terhune's saloon, a woman screamed. She
was Ephram Culpepper's woman. She died
screaming.

Ephram whirled and saw two men . . . one of whom
had just killed the woman. He fired two shots from
his Winchester. Both men died. Ephram got to his
feet, walked back and knelt beside his woman. He

nad tears in his eyes. He heard a noise. He looked up. There stood Brock.

Brock was as fast a man as Ephram had ever faced. Both had been momentarily distracted by a noise above them. They glanced up at the same time. Addie Terhune was there! She wasn't supposed to be. She was holding a shotgun. Brock drew. Ephram's arm was still sore . . . stiff . . . slow to react. Brock's shot passed through the fleshy part of Ephram's left shoulder just below the armpit. Ephram winced but even wounded, his draw was fast and accurate. Brock took a shot between the eyes.

"Ephram . . . my God . . . look out!" Ephram whirled. A shot rang out. . . loud even amidst the outside rifle fire. Ephram saw the man. Big . . . sinister looking. He was holding a smoking .44. Ephram heard the crack of wood behind him. He turned in time to see Addie Terhune's body smash into the top of the bar. It cracked and then slipped from sight. Ephram wheeled. The sinister man had holstered the gun. He was grinning.

"Hello, Preacher Man."

"Jace Kileen . . you rotten son-of-a-bitch."

"I'll cross draw you, Preacher Man . . . since you're hit an' all." Ephram holstered his gun. He realized his throat was dry. *Jeezus,* he thought, *I'm scared.* He'd seen Jace Kileen. He'd never seen a man faster. Ephram's right hand tightened into a fist, relaxed and tightened again. He swallowed, wet his lips, relaxed his hand and drew.

The barrel of his gun was clear of the holster. The shot travelled at an angle and the shell buried itself in a table leg. Ephram's mouth rippled with a grin. It opened but there was no sound. Jace Kileen put a bullet between Ephram Culpepper's eyes.

Perhaps a dozen of the marauders tried to make it
back the way they had come . . . from the south.
Morgan was there . . . he and the men with him cut
them down. Twenty—perhaps even thirty—some
wounded, managed to gather, find mounts and ride
north. Seth Rawlings let them pass. He'd seen Tom
Horn and Ketchum's citizens coming up from the
west. The marauders rode straight into half of them.
The others, with Horn leading, flanked them about a
minute later. Most fell to the ground, hands up,
quitting at last.

There were stragglers . . . eight all told. One of
them was Jace Kileen. The others scattered. Jace
rode hard and fast straight toward Boise. The fight
was over. Twenty minutes . . . perhaps a half an
hour. No one, not even the participants, could be
certain . . . but it *was* over.

Seth, Tom Horn and Lee Morgan met in Addie's
place. The evidence told the story . . . or most of it.
What remained they learned from Addie's one-
armed barkeep, Louie Mathers.

"The preacher . . . he . . . he shot that fella," Louie
said, pointing to Brock, "but . . . I never seen a man
so fast as the other one. Preacher Man called him . . .
uh, Jace . . . Jace Kileen."

Morgan reloaded, picked up the Winchester he'd
loaned to Culpepper and headed for the door.

"Where the hell you bound for?" Seth yelled.

"Boise."

"Morgan!" Lee stopped and turned around. Seth
Rawlings handed Tom Horn a badge. "You took it
off this mornin'. I'm askin' you to put it on, Horn,
and ride to Boise with me—as *law*." Morgan
frowned and then scowled at Tom Horn.

Tom smiled . . . that old, soft, friendly smile of his.

He shrugged. "May as well do it right," he said, taking the badge. Now, both men looked at Morgan. Seth reached in his pocket and withdrew another badge. He held it out. Again, Morgan's eyes met those of the old manhunter . . . Tom Horn.

"Shit," Morgan said. He walked over, took the badge and jammed it into his pocket. Just then, Josh Killerman walked through the door.

"Can't find Judge Barr nowhere."

"You got a head count on our side yet?"

"Five men so far." Killerman saw Ephram. He shook his head. "Six."

"The judge is prob'ly at the church." Killerman shook his head.

"Checked there first . . . I . . . I think he rode out for Boise."

"Jeezus," Morgan said. He pushed by Killerman and raced out.

"Somebody needs to stay here an' take charge," Tom said.

"Yeah," Seth agreed. He pulled another badge out and handed it to Josh Killerman. "You're deputized. Take over here." Tom smiled and the two hurried out.

The trio stopped at the Rocky Barr ranch. They were all certain Judge Barr would have made the same stop. They were wrong. Nonetheless, they took the time to stock up for the trip, tell the judge's foreman and his men what had happened and to rest up. Somewhere, the old judge would have to stop as well. Boise was too long a ride without rest.

Senator Tom Yeager had made quite a show for the voters in Boise. He promised them an end to the land troubles in Idaho and to the killer marauders who'd been plaguing them for months. He also made it appear he'd quit Boise to return to Washington. In fact, he was holed up in Belle Moran's private quarters in the Four Queens.

"Senator, I don't think you can expect anything this soon from Ketchum. It's a long ride in the best of weather." Yeager looked up at the well dressed man who had been serving him as a personal aide for some eight years. A former Pinkerton agent, his name was Ted Peabody.

"You still don't grasp what's happened do you, Ted? That bitch! That whore Belle. She left word at Tate Bosley's office and now I found out she rode off to Ketchum to warn them."

"Sheriff Bosley will pose no problem. I've handled that, I told you about it. He was out of town and the minute he rides in . . . uh . . . the situation will be settled. As to the woman warning someone in Ketchum . . ." the man smiled, "*who?* And what good would it do. We've nearly a hundred men to handle that."

"You can reassure me all you want to Ted . . . but until I see that whore's body . . . hers . . . and Bosley's . . . and the others . . . I won't . . . I *can't* rest easy. You seem to forget what's at stake here."

"Not at all, Senator, but perhaps you're underestimating the men I've assigned to do this job."

"Ted . . . . Goddam you . . . don't try to soft soap me anymore. I turned this whole thing to you a year and a half ago. Now, by God, I'm here in person . . ."

"They proved to be tougher than I thought. I'll admit that but it's under control now . . . settled."

"Too many people know . . . two many are involved. Tom Horn! Good God . . . ten years ago, he was a national hero. Seth Rawlings! One of the finest and oldest lawmen west of the Mississippi. And this . . ."

"Morgan?"

"Yes . . . yes . . . Lee Morgan. I've heard plenty about *him*."

"The son of some old time gunman or other. No real threat."

"You'd better be right Ted—about *everything*."

The door opened and one of Ted's men came in. He looked stern. Yeager looked from one to the other.

"*Well?*"

The man closed the door. "Sheriff Bosley . . . he . . . he's back. He arrested six of our men. He's got a half a dozen deputies and he's comin' *here*." Yeager's face paled. Even Ted Peabody reeled under the shock of the news.

"Another one you underestimated. Is that it, *Ted?*"

The other men? Where are they?"

"Gone . . . 'cept fer that gunny they call Cody."

"*Gone?* Where in hell did they *go?*"

"Rode out. I'm doin' the same." Ted Peabody reached into his coat, withdrew a Colt's model Deringer and put a single bullet into the man's head.

"Ted . . . for God's sake . . . we can't kill them all." Ted Peabody dragged the man's body to a closet, shoved it inside and closed the door. He straightened.

"Tom," he said, his voice low but firm . . . almost steely . . . "don't whine. I can't stand your whining. I've come a long way with you . . . I've got more at stake than you have. You're *somebody* . . . I'm just hired help. Now shut up, Senator . . . and I'll get us both out of this."

Both men heard the door and turned toward it. It opened and Jace Kileen walked in. He quickly explained what had happened in Ketchum.

"Those that know about you," Kileen said, "will

be here. Most still don't. You want to keep it tha
way?"

"Of course he does," Ted Peabody said. Kileen
ignored Peabody. Tom Yeager finally nodded.
"Kileen . . . I need you here to do a job." Again, the
gunman ignored Peabody and spoke directly to
Yeager.

"Cody told me, downstairs, that the law is onto
you. They'll be here in a few minutes. Now me an'
Cody will stand with you . . . for a price."

"Name it."

"To start," Kileen said, smiling and pointing at
Ted. "I want his job." Ted Peabody was incredu-
lous. He jerked his head and looked at Senator
Yeager.

Yeager's eyes never left Kileen's. "Take it," he
said, coldly. Ted Peabody reached. His hand never
got near his coat. Kileen shot him in the forehead.

"What else?" Yeager asked, his voice shaky.

"We'll settle that later. Just make certain you're
here." Kileen walked out, walked down the stairs
and had just reached the main floor when Tate
Bosley and his men walked in. Two of them stopped
dead in their tracks.

"Tate . . . that's . . . that's Jace Kileen."

"You're under arrest," Tate said. He was carrying
a shotgun and he raised the barrel until it was
leveled at Kileen. The man to Tate's right glanced
around the room. Everyone had moved back save a
young man at the bar. He downed a shot of whiskey,
set the glass on the bar and both arms moved like
whips. Jace Kileen dropped to one knee, drawing
with a speed which defied description. Tate Bosley,
Sheriff of Boise for more than eight years, died
instantly. So did his two chief deputies. Outside,
two more fled. Neither got out of sight.

"Do we bust them others out o' jail," Cody asked

Kileen.

"No need. There'll be three men riding into Boise." Kileen smiled. "Seth Rawlings is one of 'em, an' I've got an old account to settle with him." He looked at the kid named Cody. "You can have yourself a whole new reputation with the second one —old Tom Horn."

"Shit!" Cody grinned and gripped the butts of his twin Colt's.

"Who's the other one?"

"Heard his name kicked around," Kileen said, "but I don't know anything about him. Name's Morgan . . . Lee Morgan."

"I'll be waitin' right here," Cody said. Kileen nodded and went back upstairs.

"The sheriff is dead. No one else will bother you. The ones riding in from Ketchum Cody and I will handle. After that . . . I'll tell you what else I want."

"Get the job done, Kileen . . . that's all. Just get it done. I'll see to it you're well payed."

The Rocky Barr ranch was the end of the line for Seth Rawlings. Back in Ketchum, his leg had not been too important. He really didn't have to use it that much. The ride proved more than it could take. It ripped open and bled badly. Seth elicited a promise that both Tom Horn and Lee Morgan would honor their commitments and act for the law. They both agreed.

They arrived in Boise in the early hours of the morning. They rode to the sheriff's office and found it abandoned and the cells empty. Petie Wheeler limped up just as they were leaving. He motioned for them to follow him inside.

"You gents ride in from Ketchum?" They were surprised. "Plenty o' talk circulatin' about it. Most excitement in Boise in twenty year or more." Petie

had been the general clean-up man and cook at the
jail. He'd worked the entire time for Tate Bosley. He
told Tom and Lee what had happened.

"Them other two deputies . . . hell fire . . . they
rode out o' here like somebody put horse linament
on their peters. Little later . . . this here kid . . . totes
two Colt's . . . he come by an' turned ever'body
loose. They was six. Four o' them high-tailed it too."

"What about the others?"

"Went back over to the Queens. They got it all to
themselves."

"You know who all is in there?"

"Best I can figger . . . this kid . . . two o' them
what he let out an' Jace Kileen." Tom Horn let out a
long, low whistle. Morgan eyed him.

"He the old bounty hunter?" Morgan asked.

"No older'n me," Tom said.

"I thought he was dead. I figured that old barkeep
back in Ketchum was wrong."

"Yeah . . . I kinda thought mebbe he was too, but
he wasn't."

"This Kileen . . . he was good."

"The best," Tom said.

"Better than my dad?"

"I don't know if there was *any* man *better* than
Buckskin Frank Leslie. But there were a few around
just as good. One of 'em killed him."

"Yeah . . . Harv Logan."

"Well . . . Jace Kileen was right up there with all
of 'em."

"You scared of him, Tom?"

"You damned right I am. I get a chance I'll take
him out with the Creedmoor."

"It's not that kind of a fight Tom," Morgan said.
"You take your shotgun and you take out those
others . . . two of 'em anyway. I can't say what this
kid Cody will be like."

"Uh huh . . . an' you'll take Kileen?"

"I want Yeager and I don't want Judge Barr gettin' killed." Morgan turned to Petie Wheeler. "You know who Judge Isaac Barr is . . . by sight I mean?"

"Yep."

"You seen him?"

"Nope."

"Morgan . . . I've come to like you, boy . . . seen you work too. You're good . . ."

"But not good enough to take Jace Kileen . . . is that what you're leading up to?"

"That's about it."

"You got a better way? They won't come out and trail us and I don't know anybody else close by that'll go in after 'em. If we don't, Yeager gets away clean—with everything. Folks in Ketchum don't win."

"You're tellin' me ever'thing I don't want to hear, son. It's all right o' course, but I still don't want to hear it." Tom Horn walked out. Morgan frowned. Surely the old man hunter hadn't quit him. In a moment, Tom returned. He was toting his Parker shotgun.

"When?" he asked.

"In the morning," Morgan answered. "I'd like to find Judge Barr." Morgan looked around the office. "We can stay right here."

Morgan looked down at old Petie Wheeler. The old man was frowning. He wasn't certain of this young, dark eyed gunman. Morgan reached into his coat pocket, felt around and withdrew a tin star. He held it up, shook his head and then pinned it on his coat lapel. Tom Horn grinned. Petie Wheeler grinned. He shook his head.

"I'll be back in an hour," Morgan said.

14

Lee Morgan woke with a start. He wasn't exactly certain why. The only noise was the occasional snoring spells of Tom Horn. Morgan got up, turned up the lamp and rolled himself a smoke. It was nearly three o'clock in the morning. He sat down and looked over at Tom Horn. He couldn't help but wonder if he'd live that long.

His mind wandered back over the years—the years and the few miles from Boise to the old Spade Bit ranch. The day he'd come back. Scared. Knowing he'd failed. Trying to ride with the likes of Butch and Sundance and Harvey Logan. Logan! God. He was fast. Morgan's face wrinkled up as he remembered the day in the cook shack at the Spade Bit.

Lee walked in . . . bound on turning and trying Harvey Logan. Old McCorkle the cook was busy at his stove. Wait! It wasn't McCorkle. The tall man turned and there stood Buckskin Frank Leslie. Both men drew. Both men fired. Both men died. Morgan blinked and cursed under his breath as the end of his cigarette reached his finger.

He walked back over and lay down, his arms up and his hands underneath his head. Is that the way it will end? He and Jace Kileen both dead? Tom Horn snored again. Morgan closed his eyes. He saw

his father's face . . . looking up at him . . . smiling.
The red spot on his chest growing bigger with each
breath. Who would hold Morgan's head? Was he like
Harvey Logan . . . and Kileen the old time shootist?
Morgan dozed.

The rattling of the coffee pot brought Morgan
from the deepest sleep he'd experienced in weeks.
Sunshine streamed through the windows of the
sheriff's office. He caught the movement of someone
. . . Petie.

"What the hell time is it?"

"Well now . . . mornin' Mister Morgan. Seemed to
me, there fer a spell, you just might sleep out the
day."

Morgan sat up and then got to his feet. He was
irritated. "Damn it, old man, what time is it?"

"Jist past ten."

"*Ten!*" Morgan looked around. Petie walked up,
smiled and handed him a cup of coffee. "Where's
Horn?"

"Asked me to give you this." Morgan took the
slip of paper. He sat down at the desk, took a short
sip of coffee, set the cup down and unfolded the
paper.

> One of Belle's gals come by . . . said two
> fellas left early riding to Ketchum. She
> heard they was riding to kill Marshal
> Rawlings. May be they just want to split
> us. It worked. Can't let Seth get it. I'll
> dog them two and git back soon as I can.
> Watch yourself, son.
>
>   Tom Horn

"Goddamn fool," Morgan said. "They'll be laying

for him not five miles out.''

"That there is about what he said.'' Morgan looked up. Petie was smiling. "Mister Horn . . . he's been around a long time . . . he got worse than the likes o' those two. I wouldn't worry none 'bout him, Mister Morgan. It's you what's gonna face down Jace Kileen.''

Morgan checked the load in the Smith and Wesson, loaded the sixth chamber and strapped on the rig. He sat back down and sipped his coffee. Outside, the bustle of Boise seemed undisturbed by the presence of the participants of the drama. No law existed now but most citizens didn't even know it. The newspaper was afraid to send a reporter to the Four Queens. Morgan knew there would be no posse formed up in Boise. No vigilantes would ride in and shoot it out at the saloon. Doubtless, his death or that of Kileen's would go unnoticed.

Morgan finished his coffee, slipped on his coat, smiled at Petie and walked out. It was a block and a half to the Four Queens. Down Rose Hill from Shoshone, past the railroad depot and then right onto Vista. "Mister Morgan . . . Mister Morgan . . . you forgot somethin'.'' Morgan turned. Petie held up his hand and Morgan saw the glint of the sun on the tin star.

"Shit,'' Morgan muttered. He walked back, nodded at Petie, took the badge and pinned it to his coat. Then he turned back and walked to the corner. He stayed to the sidewalks but noticed that the number of people on the streets had diminished. He reached Vista, paused and glanced toward the railroad depot. He saw a little knot of men by the corner of the building. They saw him. They shuffled, nervous. One of them pointed at Morgan. They knew. He walked to the middle of the street, eyed each building carefully and then turned toward the saloon.

Up in Belle Moran's office, the door opened. A nervous little man poked his head inside. Jace Kileen was leaning against the wall, arms folded across his chest. Senator Tom Yeager was seated at the desk.

"What is it, Rollins?"

"He's coming sir . . . not the old one . . . the young one."

"Thank you," Yeager said. He swallowed. The door closed. He looked at Kileen. Kileen smiled. "Well?"

"Cody will handle him."

"And if he doesn't?"

"Then I'll know he's better than I figure he is."

"And you sent the others off on a wild goose chase after some damned old lawman."

"Seth Rawlings is a better man than you've ever seen, Senator."

"That's not the point. What if this Morgan gets by you?"

"He won't."

"I'm not in a position to risk that. . . am I?"

"You fuck with me," Kileen said icily, "and I'll live long enough to kill you Yeager . . . mark me on that."

"I . . . I don't see how . . . how *everything* could have gone wrong."

"Real easy. You had all the wrong men thinking for you."

"Are you at least going downstairs . . . just in case?" Kileen smiled . . . then he nodded. When he reached the door, Yeager said, "Get him, Kileen. Make sure you get him."

"Sure, Yeager, you just relax." Kileen walked out

and Tom Yeager wiped his brow, walked to the window and peered out. Seeing nothing at the back of the saloon, he disappeared into the sleeping quarters.

Downstairs, the kid named Cody shoved a big tin plate away from him, took two swallows of coffee and sucked some bacon out of his front teeth. He looked up and saw Jace Kileen.

"Mornin' Jace."

"Morgan's outside."

"Yeah . . . I know." Cody grinned, hefted the twin Colts and let them slip back into their holsters. Then he hefted his right leg onto a chair and tied down his holster. He repeated the process on the left side.

"I've heard he's good, Cody. Son of old Frank Leslie."

"I heard o' Leslie. Harvey Logan took him out." Cody grinned. "Now there was a fast gun . . . Kid Curry."

"Leslie killed him . . . he didn't gain much."

"Well I ain't Logan . . . an' this gunny ain't his daddy." A man at the front door backed off, swallowing. He turned and looked at Kileen and the kid called Cody. "Out front . . . that's Lee Morgan."

Cody doffed his hat. "See you in a minute Jace. Buy you the first drink o' the day." Cody walked to the front door, opened it and walked out. He closed it behind him and then turned. Lee Morgan stood in the middle of the street. The little knot of men from the depot had moved to about half a block away. Another group had formed in the other direction. All had come to see a man die. Morgan doubted that it made any difference to them which man it was.

"Well now . . . we got ourselves some new law in Boise. You takin' up for Tate Bosley are you?"

"Deputy Territorial Marshal," Morgan said,

"deputy to Seth Rawlings."

"That right. My name's Cody. That's my *first* name. Only one you'll be needin' to know."

"You're under arrest," Morgan said. At the same time, the hem of the sheepskin coat went back. Cody made his move. Both hands, both Colts . . . three shots. The first two dug into the snow and the dirt on Vista Street. They were just beneath the toes of Morgan's boots. The third shot, out of the right hand gun, went high and wild. It was fired by the reflex action of a dead man. Morgan fired only one shot. It penetrated Cody's left eye, tore it from the socket and drove it, along with a fragment of nose bone, into Cody's brain.

Cody's body smashed into the saloon's door. His left elbow went through the window. The signal from the opposite side of his brain sent the message that caused him to fire the third shot. He was already dead. His body hung on the door a moment, stiffened, teetered precariously as though seeking equilibrium and then fell foward.

A man at the window stepped back. "I never seen nobody draw that fast . . . not nobody. Not even from the old days." The man turned and looked right straight at Jace Kileen. "He kil't Cody with one shot." Jace reached up and wiped his mouth. He turned and walked to the bar.

"What'll you have, Mister Kileen?"

"Tennessee mash," Kileen replied. Then he turned and faced the door.

Tom Horn's mount pulled up short on a hillock about twenty miles outside of Boise. He dropped his head and pawed. He raised his head and snorted. A shot rang out and the animal staggered, whinnied and dropped in its tracks. The horse kicked its legs

and four more shots rang out. The animal was still.
So was its rider. All four shots had hit home.

Two men emerged from a stand of trees on either
side of the rise. They met at the spiny summit,
spoke to each other in low tones and then walked
toward their victims. Once there, they split up. One
man knelt by the animal. It was dead. The other by
the man.

"Jeezus Christ . . . he . . . he's *dead!*" The man
leaped to his feet.

" 'Course he's dead you goddam fool," the other
man said, standing up now.

"Oh shit . . . oh billy shit." The man who'd knelt
by the horse's rider turned white, his eyes grew big
and he started turning . . . 'round and 'round. "He
was *already* dead." He pointed to the man on the
horse. "It's Eddie . . . Eddie Hargrove. Oh shit . . .
Billy shit." The Creedmoor barked. The frightened
man's body was slammed into the snow, face first,
with the force equivalent to having been hit in the
head with a sledge hammer. He never moved again.

The second man stood . . . unbelieving . . . frozen
. . . numb with the realization he was about to die.
He turned on his heel . . . his brain's message finally
reaching reluctant legs. The Creedmoor barked a
second time and the whole back of the man's head
disappeared behind a shock of thick, brown hair and
a black, flat crowned hat.

Tom Horn had experienced the horse killers before
—up near Gunsmoke Gorge. He'd risen early, listened to the girl's report and then rounded up his
gear and borrowed a horse from the livery. Tom then
rode to the mortuary and, at gunpoint, found himself a cadaver. An hour in the morning air gave the
body all the stiffness required for it to sit a horse.

Horn dogged the two men's trail until it split.

Then, he dismounted, replaced himself with the body of Eddie Hargrove, dropped the reins on the horse and slapped its thighs. The horse moved off along the ridge almost at a walk. Creedmoor in hand, Tom Horn took to the trees, finally positioned himself at the split in the trail and waited.

Tom had no trouble rounding up the men's horses. He tied both of them to one horse, draped Eddie's body over the back of his own, mounted up and headed back to Boise.

The saloon door opened and Cody's body came through it. Morgan stepped in behind, quickly surveyed the scene and then looked straight at Jace Kileen.

"I think he belongs to you," Morgan said.

"I knew him." Several men in the bar moved back to the far wall. Morgan's eyes remained riveted on those of Jace Kileen. "You're pretty good."

"You're under arrest, Kileen."

"You're not *that* good." Kileen drank a shot of whiskey, wiped his mouth and stepped away from the bar. He smiled. "It's really not me you want anyway, is it, Morgan?"

"You'll do, Kileen . . . for starters . . . for Ephram Culpepper." Kileen smirked. "The old preacher man. Always thought he could take me. We were trail compadres once—a long time back."

"You're a talker Kileen . . . talk 'til you buffalo a man."

"Tomorrow, Morgan . . . right here." Kileen nodded toward a table. "I'll have the man you *really* want right over there . . . so he can watch. Take me . . . and he's yours."

"I can have him right now."

"No, you can't. I've got a man upstairs with a

shotgun on him. Any noise down here and he dies."

Morgan reacted for the first time to something Kileen had said. Kileen smiled. Morgan said, "What's the difference Kileen? Today or tomorrow it'll end the same way."

"True . . . but I sent two men out to fetch back Seth Rawlings. You see . . . he's the man I want. You're in my way getting to him just like I'm in yours getting to who you want. Tomorrow . . . Rawlings will be here . . . alive. After I've settled him, you'll have your chance."

"You sure about those men you sent out . . . sure they'll make it?"

"Why shouldn't they?"

"Because Tom Horn found out about them. He rode out of Boise less than an hour behind them, Kileen. Now surely . . . I don't have to tell *you* about Tom Horn." Now it was Morgan's turn to get a reaction. He did. Kileen's face paled. Morgan had a little edge. "I'll make you a deal," he said, smiling, "if Horn rides back in anytime today, I'll be back for you. If not . . . we'll do it your way . . . Seth Rawlings and all."

"Done," Kileen said. His voice did not carry in its tone his earlier conviction. Morgan backed to the door, stepped over Cody's body and outside. "I'll enjoy taking you, Morgan. You might offer some serious competition." Morgan didn't reply.

Judge Isaac Barr had risen early that same morning as well. He had been staying at the home of Ada county prosecutor, James Bidwell. It was located in nearby Nampa, Idaho. Bidwell was more than a little cornered with his old friend's state of mind.

"Judge . . . for God's sake . . . you can't ride into

Boise until I hear from Tate Bosley. We don't know the situation."

"Jim," Isaac Barr said, putting his hand on Bidwell's shoulder, "are you going to stop me at gunpoint?"

"For God's sake . . . no!"

"Then you can't stop me at all. You know it and you know why."

"This man Morgan . . . and Tom Horn . . . Tate and his men . . . they can handle things."

"You were supposed to hear something yesterday from your assistant. You didn't. Something is wrong."

"Judge . . . he could have gotten tied up with anything. At least give it one more day."

"No Jim . . . I'm sorry . . . I can't. I just simply can't."

Judge Bar ate a small breakfast, finished dressing and asked the stable boy to ready his horse.

"At least take my buggy."

"I'll ride in. I want to see Yeager's face just once before I die. I want to see how he must look . . . how he must *feel* about the man he's become . . . and what he . . . what he's done to me . . . and mine."

"My God, man! Stop torturing yourself. You don't know for sure about Morgana. No one has seen her. No one has heard anything."

"Goodbye, Jim, and thank you," Barr said. Jim Bidwell watched Isaac Barr ride away. Immediately, he dressed, readied his buggy and set off behind the judge.

Lee Morgan sat in the sheriff's office and cleaned his weapons . . . twice. His mind kept going back to the kid named Cody. Had Morgan drawn as fast as he could have? He shook the thought away. But it came back. If he had, Cody had come close. Surely Jace Kileen was faster . . . much faster. If Morgan hadn't used all his speed how much more could he call upon? He didn't know.

Buckskin Frank Leslie told him once that the difference between living and dying in a gun fight was often no more than to be willing to die if that's what had to be done. Most men, he'd said, weren't willing. Sometimes they recognized it only at the last moment. A split second of time in their lives when their minds ask the silent question. During that moment—that ever so minute speck of time—their opponent had the edge.

The door opened and Morgan looked up. "Mornin'," Tom Horn said. Morgan poured the coffee, Tom did the talking. Morgan then told Tom what had happened over at the Four Queens.

"Kileen feels pretty safe right now," Tom finally said. "If he's to be taken, now's the time."

"If I don't make it," Morgan said, his voice even in tone and almost passive about the subject, "bury me next to my dad. That cemetery—at least the rights to use it—that stayed with me when the Bit was sold." Horn just nodded. He loaded the Parker and put his coat and hat back on. Morgan frowned.

"I'll back you against anybody else that might figger to make a name fer themselves."

"I lose," Morgan said, grimly, "Kileen might just kill you too."

"Doubt that. Kileen is an old timer. Got a code. Like your daddy had. Knows he could kill me face-to-face an' he don't fight no other way. He might send somebody after me . . . like them two this mornin' . . . but he won't do it."

"What if you're wrong Tom?"

Horn grinned. "Got another hold up there by your

daddy?'' Morgan shook his head and walked out. Horn fell in beside him.

A block and a half away, the door at the Four Queens opened. A man rushed inside, looked around and then hollered, "Jace Kileen in here?"

"Here," Kileen replied. He was in a far corner, seated with three other men. They were playing poker. Kileen stood up.

"That fella Morgan is on his way over," the man paused, drew a deep breath and then added, "Tom Horn is with him." No one really saw the expression on Kileen's face but a moment later, he turned to the men at the table and smiled.

"Sorry, gents, you'll have to excuse me for a few minutes." Out on the street, the word spread even faster than it had earlier. In part, it had come from the undertaker. Tom Horn had dropped off three bodies, apologized for his earlier theft and payed for all the preparations. By the time he and Morgan turned onto Vista, quite a crowd had gathered.

Uptairs in the saloon, Tom Yeager was in the living quarters. There was a window which overlooked Vista Street. He heard the commotion, pulled the curtain back, looked out and sucked in several short gasps of air. He hurried out of the room, through the office, into the hallway and stopped at the head of the stairs. Jace Kileen was just opening the front door.

"Kileen!" Jace paused for a second but nothing more. He said nothing and he did not acknowledge Yeager's single spoken word. He walked out and into the street. Tom Horn and Lee Morgan were about seventy-five yards away. Horn stopped. Morgan did not. Horn walked to the side of the street, scanning the nearby buildings for signs of any back-up men. He saw nothing but cocked both barrels on the Parker.

Morgan had slowed his pace just a little . . . but he was still walking. 65 yards . . . 60 . . . 55 . . . 45. Jace Kileen moved his coat tail and exposed the butt of his pistol. A faint smile rippled across his thin lips. Still Morgan came at him. 30 yards . . . 25 . . . 20. Kileen spread his feet slightly and his shoulders visibly sagged as the tension flowed from them.

"Your round," Kileen said. Now, he was smiling . . . a broad, almost beaming smile. Lee Morgan said nothing and never broke his pace. 15 yards . . . 14 . . . 13 . . . Jace Kileen's brow wrinkled ever so slightly. 12 yards . . . 11 . . . 10 . . . Kileen said, "Morgan . . ."

There were twenty-seven witnesses to what occurred. A dozen of them were in positions to see every detail of the scenario. Some would speak of it for years. None would ever forget.

At eight yards distance . . . 24 feet . . . Jace Kileen's mouth opened. He faced more men in his life than Lee Morgan probably knew. He'd never experienced a man who didn't stop . . . who wouldn't stop . . . who ignored everything except the barest necessity of life . . . breathing! Kileen recognized an iron will . . . a steel-nerved determination to do what no one would believe *could* be done.

This recognition required thought . . . emotional action and a pause for reaction. Given a lesser man than Lee Morgan . . . Kileen's skill and speed with a gun would have offset the lost time. Kileen suddenly realized that Lee Moran *wasn't* a lesser man. Kileen's hand moved with the same smooth flow, the same practiced style that it had for twenty-five years. He was no slower—no less accurate—he was just a split second later in starting.

Morgan's little Smith and Wesson cracked loudly —*twice!* The first shot already fading by the time the second was fired. Between them, almost unheard, Jace Kileen fired. Kileen's bullet traced an angled trajectory and cut a groove of flesh from the upper inside of Lee Morgan's left thigh. Kileen lived long enough to realize it.

Morgan's first shot shattered Kileen's sternum. Bone fragments pierced his right lung and severed a number of blood vessels. Morgan's second shot was a few inches off target. He hadn't allowed for the backward movement of Kileen's body. The bullet entered Kileen's jaw just beneath his chin. It traveled upward, pierced the back of his tongue, passed through his head and exited at the base of his skull.

Lee Morgan was still walking. He did not stop until he was standing over Jace Kileen's motionless form. In his mind's eye, Morgan saw the face of Kid Curry . . . Harvey Logan . . . dead at the hand of Buckskin Frank Leslie. A moment later, Morgan saw Kileen's face. His eyes fluttered, his right leg twitched and the crotch of his denim showed a dark blue, wet spot which continued to spread.

Morgan holstered the S and W, turned, winced in pain and staggered slightly as he took a step. Tom Horn moved toward him at a trot. Lee regained his balance and smiled . . . moving off toward the door of the Four Queens. He could hear disjointed words . . . parts of sentences . . . bits of comment.

"See that . . . fastest man alive . . . Kileen was scared . . . Morgan . . . Frank Leslie . . . Jeezus that was somethin' . . . never believe . . ." Morgan reached the door, Tom Horn reached Morgan.

"You're good boy . . . I believe you're better'n ol' Leslie." Morgan looked at Tom Horn and a half smile crossed his lips. He said, "I was better than Jace Kileen and that's all the better I had to be."

The two men went inside after Tom Horn ordered one of the bystanders to fetch the doctor.

Upstairs, U.S. Senator Thomas Yeager poured himself a straight shot of whiskey, downed it with a shaky hand and slumped into a chair. He sat staring at the wall. Somewhere behind him a door opened and closed. He didn't hear it.

15

Just forty-eight hours before the gun fight that
would keep all of Boise talking for years, U.S.
Marshal Seth Rawlings had crawled into a buggy
seat. Most who were nearby were protesting loudly
about his action. He ignored them as did his
companion, Belle Moran. A few minutes later they
set out for Boise.

"You know," Belle said, "I agree with those folks.
I don't think you should make this trip."

Seth looked at her and smiled. "But you understand . . . don't you?"

She nodded. "How long you known Morgan?"

"More years than I'll admit to," she replied.

"He's not that damned old." Seth realized, too
late, what his observation inferred. He grinned at
his lack of tact.

"I'll let that pass," Belle said.

"You know his daddy?"

"Uh huh. God . . . there *was* a man."

"A gun fighter."

"A *man* first." Belle glanced over at the aging
marshal. "His kind were needed back then. You
were around. You know it."

"He walked on both sides of the law. Don't make
him any less guilty than a man who never walks but
the wrong side."

"You don't believe that tripe, Seth. That's putting Buckskin Frank Leslie in the same box with Jace Kileen."

"Wasn't he?"

"Hell *no*. Kileen does what he wants to do. Frank," she smiled, wistfully, as she thought about him, "he did what he *had* to do."

"Mebbe."

"You were lawin' even then, Seth. How's come you never went after him if you thought he was so damned bad?"

"Never knew it was him . . . not fer sure anyways . . . not 'til Harvey Logan rode in an' killed him. Then . . . well, it all come out."

"An' his son? When did you meet him?"

"Same time. Greenhorn kid . . . scared . . . madder'n a swatted hornet and frustrated as to what to do about it."

Belle frowned. "Is he good enough to take Kileen?"

"Yeah," Seth replied without hesitation. "He's good enough." He looked into Belle's eyes now and added, "But I'm not sure *he* knows it."

"And you . . . are *you* good enough?"

"No. Never was. Mebbe that's one reason I didn't go after old Frank Leslie. Mebbe I knew even then I wasn't the same cut."

"I've heard you're one of the best."

Seth smiled. "One . . . that there's the key word . . . one o' the best. I don't use a gun the same way those men do . . . or did. Makes me vulnerable."

"You knew a lot of them didn't you . . . the old timers?"

"Yeah . . . most. Hickok . . . Earp . . . Masterson. Doc Holliday too." Belle smiled and raised her eyebrows. "I heard he was about the handsomest devil around."

"I s'pose any woman would have thought so."

"Who was the best . . . the very, very best?"

"Don't think I can answer that one Belle. Don't think *anybody* can. I reckon four come to muh mind first if'n I think back. Hickok . . . Holliday . . . Frank Leslie and J.W. Hardin."

"But you can't pick the best huh?"

"Nope. Coolest heads were on Holliday's shoulders . . . an' Leslie's. Flat out speed? Prob'ly Johnny Hardin. Accuracy? No doubt about that . . . James Butler Hickok."

"And what about Lee Morgan?"

"He's got a ways to go yet . . . gotta live more years."

"Kileen?"

"Couldn't have taken a single one o' them I jist mentioned. Neither could Morgan, but he's got the coolest head if he'll just use it."

"I saw Hardin once," Belle said, "down in Abilene. I was just startin' out. Fella name of Deke Brokaw an' a couple o' friends o' his decided mister Hardin would stake their reputations.

"I remember hearin' 'bout a Brokaw."

"Hmm. He was real good. Called Mister Hardin out while he was standin' at the bar. Hell, Hardin had a glass o' whiskey in his left hand when Brokaw drew. Hardin killed him an' never spilled a drop. Then he drank the whiskey, walked to the door, turned back around an' called out the other two. They were at opposite sides o' the room. He killed 'em both. One shot each. Then he just walked out."

"I'd like to git Lee Morgan to deputy for me—permanent." Belle looked surprised. The statement had come from nowhere. Seth was looking at Belle. "Would you help me?"

"Hell, he won't listen to me."

"He might. He come back to Idaho to stay. Got no ranch now. He'll need somethin'."

"Lee's a drifter an' he's got no use for lawmen."

"He'll end up on some street, suckin' air through a hole in his chest. They'll mount 'im on a plank board an' charge ten cents to git a look see."

"I'll talk to him Seth. I'll try."

Morgan walked back to the sheriff's office and changed his britches. He reloaded his pistol and then went back to the Four Queens. He'd left Tom Horn there to make certain no one left. Tom recruited a youngster to keep an eye on the back way out.

"Your man's upstairs," Tom said.

"Do me one more favor." Horn looked quizzical. "Walk over to the newspaper office and bring back a reporter. They'll come if you ask 'em to. I want to tell the story. All of it. I want it out before that Senator is brought down."

"No need," Horn said. "Soon as they heard Jace Kileen was dead, their man came runnin'. Howard Bracken is 'is name." Horn pointed. "That's him . . . fella at the end o' the bar. He owns the newspaper."

"Mister Morgan," Bracken said, smiling and extending his hand. Morgan shook it. "I'd hoped to get a chance to talk to you. I've heard some disturbing stories."

"About Idaho's real honest to God Senator?"

"Yes. I've known Tom Yeager a long time. Like to think I helped him get elected."

"Nothing wrong with that . . . then."

"Can you prove what you're claiming?"

"He can."

"Sure," Bracken agreed, laughing, "if he'll admit

it."

"He'll admit it."

"At the point of a gun? He's no Jace Kileen and I've not heard or seen anything to prove a connection between the two."

"Your senator friend was supposed to have left town. He didn't."

"So I gather, but that doesn't prove much except that he's still in Boise . . . upstairs."

"Why don't I tell you what I know. Then we'll see about proving it."

"Shall we?" Bracken said, pointing to a table. Morgan nodded.

Howard Bracken listened, questioned and wrote for more than two hours. He heard about the marauders, the professional hired on both sides, the fortress at Gunsmoke Gorge and the trail which had led, finally, to this meeting.

"I don't think you conjured all this up, Mister Morgan," Bracken finally said, "but I'm wondering if a deputy an' a kind of unofficial one at that, can carry on from here?"

"I can answer that question, Howard." Morgan and Bracken both jerked their heads around and saw Seth Rawlings at the door. Beside him was Belle Moran. "I'd have been here sooner but we stopped off at the courthouse." Seth handed Bracken a paper. Bracken looked at it. It was a warrant for the arrest of Senator Thomas Yeager.

Morgan looked down at Seth's leg. Blood was soaking through his britches. "Get the doc back," Morgan said to Tom.

"I'll live."

"Yeah you will . . . if I have to shoot you so the doc can fix you up again." Seth laughed for the first time in weeks. "I want the arrest."

"And I want you permanent," Seth said. Belle looked shocked. "I'll do my own dirty work," Seth said to her. He looked back at Morgan.

"No deal."

"You're a hard-headed son-of-a-bitch, Morgan."

"No offense in this refusal," Morgan said. "There's too many things to remember in Idaho for me. I might get to thinking about them and get myself shot . . . or worse . . . somebody else."

Seth winced . . . looked at his leg and then sat down. He looked up. "I can't argue the logic in that, damn it! As for the arrest, it's yours. You sure as hell earned it."

"I sent a boy for the doc," Tom said.

"Will you back me upstairs . . . just in case?" Horn nodded.

"Ladies and Gentlemen . . . please . . . your attention . . . please." Everyone turned to the sound of the voice. There, at the top of the stairs, was Senator Thomas Yeager. His arms were up in the air. Some of the crowd gasped. They knew only what they had already heard—that Yeager had left Boise.

"A terrible, terrible thing happened this morning in Boise. Something that civilization can no longer tolerate. A shooting in the street. Gunplay reminiscent of a quarter century ago." He coughed and cleared his throat.

He put his arms down. "I came to Boise to personally put an end to the marauding raids on helpless ranchers . . . to restore law and order to this great state. Instead, I found myself the participant . . . and the victim . . . of a vile intrigue which reaches to the very seat of our nation's power."

Seth, Morgan, Horn and many others moved nearer the steps. At the very forefront was Howard Bracken. Moments later, a photographer appeared and pushed his way through the crowd.

"Some of my own aides were involved in these criminal acts. I found myself fearful . . . desperate. I grasped at even the most feeble straws of credibility. As a result, I fell under the influence of evil men . . . men like Jace Kileen . . . a man named Brock and my own, personal aide, Ted Peabody."

The crowd gasped. Others from the street had pushed their way in. Yeager was in his element and he was *winning*.

Morgan started to go upstairs. A firm hand gripped his arm. He turned. It was Seth. "Not here," he said, softly, "and not now."

"The bastard is lying."

"But he's doing it on his ground," Seth said, "and if you face him now he'll be a hell of a lot tougher opponent than Jace Kileen was. He's got a power that beats hell out of a Colt's revolver." Morgan studied Seth's face. Somehow, he wasn't exactly certain why, Morgan knew Seth was right.

"Even as these events were unfolding—tragic as it may be—I had to allow them. Men like Mister Morgan . . . our fine Sheriff, Tate Bosley and his deputies . . . and U.S. Marshal Seth Rawlings bought me the most precious commodity a politician can have . . . *time*. Now with these heroic deeds and the law quietly at work behind the scenes, justice has prevailed. Ladies and gentleman . . . law and order have won. Idaho is at peace with itself."

A cheer went up, along with hats. Guns were fired into the ceiling and as the word spread to the outside, the scene became a melee of joy. When order was restored, allowed simply to run its course, the crowd finally settled. Senator Yeager, smiling broadly, concluded.

"Formal tributes and a proper ceremony will be

announced. For now, I ask you to return to your
homes and allow me to return to Washington. There,
I will formalize the report and see to it that formal
charges are leveled at those still free who raised
their hands against our sovereign state.''

Amid the din of more cheering, Senator Thomas
Yeager retreated to Belle Moran's office. In a few
moments, he would walk down the stairs, through
the crowd, down to the train depot and depart Boise.
He would do so with the blessing and protection of
its citizens. Anyone moving against him would be
dealt with harshly.

"Get out that damned warrant," Morgan said.

"It's not worth the paper it's written on . . . not
now it isn't."

Howard Bracken overheard the comment and
turned to Lee Morgan. "The good marshal is right,
Mister Morgan. Even if every word you told me this
morning is gospel."

"You doubting it now?"

"I never doubted anything," Bracken said. He
pointed upstairs. "I don't doubt what he said. In
neither case does that imply that I believe it. I've
heard it. Now, I'll do my best to sort it out . . . to
squeeze from the fruit . . . the juice of the truth."

Morgan said, "You've got a fine way with words,
Mister Bracken, but you're one gullible son-of-a-
bitch." In an instant, Morgan had grabbed the
arrest warrant from Seth's hand and gained the top
of the stairs. He drew the S and W, fired one shot at
the ceiling and then holstered the gun.

"Some of you know me by name . . . some don't
know me at all and I'd guess that most don't give a
damn either way . . . but now you'll listen to *me*." He
held up the warrant. "This paper is a warrant issued
by your own local, lovable, Judge Tyrone P. Riddle.

's a warrant for the arrest of the man you just
ard . . . of Senator Thomas Yeager." Morgan
aused. The reaction was one of stunned silence but
e did have the crowd's attention. Howard Bracken
as quietly impressed.

"I don't believe," Morgan continued, "that the
idge would have issued this warrant without
ause. It's my job to serve it and make the arrest."
le heard some moans and grumbling. He waited.
We fought a war a few years back over this very
ing . . . the right of a state to conduct its own
usiness. Granted, there were men who abused the
ght . . . treated fellow human beings badly . . . but
ie issue when settled, still restored the right of
cal law."

"What's any o' that got to do with Yeager? He's
o crook."

"Maybe he's not," Morgan snapped, "but if he's
ot . . . let me prove it in Idaho . . . not Washington.
et the law . . . your law . . . work. Hell, it wasn't
Vashington where these bastards burned out
anches, it was Idaho. Is he above it because he's a
enator? Am I . . . or Seth Rawlilngs here . . . are we
bove the law because we wear badges?"

The crowd mumbled, there were isolated shouts of
No!" and then a ripple of support which turned
ito a wave of cheering. One man then shouted
bove the din.

"My ranch was burned out . . . my family killed.
.et Yeager answer *that* in court . . . here . . . do it
ere in Idaho."

"Yeah . . take him in, deputy. Let's find out."

Morgan nodded and walked to the bottom of the
tairs. Howard Bracken smiled. "You're an eloquent
on-of-a-bitch," he said. "I didn't think you had it in
ou."

"I probably spoke out of turn," Morgan said. H
turned to Seth. "Well?" He was holding out th
warrant. Seth looked at it, at Morgan, at Howar
Bracken and then back to Morgan.

"Serve the goddam thing," Seth said.

Morgan turned and started up the stairway. Hal
way up, he stopped. He looked down a moment an
then he turned back to the crowd. "One mor
thing," he shouted. The crowd turned silent. "Ton
Yeager will remain innocent of anything until th
law finds him guilty. Some of you will be asked t
judge him. Do it from the evidence . . . not from
anything anybody . . . him or I . . . have said."

"What's he charged with, Deputy?"

"The warrant says fraud, abuse of the power of an
official office and conspiracy to commit murder. I'll
arrest him and I'll stand against any man who tries
to interfere with the legal procedure after that." No
one, particularly those who witnessed Morgan's
confrontations with Cody and Jace Kileen, cared to
argue with him. He turned back.

The shot seemed very loud. So did the woman's
scream. A door slammed shut. Morgan cleared the
rest of the stairs two at a time. He rushed to Belle's
office . . . gun drawn. He stepped back and kicked
the door open, pistol at the ready. There was
nothing but silence. He entered the room.

U. S. Senator Thomas Yeager was seated at
Belle's desk. His left arm was on the desk and his
head rested on it. His right arm dangled at his side.
There was a thud behind the desk. Morgan walked
over.

"God damn," Morgan exclaimed. The pistol, a
tiny wisp of smoke still curling up from its barrel,
had fallen from his hand. A steady stream of blood
flowed from Yeager's right temple. He turned and
walked out of the office . . . checking in both

irections in the corridor. He saw nothing. He
eard nothing. He wondered about the door he'd
eard slam. He walked back to the stairway.

"Morgan! What happened up there?" Bracken
sked. Seth Rawlings seemed to know. Tom Horn
vas helping Seth start up the stairs.

"Yeager is dead. He put a bullet in his head or so
t appears." The crowd chattered but there was no
outburst. Seth and Tom were about half way up
vhen Seth stopped dead in his tracks. He was
ooking up and to his left. Tom followed his line of
rision. Morgan looked puzzled.

"You killed him . . . you *bastard!* You drove him to
t!" Morgan wheeled but he didn't draw his gun. The
roice belonged to a woman. He saw the shotgun
irst, both barrels levelled at his chest . . . ten feet
away. Holding it was Morgana Barr.

"Morgana . . . don't!" She glanced at Seth, spat in
ais direction and raised the shotgun. Another shot
echoed through the corridor of the Four Queens
saloon. It came from the darkness just behind
Morgana Barr. Her eyes grew big . . . her mouth
dropped open and the shotgun dropped from her
aands and clattered to the floor. She staggered and
hen fell, face forward.

Out of the shadows . . . dazed by what he had seen
and what he had done was Judge Isaac Barr. He
dropped to his knees beside the body of his dead
daughter. The daughter he'd just killed. He was
sobbing. No one else moved. The old judge
struggled back to his feet and slowly, very slowly,
raised the pistol.

"Isaac . . . Jeezus . . . no!" Morgan lurched
forward. Judge Barr looked down and then up. He
turned the gun end for end and handed it to Morgan.

"It's over," he said softly. "It's finally all over."

In fact, it wasn't over.

16

Two trials were held in the district court in Ada county Idaho that year. The first was held *in Absentia*. The accused was U.S. Senator Thomas Yeager. At the conclusion of the more than two months of testimony, much of it from participants such as Tom Horn, Lee Morgan and the rancher's association members, Yeager was found guilty on all charges. Two weeks later, Judge Isaac Barr was brought to trail on charges of murder in the death of his daughter.

The jury heard two weeks worth of testimony . . . much of it from the judge himself. The juror's were finally sequestered to ponder the judge's fate on the 22nd day of December at just past noon.

"What do you think, Seth?" Morgan asked after they got back to the sheriff's office.

"Can't do much more than find him guilty. Hell, he shot her in front of a whole goddamn room full of witnesses . . . and admitted it to boot."

"Did he ride in with that in mind?"

"Nope. Manslaughter . . . that's what they'll find." Seth looked at Tom Horn.

Tom nodded and said, "Sentence him to jail an' then suspend it."

"I hope you're right," Morgan said.

"They will . . . no doubt. The one thing about this

194

ountry that I got great faith in is the legal system.
Seen it work good for near forty years. It's slow but
t works."

"You've never seen it fail?" Morgan asked Tom.

"Nope. Leastways not where a man's life is
dep017endin' on it. Never knowed a man hanged that
didn't deserve to be—by the law I mean."

"There's always a first time."

"You're a cynical bastard," Tom said, grinning.
"I s'pose it could happen but I don't think I'll ever
see it. Mostly men are fair. They try. Anyways,"
Horn added thoughtfully, "even if a mistake was
made . . . even if a man died . . . the system shouldn't
be thrown out. It serves more right than wrong.
That's the best anybody can hope for."

"He's had enough punishment anyway," Seth
said. He hit on his leg, sore and still stiff from the
gunshot wound. He sat down. "I don't know if I
could have done what he did. Killed his own flesh
and blood. God! What a decision to make!"

"Yeah," Morgan said, "I know. I made it once. I
went looking for my father. I hated him then. I
wanted him dead. I had my chance. I figure he'd
have killed me too . . . mostly out of reflex action . . .
but I couldn't do it."

"I guess old Isaac figured she'd done enough.
He'd suspected for a long time . . . wasn't certain of
t 'til he sent you that note to back off."

"Yeah . . . he figured she'd backshoot me the first
chance she got."

"That was one I couldn't figure," Tom said.
"How's come you s'pose she didn't?"

"The only thing I could ever make of it was that
she thought I'd do more good for the marauders
than bad. I had all the right contacts with all the
right people . . . Killerman . . . Strada . . . her daddy .

. . even the law. Besides, she knew about Brock and
Cody and Jessup.''

"An' Jace Kileen.'' Seth shook his head. "That's
one I regret missin'.'' He looked up at Morgan.
"You give anymore thought to stayin' on?''

"Yeah.''

"And?''

"No good. I told you why. It still holds.''

"What then? And where?'' Lee Morgan shrugged.
The door opened. Seth's new deputy, George Tyson,
stuck his head in the door.

"Jury's in.''

"Gentlemen,'' Judge Riddle said, "have you
reached a verdict?''

"We have, Your Honor. We find Judge Isaac Barr
guilty of the second charge of manslaughter.''

Judge Riddle thanked the jury, set sentencing for
two weeks hence and closed the case.

Back in his cell at the county jail, Isaac Barr
asked Seth, Lee Morgan and Tom Horn to visit him.
They complied.

"I'm hoping that you, Morgan, and you Mister
Horn, will stay in Boise for two more weeks until
I'm sentenced.''

"If you'd like, Judge. I'll stay,'' Morgan said.

Tom Horn grinned. "Seems I can't rightly
recollect a passle o' invites from anybody wantin' to
see me lately. I'll stick around.''

"Good. Then the lot of you are invited to the
Rocky Barr on that day. We've some celebrating to
do and some settling of accounts.'' All three men
looked somewhat stunned. Judge Barr smiled. "If I
were on the bench, I'd give myself a suspended
sentence . . . with probation time.''

Judge Barr, quite out of character, swelled

himself up and said, tongue-in-cheek, "And I am, by
Godfrey, a better judge than old Riddle." They all
laughed.

Seth released Isaac from his cell each evening and
they sat and played checkers. On one such an
evening, three days before Isaac was to be
sentenced, the door opened. Riley Preston, Ada
county's Democratic chairman, walked in.

"Gentlemen . . . good evening," Isaac smiled,
wryly. Seth frowned. "May I," Preston said,
gesturing toward a chair. Seth nodded, Riley sat.
"We have an unexpired Senate term to fill . . . about
eighteen months worth. We've been wrestling with
the problem but during the past three weeks . . .
thanks to Isaac Barr's suggestion . . . we've taken a
poll and reached a solution."

"Well . . . I'm proud of you," Seth said, dryly,
"but what brings you here?"

"The voters we polled picked from five names on a
list. One man got more votes than all the rest
combined. Now Isaac here . . . he couldn't be
considered of course." Seth frowned and looked at
both men. They were looking back . . . and both
smiling. "You won, Marshal."

"Bull dung!"

"See for yourself." Preston handed Seth the day's
issue of the Boise paper. The news report confirmed
what Preston had just revealed.

"I'm no goddam politician. I'm a lawman."

"With that leg," Isaac said, pointing. "Besides,
you're too old to ride all over the circuit. George
Tyson isn't. He's been a good deputy and he'd make
a good territorial marshal."

"Well . . . I won't do it," Seth said. "Too damned
old or not." Preston got to his feet, slapped Seth on
the shoulder and said, "Fair enough, Marshal. Now

all you have to do is tell the folks you've turned
them down and then ask them to vote for you again
for the sheriff's job you wanted.''

"You're blackmailing me!"

"That's a fair assessment, Marshal . . . only it's all
very legal." Preston waved his goodbye as he went
out.

"Isaac . . . you old bastard . . . this was your
doing."

"Yes . . . it was. And I'll tell you something else.
You won't get the marshal's appointment again
either. I'll see to that." Isaac grinned. "You'll have
to retire. You can ride out to my ranch every day.
We'll sit and grow old and play checkers."

"The hell we will!"

The sentence came down from the bench almost
exactly as it had been predicted by both Tom Horn
and Isaac Barr himself. It was all over by eleven
o'clock in the morning. Isaac had added to the list of
names of those invited to his ranch, that of Judge
Riddle. Even before anyone left for the Rocky Barr
ranch however, there was to be another round of
celebrating at Belle Moran's Four Queens saloon.

Isaac Barr had returned to the home of Jim
Bidwell in Nampa. He would return to Boise that
evening for Belle's celebration. Tom Horn was out
of town as well, negotiating the purchase of some
new horses. Lee Morgan had been given quarters in
Belle's place . . . not always alone. On this day, he
was at the livery. Seth Rawlings was more or less
cleaning up the paper work which was now almost
as important as keeping the peace. He'd about
decided to accept the political offer made to him
although he had not yet admitted it aloud.

The door to Seth's office opened and Seth looked

up. Belle Moran stepped in looking scared as hell. She looked back over her shoulder, then she closed the door.

"Belle?" Seth got to his feet.

"Oh Seth . . . Gawd A'mighty . . . I thought it . . . it was over."

"Belle . . . you ain't makin' much sense."

She swallowed, steadied herself on the back of a chair and then moved around in front of it and sat down.

"Three men just walked into my place, Seth, an' took it over. They ran ever'body out an' told me to . . . to fetch the deputy."

"George?"

She shook her head. "Lee. Oh Seth . . . one of 'em is Bryce Kileen . . . Jace's brother. I . . . I don't know the others."

"Jeezus!" Seth thought for a moment. "You see George?"

"No. Seth . . . what . . ." the old marshal held up his hand. He turned, walked to his gun case and pulled out a shotgun.

"Seth!" Belle got to her feet. Seth whirled around. frowning.

"Damn it Belle . . . don't say anythin' . . . you hear me . . . nothin'. I'm still the marshal here an' George Tyson is my deputy . . . not Lee Morgan . . . not anymore. Horn neither. If I can't keep the goddam peace in my own territory, I'd make a piss poor Senator, wouldn't I?"

Belle looked up, tears in her eyes. Still, she knew better than to argue. It was neither the time or the place. Seth loaded the shotgun, put on his heavy coat, pulled on his old, beat up hat and walked around the desk. He leaned down and gently kissed the top of Belle's head. Then, he walked out.

Seth's deputy, George Tyson, had just served some papers on King Gilman over at his feed store. George had mounted up and was headed for the office. Howard Bracken from the Boise newspaper waved him down just half a block away. Bracken had just come from Belle's. He'd gone over to assist with the plans for that night's celebration.

"Mister Bracken," George said smiling, "what can I do for you?" Bracken looked stern.

"Find Lee Morgan. Tom Horn too. Do it fast, George."

"Well Mister Horn's out o' town," George said. "An' last I knew, Mister Morgan was over to the livery barn. What's wrong?"

"Trouble, Deputy. Jace Kileen's brother is down at the Four Queens. He's got two gunmen with him."

"Oh shit!" Tyson yanked his mount's head around, dug his spurs into the animal's flanks and galloped toward the livery. Belle Morgan had regained her composure and was now stricken with the reality of what she had done. She found a pistol . . . an old Navy Colt's. She loaded it, slipped it in the folds of her shawl and hurried off toward her saloon.

Seth Rawlings had just stepped onto Vista Street. He crossed it and started toward the Four Queens. Three blocks away, Tyson galloped up to Lee Morgan who had just emerged from the livery.

"Kileen's brother and two gunmen at Belle's place." Morgan sprang onto Pacer's back.

"Get Seth. Meet me there. Do it, George . . . right now!" Tyson nodded, wheeled his mount and rode off. Morgan spurred Pacer and galloped toward the saloon. He rounded the corner onto Vista with Howard Bracken just behind him. Both saw Seth. The old marshal was just in front of the saloon's doors.

"Seth! Wait!" Seth turned. The bat wings pushed open and a tall, dark haired man stepped out. Seth's head jerked around. The man was carrying a shotgun. He brought it up, stock first, with a sweeping motion from right to left in front of him. The end of the stock caught Seth's jaw and sent the old lawman reeling. He fell from the boardwalk and into the street. He lost his own weapon and lay sprawled, helpless and dazed, at the man's mercy. The man with the shotgun heard the riders to his left, looked up and fired from the hip. The shots struck nothing but forced both Morgan and Bracken to rein up. They dismounted. The man disappeared back inside.

"Morgan," Bracken hollered. "Look!" Morgan did. Toward the other end of the block, Belle Moran came around the corner at sort of a run. She crossed the street and disappeared toward the back of the building.

"Damn," Morgan said. "She'll get herself killed." The tall man stepped out again, the shotgun leveled at Seth.

"Where's Lee Morgan, old man?"

"I'm right here," Morgan shouted. The man glanced up, grinned and turned back to look at Seth. Seth was now trying to sit up and, at the same time, reach his pistol. The man brought the shotgun to his shoulder. Morgan drew. A shot ran out from the opposite end of the street. A rifle! The man's grin faded. He staggered. The shotgun discharged harmlessly into the air. The man fell back through the bat wing doors. Morgan, Bracken and Seth all turned toward the sound of the rifle. George Tyson was walking toward them.

Morgan, in a crouch and moving fast, emptied the

Smith and Wesson into the big, plate glass window just to the left of the door at the Four Queens. He could only hope to God, he'd hit no one unless it was one of the two remaining gunmen. In any event, Tyson and Bracken got Seth, who was growling at them as usual, to his feet and out of the way. His jaw was broken.

Morgan pressed against the building, reloaded the pistol and Tyson scooped up Seth's shotgun and tossed it to Morgan. Morgan holstered the pistol. Bracken moved down the block, helping Seth. Tyson squeezed into a doorway across the street.

Inside the saloon, Belle Moran started down the stairs. She was wearing a low cut, emerald green, satin dress. Her left hand was tugging at the bodice, pulling it lower, revealing more of her creamy, ample bosom. Her right hand, behind the folds of the dress, concealed the old Colt's.

"You gents want a drink—it's on the house?"

The tall man who had been shot was not dead. A second man, stocky of build and dirty looking, was crouched down examining the tall man's wound. He stood up, turned, drew a pistol and pointed it at Belle.

"Reese," a man at the bar yelled, "is that any way to treat a lady? Particularly our hostess."

"She's the one brought the goddam law in, Bryce."

"Take care of Shell," Bryce Kileen said, smiling. "I'll take care of the lady."

Belle moved behind the bar, stopped and smiled. She let out the breath of air she'd been holding when she saw the man named Reese holster his pistol.

"What'll you have?" Belle asked, realizing the shakiness in her own voice. Bryce Kileen, a sinister smile on his face, leaned foward, grabbed a handful of Belle's hair, jerked forward, hard and twisted.

"I'll have that pistol you're hiding . . . you goddam whore!" Belle had brought her arm up reflexively, and Kileen now grabbed it and twisted. Belle let out a cry of pain. Kileen took the gun and then shoved Belle backwards. "You get over to the front door and you tell Lee Morgan to come inside if you want to stay alive."

Belle nodded. She couldn't help but wonder how Bryce Kileen had known about the pistol. A moment later, she got her answer. As she walked past the stairway, she caught a faint movement above her on the balcony. She looked up. Kileen had two more men up there!

Reese walked to the bar. "Shell took one through the side. Got the bleedin' stopped. Bullet went clean through. Think he's got a busted rib. He'll need a doc."

"We'll get one," Bryce said.

Belle shouted. "Lee . . . they . . . they want you inside." There was no answer. "Lee . . . it's Belle . . . they . . . ." She stopped. Tyson was in a doorway exactly opposite her, across the street. He was motioning to her to come through the door.

Belle took a deep breath, pushed hard on both bat wing doors and hurried through. Instantly, Lee Morgan had her by the arm, jerked her aside and pushed her down. Two shots smashed into the doors where, a moment before, Belle had been standing. Morgan, in a crouch, wheeled himself in front of the door and fired . . . up . . . toward the top of the stairs. He heard a grunt, the clatter of a gun against wood and a body bouncing down the stairway. Morgan threw himself in the opposite direction and came back to his feet . . . his back pressed against the wall on the opposite side of the door.

"Belle . . . stay close to the buildings until you get
to the corner . . . then go like hell . . . get to the depot.
Stay put!"

Belle didn't argue. She paused when she reached
the alley way which led to the back of the saloon.
She turned back to wave at Morgan. Instead, she
saw George Tyson. His eyes were big and round. He
raised his rifle and fired. The shot was so close, Belle
could hear the bullet splitting the air ahead of it.
The other man who'd been on the balcony had
slipped out the back, worked his way along the alley
and was waiting to kill her as soon as she stepped
into view. Tyson killed him but not without sacri-
fice.

George had to show himself in order to make the
shot. Across the street in the Four Queens, Reese
had just moved to the broken window and peered
out. Tyson was a full, close target. Reese drew and
fired. Tyson went down, critically wounded. Reese
dived for cover. Morgan put three rounds through
the window. None hit home.

"Kileen . . . you bastard . . . walk out. . . you and
me . . . same as with Jace." Morgan waited. No
reply. "You got one man shot up, two dead. Let's
settle it."

"Fuck you, Morgan." Morgan turned. Belle was
still at the corner. She was crying. She was looking
at Tyson writhing in pain across the street.

"Belle," Morgan shouted, "go on . . . now . . . do
what I told you to do." She finally moved . . . slowly
. . . in a daze.

"Morgan!"

"Yeah, Kileen . . . I'm still here."

"You got a marshal with a busted jaw an' a dyin'
deputy out there. You ain't a goddam bit better off
than me. Why don't *you* come in?" Kileen laughed.

"Fuck you," Morgan said. Inside the saloon, Reese had worked his way back to the bar. Bryce Kileen was now at its far end where cover was but a few feet away.

"Get on up stairs. We got nobody coverin' the back." Reese nodded. Kileen took a bottle, moved to a corner table, upended the table next to it so that he would have some handy cover, sat down, uncorked the jug and took a long pull. "Let 'im know we're in here," Kileen hollered at Reese. Reese was about half way up the stairs. He turned, drew and fanned four shots into the bat wing doors. He grinned, holstered the pistol and turned back.

"Oh Jeezus," Reese shouted. His eyes were big, his mouth still open, his gut tightened into a ball of fear. His eyes were level with both barrels of a Parker shotgun. He might have seen the powder flash as they discharged . . . then Reese's head disappeared.

"Just Kileen now," Tom Horn said, "all by himself, Morgan."

"I'll be goddamned," Morgan whispered to himself, grinning. "That ol' son-of-a-bitch always manages to be in the right place at the right time." Morgan loaded the Smith and Wesson, holstered it, turned, pushed through the splintered bat wings and moved into the center of the saloon. Bryce Kileen was on his feet. He set the empty jug back on the table. Shell tried to draw. Morgan killed him.

"Seems like your hand," Bryce said, grinning.

"Make your move, Kileen."

"Oh no . . . no, Mister Morgan. I don't think so. Man with the shotgun up there . . . whole goddam town ready to string me up . . . even if I killed you, I got no way out. No sir, Mister Morgan. You'll have to take me in an' do it the hard way. I'll be around.

Mebbe I'll break out. Mebbe I got more men waitin'
outside o' town. Hell, I ain't shot nobody in Boise,"
he laughed, "mebbe they'll find me innocent an' I'll
jist ride away. Anyway . . . you'll never have to stick
around to find out . . . or keep lookin' over your
shoulder."

Morgan looked toward the balcony. Tom Horn
stood there, cradling the Parker. Their eyes met.
Tom had seen the expression before . . . many times
. . . mostly on his own face. Now, seeing it on someone else's . . . it bothered him. He frowned and,
almost imperceptibly, gave a negative shake of his
head. It was too late.

Lee Morgan drew the little, short barreled Smith
and Wesson he'd gotten from drummer Mason.
He'd probably never made a faster or smoother
draw . . . even though no one was drawing against
him. He was just as accurate as he was fast. Kileen
died instantly, a bullet between his eyes.

Epilogue

Tom Horn lied about the last few minutes at the Four Queens saloon in Boise, Idaho. He told Seth Parker there had been a shoot-out. Tom then rode out . . . Wyoming bound . . . riding to his own destiny. Seth would have believed the lie . . . save for one thing. Lee Morgan left a letter which told the truth. He hadn't been wearing the badge that day. He'd quit the law. He gunned down Bryce Kileen in cold blood. Then, he rode out.

Seth Rawlings was faced with one, final, painful duty as a U.S. marshal. He knew Morgan would understand. Seth had to do it. Once again, sheriffs' offices would all possess a wanted poster on Lee Morgan. *Wanted: For the Murder of Bryce Kileen in Boise, Idaho.* Seth did his duty, resigned and became one of the state's most respected senators. George Tyson survived his wounds and lived out his life as a United States marshal.

Belle Moran sold the Four Queens about a year later, moved to San Francisco, flourished for a few more years and then disappeared into obscurity.

Judge Isaac Barr died, quietly, at the Rocky Barr ranch about eighteen months after Idaho's darkest period ended. The coroner said his death was from heart failure. Many believed his heart was simply broken and never mended again.

The initial manhunt for Lee Morgan was ambitious and extensive. Morgan anticipated his pursuers. Well supplied, he stayed hidden until the search for him had become more passive than active. Summer had returned to the Idaho wilderness before he stirred again. He rode Pacer slowly to the summit of a spiny ridge on a fine, sunny morning in July. He stopped, stood up in the stirrups, turned and took his final look into the rocky fortress at the base of the Bitterroots. Then, he rode away from Gunsmoke Gorge.

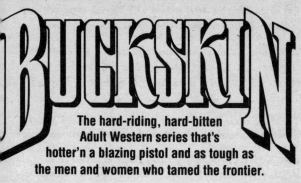

BUCKSKIN

**The hard-riding, hard-bitten
Adult Western series that's
hotter'n a blazing pistol and as tough as
the men and women who tamed the frontier.**

27: DOUBLE ACTION by Kit Dalton. Ambushed and left
with amnesia, Lee Morgan swore he wouldn't rest until he had
killed the cowards who had attacked him.
_2845-X $2.95

28: APACHE RIFLES by Kit Dalton. Working as a scout for
the U.S. Army, Lee Morgan tracked the deadly Chircahua
Apache — and found a dangerous Indian maid who had eyes for
him.
_2943-X $2.95

29: RETURN FIRE by Kit Dalton. Searching for a missing
prospector in Deadwood, South Dakota, Lee Morgan found the
only help anyone would give him was a one-way ticket to boot
hill.
_3009-8 $2.95 US/$3.50 CAN

LEISURE BOOKS
ATTN: Customer Service Dept.
276 5th Avenue, New York, NY 10001

Please add $1.25 for shipping and handling of the first book and $.30 for
each book thereafter. All orders shipped within 6 weeks via postal service
book rate.

Canadian orders must reflect Canadian price, when indicated, and must be
paid in U.S. dollars through a U.S. banking facility.

Name _____

Address _____

City _____ State _____ Zip _____

I have enclosed $ _____ in payment for the books checked above.

GUNSLICK

The bawdy Adult Western series that's
more fun than a Saturday night shootout!

#1: A MAN PURSUED by J.G. White. After two years in jail, Matt Sutton was thinking of three things: women, money, and a new life. He had the woman and the money, but some dangerous people stood between Sutton and a new life — people who shot first and asked questions later.

__2916-2 $2.95

#2: THE RAWHIDERS by J.G. White. On the road to California, Sutton's bedmate Diana was captured by a gang of horsethievin' cutthroats. And Sutton was willing to do anything to get his woman back — even die.

__2926-X $2.95

LEISURE BOOKS
ATTN: Customer Service Dept.
276 5th Avenue, New York, NY 10001
Please add $1.25 for shipping and handling of the first book and $.30 for each book thereafter. All orders shipped within 6 weeks via postal service book rate.
Canadian orders must reflect Canadian price, when indicated, and must be paid in U.S. dollars through a U.S. banking facility.

Name _____
Address _____
City _____State _____ Zip _____
I have enclosed $ _____in payment for the books checked above.
Payment <u>must</u> accompany all orders.   ❏Please send a free catalogue.

Get more for your money with special Double Editions of the wildest Adult Series around!

More gunslinging gangs, more wild women, more non-stop Western action!